Meg's lips pinched, and she raised her chin to a stubborn little point. "Are you as sinful as they say you are?"

The duke smiled at her daring. "Probably more so, since most of my sinning is done behind closed doors." She blushed again, and his grin deepened. "Yes, you are definitely innocent. Far too innocent for my taste." But the desire to touch her didn't go away.

"Don't men expect the ladies they marry to be innocent?"

"True enough, Duchess. But I'm not like most men. Have you ever kissed a man?"

She kept her eyes locked on his. "I kissed you," she said tartly, and he barked a laugh. He got up from his chair, crossed the room, and sat beside her.

"No, Duchess, that miserable peck in the church was no kiss at all. I shall have to teach you better than that."

He slid his knuckles over her cheek, his touch light, teasing. Her skin was hot, and soft as silk. She lowered her gaze and her lips parted.

His mouth descended on hers.

/ALL

How to Deceive a Duke

AVON

An Imprint of HarperCollins*Publishers*

This is a work of fiction. Names, characters, places, and incidents are products of the author's imagination or are used fictitiously and are not to be construed as real. Any resemblance to actual events, locales, organizations, or persons, living or dead, is entirely coincidental.

AVON BOOKS
An Imprint of HarperCollins*Publishers*
10 East 53rd Street
New York, New York 10022-5299

Copyright © 2012 by Lecia Cotton Cornwall
ISBN 978-0-06-220241-3
www.avonromance.com

First Avon Books mass market printing: December 2012

Avon Trademark Reg. U.S. Pat. Off. and in Other Countries, Marca Registrada, Hecho en U.S.A.
HarperCollins® is a registered trademark of HarperCollins Publishers.

Printed in the U.S.A.

10 9 8 7 6 5 4 3 2 1

To Kevan and Tessa. Thank you!

How to
Deceive a Duke

Chapter 1

Marguerite Lynton winced as her elder sister's teacup fell to the floor and shattered.

There was nothing she could do about it in front of their esteemed guest. If the carpet that usually graced the floor of Wycliffe's salon had been in place, then Rose's cup would still be whole, but the rug had been rolled up and sold that morning, just hours before the Duchess of Temberlay's unexpected arrival. She had come to ask Rose a very important question, which was happy news indeed, since the tea service was next on the list to be sold, and a diminished set would fetch considerably less.

The silence stretched as the duchess—and everyone else in the room—waited for Rose's answer.

"Well, young lady, will you marry my grandson or not?" The duchess regarded Rose's stunned expression and ignored the shards of china at her feet. Still her sister said nothing, and Marguerite glanced at the mantel where the clock had once stood, wanting to know the exact moment their fortunes had suddenly changed for the good, but the clock, like the rug, was gone.

She bit her lip. The duchess's offer couldn't have come

at a better time, or been more generous, and Rose was sitting there in gape-jawed silence.

It was a pity the groom himself had not come to make the offer of marriage, but had sent his grandmother instead. She would have liked to see the infamous Nicholas Hartley, Duke of Temberlay, in the flesh. They'd only seen caricatures, and every one portrayed him as devastatingly handsome. Marguerite's toes curled. Temberlay was said to be the wickedest rake in London, and now her sister was about to become his duchess. Rose had dreamed of a wealthy prince on a white horse, and now the nearest equivalent had appeared, all she could do was sit there, when all she had to do was say—

"No!" Rose's anguished moan echoed off the bare walls.

Another teacup hit the floor. Marguerite's mother shot to her feet from her seat beside Rose, her face a mask of horrified shock. Marguerite glanced at the cups the duchess and Uncle Hector still held, waiting for their reaction, hoping the china didn't bear the brunt of their surprise too.

"No?" Flora Lynton, the Countess of Wycliffe, stared at her eldest daughter. "No? Rose, you can't say no!"

"Young lady, are you truly saying you will not marry my grandson?" the duchess demanded, her tone gravel against Flora's dismayed warble.

"Of course she isn't saying no, Your Grace!" Flora cried, twining her fingers in Rose's collar. "Are you?"

"No," Rose said mulishly. "I mean yes, I'm saying no."

Marguerite cast a pleading glance at her uncle, her father's stepbrother, seated near the fireplace. He was usually the voice of reason, but he looked as stunned as Flora.

"Uncle Hector?" she whispered, trying not to attract the duchess's attention, but the sharp black eyes swung toward her, swept over her russet hair and her shabby gown, and clung for a long moment of inspection. She felt her skin heat from toe to hairline under the bold appraisal.

Hector recovered himself and rose. "In this case, Flora, I would suggest—" He was cut off by a loud sob.

Before their eyes, Rose transformed from the family beauty to a wailing child. Her pert nose turned beet pink and began to swell. Her cupid's-bow lips stretched wide and thin as she screeched like a scalded cat. She was shaking so hard that blond curls were working their way loose from her coiffure.

"Why me? Why do *I* have to marry him? Why not Marguerite or Lily?"

Flora stamped her foot, and shards of china crackled. She tightened her grip on Rose's collar. "Be quiet this instant! Her Grace will think you are ungrateful!"

But she kept right on wailing, and Marguerite watched her mother's complexion turn as red as Rose's. In a moment she'd be crying too.

"Mama, perhaps you should take Rose upstairs to compose herself in private while I order more tea for Her Grace," Marguerite said, taking control of the situation.

She led her sister to the door, and her mother followed, trying to curtsy and walk and apologize at the same time. "Please excuse us for just a moment, Your Grace, we'll be back within—" Flora glanced at the absent clock and her eyes filled with tears.

"Papa's watch is still upstairs, Mama," Marguerite reminded her, and Flora nodded and left the room.

Marguerite shut the door and took her mother's place on the settee, ignoring the naked speculation in the duchess's eyes. "More tea, Your Grace?" she asked calmly as something crashed in the hallway. Hopefully it wasn't anything valuable.

"Perhaps I should take my leave if the young lady isn't interested," the duchess said.

Marguerite forced a placid smile, as if tantrums and tea with duchesses happened every day at Wycliffe Park. "They will only be a moment. Do try the tarts," she said, offering the plate. Their housekeeper, Amy, had baked them that morning from the last of the winter apples.

The duchess ignored them. "And which one are you, assuming you are one of the girls Lady Rose mentioned?"

Hector snapped to attention. "May I present Lady Marguerite Lynton, Your Grace?"

"The second sister then," the duchess said flatly, as if she was of no further interest. Marguerite felt hot blood creeping up her face. It was true that she looked nothing like Rose or her lovely mother and pretty younger sisters. They were four perfect blond beauties, while Marguerite resembled her late father, russet-haired and plain, the only weed in Wycliffe's garden of flowers. At least she had been given brains to make up for her lack of looks. She kept her chin high.

"And what of the third sister?" the duchess asked Hector, obviously dismissing Marguerite as anyone's bride.

"Lily is only ten, Your Grace, and still in the nursery," he replied.

"Then perhaps I have indeed wasted my time coming today." She rose to her feet.

Panic propelled Marguerite up as well. "Wait! Rose simply needs a moment to compose herself. She is so delighted by your—er, your grandson's—proposal, she is overcome."

The oak panels of the door did little to muffle Rose's distant screams of protest. "Is your sister always this demonstrative?" the duchess asked, taking her seat and examining Marguerite again.

"Quite the opposite, Your Grace. Rose is known for her sweet and gentle nature."

The duchess snorted a laugh. "God help her then. My grandson will eat her alive!"

"An offer of marriage from the Duke of Temberlay would surprise any girl," Marguerite bristled. "It was even more unexpected here, being as we are only recently out of mourning for my father."

"Not to mention penniless," the duchess added. She raised her hand for silence as Marguerite opened her mouth to protest. "I do not expect a dowry. I chose Lady Rose because of your father's reputation. Nicholas must marry a woman of sterling character—chaste, demure, and titled. I understand the earl strictly educated his daughters to be clever, yet not too clever, and impeccably moral. He believed young ladies should be carefully bred to be perfect wives for peers of the realm, and to improve the moral and intellectual fiber of future generations, did he not?"

"That *was* Papa's philosophy," Marguerite murmured.

The clever-but-not-too-clever part certainly described her sisters. As Papa's Plan for Raising Perfect Ladies dictated, they sang and played the pianoforte—before it was sold—they painted tolerably in watercolors, and they could make graceful curtsies. But they were not sensible girls, and not one of them was likely to improve the intellectual fiber of anything.

If Rose rejected the duke's proposal, things would get worse. Wycliffe Park would have to be sold. Marguerite would have to find work as a governess or companion to support her mother and sisters. But if Rose accepted the proposal, the Temberlay fortune would provide for them all, and even ensure that Lily and Minnie had rich dowries when the time came. She blessed the fact that a man as wealthy and eccentric as the Duke of Temberlay could afford to select a bride like Rose, solely for her beauty, without a fortune to bring to the match.

"Has Lady Rose had other offers for her hand?" the duchess asked. "She's a pretty girl, and appears healthy enough, even if she lacks sense."

Marguerite raised her chin at the old lady's bluntness. "Rose has a great many admirers, Your Grace, but she has not made her formal debut." The duchess was staring again, and Marguerite felt as if the old lady could see inside her head and read her thoughts. She lowered her gaze to her hands, tried to look demure.

"And you, young lady, do you also have 'admirers'?"

Marguerite looked up again, her temper flaring. It was true enough that no one noticed plain Marguerite when lovely Rose was in the room, but she did not appreciate the duchess's reminder of it. Papa had despaired of ever finding a man of title to marry her, and the sting of that fear went even deeper coming from a complete stranger.

"Admirers? Of course I have. Dozens."

"And have you come out yet?" the duchess asked, and Marguerite felt hot blood rise from her toes to her hairline.

"Perhaps once Rose is married, eh, Meg?" Hector said. "Perhaps Rose—or even Her Grace—will sponsor your debut next Season."

"Yes, I daresay when my money fills your family's empty coffers you'll be a prime catch," the duchess added.

Pride prodded Marguerite's temper. "Or the connection may worsen our chances. We have heard of your grandson, even here in Somerset. Who in England has not? They call him Devil, do they not? We've read about the women and the scandals he causes with just a wink of—"

"Meg!" Hector said, stopping her, but the duchess laughed.

"Odd. Your father was a reformer, a crusader for the purity and morals of English womanhood. You don't mean to say that he let you read the London scandal sheets?"

Of course he didn't. They purloined them from their maid, read them in secret. Papa would be horrified. Meg felt herself flush. "My father has been dead for over a year."

The duchess did not offer condolences.

"As for my grandson, they do indeed call him Devil. The name suits him. If his brother had not died, I would be content to leave Nicholas to his women and his drink, but he is now the Duke of Temberlay, and he must reform. His bride and his heirs will be impeccably respectable even if he is not."

Marguerite laughed before she could stop herself. Hector cleared his throat and she dropped her gaze. Rose was hardly the type to turn a rake into a paragon.

The door opened before the duchess could take her to task for her rudeness, and Rose entered with Flora at her back. She stopped in the doorway and stared at the floor. Her mother prodded her forward.

"I accept," she murmured, but her shoulders began shaking again.

The duchess's eyes filled with heartless triumph. She didn't offer a single word of comfort or congratulations. Marguerite rose to take her sister's hand before she said something unforgivably rude to their guest.

"Come, Rose, we'll go upstairs and get a cold cloth for your eyes."

"She'll need to come to London for fittings immediately, and I expect her to—" the duchess began instructing Flora, and Marguerite closed the door on the rest of her commands and led her sister away.

So Rose was to marry the Devil Duke of Temberlay. She glanced at her sister's tearstained face, the picture of misery.

Lucky, lucky Rose.

"Thank heaven she's gone," Meg said half an hour later, watching from the bedroom window as the Temberlay coach rumbled down the driveway.

She turned to her sister, still curled on the bed sniffling. Sodden handkerchiefs littered the floor like blossoms around a coffin. Rose couldn't have looked less like a bride, or the beauty their father had petted and adored.

"When is the wedding to be?" Meg asked, offering a fresh handkerchief.

"Mama said the duchess wants it done at once. She's given us just enough time to get a wedding gown made up, and within a fortnight—" Her face crumpled and fresh misery soaked the linen. "Oh, Meg, what will I do? It will look very improper to wed in such haste, and to a man like *him*! Everyone will think that I am—" Tears made further speech impossible. "Papa would never force me to marry such a man. I daresay he'd forbid it!"

Meg shut her eyes. Their father was dead, and while his expectations for his daughters were all well and good while he was alive, he'd left them penniless, alone, and without provision for dowries or husbands. They were on their own, and must do what was necessary to survive. It was time to be strong and practical rather than romantic, but Papa hadn't taught them that, hadn't thought it would be necessary. Rose was no more than a lovely possession. First, as Papa's pampered daughter, then in marriage, she would be like a fine horse or a breathtaking marble sculpture of a goddess, an object of admiration, but not expected to think or to manage anything more complicated than a dinner menu. Wycliffe's philosophy called for the perfect wife to smile and bear heirs without demur, and in return she would be adored and pampered and kept safe from the harsh aspects of the real world. Rose was quite right. Nicholas Hartley was exactly the kind of man their father's theories railed against, but there was no choice. They *needed* this match.

Meg squeezed her sister's icy fingers. "They say he's handsome, and rich, and very skilled at—"

"Marguerite Lynton!" Rose gasped. "It was amusing to read about him in the scandal sheets, to laugh at his antics, but *marry* him? The mere thought of him touching me makes me ill. God knows where his hands have been. Last I read they were around Lord Grimsby's wife! And we don't even know for certain that he's handsome. We have only drawings in Amy's scandal sheets to go by." She smoothed a hand over her cheek, as if marrying an unattractive duke would be an insult to a penniless beauty like herself.

Meg resisted the urge to roll her eyes. "But if every woman in London wants him, surely that suggests he *must* be handsome," she replied. And charming, and very, very good at—

"Oh, Meg, what a fool you are! Did you read of his latest scandal?" Rose leaped off the bed and retrieved the page from the bottom drawer of the dresser, where it was hidden under a pile of thrice-darned stockings.

"How could I have missed seeing it there?" Meg murmured as her sister thrust the crumpled page at her.

According to the latest gossip, a mere month out of date, Temberlay had fought a duel with a rich merchant who claimed that Devil had debauched his wife. The caricature showed him with horns, a forked tail, and a bullet clenched between perfect teeth while the merchant's buxom wife shielded him from her husband's brace of pistols. Behind her, a dozen London beauties tried to catch Devil's roving eye.

Meg swallowed. Until the duchess had come to call, the Lynton sisters had laughed at his outrageous exploits, but now it was serious. *He'll eat her alive!* Meg heard the echo of the duchess's cackle in her mind and looked again at Rose, who was picking the lace off the edge of the handkerchief.

Rose had far more experience of men than she did. The local lads had come to call after Papa's death. There were poems and flowers and billets-doux left at the kitchen door daily for Rose. She had even allowed a lad or two to hold her hand. Rose loved to be the center of attention, and she played with her admirers as other girls played with dolls.

Meg had only her imagination of what a poem written in her honor might say, and what it would be like to be kissed by the Devil of Temberlay, loved by him. Her face flamed at such improper thoughts, and she turned away to fetch another dry handkerchief for Rose. In a fortnight, he'd be her sister's husband. Somehow she doubted a man with a soubriquet like Devil was the type who wrote poetry, and Rose would wither and die if she was not the center of his world.

The countess swept into the room without knocking, and Meg pushed the scandal sheet into her pocket.

The countess looked at Rose in annoyance. "Still sulking? I had hoped you would understand what is at stake. Hector says if we do not have money soon, we will lose Wycliffe Park entirely. Would you see us all crammed into a tiny cottage in the village? I'd be a laughingstock, and poor Marguerite would be forced to find paid employment to support us!"

Meg stifled a frisson of annoyance. There was no talk of *Rose* going to work. Rose was too silly to be anyone's governess, and too lovely to use her hands for anything but waving to admirers.

"You won't get a better offer than this," Flora warned. "If you reject a duke, other gentlemen will think you overly particular, and no one at all will want you."

Rose burst into fresh tears. "I am to be sacrificed!"

Flora's complexion reddened. "You are marrying a duke! That's hardly torture!"

"He's the devil!" Rose moaned.

To Meg, he seemed more like a hero on a white horse, riding to their rescue in the nick of time. She hated the privations they'd been forced to endure in the year since her father had died. She had taken control while her mother retreated into nervous illness and grief. She was the one who sold the silver and the paintings and dismissed the servants one by one so her mother could afford to live the life she was accustomed to for as long as possible. Mama was the perfect example of Papa's philosophy. Without Meg's practicality and Hector's advice, they would have lost Wycliffe much sooner than this.

"Get up and dry your tears at once," Flora ordered Rose. "We must leave for London tomorrow at first light to see about having wedding clothes made." When Rose continued to stare at the wall mutinously, she turned to Meg. "You had better come as well, Marguerite. I'll need your help. Once Rose is married, and we have funds again, we'll hire more staff, but until then, I must continue to depend upon you to manage things."

Meg felt excitement rush through her. Not only was

that the closest thing to a compliment her mother had paid her for her hard work since Papa's death, it meant she would see London, attend the wedding, and meet the Devil of Temberlay in the flesh. "Oh, Mama—"

"Rose, will you wear the blue gown or the yellow?" Flora asked.

"Don't sacrificial virgins wear white?" Rose asked.

Flora threw up her hands. "Marguerite, you do the packing. Rose is far too overcome by joy to see to it herself."

"Obviously," Meg muttered.

Flora moved to the bureau, only to be distracted by the mirror. She smoothed the wrinkles from her forehead. "Rose will make a beautiful bride, and I shall stand out as her radiant mama," she said, as if trying to convince herself. She swept out of the room, calling for Amy to see to her own packing.

Meg laid the gowns on the bed. They'd both worn every gown a hundred times, and she hated all of them. Now Rose would have an entirely new wardrobe, fashionable and lovely, and never have to share her clothes again. A shimmer of jealousy crept up her spine, and Meg tightened her fist on a particularly hated sprigged muslin. She let go so she wouldn't need to press the wrinkles out of it and forced a smile.

"You'll wear pretty clothes and go to parties and balls." She looked critically at a faded green gown with a small tear on the sleeve. "No more turned hems or darned stockings."

Rose sniffed. "I'd rather wear rags and be a spinster than marry the Devil of Temberlay." She snatched the gown out of Meg's hands and tossed it to the floor. "I won't do it."

Meg picked up the gown. "You've already agreed!"

"Then I shall un-agree! Why should I sacrifice myself just so Mama can have more servants, sell myself like a—"

Meg's eyes widened as her sister's mouth formed the word but didn't dare to say it aloud.

"But it's not just for Mama. Think of Mignonette and Lily. Think of—"

"Why? No one is thinking of me!" Rose whined.

It would take hours of careful explanation to get her sister to see reason. Meg picked up the gowns and the sewing basket. "I'll go and work in the library. Get some rest. You'll feel better in the morning."

She shut the door and stood in the quiet of the hall, trying to quell the dark little demons of jealousy and envy. Rose would cry all the way to London, but once there, trying on pretty clothes and attending parties, she would feel differently about becoming a duchess.

And Temberlay? Was he awaiting his bride, anticipating the wedding night? Meg's stomach quivered. She set the gowns on the stair railing and took the scandal sheet out of her pocket. She looked down at the handsome face with a sigh, and ran the tip of one finger over his grinning mouth, and down his broad chest, the impossible length of his booted legs . . . was he really as wicked as he was drawn? She shut her eyes. She felt wicked just thinking about him, especially now. She picked up the gowns and headed downstairs.

A deal with this devil might be well worth the cost.

Chapter 2

"There's a rumor afoot you're getting married."

Nicholas Hartley, the infamous Devil Duke of Temberlay, opened one sleepy gray eye and fixed his gaze on the naked woman draped over his chest. The rumor was true enough, but he didn't want to discuss it, especially now.

His latest mistress had hair so blond it was almost white. It made her famous, both on stage and in bed, since every man in London wanted to know if the color was entirely natural.

It was.

Angelique's expressive green eyes remained fixed on him, her curiosity evident. She was jealous, if the scratch of her nails on his chest was anything to go by. He picked up her hand and put it where it could do some good, and grunted when she squeezed his cock.

"They say she's the daughter of the late Earl of Wycliffe. Wherever did you meet her, Devil?"

He hated when she called him Devil. The nickname had been earned in war, for braver deeds than the *ton* used it for now. He also frowned at the other name. Wycliffe. *Had* he met her? He'd been out of England for nearly three years, and home for mere weeks.

He tried to focus on his very talented mistress, rather than wondering about the bride his grandmother had arranged for him. He was surprised at Granddame's alacrity. It had been less than a week since she'd insisted he must marry, and since he had no choice, he'd given her carte blanche to make a match. He'd assumed she would confer with him before reaching a final decision. Once again, he had underestimated her.

"Is she pretty?" Angelique persisted.

He had no idea. Given his grandmother's hatred of him, he rather doubted she was. But he needed Granddame's fortune to support the estate his brother had left bankrupt. Marriage was simply a necessary bargain to maintain the dukedom. He shifted on the sheets, shut his eyes, told himself he didn't care who she was.

"Will she do this for you?" Angelique asked. Her hair brushed his stomach, and he gathered the silk of it in his hand so he could watch her work. She lifted her head again, much to his annoyance.

"Am I invited to the wedding?"

Was *he*? His grandmother hadn't so much as left a note to inform him of the arrangements.

He forced away his annoyance at the whole situation, and slid his hand between Angelique's thighs, and she purred as he stroked her, all other thoughts gone at last from her pretty head. He waited until she cried out, then lifted her to straddle his hips.

She laughed. "You are a devil! I'm due at the theater for rehearsal in less than an hour. There's no time."

Nicholas flipped her onto her back and grinned, "There's always time for this, Miss Encore." She arched against him with a mewl of need.

"Just once more, then, but hurry—" She rolled her

hips, tried to make him move faster, but he held still, teasing her.

"Hurry, Miss Encore?" He tweaked her nipple and she cried out in delight. "Not on your life."

With Angelique well sated but very late for rehearsal, Nicholas strolled into White's Club. Viscount Sebastian St. James was waiting for him, seated in a comfortable leather chair, drinking with several other gentlemen of the *ton*.

"Not your usual crowd, St. James," Nicholas murmured.

He was sitting with Charles Wilton and Lord Augustus Howard. The gentlemen were only vague acquaintances. Their smiles faded as Nicholas sat down.

"I'd about given you up," Sebastian said with a drunken grin. "We were just talking about you."

Nicholas's spine prickled. "Oh?"

Wilton smiled, but his eyes remained cold. "We were about to mount a wager as to what was keeping you, but St. James felt there was no point, since Angelique Encore is your new ladybird. It was all too obvious." There was an edge to his tone that tightened Nicholas's gut.

Augustus Howard waggled his gray brows. "We decided instead to bet on what time you'd arrive. Unfortunately, you're some hours earlier than my prediction."

"Trouble with—" Wilton pointed at Nicholas's lap.

"No, never, not Nicholas!" Sebastian cried. "My guess is Angelique had a performance this afternoon—" He elbowed Nicholas in the ribs. "Or should I say *another* performance?" Nicholas refrained from rolling his eyes.

Wilton smirked and sipped his drink, as if he knew a secret joke.

Lord Howard leaned in. "I hear your days of merriment are soon to come to an end."

Ah, so that was the secret joke. His wedding. Nicholas set his jaw, making ready to endure more questions and ribald jests.

Howard pursed his brandy-sodden lips in an ugly pout. "Since you're to hang in the parson's noose before the month is out, will you bequeath the lovely Angelique to me?"

Nicholas sipped his whisky to hide his surprise. Within the month? That soon? He felt the imaginary noose tighten, imagined his grandmother cackling as she tugged on his leg to hasten the drop.

"Doesn't anyone have anything better to talk about?" he asked. "I hear Napoleon is safely ensconced on Elba, never to terrorize the world again." But these men were different from the officers he'd known in Spain. His comrades had been sober and keen in battle, but after, once the dead and the living had been accounted for, they wagered and whored and drank as hard as these idle lords. But they did it to remind themselves they were still alive, and to forget that good men died every day. He looked at Wilton, Howard, and even Sebastian. What did these silly fops have to forget?

Boredom, he supposed.

He'd been back in England for five weeks, and he had not met a gentleman of rank with a useful occupation, or one who stayed sober past noon, if they were awake that early. He also remembered being one of the worst of them, the most incorrigible rake, the wildest, the drunkest, the most ridiculous rich, bored lordling of the bunch.

But that was before he went to war.

He was a different man—harder, stronger, and smarter. Yet they expected him to be the same drunken fool.

Charles Wilton raised his brows. "Napoleon? Not interesting enough. Not when the Devil is about to be shackled to the daughter of the virtuous Earl of Wycliffe. What's she like?"

Nicholas kept his expression bland, as if he knew all about her and didn't care that she was—what? Ugly? A stranger he must wed and bed within the month? He shifted uncomfortably, realizing he did care after all. Slightly.

He wished himself back in Spain, where the world made sense. If not for his brother's sudden and mysterious death, he wouldn't be here at all.

And if his grandmother had not insisted he remain in London, he would have retired to Temberlay weeks ago to calculate the full damage of David's mismanagement, and to discover just what had happened to his brother. The accident that killed him seemed to be the greatest secret in London, the details as deeply and hastily buried as David's corpse.

He worried about his grandmother when news of his brother's death finally reached Spain in a solicitor's letter, months after it had happened. She'd raised David, doted on him. Even in her terrible grief, she had managed the dukedom as best she could.

Or so he thought.

She had rushed at him the moment he'd arrived home, a virago in black bombazine. She'd slapped his face with the full strength in her arm, blamed him for everything that had befallen her, from David's death to the ruin of the dukedom. She had squelched the scandal, and hidden the details of how her beloved grandson had died, but she hissed them in Nicholas's ear.

He sipped his whisky and let it burn.

David had died in her arms after a duel, carried home

barely alive, his body riddled with wounds. "It's all Nicholas's fault," were his last words.

Nicholas had no idea what that meant. Unfortunately, he'd found nothing to explain it. No witnesses, no bystanders, no gossip at all . . . but he would. Finding other people's secrets was what he was best at. Which made the total surprise of his own wedding all the more unbearable.

Sebastian spilled his drink. Nicholas watched the brandy soak into the swirls of the club's Turkey carpet.

His grandmother had refused to allow anyone to clean David's blood from the rug in her study. It had been there when she called him into that room and insisted that he must do his duty and marry. Over his brother's blood, she'd told him the estate was ruined, that only her personal fortune was keeping them. She would continue to pay only if he agreed to marry where she wished.

He respectfully took her money for debts and current expenses, and agreed to the wedding, but refused to let her manage his estates.

"They say Wycliffe raised his girls to be pillars of feminine virtue and modesty!" Sebastian said, and grinned encouragement at Nicholas, as if he truly expected him to add more details. Nicholas sent him a flat look of warning, but Augustus Howard laughed.

"That doesn't bode well for you. Wycliffe was an ugly little man who used to scream about moral decency and the tender sensibilities of English womanhood in the House of Lords. Didn't he try to introduce a bill to force the female aristocracy to take vows of chastity, order, and virtue?" He shuddered and grinned at Nicholas.

"Ugly men have ugly wives in my experience, and ugly daughters." Wilton finished his drink and signaled for another. "Perhaps you'd better keep Angelique after all, if you can afford her."

Now what would Wilton know about his financial affairs? Perhaps it was merely jealousy. It was well known that Wilton had banished his wife to the country, and spent his evenings in the lowest brothels in London.

Sebastian mistook his silence for an invitation to keep up Nicholas's end of the conversation. "Not to worry, gentlemen. I know for a fact that Nicholas can bed anything, no matter how ugly. He once won a bet that he couldn't keep it stiff long enough to—"

"St. James," Nicholas murmured the warning. He'd come home from Spain to find dozens of such legends about him, none of them any truer than this one. He made it a policy to neither confirm nor deny what was said about him, but silence only seemed to make the rumors more prevalent, and infinitely wilder.

"Bedding an ugly wench once on a bet is one thing, but night after night until an heir is born?" Wilton grinned with delight. "You have my condolences." He raised his brandy in salute and downed it at a gulp. His eyes narrowed when Nicholas didn't join the toast. "But perhaps she's not so bad. What *is* your bride like, Temberlay?"

Nicholas tightened his grip on his glass, let the cut crystal points dig into his flesh, but the anger remained. He did not want to be a duke, did not want to marry. He wondered if his grandmother had intentionally meant to make a fool of him in front of men like Howard and Wilton. "A woman like any other, I suppose."

"You suppose?" Wilton prompted.

"All cats are black in the dark!" Sebastian chirped, and Nicholas sent him another quelling look, which Sebastian failed to heed. "It's an arranged marriage, gentlemen.

Nicholas's grandmother wants a grandchild to dandle on her ancient knee before she turns her toes heavenward. Isn't that so, Nick?"

Nicholas ignored him.

"Will she be attending Lady Melrose's ball on Thursday?" Howard asked. "The entire *ton* will be there. It would be a good time to show her off, prove she isn't hideous."

"I won't be going," Nicholas replied.

Howard looked shocked. "You did receive an invitation, didn't you? Surely your reputation is not so tarnished that—"

"It's probably Miss Encore's night off," Sebastian said in a stage whisper that would have done Angelique proud.

Nicholas had had enough. He picked up his hat. "Gentlemen, if you'll excuse me, I have another appointment."

Sebastian was at his heels before he reached the curb. "You're like a bear with a sore head! Are you unhappy with the match?"

"You know everyone in London. Who is she?" Nicholas asked.

"Who? Wycliffe's daughter?" Sebastian frowned. "Never been seen in London as far as I know. They've been in mourning since the earl died last year."

"They?"

Sebastian grinned. "I have two sisters, both notorious gossips. The earl has four daughters . . . or is it five?" He stroked his chin. "What was it Delphine said to Eleanor? They were laughing when they heard you were—" He winced. "Sorry, old man, but no one is talking of anything else."

"What did Delphine say?" Seb's twin sister was the worst gossip in the family, which probably accounted for why she remained unmarried well into her second Season.

"Flowers . . . something about flowers. Ah yes. They are all *named* after flowers! Blossom, Tulip, Cowslip . . ." He dissolved into drunken laughter at his own joke.

Nicholas frowned. "Which one is my bride?" he asked, his heart sinking. He was about to be saddled with a silly country virgin, precisely the kind of female he despised.

Sebastian's eyes popped. "You mean you don't know?"

Nicholas was forced to shake his head. "My grandmother is the one who wanted me married, so I told her to arrange it. Apparently, she has."

"Indeed," Sebastian said soberly. Nicholas turned toward his coach, but Sebastian caught his sleeve. "Look, I'll make inquiries, shall I? I'll ask Delphie and Eleanor. If anyone has any information, they will."

Nicholas looked at his friend. He was drunk, probably wouldn't even recall the conversation, especially if he went back inside to drink some more. Still, if Nicholas started asking questions himself, he'd look like an even bigger fool than he felt.

"I trust you'll be discreet," he said.

Sebastian laid a hand on his heart. "What would you like to know?"

Nicholas hesitated. Nothing. Everything. He wished again he were back at war, but the war was over, and David was dead, and he was the Duke of Temberlay. That meant marriage and children and becoming a pillar of English society, all the things he detested.

"Don't tell me you're nervous, Nick!" Sebastian scoffed.

Nicholas opened the door of his coach. "Of a woman named after a flower? Not a chance."

He'd eat her alive, and spit out the petals.

"D'you suppose he knows anything? He's not the gullible fool his brother was," Augustus Howard said as he boarded Wilton's coach.

"You seem worried. About what?" Wilton asked, knocking on the roof of the coach, giving the order to drive on. "He's as big a fool as his brother." He regarded his companion's nervous expression coldly. "Don't you find the irony satisfying? Temberlay is about to marry the daughter of the man who helped kill his own brother. I doubt he even knows."

Augustus frowned. The afternoon sun streaming into the coach emphasized his wrinkles, the paunch under his waistcoat.

"You got a pretty little wife out of it, didn't you?" Wilton asked. "How is sweet little Claire? Still pining for her true love every time you touch her?"

"I love my wife. You didn't love yours," Augustus shot back.

"We both got what we wanted. Revenge is sweet, don't you think? Perhaps we can yet destroy Nicholas Hartley for his sins. He's home now."

"His brother paid the debt!" Augustus hissed.

Wilton shot him a cold look. "It's not enough. David was merely a substitute, since Nicholas wasn't here. He is now."

Augustus swallowed, and Wilton smiled coldly. "Go home to sweet little Claire, old man. Take her to bed, and be glad it wasn't your wife he ruined."

"When will this end?" Augustus moaned.

Wilton turned to look out the window. "When I say it's over."

Chapter 3

"**W**here's your sister, Meg?" Amy asked, opening the bed curtains with a swish. Meg squinted at the housekeeper and shut her eyes again. She had nightmares about her father's death. When her dreams were at their worst, Rose often slept in the dressing room for a little peace. The nightmares were a secret they shared. If Mama found out, she might ask what they were about, and if she knew, it might well send her back into her shadow world of grief and pain.

"She's probably in the dressing room." She stretched, and recoiled as her foot touched the icy sheets on Rose's side of the bed. She pulled the coverlet closer and curled into a warm ball.

Amy went to check and returned to poke her again. "No she isn't! Lord Bryant is downstairs with his coach, and your mother is waiting on you and Rose in the breakfast room. She sent me up here to fetch you."

Meg sat up, and stared at her sister's empty pillow. The valise she'd carefully packed for her sister the night before was gone. Meg looked around the room, instantly awake.

She pulled on her robe. "Did you check the library? The kitchen?"

Amy set her hands on her hips. "I just came from the kitchen!"

Flora burst in. "Marguerite, you're still in bed! It's past eight, and we must leave immediately. The roads are—" She bustled into the dressing room, and came right back out again. "Where's Rose?"

In the doorway, John, their manservant, waited to carry the luggage downstairs.

Meg felt a moment's panic, and squelched it.

"She isn't here, my lady," Amy informed her. The countess's eyes widened.

"She's probably downstairs somewhere," Meg soothed. It was too soon to worry yet. "Did you look in the conservatory and the ballroom?" she asked, directing the question to John. "She always liked to play there."

Flora put her fingers to her temples and shut her eyes. "Those rooms have been locked for months, and she's not a child anymore. She's almost a married woman, and this is no time for games!"

"John, Amy, go and see if you can find her," Meg directed the servants. When they'd gone, she put her arm around her mother and led her to a chair. "I'm sure there's nothing to worry about. Rose is probably flitting from room to room, looking at herself in every mirror, trying to decide which one makes her look fairest. She'll be back momentarily, demanding John take down her favorites and ship them to Temberlay Castle."

Footsteps thundered up the hallway, pounded in Meg's chest, and she gripped her mother's shoulder and stared at the door, waiting for bad news.

The countess let go of the breath she was holding as her two youngest daughters raced into the room in their nightgowns. They climbed on the bed and began jumping. Meg swallowed a sigh of relief.

"Girls, get down—" she said, trying to catch them.

"Has Rose gone already?" ten-year-old Lily asked. "I wanted to ask her to bring me a present from London."

"I want a hair ribbon and a doll," seven-year-old Minnie added.

"Do stop jumping," Flora snapped. "Can't you see there's a crisis?"

"What's a crisis?" Minnie asked. "Is it a sweet? I want sweets from London too, like the sugared almonds Papa used to bring."

"I'm surprised you remember that." Meg took a moment to smile reassuringly at her little sisters as she lifted them off the bed and set them on the floor. She kissed them on the tops of their blond heads. "Go down to the kitchen for breakfast. You're giving Mama a headache." She hurried into the dressing room and pulled on the first gown—the only gown—she could find. Their best dress, the one Rose was to wear this morning, was gone. Meg's fingers trembled as she fastened the buttons. Her sister never got out of bed before being called at least twice. Meg fixed her expression into a placid smile for Flora's sake.

John returned as she was tying her hair back with a ribbon. "No sign of her, my lady," he reported to Flora, and sent Meg a worried glance. Meg felt her smile slip a little.

Flora's eyes widened for a moment, but she shook her head. Meg watched as she smoothed her fingers over her forehead. It was one of her mother's rules. Frowning caused wrinkles, and wrinkles were to be avoided at all costs. She settled back into the chair, and arranged her skirts to elegant perfection. "She's here somewhere, I'm sure of it. I will simply sit right here and wait for her to return."

Hector appeared in the doorway, his expression grim. Meg felt her heart climb into her throat, knowing it was bad news, hoping her sister wasn't hurt, or worse. "You'll have a long wait, Flora. A lad from the village just delivered a note. Rose is gone. Eloped, she says." Meg's heart dropped again, hurtling to the floor like a stone. It was worse indeed.

Hector held out the note, but Flora recoiled in horror.

Meg stood in stunned silence for a moment, staring at the letter in her uncle's hand. The ink was blotched with tears. Or was it only rain? She glanced out the window at the weather.

Sunny. Her stomach knotted.

"It's not true," Flora murmured. "It can't possibly be true!" She looked from Meg to Hector. "What am I to do now?"

Meg took the note and read it. Rose would not, could not, marry a man like Temberlay. She would rather face death and—Meg slid it into her pocket without finishing it, bitterness filling her throat. Now they'd all face death, or poverty. Her sister was the most selfish creature on earth. Still, she glanced at Rose's side of the bed with a twinge of fear. The future she'd chosen might turn out to be far worse than marriage to a duke with a rogue's reputation.

She squeezed her mother's hand, worried herself now, for Rose, for Flora, for her sisters. Hector patted Flora's shoulder as she began to blink back tears. "We'll find her before things go beyond redemption," he said. "She can't have gotten far."

Flora looked at Meg, her blue eyes sharp as a needle. "Who would Rose elope with?"

Meg shrugged. "How would I know? She had a dozen young men who—"

"A dozen?" Flora cried. "Oh, Hector, I'm going to faint!"

Hector ignored the threat. "Can you narrow it down?"

Meg shook her head, and Flora's eyes narrowed. "Come now, you've shared everything for over a year, clothes, this room, that bed! Surely you know her secrets!"

Was this her fault? Meg hadn't wanted to hear Rose gloat over her admirers, spin her romantic dreams. She'd pretended she didn't care, ignored her sister's attempts to whisper her secrets in bed at night. Guilt coiled through her like smoke. "Not this one."

Flora put a hand to her mouth. "Think of the scandal! What will the duchess say?"

Meg read dismay in Hector's eyes before he turned to soothe Flora. "I'll go myself, and bring Rose straight to London when I find her. In the meantime, Meg is close to her sister in size. She'll do to have the wedding gown fitted." He pressed his handkerchief into Flora's hand.

Meg felt her knees turn to water. "Me?" she whispered.

"Hector's quite right. The wedding is a fortnight away, and there's no time to waste," Flora said, rising now the decision had been made. She smoothed her curls and set her bonnet on her head like a soldier preparing for battle. "I'm going to wait in the coach. Do hurry."

"Is there anything else you can think of? Anything at all?" Hector asked Meg.

Meg looked again at the tear-stained note, scanned the last few lines. Rose didn't name her intended husband. If only she'd listened, hadn't been jealous. She racked her brain. "The last lad she mentioned was an ensign in the navy. I don't recall his name. Edwin, possibly. He wrote her several letters, but I didn't—she wouldn't let me read them."

Hector kissed her forehead. "Don't worry," he said, and helped her into her cloak. "I'll find her." He pulled a card from his pocket. "You'd better take this. It's the mo-

diste the duchess recommended. At least you'll have the
pleasure of trying on the gowns. I'll join you in London
in a day or two."

Meg read the worry in her godfather's eyes as she took
the card. There'd been so many problems he hadn't been
able to fix since Papa's death. Was this one more?

He smiled, tried to reassure her. "Go on, before your
mother starts to fret."

Meg's heart was pounding as Hector handed her into
the coach.

"You'll find her, won't you?" Flora asked him.

He gave her a reassuring smile. "Of course."

Flora lowered the window of the coach and watched
him mount his horse and ride away at a gallop. Then she
shut her eyes and lay back against the squabs with a sigh,
pale and worried. Meg leaned over to shut the window
against the cold breeze, and wrapped a rug around her
mother's knees.

Rose's disappearance on the eve of their salvation was
tragic. She might be in danger, and her mother was on
the verge of another nervous collapse. Flora had lost her
husband, her fortune, and now her eldest daughter. She
stood to lose her home too. Meg would have to find a way
to protect her from all of it.

Hector would find Rose in time for the wedding.

He must.

Guilt nipped at her as the coach moved through the
gates of Wycliffe Park and turned onto the London
road. She should be worried, not excited, but she was.
She would see the sights of London, visit the fashionable
shops, and stay in Lord Bryant's town house. And she
would see the notorious Devil of Temberlay in the flesh.
That promised to be an adventure in itself, and perhaps
the one she was looking forward to most of all.

Chapter 4

Lady Julia Leighton lifted her heavy veil and got to her feet as Nicholas entered the salon. He noted the dark circles under her eyes, made all the more startling by her pallor.

He crossed and kissed her forehead, and escorted her to a comfortable seat. "Have you been waiting long?" he asked gently.

His brother's fiancée had been heavily pregnant the last time he'd seen her, just days after his arrival home in London. She'd written to him to explain why she'd betrayed David with another man, and to ask for help. He'd gone to see her, given her money, arranged for a house, a midwife, and a nurse for the child. He could not see her as a fallen woman. Julia had always been like a sister to him, and if things had been different, she would have been David's wife and Duchess of Temberlay. His mouth twisted. He had always pictured Julia in that role, but now a stranger, his own unknown, unwanted bride, would take her place. He sat across from Julia to stem the sudden rage he felt.

"The child is well?" he asked.

"Yes, thank you," she smiled. "He's growing very fast.

I've come to say good-bye, Nick. I'm leaving London. My father found out where I was staying and insists that I cannot remain in Town. In fact he prefers I leave England." She looked up at him with a sad smile. "He told everyone I was dead, you see. My ghost walking the streets of Mayfair would be a rather difficult thing to explain." She rose to her feet, pulling her dark cloak more closely around her, her hands white flowers on the black velvet. "I owe you my thanks for all you've done—" She choked back a sob. "You've been most kind, Nicholas, in spite of everything."

He rose as well. He couldn't let her go this way. He'd known Julia since she was a child. She and David had been betrothed on her eighth birthday. He'd been as shocked as anyone else, but he didn't only blame her. "Where will you go?"

"Perhaps France, now the war is over," she said with false brightness. "Maybe Italy. My own grand tour."

"With a two-month-old child?"

Her smile fled. "I just wanted you to know that I regret what I did, Nicholas, my stupid, foolish behavior. I hurt David, and my parents. But I do not regret Jamie. My son is the love of my life. I thought my father might—accept him, after my brother's death, but he only wants me dead too."

He stared at the uncertainty in her face, visible in her eyes, even if she kept her jaw set with fierce determination. She didn't have a clue where she was going.

He took her hands. Her fingers were ice in his. "Julia, don't leave Town just yet. Wait a few days. I'll make some arrangements—"

"You've done far too much already," she said, and tried to pull her hand free, but he refused to give it up.

"My brother loved you."

There was doubt in her eyes. "Did he? Like a sister, perhaps. It's my fault he's dead. He fought that duel for my honor, although I had no honor left to fight for. He'd be alive if I hadn't—"

"He would have married you anyway if he lived."

She raised her chin, and curled her fingers in his. He felt the scrape of her nails on his palm. "I would not have let him."

Despite her downfall from earl's daughter to ruined woman, she was still the girl he remembered. The blackguard who seduced her had suffered no such fate.

"Tell me his name, Julia," he asked again. "Who is Jamie's father? Was he the man David challenged?"

"It doesn't matter, Nick. I have not seen him since that night—" She shut her eyes, blushed. "What would you do if you knew? Another foolish duel? I could not bear it if you were killed too, for my stupidity."

The blush added color to her pale face for a moment, made her look like the pretty woman she'd always been.

"Then allow me to speak to your father again."

"No. I cannot bear to see the disgust in his eyes again."

Desperation filled him, a need to protect her. "Then marry me, Julia."

It would fix everything, surely. With Julia by his side, as his duchess, his wife, being Duke of Temberlay might be bearable. She was his friend, his sister.

He realized at once it was a mistake.

She looked up in surprise, her dark eyes wide. Then she smiled sadly. "I hear you're already betrothed, Nicholas. And your grandmother would never allow you to marry a fallen woman. I thank you for the offer, but no."

Frustration warred with relief in Nicholas's breast. He didn't want to marry anyone. He wanted exactly what he couldn't have, the past back again.

She set his hand aside and got to her feet, lowering the veil again, moving toward the door. "I hope you find happiness in your marriage."

"Wait," he said. "Promise me you'll wait a few days, Julia. Don't leave London yet. Let me make some inquiries."

She lowered her eyes to her hands. "Thank you. I find I must accept your kindness yet again. I really must learn to stand on my own two feet. Three days, then I must be gone."

When she'd gone, he wondered what might have happened if she had accepted his proposal. It would have been so simple, so tidy, for both of them, a comfortable, companionable union. But Julia was right, his grandmother would never accept her now. Instead, he was tied to a woman he'd never even met. Anger flared again at the senseless mess David's death had created.

He poured a glass of whisky and stared into the amber depths, and thought of the bride his grandmother had chosen for him, a woman willing to take a husband she'd never met for a fortune and a title. How was that any less terrible than what Julia had done?

He set the drink down untouched. His bride didn't realize what she was getting along with that fortune. The new duchess had indeed made a deal with the devil.

He'd make her earn every penny.

Chapter 5

"**A**h, my dear mademoiselle, the pink silk is *parfait* for your coloring! It makes you glow, and that will make your bridegroom a very happy man!

The duchess's modiste was very small and very French. She flew around the shop on tiptoes, gathering samples, snapping her fingers at her assistants like a magical fairy, and like magic, when she draped the length of pale pink silk over Meg's shoulder, Meg was instantly transformed from plain to princess. Meg stared at her reflection in awe. The color brought out the golden glow of her skin, the rich red of her hair. It made her look dramatic, and, she almost dared to think it, beautiful.

"Who is the lucky gentleman?" the modiste asked, cocking her head and examining Meg in the mirror as she tucked and pinned the silk.

"The Duke of Temberlay," Meg replied without thinking. Interest lit like a flame in the Frenchwoman's eyes.

Flora's face appeared over Meg's other shoulder in the glass. "Would the color suit her as well if she were blond?"

The modiste pursed her lips. "My lady is thinking of herself, perhaps. I would suggest a deeper shade of pink for you."

"Then make up the gown in the deeper shade," Flora commanded.

The modiste squinted. "But the young lady is *magnifique* in the paler shade. To change the color would be a mistake."

A bolder pink would pick up the color in Rose's cheeks, the blue of her eyes, the sweetness of her lips. Meg pursed her own lips. If her sister had wanted to choose, she should not have run away.

"Where is Lady Rose this morning?" asked a voice behind them. Meg turned to find the Duchess of Temberlay standing behind her.

Flora gasped and laid a hand on her heart. The duchess ignored the reaction. She perched on a chair and regarded Meg.

Meg resisted the urge to raise her hands over her chest. She was clad only in a slip of muslin, held together with pins and marked with her measurements. She felt a blush rise over every exposed inch of her under the old lady's scrutiny.

"Rose has a dreadful cold," Meg managed the lie without flinching. "Since we are the same size, and there is so little time to get the wedding gown made, she asked me to attend this fitting for her."

The duchess's lips pouched. "She is still unwilling, then."

"Not at all, Your Grace," Flora gushed. "Rose is simply delighted to be marrying the duke now she's had time to recover from the honor of your—his—proposal. Simply, utterly, completely—" Meg winced. Flora's false smile was entirely too bright.

"So you've said, Countess." The duchess turned her attention back to the modiste.

"Try green on her, Mathilde." Three assistants rushed

forward with a dozen bolts of green velvet, silk, and damask. "That one." The duchess selected a mossy velvet. "Make a riding habit, something dramatic. Line it with russet, or scarlet. I'll trust your suggestions on day gowns, but I want something splendid to go with the sapphires."

Meg found herself surrounded by assistants, and swathed in luxurious cloth.

"Sapphires?" Flora asked.

"The famous Temberlay sapphires," the duchess informed her. "The new duchess will wear them at the first ball she attends with Nicholas after the wedding."

Mathilde draped Meg in ice blue satin. "I have seen the sapphires. They are *magnifique*!" she whispered, kissing her fingers and rolling her eyes dramatically.

"Such jewels will overwhelm poor Rose!" Flora murmured. "She is more suited to pearls and diamonds."

"The yellow diamonds will bring out the hazel of her eyes," the duchess mused.

"Rose's eyes are blue, Your Grace," Flora warbled. "Have you forgotten?"

"I have forgotten nothing, Countess." She didn't take her eyes off Meg for an instant. Meg grew indignant under the bold stare.

"Have you come for gowns of your own, Your Grace?" she asked, standing tall in the flood of shimmering blue satin. The color didn't overwhelm *her*. It made her hair glow like embers, and turned her skin to rich cream.

"I have plenty of gowns. No one looks to see what I am wearing anymore. They'll be watching the new Duchess of Temberlay. I expect her to make a grand impression."

She slowly circled Meg, examining her from every angle. "Tell me, is your sister a brave woman, Lady Marguerite?"

Meg shrugged, and had to catch the slippery fabric as it slid off her shoulder. "I don't see why—"

"Don't shrug," the duchess admonished. "It is an unbecoming mannerism."

Meg's chin came up at the correction. "Why would Rose need to be brave? She is getting married, not going into battle."

The duchess's cold obsidian eyes bored into Meg's in the mirror. "She is marrying the most notorious rake in London. She might indeed find it a battle. She must appear on his arm in public and remain graceful and serene, no matter what scandals Nicholas throws in her face. Is she brave enough to do that?"

Meg lowered her gaze before the duchess could read the answer in her eyes. Rose had run away to avoid that very thing. Would pretty clothes and sapphires be enough to comfort Rose when her husband went to another woman—or a score of other women? Meg met the duchess's eyes in the mirror, about to plead Rose's innocence, but the smirk on her face goaded Meg.

"Of course she's brave. Rose will make a magnificent duchess."

The duchess let her gaze travel over Meg again. "And you, Marguerite Lynton, are you brave?"

"Surely my character is not at issue, Your Grace."

The duchess leaned closer, her dark eyes boring into Meg's. "I read the scandal sheets too. They say he is a powerful lover," she whispered. "But not an easy one. He expects as good as he gives in bed."

Meg's eyes widened. She should be scandalized by the duchess's boldness, but she clutched the blue satin against her breast and waited to hear more. The old lady stepped back and laughed. "What an interesting reaction from such a chaste young lady—you're not shocked. You're curious."

"Marguerite!" Flora gasped. Meg dropped her gaze at once, and mortification heated the satin. She was shocked now. What an odd comment from Temberlay's own grandmother—it was as if she were speaking of a stranger rather than a beloved grandson. She glanced at the old lady. The look in her eyes was cold, calculating. She gazed at Meg as one might examine a broodmare, contemplating the creature's lines and her fitness as a match for the stallion. Meg's breath caught in her throat.

The duchess turned away and pointed to a bolt of cloth. "That sheer silk, Mathilde. Make something wicked for the wedding night."

"Is there something . . . thicker, perhaps?" Flora asked. "Rose takes cold easily."

"The very reason she is not here today, I believe," the duchess replied. "Make a pelisse in the blue-gray velvet, and a walking gown in that pewter brocade," she continued directing the modiste, who flew around the shop collecting fabrics at the duchess's nod. Soon Meg stood knee-deep in a rising tide of cloth.

"Wait—" Flora warbled, but the modiste grinned.

"Have no fear, Countess. Her Grace has exquisite taste. This young lady will make a lovely bride!"

Meg tried to step over the pile. "But I'm not—"

The duchess dropped her walking stick with a clatter. An assistant and Flora both bent to retrieve it, knocking their heads together with a cry of pain. Another shop assistant hurried forward to steady a pile of pattern books that threatened to topple as Flora staggered back.

Unperturbed by the chaos, the duchess picked up the stick herself.

"Yes, I think you must make up the wedding gown in the pale pink silk, Mathilde, not the darker shade. Good day, Marguerite. I have no doubt I will see you at the wedding."

She swept out of the shop without a backward glance, and Meg's stomach fluttered.

Poor, poor Rose.

Chapter 6

Lord Bryant arrived home the night before the wedding, rumpled, exhausted, and unshaven from days of hard travel.

He came alone.

Meg read the defeat in his eyes as he entered the drawing room. A grim shake of his head sent Flora to the floor in a flood of noisy tears. Meg rang for the maid and bundled her mother upstairs with a reviving glass of sherry. The maid returned a few minutes later for the decanter.

"Did you find any sign of her at all?" Meg asked.

Hector sank into a chair as if it was the first rest he'd taken in days. "The Edwin you mentioned turned out to be Edwin Ramsey, a midshipman in the Royal Navy. He married last spring, and has not seen Rose since. He suggested I call on Peter Markham, a young army captain stationed in Devon. Captain Markham directed me to Lieutenant Phillips. It went on that way for some days." He pushed a hand through his hair. "The trail simply ended. There was nowhere else to look. If she eloped to Scotland, then surely she's married over the anvil by now. I didn't have time to search there too. There are as many men in Scotland as England, and I fear most of them have probably written love letters to your sister at some point."

Meg's stomach knotted. "But the wedding is tomorrow!"

Hector shut his eyes. "I know."

Meg poured him a glass of brandy, her hands shaking. They faced shame, scandal, and a return to penury somewhere. It wouldn't be at Wycliffe Park.

Hector took the drink with a nod of thanks. "I'll go and see Temberlay myself in the morning and try to explain."

Meg sat on the edge of her chair. "Wycliffe will have to be sold at once."

"That's all you can say?" Hector frowned. "No anger over your sister's betrayal? If she'd stayed, you wouldn't be in this situation. I know you're worried about her, and we knew she was a silly, vain creature, but now—"

"It won't bring her back!" Meg said.

Hector shut his eyes, rubbed them with a thumb and forefinger. "You have a cousin in Kent. You could go there, perhaps."

"Her family is not wealthy. She couldn't afford to keep all of them," Meg replied.

"You never include yourself, do you? You're facing the necessity of going out to earn your bread, and probably theirs as well, and you aren't angry?"

"Of course I'm angry!" Meg said, rising to her feet. "I wish that Rose had done the right thing, and stayed, but she did not. There's Mama and the girls to think of now."

"If your father had not been so blindly stupid—"

Meg held up her hand to stop him. Papa was dead, and that's all there was to it. She couldn't think of that now, couldn't let the sadness overwhelm her. She felt the sting of tears behind her eyes, and forced them away as she always did when she thought of him. There was no time to cry, and hadn't been since the day he'd—*no!* She swallowed the rise of her stomach. "The duchess is sending her coach tomorrow at eleven o'clock to take Mama and Rose to the church," she said, changing the subject.

Hector's face twisted. "I said I'd see to it in the morning!" he said harshly, then his face fell. "God, I'm sorry, Meg. It's not your fault. Go to bed and try not to worry."

She sent up a prayer for her sister as she climbed the stairs, wished her safe. She passed her mother's door, heard her sobbing. She paused with her hand on the latch. Flora was about to lose everything yet again. First she had faced her husband's death, followed by the discovery that he had left his family penniless. Then Rose had disappeared, and left her family to face the scandal.

Anger flared, and she let go of the latch and stepped away. What was there to say? Flora would be inconsolable for days. She cursed her sister's inconsiderate behavior. What did it matter that Temberlay wasn't to Rose's taste, that he wasn't a fawning young officer willing to fall at her feet in adoration? His money would have gone a long way to make him bearable. Rose would only have had to put up with him long enough to give him an heir, and how long could that take? After that, well, husbands and wives lived apart all the time in fashionable circles. Rose could have lived her own life, chosen her own amusements, and had the full enjoyment of Temberlay's vast wealth.

She went into the bedroom that had been prepared for Rose. The wedding gown was hanging up so it wouldn't get creased, and in the pale light shining in from the street outside, the dress greeted her like Rose's ghost. She crossed and touched it, and the silk warmed under her fingers like living flesh. The dress was lovely, a confection. Madame Mathilde had outdone herself. How sad that no one would ever wear it.

She took it down and held it against her chest, and looked into the mirror. In the dim light, the transformation was remarkable. She might have been Rose, if her hair was blond. How often had her father despaired that she was not like the rest of his perfect blossoms? She was the wildflower among roses. But in this moment, she looked like a bride.

She wondered what it would feel like to be *his* bride.

She would probably never wed. She faced a future as a spinster, governess to other women's children.

Fiercely, she stripped to her shift, and put on the gown. The silk sighed as it slid over her body.

She lit a candle, and turned to the mirror again. It fit like it had been made for her. A wry smile twisted her lips. It *had* been made for her. It wasn't Rose's dress—she had never even seen it. Would she have changed her mind about marrying Temberlay if she had?

Meg gathered her hair and piled it atop her head, arching her neck, pursing her lips, posing. On a whim, she picked up one of the lacy negligees the maid hadn't packed yet, and draped it over her head. The scalloped hem dipped over her eyes, and only her lips showed.

Meg's heart stopped. She blinked. The layers of white lace slipped from her fingers, and her hair tumbled around her shoulders. She stared into her own eyes in the mirror.

Did she dare?

If she were caught, the scandal would be even worse. But if she succeeded . . .

She found pins, fixed the makeshift veil more firmly in place, and looked again.

Chapter 7

"**W**here is he, St. James?"

Sebastian St. James shook his head to clear it as he faced Nicholas's grandmother. It was like being cornered by a tiger, the man-eating kind that didn't bother with niceties like "good morning" before devouring a chap whole.

"Isn't he here?" he squeaked, and cleared his throat. He'd just arrived at Hartley Place to accompany Nicholas to his wedding. Although it was nearly eleven o'clock, it was far earlier than Sebastian usually rose, especially after a night of hard drinking. Finding the dread Duchess of Temberlay seated in a chair in the middle of the entrance hall brought on the shakes. He licked his lips, plucked his hat off his head, and held it over the vital parts of his anatomy like a shield.

"You know very well he is not here. Where is he?"

His lips moved, and his jaw flapped like a trout's, but no sound came out. He tried to think of a polite excuse, but there wasn't one. "He was out celebrating the, um, happy occasion last night. He gave me his word that he would be on time this morning . . ." It was obvious that she didn't believe a word, and he let the falsehoods trail off.

He shifted his feet like a disgraced schoolboy, and tried to think of a better explanation for Nicholas's absence, but his head was pounding. They'd visited three parties, and it had been well past four when Sebastian had tumbled into the nearest coach and ordered the driver to take him home. He'd woken in his own bed this morning, so it must have been his coach. He assumed that Nicholas had gone on without him. The man had the constitution of a warhorse.

"He will be late for his wedding if he does not walk through that door in the next five minutes," the duchess snapped. "Do you know where to look for him? With that actress, perhaps?"

Sebastian blushed. The old lady was remarkably well informed. Of course, she didn't like her younger grandson, and probably believed every scandalous tale about him out of sheer spite. "Oh, I don't think he would—"

She banged her walking stick on the marble tiles, and the sound echoed through the cavernous hall. Sebastian winced. "Don't be a fool! I can read, and I can hear perfectly well. Temberlay's habits are the talk of every fashionable salon in London, and a good many disreputable ones as well. Go and find him."

"Your pardon?" he squeaked again.

"Find him! Drag him to the church in whatever condition you find him, drunk or sober, naked, if necessary," she bellowed, and the echo rang in his head like a hammer blow. He began to back toward the door, trying to bow and escape at the same time.

The door opened before he could reach it.

"St. James, there you are! I was afraid you'd be late." Nick's companionable slap on the back nearly floored him, and Sebastian wheezed. Nicholas was tousled and unkempt, still in evening clothes, his cravat loose, his waistcoat missing a button, looking every inch like a man who had spent the night reveling in every manner of debauchery. He grinned at his grandmother. It was a smile Sebastian knew well, the one he saved for charming the most difficult of female conquests. The duchess glared back malevolently, completely unaffected.

"You fool! You have only minutes to bathe, shave, and dress. You will not be late for your wedding, Temberlay."

Nicholas bowed over her hand, but she snatched it out of his grip.

"I'll be there, Granddame. If I'm not, you and Daisy may start without me."

Sebastian almost smiled at his daring and his fortitude, but it hurt too much. Nicholas took the stairs two at a time, calling for his valet.

Sebastian followed more gingerly.

"You will make sure he's on time, St. James. Is that clear?" the duchess called after him. "The wedding is at eleven." She rose, and swept him with a look of disdain. "Perhaps I'd better see to it myself that he gets there," she said. Sebastian tried Nicholas's rogue's grin. It felt like death's grimace.

"Please, Your Grace, I'll see that he arrives on time. He'll want to ride, and the fresh air will do him a world of good." Or it would make Nicholas's own hangover all the more painful, Sebastian hoped.

"He has fifteen minutes, or I will go upstairs and drag him down, d'you hear?"

Her words thundered around the domed ceiling and smacked him across the head.

"Perfectly, Your Grace. I'll go up and hurry him along." He fled before she could threaten castration if he failed, probably his, since she wanted heirs.

Sebastian shut the door of his friend's chamber and leaned on it. Nicholas's hair was wet from a hasty bath, and his valet was preparing to shave him. "Lord, Devil, your grandmother is a dragon!"

"She's a woman like any other. You just need to know how to charm her, manage her," Nicholas said.

"Oh? And if you know how to handle her, then why do we find you about to hang in the parson's noose this fine morning? It seems she's the one who has managed you right into matrimony."

Nicholas sobered. "Let's give her the full joy of it, shall we?" He crossed the room to sip the coffee awaiting him on a tray.

Sebastian looked at his watch and grimaced. "I need to rush you along, old chap, or no one will have any joy at all. Her Grace will have my head boiled and served at the wedding breakfast if you're late." He strode to the wardrobe and threw open the mahogany doors. "What coat will you wear?"

"What do you suggest, Partridge?" Nicholas asked his valet.

"Dark blue or gray would be most appropriate, Your Grace. Something elegant and dignified."

Nicholas set his cup down and grinned. "D'you hear that, Seb? In that case, I'll take the green one. Pair it with the red striped waistcoat."

Sebastian winced as Partridge took the items out of the wardrobe. The coat was a vivid shade of emerald, more suited to an afternoon at the races, and even there it would be pushing the limits of good taste. "You're quite certain this is the coat you meant, sir?" Partridge asked.

"The very one," Nicholas replied. "With black breeches and boots. What do you think of that?"

"You'll knock her eye out, Your Grace," Partridge intoned soberly.

"That's the very idea. Like a good horse, she needs to know who's riding her, who holds the whip. I mean to show her that from the very start."

Sebastian wondered how the god-awful outfit was meant to accomplish that, but there wasn't time to discuss it. He watched the clock as Partridge tied Nicholas's cravat with his usual precision, and helped his master into the nauseatingly bright waistcoat. The coat was almost a blessing, since it hid some of the stripes.

Nicholas took his top hat from Partridge and turned to go, going down the stairs at a run. Mercifully, the duchess had left her post.

"Her name is Rose," Sebastian panted. "Not Daisy."

A footman opened the front door and Nicholas sailed through it. "Rose," he repeated in a wicked drawl.

"Rose," Sebastian confirmed, and squinted at the merciless midday sun. Nicholas was grinning his Devil grin, and Sebastian felt his stomach lurch. He almost pitied the bride.

She was in for one hell of a day.

Chapter 8

$\sim\!\!\infty\!\!\sim$

Flora was still crying when Meg descended the stairs the next morning, dressed for the wedding. She followed the sound of her mother's sobs to the breakfast room, and opened the door. Hector was patting her hand and doing his best to comfort her.

He drew a surprised breath and leaped to his feet.

"Rose!" Flora slid to the floor in a faint. If she expected Hector to catch her, she was disappointed. He was staring at the bride before him, looking a little pale himself. Meg lifted the veil an inch and regarded her mother.

"What the devil do you think you're playing at, Marguerite?" Hector bent to rub Flora's limp wrists. "Look what you've done to your poor mother. We thought you were Rose."

Meg folded back the veil entirely. "I'm not playing at anything. I'm going to marry the Duke of Temberlay in Rose's place. He needs a wife and we need his money."

"Are you out of your mind?" Hector dropped Flora's hand and rose, stepping over her prostrate form to reach Meg. "This isn't a game!"

Meg sat down and buttered a triangle of toast, though she wasn't hungry. The butterflies in her stomach felt more like birds of prey. "Of course it's a game. Temberlay has not once shown his face at the door, or sent a note or even so much as a flower, and we've been in Town for a fortnight. He obviously doesn't care whom he marries, so I shall do as well as Rose. If he wishes to play games, then I will play to save this family from poverty."

"But the duchess will care! Meg, I can't let you do this—" Hector began, but Flora gripped his ankle.

She sat up and looked at her daughter. "You would do this, Marguerite? You're willing to marry him in your sister's place?"

Meg read the conflicting emotions in her mother's blue eyes. There was fear there, and hope as well. The carrion birds circled her stomach again. "Yes, Mama. I'll marry him. There's no other choice. We can't have Minnie and Lily growing up in debtors' prison." The jest sounded hollow.

Flora got to her feet, and her eyes moved over the gown and the veil. "You're doing this for me? For your sisters? Marrying a stranger? I mean, managing the servants and selling off the silver is one thing, but this—" She looked at Meg as if she were seeing her for the first time.

Meg felt tears sting her eyes. She forced a smile. "I have no wish to be a spinster governess for the rest of my life!" If she married Temberlay, there would be no more need to sell Wycliffe's valuables. Perhaps she could even buy back a few things, like Papa's horses and her mare. Of all that they'd lost, they meant the most to her.

Flora blinked at her.

"I still say this isn't a good idea. It will not be an easy marriage for you," Hector murmured. "Rose would have managed it, despite her tantrums. Give her a shiny necklace to play with and she forgets everything else. You deserve more, my dear, and I'm not sure he's the kind of man to give you that."

Meg set the toast down, unable to even pretend to eat now. "It *will* be easy. I want nothing but his money," she lied. "I shall simply lay down the rules from the start."

"From what I know of Nicholas Temberlay, he's the one who makes the rules," Hector warned.

She raised her chin. "He won't get his way this time. I will marry him and provide him with an heir, and I will make it clear that I won't have daily scandals thrown in my face."

Flora shook her head. "Pretty though you look today, you're not the kind of woman to reform a rake. You haven't the experience—the feminine wiles—it would call for. You're clever, but he's out of your league, dear."

"Nonsense. Once I've given him a son, we'll live apart. I will have a generous income to support you and the girls, and he will have his freedom. It should only take a few days, weeks at most. I was raised on a farm with horses. When a foal is wanted, it takes little time."

Hector turned scarlet. "You think—"

Flora laid a hand on his sleeve. "Perhaps a mother is better qualified to handle this part, Hector."

He looked relieved. "Fine, shall I leave?"

"Yes," Flora said.

"No!" Meg countered.

"Marguerite, there is more to know about marriage than I feel comfortable saying in front of your father's stepbrother!" she whispered.

"But he's my godfather!"

Flora actually blushed. "You have had a very sheltered upbringing. Do you even understand how a woman gets with child?"

Meg raised her brows. "Of course. Papa's Thorough-breds did it all the time."

Hector made a strangled sound and began edging toward the door, but Flora grabbed his arm, keeping him by her side. "It's different between a man and a woman, Marguerite. Especially *that* man! You heard what the duchess said." She was blushing again. She tugged Hector's sleeve. "Tell her, Hector."

"Tell her what?" he asked, looking horrified.

"What they *say* about him!"

Hector looked miserable. "She already knows he's a rake and a gambler and a—"

Flora snorted like one of Lord Wycliffe's horses. "Of course she knows that! She and Rose read Amy's scandal sheets."

"Mother! How did you find out?" Meg asked, but Flora refused to be distracted.

"You know what I mean, Hector. There are rumors about his *predilections,* his *prowess* as a lover. They say he is—" She broke off and held her hands in front of her, a foot apart. Meg frowned.

Now Hector was blushing. He put a hand under Flora's elbow and firmly escorted her into the hallway.

Meg crept to the half-open door to listen.

"Flora, you can't tell a virgin bride on her wedding day that her husband is—" He whispered a word Meg couldn't hear.

"I wish Marcus hadn't insisted the girls be raised in total ignorance of these matters. She needs to know, Hector."

"Why? She'll find out in her own good time. I trust he isn't a savage. Just tell Meg the things your mother told you," Hector advised.

"She told me to lie still and pretend I was asleep," Flora murmured.

Meg opened the door. "Is that all there is to it? Lying still?"

Flora let out a nervous whoop of surprise. "Well, yes and no," she began.

She was interrupted by a discreet cough.

"The Temberlay coach is here, my lord," the footman said.

"Already?" Flora gasped, but Meg stepped forward.

"You may tell the coachman we'll be ready shortly."

Hector's butler followed, bearing a bouquet of pink roses. Meg's heart leaped, hoping they were from Temberlay. "With the compliments of Her Grace, the Duchess of Temberlay," he told her.

"Oh." Meg took them with a frizzle of disappointment.

"May I offer congratulations, my lady?" the butler said.

The birds flapped against her ribs again. "Ask me later."

Chapter 9

The coach pulled up at the church of St. George's Han-over Square, and Meg took a deep breath, and looked up at the gray facade of the old church.

The building stared back with sober disapproval of her deception. She lowered her eyes to the bridal bouquet.

Roses for Rose.

She tugged the makeshift veil forward, covering her face from her forehead to the tip of her nose.

"Lovely veil, dear, but I don't recall buying it. Where did you get it?"

Meg leaned forward and whispered in her mother's ear, and Flora's hand flew to her mouth. "What do you intend to do, take it off and wear it later?"

"The veil we ordered for Rose was too thin. You could see right through it." Her stomach fluttered. "Is he here yet?"

Flora scanned the street. "There's not another coach in sight," she said indignantly. "He should be waiting for you."

Hector took their arms and hurried them up the steps. "Under the circumstances, I think it's better that he's late. Marguerite is not Rose, and that's who he'll be expect-ing."

"As if he'd know one of us from the other!" Meg muttered, but her stomach quailed. Even if he hadn't met either sister, surely the duchess would have told him of Rose's legendary beauty the moment the betrothal was arranged. She swallowed. Temberlay, a man seen with only the finest London beauties on his arm, was about to marry the plainest Lynton sister. Her lips twitched. She was, no doubt, the first plain woman who even dared *speak* to him.

A coach turned the corner, and Flora craned to look. "Is that him?"

Meg's throat was as dry as dust as the coach came toward them.

"Come on, Meg, there's no time to lose. Temberlay may not know the difference between you and Rose, but the duchess will. If she puts a stop to this wedding the minute you walk in, we'll look like even bigger fools than if we'd just admitted Rose ran away," Hector said, tucking her hand under his arm, and placing the other firmly on Flora's back to hurry them inside. "It's bad luck if the groom sees the bride before the wedding. In this case, very bad luck indeed."

He put them into a little room off the main porch. "I'll come and get you when it's time," he said as he shut the door.

"Are you nervous?" Flora asked. She plucked a rose from the bridal bouquet and shredded it.

Meg pressed her knees together to keep them from shaking. "No, not in the least."

"I was sick twice before I found the courage to walk down the aisle on my wedding day, and I knew your father. You're about to wed a complete stranger, and—" Flora's face crumpled. Meg caught her as she burst into tears.

"You'll ruin the silk, Mama," she said gently.

Flora dabbed at her eyes, and Meg looked around the tiny storeroom. It was filled with prayer books and hymnals in teetering piles. A small, round stained glass window high above the floor showed St. George gazing up to heaven. He looked much comforted by what he saw there, but Meg followed his gaze to the stone ceiling and saw only cobwebs.

"Mother, what did you mean about his prowess as a lover? What *do* they say about him?" she asked. "I don't think it was in the scandal sheets, whatever it is."

"It's his *size*, he's reported to be very—" She began crying anew.

"Is he tall, then?" Meg mused. "I'm a tall woman, and I'd like him to at least be as big as I am."

Flora looked up through red-rimmed eyes. "He's not *tall*, Marguerite. It's his—"

A commotion on the porch broke the silence outside their hiding place. A horse cried out, and hooves clattered on the stone steps. The main doors of the church banged open and hit the wall with a terrifying crash. Flora shrank back, and grabbed Meg's arm.

"Where's my bride? Let's get on with the wedding!" a male voice shouted.

Meg shut her eyes in dismay, and the birds in her stomach died of fright and dropped like stones, one by one. "I take it he's arrived."

Flora gripped Meg's shoulders. "It's not too late. We can slip out the door and down the steps. No one will notice if we hurry."

For a moment, Meg was tempted. Other men were shouting now, and the horse was screaming its own objections. Someone was laughing. Her groom, no doubt, living up to his devilish reputation.

She stared at the door latch, then glanced up at St. George. He dared her to flee. She pursed her lips. She hadn't run when her father had sold her beloved horses without even telling her. She hadn't run when he died, and her mother collapsed into grief. She had gone forward, done what was necessary.

"You and I and Lily and Mignonette will notice when we have to leave Wycliffe," she said.

There was a heavy thump on the door, and Meg crossed to open it a crack, only to be confronted by the horse's panicked eyes as several Temberlay footmen hustled it down the steps. There was no sign of the animal's rider. Her heart thumped and her stomach churned, and she knew exactly how the poor horse felt. She had no more right to be here than he did. "I will go through with this wedding," she informed the horse, and her mother.

Hector arrived, breathing hard, looking angry.

"What's he playing at?" Flora demanded. "Does he mean to carry her off over his saddle?"

Hector straightened his coat with an angry jerk. "If you wish to reconsider, Meg, I will be pleased to go and explain everything to the duchess."

Meg's heart climbed her throat. "Is he as bad as that?" she croaked, then held up a hand. "No, it doesn't matter. I'm not leaving. He's playing his game, and I'm playing mine. My stakes are higher."

She stiffened her spine. She felt more like a soldier marching into battle than a bride. Hector squeezed her hand, and she read admiration in his eyes, and uncertainty. It made her shiver.

"I'll escort your mother to her seat and come back for you in a moment," he said.

Alone, Meg chewed her lip. She lowered the veil over her eyes with shaking fingers and picked up the bouquet.

The overwhelming fragrance of roses filled the room like her sister's ghost, reminding her she wasn't really the bride. And yet she was. She squeezed the stems, and a thorn pricked her finger. She felt the sting, watched the blood bloom across the pristine white silk of her glove, and tried to block out the hammering of her heart. Then Hector was back again, and it was time to let him lead her into the cool dimness of the church.

"You look lovely, Meg. Your father would have been proud, and—"

She stopped listening to the murmured reassurances.

She was looking at the Devil Duke of Temberlay. Nicholas Hartley. Her groom.

He was indeed tall, and elegantly slim. He wore an odd emerald green coat, and a gypsy-striped waistcoat. His hair was dark, nearly black, and curling over his collar. It was impossible to tell the color of his eyes, but she imagined they must be an exotic shade of green to match the coat. Why else would a man choose such an outlandish outfit?

Her stomach fluttered as she drew closer. He was very big indeed, broad shouldered as well as tall. He wore black breeches and polished Hessians, and they outlined every muscular inch of his long legs. Her gaze traveled up to his face. Even from here, she could see the anger in the hard set of his jaw, the forbidding frown. The coldness of his gaze chilled her, made her tremble.

Hector shook her gently, and she realized she'd stopped walking and was standing in the middle of the aisle like a ninny. She swallowed, forced herself to take the last dozen steps forward, counting them as she went.

Hector bowed stiffly, and offered Meg's hand to Temberlay. He waited a long, insulting moment before he accepted it, and she felt hot blood rush to her face. She stared down at his hand, tanned and brown against her white glove. A thin white scar ran up the length of his thumb to disappear under his cuff. How did a man get such a scar? It spoke of blood, and daring, but just as likely it was a love bite, or a fall he'd taken while drunk.

His grip was firm and impersonal as he led her the last few steps to face the bishop.

Meg turned her face forward, trying to ignore the tingle that raced up her arm from his touch. She concentrated on the churchman's untidy ruff of white hair. He intoned the ceremony in a rich bass voice, and the words echoed through the church, daring anyone to decry the match that God had ordained.

Meg stared up at the saints in the stained glass windows, holding her breath, waiting for them to descend and denounce her as a fraud, but they remained silent.

She repeated her vows, her stomach knotted against her deception, stumbling only a little as she whispered her own name in place of her sister's. She glanced sideways at the stranger by her side, but he was staring at the wall, looking thoroughly bored. Annoyed, she tried to withdraw her hand from his, but his grip instantly tightened like iron, though he did not move otherwise, or even look at her.

He spoke his vows in a deep growl that vibrated over her nerves. He promised to take someone named Daisy to wife. This time, when she glanced up at him, he had the audacity to smile, a grin of pure, breathtaking devilment. She drew a breath and almost forgot to exhale. This was the Devil of the scandal sheets, the rogue, the lover, the rake . . . and with the final "I will," her husband.

She thought of everything that meant, and her skin grew warm, the heat radiating from their joined hands, spreading through her limbs like fire. It was too late for regrets. She swayed, and his grip tightened again, silently commanding her not to dare to swoon. She'd never swooned in her life, but if ever there was a time for it, this was probably it. She straightened her spine instead.

Nicholas felt her sway, and refused to let her faint. It was a silly female trick he detested. Her fingers were icy in his, and he could feel her pulse racing under his hand. She was nervous, perhaps even afraid of him.

Good.

He frowned at the heavy veil she wore, felt pity and dismay. She must be hideous.

All he could see of her face as she walked up the aisle was her mouth. She had full lips, sweetly pink, damp and parted. He watched in fascination as she caught her lower lip between white teeth the moment she saw him. He let his gaze roam over the rest of her. Her gown was a shade of pink that resembled a blush. It almost matched the color of her skin, making it appear from a distance that she wore nothing at all. She was tall, but her figure was impossible to gauge behind the massive bouquet of roses. His gut churned with frustration, and anger—at her, at his grandmother, at himself for agreeing to this sham.

He frowned, and she stopped in her tracks.

Hector Bryant tugged her forward, and her pretty mouth set itself into more determined lines as she came the last few steps toward him. The pulse in her throat throbbed, and the roses shivered against her bosom. In any other situation, he would have been sorry for her fear, done his best to soothe it.

But this woman had chosen to marry a stranger, and she was being well paid for it. She didn't need his pity.

She glanced back at Hector as she put her hand in his,

and he noted the slimness of her waist, the delicacy of her figure as she turned. He tightened his grip on her hand, and she looked up at him. At least he thought she had. He couldn't be sure through the heavy layers of lace that fashioned her veil.

She took her place beside him and squared her shoulders like a soldier going into battle, finding comfort in her own courage since he hadn't offered any. He felt a surge of admiration that belonged on a battlefield, and shook it off.

He could smell her perfume over the scent of the roses, something soft and enticing, slightly spicy, definitely intriguing. He turned away, studied the rear door, wondering what would happen if he bolted through it, left her here. He didn't hear a word of her breathless vows.

When the time came to lift the veil and kiss her, he held his breath, steeling himself not to flinch, no matter what she looked like. Not for her sake, but because he wouldn't give his grandmother the satisfaction. He could feel Granddame's gaze on him like a blade at his throat.

He braced himself and lifted the veil.

He stared down at her. She wasn't hideous.

She was beautiful.

He met wide eyes that held a kaleidoscope of colors, gold, brown, and green, set in a lush fringe of copper-tipped lashes. Her features were delicate, perfectly formed, her nose dusted with faint freckles that suggested she spent time outdoors and didn't always wear a bonnet or carry a parasol. Under his scrutiny, she blushed. He was trying to recall the last time he'd seen a maidenly blush when his eyes found her mouth.

Her lips were parted slightly, perhaps in awe of him, perhaps in anticipation of the kiss that would seal their vows.

He lowered his head, intent on that unexpectedly glorious mouth, but the instant his lips touched hers, she slammed her mouth shut, and the kiss was disappointingly hard and unyielding, a virgin's kiss. He frowned as she pulled away and dropped the veil back over her face. He felt as if a curtain had been drawn too soon on what he'd hoped would be a very tantalizing performance. Disappointment warred with anger as he turned to face the bishop.

Meg barely heard the last few words the bishop spoke over them. She was trembling when Temberlay led her down the aisle, her wrist clenched in his fist. She had to run to keep up with his long strides. All she could think of were his eyes. They weren't green. They were gray, and as cold and forbidding as the winter sea. A dozen emotions had passed through the depths of his eyes as he stared down at her—resignation, surprise, curiosity, and something she couldn't name that made her intensely aware that she stood just inches from the heat and power of a male body for the first time in her life.

When he bent to kiss her, she felt the soft exhalation of his breath on her mouth, smelled the spice of his soap, the tang of leather, and she was more afraid in that moment than she'd ever been in her life. She slammed her eyes shut and puckered. He pulled back with a frown and she read confusion and anger in his eyes. Hot blood filled her cheeks, and she pulled her veil back over her face to hide her dismay.

He grabbed her wrist without a word and strode down the aisle, dragging her behind him.

Her mother sobbed as they raced past, the sound of her grief echoing off the vaulted ceiling. Hector looked grim.

The duchess stood stiffly silent in the family pew. If she knew, she gave no sign that her grandson had married the wrong woman.

The rest of the church was nearly empty. Other than immediate family, no one at all had been invited to the wedding.

Realization shook her anew as the bells began to peal. The man dragging her out of the church at a dead run was her husband. For better or worse—probably more the latter than the former—she was married.

The Devil of Temberlay was not so amusing now.

She glanced up at St. George as they swept out of the church and whispered a prayer, but the saint had slain *his* dragon, and she was on her own.

Chapter 10

Temberlay dragged her down the steps, his grip like iron. Meg flinched as handfuls of wheat hit her like hail. She tried to tug free to slow down, but he hurried on, ignoring her struggles.

He reached the nearest coach and opened the door. "Hartley Place, Rogers," he ordered as he thrust her into the dark interior.

She perched stiffly on the plush seat, and he settled himself across from her. She examined her husband from under the veil as the coach lurched away from the curb. The velvet squabs were dark green, which made his coat look all the more garish. She felt a bubble of hysterical laughter catch in her throat, though aside from his attire, there was nothing at all amusing about him. The caricatures didn't begin to do him justice. He was better-looking, bigger, and far more dangerous in person. He bore no resemblance at all to the playful rascal in the scandal sheets.

"You can take off that veil now, Daisy," he said, and she stiffened at his insolent use of the wrong name. Even Rose would have been better.

"Daisy might take hers off, but I have no intention of

doing so," she said, and bit her lip. She sounded like a prim little fool.

He sent her a lazy smile that turned her insides to jelly. Men smiled like that at Rose, not Marguerite. He plucked a rose from her bouquet and brought it to his nose in a polished gesture.

"If I call you Rose, and ask nicely, will you comply?"

Suddenly Meg did not want to be called by her sister's name. Not by this man.

"No," she said stubbornly.

"Surely I've earned the right to look at you. I married you, and you've been well paid for the honor of becoming Duchess of Temberlay," he said coldly.

"Not well enough paid to endure insults! Are you drunk?" She'd read that he drank four bottles of wine at breakfast, switched to whisky, gin, and stout at lunch, and enjoyed countless glasses of champagne by night.

He raised his brows. "Not at the moment, but I intend to remedy that as soon as I get home. I wonder when I'll need the solace of drink more—before or after I bed you?"

Her stomach flipped. Something in his eyes told her this would be very different indeed from the mating of horses, or from the casual kisses Rose had described, or anything else in her narrow realm of experience. She would not let him know that, however. She raised her chin and bluffed. "Let's make it before, shall we? I hear that drink renders a man incapable." She'd seen that tidbit in a scandal sheet somewhere, hadn't she? He laughed, hardly the response she'd hoped for.

"That's never been a problem for me," Nicholas drawled. She was quick-witted, at least, if tart-tongued. He watched her incredible mouth work. Her mouth rippled in trepidation as she wondered if she'd gone too far. Even with the rest of her face hidden, that one feature betrayed a dozen emotions. He'd read disapproval, fear, pride, and determination, all from observing nothing more than her lips. It was fascinating, made him wonder what it would be like to kiss her properly.

Was she as untried as rumor reported? "Have you been disappointed by an inebriated lover in the past? Show me the cad, and I'll call him out on your behalf."

Her lips gaped in maidenly mortification. Was she blushing under the veil, or on the verge of tears? To his surprise, she laughed, and clapped a hand over her mouth.

He frowned. He wanted to discomfit her, not amuse her. He picked up her hand and pulled off her glove, and tossed it out the window for effect. Her smile faded, and her lips trembled when he touched her.

He looked at her hand. Her fingers were cold and stiff, though long and delicately made. Her skin was tanned, and he felt a roughness on her palm and turned her hand to look at it. Her skin was calloused and red, as if she scrubbed floors for a living.

Another curiosity. Ladies did not have rough skin, or freckles. Aside from the fact she had pretty eyes, work-worn hands, a delectable mouth, and a quick tongue, he knew nothing about her at all.

She clenched her hand, tried to draw back, but he opened it again, and brought it to his lips, and kissed her palm and her fingertips. He felt the tremor run through her, heard her sharp intake of breath. Her lower lip caught in her teeth. Intrigued by the reaction, he let his lips linger on the hectic pulse point in her wrist. When he slid his hand along her arm, seeking the soft skin at her elbow, she gasped and pulled away, hiding her hand in her lap, her chest heaving, lips parted in surprise.

He shifted in his seat. The erotic teasing had unsettled her, but it also had an unexpected effect on him. Perhaps it was the fact that her face was hidden, or that she was a stranger and an innocent, though he had never found virgins to his taste before. He sat back, crossed his legs to hide his arousal and reminded himself that this was duty, not pleasure. Tantalizing as she was to toy with, she was still likely to prove a disappointment in bed. He stared out the window and did his best to ignore her, but her perfume tugged at his curiosity, and the sound of her breath and the rustle of her gown made him intensely aware of her.

Meg's hand tingled. Actually, everything tingled. He'd only held her hand, yet she felt his touch *everywhere*. The look in his eyes made her feel naked. Under her clothes her body pulsed and throbbed. She was out of her depth, drowning in sensation, and he had merely kissed her fingers.

She drew a shaky breath and gazed at him from the feeble sanctuary of her veil, imagining what else was to come, but he was staring out the window with a world-weary expression as if he'd forgotten her. His hands lay folded in his lap. She imagined those long fingers caressing her skin, his body joined to hers. His hands, his thighs . . . She shut her eyes and gave an involuntary moan. He shot her a look, his brows rising into his hairline.

"Pardon?" he asked.

"Nothing," she murmured, and clutched the roses tighter, suddenly anxious to be out of his overwhelming presence. By tomorrow it would be over—the wedding, the bedding, everything but the gossip. Surely his— their—hasty marriage would be the talk of London as soon as the notice was published in the respectable pages of the *Morning Post*. She shut her eyes, imagining the wicked delight the scandal sheets would take in her marriage if—when—her deception was discovered. Vultures swooped in her chest again.

The coach pulled up beneath the portico in front of Hartley Place, and Meg looked out at the imposing town house. The Temberlay crest, a snarling wolf poised over the body of a slain doe, was carved in stone above the front door. She gazed up at it in horror for a moment, wondering if she dared to see this through. It was wrong to deceive him, even for so good a reason. Surely Temberlay would eat her alive when he discovered he'd been tricked into marrying the plain Lynton sister, cheated out of the beauty he expected. She felt pity for him, and a pang of guilt. The poor man expected a swan, and he was getting the ugly duckling, the daughter Lord Wycliffe himself had said no one would ever want.

And when her deception was discovered, the duchess would no doubt be pleased to assist her grandson in making a meal of her. They'd add a fork and knife to the coat of arms to warn away future generations of foolish virgins.

The door opened and two rows of footmen marched out, wearing impeccable livery, and stood between the coach and front door. Nicholas climbed out of the vehicle in a lithe movement. To her dismay he walked straight up the steps without offering his hand, or even bothering to glance back at her.

Her pity faded and guilt turned to acid. She felt herself flush under the curious eyes of the servants. She stared at

Temberlay's broad back, and waited for someone to point and laugh and send the coach away with her still inside it.

Instead, a gloved hand appeared and she took it and climbed out. The decision had been made, the vows spoken. There was no turning back. She must begin as she meant to go on.

She pasted on a gracious smile and nodded at each footman as if she belonged here. For better or worse, she was from this moment on the Duchess of Temberlay.

Chapter 11

Temberlay went through the front door without pausing, and Meg followed him into a magnificent entry hall that seemed to be carved from one enormous block of marble. The ceiling soared three stories above the floor. A grand staircase soared heavenward. She gaped like a tourist.

Temberlay's hat sat on a mahogany table, and she could hear the click of his boot heels echoing from one of the myriad corridors that led off the entry. The front door closed behind her and the footmen melted into the walls. As the sound of footsteps faded entirely, she clutched the bouquet to her chest, unsure of what to do.

"Good afternoon, Your Grace. I'm Gardiner, the butler." She hadn't heard him approach, and she wondered for a moment if he'd appeared straight out of the marble. "Welcome to Hartley Place. If you will come this way?" He indicated one of the corridors with a gloved hand.

Unlike his master, the man didn't make a sound as he moved over the marble floor. He opened a pair of doors that led to a salon.

Temberlay was lounging in a chair, his booted feet propped on a delicate tea table, a tumbler of golden liquid in his hand. He tossed it back quickly and held out the empty glass to Gardiner, who silently refilled it.

Her husband didn't invite her to sit, so she did so on her own, choosing a settee as far from him as possible.

"May I offer you some tea, Your Grace?" Gardiner asked, and she looked at Temberlay.

He tilted his head mockingly. "Gardiner means you, Duchess. Do you want tea? I never touch it myself."

She wished the floor would open and swallow her. She managed to smile at the patient butler. "Thank you. Tea would be most welcome."

He bowed and glided out, closing the doors behind him. Alone in Temberlay's disturbing presence, Meg listened to the tick of the clock. It was barely noon. She had been married less than an hour.

"Isn't it hot under that veil?" he asked, and she jumped. It was indeed, and she couldn't hide her face forever. She set her bouquet aside and raised the lace, folding it back from her forehead with nervous fingers. He regarded her with lazy interest, offering no hint of either approval or disappointment. She held his gaze boldly, though she could feel her skin growing hot. She looked away first and studied a landscape above the mantel as if it were the most fascinating painting on earth.

No, he hadn't been mistaken at the church. She *was* beautiful. The realization that he'd be bedding her in just a few hours caught him in the gut with an unexpected rush of lust.

"You're hardly what I expected," he said. "How old are you?"

"Twenty," she said, her eyes returning to his. Crisp, intelligent, beautiful eyes. "And you?"

"Thirty-one in years. Far older by experience," he quipped, and was rewarded with another blush, though she didn't seem to know how to reply, and they lapsed back into silence.

He watched her eyes wander the room, taking in the furnishings, the art, the wallpaper, everything but him.

"No, you're not what I expected at all," he said again to make her look at him. Her brows rose toward the edge of the lace.

"And just what did you expect, Your Grace?"

"A woman short on looks and wit, wide of hip."

Her lips twitched, and she lowered her eyes again. What was she thinking?

"Rose," he tested her name on his lips. She didn't answer. "Rose," he said again, and she looked up with wide-eyed surprise. "Are you truly as innocent as I've heard?"

Her lips pinched, and she raised her chin to a stubborn little point. "Are you as sinful as they say you are?"

He smiled at her daring. "Probably more so, since most of my sinning is done behind closed doors." She blushed again, and his grin deepened. Not so daring after all. "Yes, you are definitely innocent. Far too innocent for my taste." He sipped the whisky, let it burn, but the desire to touch her, to see if her cheek was as warm as it looked, didn't go away.

"Don't men expect the ladies they marry to be innocent? Even the women you share your bed with now were innocent once."

Touché. "True enough, Duchess. But I'm not like most men. Have you ever kissed a man? A boy, even?"

She kept her expression flat, her eyes locked on his.

"I kissed you," she said tartly, and he barked a laugh. He got up from his chair, crossed the room, and sat beside her. She held his gaze like a doe before a hungry wolf, but held her ground.

"No, Duchess, that miserable peck in the church was no kiss at all. I shall have to teach you better than that."

He slid his knuckles over her cheek, his touch light, teasing. Her skin was indeed hot, and soft as silk. She lowered her gaze, and her lips parted. She didn't pull away, though he could feel her trembling.

His mouth descended on hers, and she made a small noise that might have been fear or desire and raised her hands to his chest. The sweet sound shot straight to his groin. She didn't push him away, and he brushed his lips over hers and hovered over her mouth, waiting until her eyes drifted shut, and her lips parted. Her fingers curled against his chest.

He kissed her again, firmly this time, his lips mobile, insistent. She tasted of roses—or perhaps it was the scent of her bouquet—and honey, and innocence. He drew her lower lip into his mouth and she stayed still, allowing it. He moved his lips to her cheek, then over her jaw to the pulse point at the base of her neck and kissed her there too. Her heart was beating like a trapped bird. When he found her lips again, she sighed and kissed him back, tentatively, inexpertly, and he realized that innocence appealed to him after all.

He drew back in surprise, read the same emotion in her misty gaze. He got up and returned to his distant seat, and she raised shaking fingertips to her lips.

He forced himself to look bored. He crossed his legs and sipped his whisky, trying to eliminate the taste of her, to calm the desire to seduce her right here in the salon. What would Granddame say to that when she arrived home to congratulate the happy couple? She'd cackle in victory, urge him on, since nothing mattered but getting a bloody heir.

"Did you like it?" he asked.

Meg ran her tongue over her lips, tasted whisky. Yes, she'd liked it. She didn't dare reply. A request for more hovered on the tip of her tongue.

"You're trembling," he said. "I must admit even I found it intriguing. I hadn't known a woman of twenty could be so entirely untouched. I have you to teach and mold as I wish, don't I?"

Indignation pricked her. She stiffened her limpid spine and leveled a glare at him. "I am not interested in being molded, Your Grace. This is duty only."

His eyes hardened. She was Granddame's creature, then. The money, he reminded himself. He still needed his grandmother's money to run his estates. For the time being, much as he hated it, he must play her game. "Then we understand each other. Once this sham of a marriage is consummated, as unpleasant as that may be for us both, you will retire to Temberlay Castle to live."

"I intend to return to Wycliffe Park as soon as possible."

Temberlay rose, and Meg watched him prowl toward her, his eyes cold, and her heart climbed into her throat, but he didn't touch her. He merely leaned on the fireplace. "I am not used to having my orders disobeyed. My time in the army, I suppose."

She got to her feet too. "This is not the army."

He ran his eyes over her body, and she felt it like a touch. "Christ, they should have sent you up against the French in Spain. Napoleon would have run screaming to hide under his bed and troubled Europe no more. Are all your sisters like you? I suppose I should be glad you wish to retire to the country. Imagine if you'd expected to stay in Town. The *ton* would have a field day with you."

Her eyes widened. It was the kind of thing her father

might have said. "How dare you—" she began, but the doors swept open.

"The Countess of Wycliffe and Lord Hector Bryant," Gardiner intoned, but Flora was already racing across the room toward her.

Nicholas watched the mother of the bride dissolve into tears more appropriate for a wake than a wedding. The bride herself was dry-eyed and strong.

Lord Hector Bryant bowed stiffly, his eyes wary as he offered terse congratulations and shook Nicholas's hand. He accepted with a crisp nod.

No one at all, it seemed, was happy. Except perhaps Granddame. She hadn't arrived to enjoy her victory as yet.

"Where is my grandmother?" he asked Gardiner.

"She has gone upstairs to rest, Your Grace. She pleads a slight headache."

Nicholas frowned. Granddame had the constitution of an army draft horse. She did not get headaches. She probably had a scythe of her own, and would do fierce battle with the Grim Reaper when he came for her. He felt a prickle of suspicion climb his spine. He dismissed Gardiner.

"The wedding was—" The countess struggled for the right word. "—brief." She regarded him as if he were a man-eating tiger that hadn't been fed.

"Mercifully so, Countess," he replied, and smiled charmingly when Flora gasped.

"Mother, do sit down," his bride said. "Gardiner will be bringing tea shortly."

But Flora was bristling with indignation. "Your audacity, Your Grace, is quite—" but her daughter's hand on her arm stopped her. He was about to bid her continue when the doors opened again.

"My apologies, I'm late," Sebastian said, grinning like a fool. His eyes fell on the bride, and he swept toward her. He sketched a bow, and kissed her hand with an exaggerated flourish. "My congratulations, Your Grace. I wish you well of Nicholas."

She looked at Nicholas expectantly.

"May I present Viscount St. James?" he said tersely. "Sebastian, sit down." He didn't like the gleam in Seb's eyes as he ogled her.

His bride simply raised her brows. "You make it sound as if I can expect difficulty with my husband, Viscount St. James."

He grinned again, and actually giggled. "Difficulty with Nick? Not at all. In the right hands, he's quite malleable."

Flora gasped, and his bride's expression declared instant dislike for the viscount.

"St. James, have you been drinking?" Temberlay asked.

"I stopped at the club on the way back to spread the happy news of your nuptials." He turned back to the bride. "I understand you have sisters at home, Your Grace. Are they all as lovely as yourself? May I call you Rose? Calling you 'Your Grace' makes me think of Nicholas, and I'd much rather think of you," he purred.

The countess clenched her fist.

The new duchess took her mother's hand and tucked it into her own. "No, you may not," she said. Sebastian's grin faded and he blinked like an owl at the set-down.

Nicholas watched Hector rub his chin, trying to hide a smile, and felt a grudging admiration of his own. Poor Sebastian. He'd made the mistake of assuming Rose Lynton was a witless country bumpkin. He'd thought so himself, but she had passed this first test, and had come out every inch a duchess.

Gardiner returned with tea, and Rose indicated with a nod that he could pour out.

"Would you care for tea, Your Grace?" she asked him.

"No thank you. I have business to attend to this afternoon, and I must go."

"Business? Today?" the countess gasped. "No wedding breakfast? Not even champagne and a toast to the—happy—couple? This is a shoddy affair!"

His bride's cheeks colored, and she dropped her gaze, but said nothing.

"Duty before pleasure," he said. "Though I'm sure Gardiner would be happy to bring you some champagne if you wish it."

The new Duchess of Temberlay looked up at that, her hazel eyes molten pools of dignity. "No, I think not. I wouldn't dream of keeping you here if you have business to see to, Your Grace. You may go. Good afternoon."

He felt his skin heat at her audacity.

She turned her back on him and made a bland comment to her mother about the warmth of the weather, as if she'd already forgotten him. Her mother's eyes were round as millponds, and Hector and Sebastian were looking from her to Temberlay and back again, waiting for his reaction.

He put his hands on her waist and picked her up with ease, turning her to face him. He caught her gasp of surprise in his mouth. This kiss wasn't the slow, tentative peck he'd given her on the settee. This was ravishment, pure sex, an onslaught she wasn't prepared for. She pressed her fists against her chest, tried to shove him away.

He heard her mother's warble of dismay, and Hector's exclamation of surprise. His tongue slipped into her mouth when she opened it to protest, sparred with hers. The intimacy was stunning, unbelievably . . . delicious. She stopped fighting as his mouth moved expertly over hers. Her knees weakened and she sagged against him. She slid her arms around his neck, and he drew her closer, pressed her body to his.

"For pity's sake!" Flora cried, and his bride pulled away, suddenly remembering where she was.

No one else in the room said a word.

The hazel of her eyes was gone, subsumed into the black of her pupils. She stared at him for a moment before she wiped the back of her hand across her lips. He leaned in again, and heard her expectant intake of breath. His mouth watered, but he put his lips to her ear instead, and kissed the lobe.

"Rest well this afternoon," he murmured. "You'll need your strength tonight." He stepped back, and she put her hand on the back of the settee to steady herself. He gave her a rake's grin, the kind of smile even an innocent could recognize as masculine superiority. He'd won that round, and she knew it.

Without another word, he turned and strode out of the room, with Sebastian at his heels.

Meg watched him go, bemused, and baffled. What on earth had just happened? The world had tilted on its axis, forever changed with one simple kiss. But it wasn't simple. There was more. She thought of the night to come, felt her stomach coil with smoke. He was the master of this game indeed, and she didn't even know the rules.

Chapter 12

Flora watched Temberlay leave after ravishing poor Marguerite before her eyes. "Well, I see all the stories I've heard about that man are true!" she snapped.

"What do you think of your new husband, Meg?" Hector asked, but she was staring at the door with her mouth open.

Flora shook her daughter's arm. "Perhaps you *should* get some rest this afternoon."

Marguerite turned to look at her, her eyes still wide. "You will return for dinner?" she asked. "There will be a wedding supper, surely."

"Are you certain you wish to remain in this house, married to that man? Hector could still arrange an annulment," Flora said. "Even after that kiss."

"All I would have to do is admit I am not Rose. If the marriage is to be valid, then it must be cons—"

Flora held up her hand. "I cannot bear to think of it!"

"Is it so terrible?" Meg asked.

Flora felt Hector pinch her arm to silence her. "Temberlay may not be what he appears, Meg. There are other, better, stories about him too."

Flora pulled her arm free indignantly. "From what I've

seen here today, they can't possibly be true!" She read the reproof in Hector's eyes and glanced at Marguerite's pale face. Her eyes were on a statue in the corner of the room, a Grecian maiden tied to a stake. She reminded herself that Marguerite was sacrificing herself for the sake of her family.

"I'm sorry, Marguerite. I'm all nerves and hysteria today. Of course he will make a good husband." She tried to feel it, but her conviction melted like butter.

She was thankful that Rose had not married him. She would have wilted under the man's insults, and that kiss would have killed her outright. Flora embraced her daughter, kissed her hot cheek, felt her cling for a moment before she stepped back and squared her shoulders.

"I will see you both at dinner," she said with the kind of bright tone she used when things couldn't be worse. Flora had no idea what to say, how to help, though she wished she did, now of all times. She might have with Rose, but Marguerite was stronger, smarter, the one she leaned on now Marcus was gone. She struggled for the right maternal words to say. She'd been a bride once, facing her wedding night with the same fears Marguerite had now, but the fierce bravery in her daughter's eyes stopped Flora. She knew that look, Marguerite at her most determined, her most capable. Perhaps everything would be well after all, and she needn't worry.

Hector caught her arm.

"Come, Flora. I'm sure Meg has things to do this afternoon, and we must go."

He took her elbow firmly and led her toward the door.

"I should like a tour of the house, please," Meg asked the butler when he returned.

He bowed. "Shall we start with the library?"

The breakfast room, den, drawing room, and sitting room were all on the way to the library, and each room was filled with roses—pink, red, yellow, and white. The lavish arrangements had obviously been prepared especially for her—well, for *Rose*—and every blossom reminded Meg that she was a fraud.

She decided she hated roses.

There weren't any flowers in the library. Bookshelves soared to the ceilings in the vast room. It was *his* room, she could see at once, though she couldn't imagine him with a book in his hand. There were decanters on a small mahogany table near the desk, deep leather chairs, and the room smelled of tobacco.

The bust of a soldier glowered at her, warned her away, standing guard in Temberlay's absence.

"An extensive library," she said, aware that Gardiner was awaiting her reaction.

"If there is anything in particular you wish to read, you need only ask His Grace. Most of the books are from his own collection."

"You mean the late duke, I assume?" she said. Surely this Temberlay did not read. Wherever would he find the time?

"I mean Duke Nicholas, ma'am. The late duke did not enjoy reading." He pointed to a portrait of a gentleman who resembled Nicholas only slightly. "That's the fifth duke."

"Is there a portrait of my, um, husband?" she asked.

"Not as yet, Your Grace. I'm sure there will be in time. There are many fine family portraits at Temberlay Castle."

She walked around the room. A statue of a naked nymph graced a pedestal near the window. She grinned at

Meg with cheeky delight. Now that spoke of Temberlay.

"His Grace encourages the staff to read his books whenever they wish. He has only just finished shelving the many books he brought back from Spain."

"Oh?" Meg looked at the butler, read the admiration in his eyes.

He led her to a space on the shelf and pointed. "His Grace served with Lord Wellington on the Peninsula for three years. He is a true hero. You may have read about his service in the *Times*."

Meg touched the cool leather spines, reading the titles. Her father believed war was an improper topic for ladies and forbade any mention of it. The *Times* too was forbidden. She had heard of Napoleon, of course, but she knew nothing of the battles, or the heroes. She took out a book of paintings of the Spanish landscape.

He offered her another book. "If I may be so bold, I recommend this one—a tourist's guide to Spain and Italy, written in the last century, before the war. Shall I send both books up to your apartments?"

"Yes, thank you," she murmured, already lost in exploring the shelves as he crossed the carpet silently to pull the bell. There were thousands of books on every topic— science, architecture, gardens, mathematics, and history. She felt a thrill run through her. She had been forced to sell most of Wycliffe's library, and she missed the pleasures of good books. Despite her father's strict rules, she had spent hours reading.

She stopped at a book on horses, felt again the pang of loss. The paintings reminded her of her father's fine stable of Thoroughbreds. They had been the first things that had to be sold— Arabella, her foal, and the Wycliffe Arabian—just days before his death. They'd been her father's pride, her joy, and she dreamed of having them back again. Wycliffe's stables had been famous, and she'd loved the horses. They hadn't cared that she had red hair instead of blond. She ran a fingertip over the painted fetlocks of a fine stallion, so like the Arabian.

"Your Grace?"

She turned at the sound of a timid voice. A young maid curtsied. "I'm Anna. Mr. Gardiner has asked me to assist you." She came forward and tucked the stack of books under her arm. "If you'll come this way? Mr. Gardiner said tea would be sent up to your apartments shortly. Cook also baked some cakes for you this morning. She is very excited about the wedding supper, since there was no breakfast this mor—" She paused. "I'm sorry, Your Grace. My tongue runs away with me at times. It is not for me to question arrangements."

Nor was it up to her, apparently. "Perhaps I might see a copy of tonight's menu?" Meg asked. "Not to make changes, of course, but simply out of interest."

They reached the second floor, and a pair of footmen swung open a set of double doors as they approached.

She stepped into an elegant sitting room. Anna bustled to the windows and opened the drapes, letting sunlight fill the room. "There's a lovely view of the garden," she said, and crossed to open another set of doors, which led to the bedchamber.

Like the sitting room, the bedchamber was done in shades of pink and green. Luxurious damask curtains draped a huge bed that occupied one entire wall. The head of the bed bore the ducal crest, embroidered and framed, and Meg winced. The hind caught in the wolf's merciless clutches was out of place here, or perhaps it wasn't. This bed was designed for the grand task of breeding heirs.

With Temberlay.

Her stomach climbed the back of her throat, and she

stared at the bed. His ravishing, stunning kiss still burned on her lips. He said he planned to teach her things in this bed, intimate things she couldn't even begin to imagine. Or could she? A shiver, half fear, half anticipation, crept up her spine. Hadn't she imagined exactly this when she gazed at the scandal sheets?

She pushed the wicked thought away. Scandal sheets and imagination were one thing, but bedsheets and Temberlay in the flesh were something else entirely. She ran her hand over the fine bed linens, tempted to tie them in knots and escape out the window. He would be naked, as would she . . . She gulped.

"This is the dressing room. It connects to His Grace's suite," Anna said, opening a smaller, narrower door. "Beyond that are His Grace's apartments."

Meg stared at the door that led to his rooms. Would he stride through it tonight, come to her? Or was she expected to go to him? She wished her mother had stayed, so she could ask.

She returned to her sitting room, where a tea tray already waited.

"Is there anything else I can bring you, Your Grace?" Anna asked.

Rest well this afternoon. You'll need your strength tonight. His words echoed in her mind. Meg swallowed the lump in her throat and shook her head.

She let Anna unpin her veil and loosen her hair before she left. She turned to the light luncheon Cook had kindly provided as the staff left and shut the door behind them. There was enough bread and cheese and sweets to feed an army of duchesses. Did they too expect she would need her strength? Her cheeks burned. A copy of the menu for the wedding supper, sent up along with her tray, confirmed it. Seven courses of fish, fowl, vegetables, sauces, meats, and pastry had been planned.

She imagined Amy in the kitchen at Wycliffe, working alone, and wondered just how many servants were required to produce a meal of this caliber. She hadn't even asked about the guest list. Perhaps there were several dozen people expected. Her stomach quailed and she put down the apple tart she'd been about to eat.

She tiptoed to the connecting door to his apartments and put her ear against it. Would it be locked? She turned the latch, and the door opened.

The scent of his soap reminded her she was trespassing. His dressing gown hung behind the door, his brushes sat on the table. She crept to the wardrobe and opened it, expecting to find a dozen other outlandish outfits, but to her surprise, his clothing was sober, well tailored, and the height of refined elegance. She ran her fingers over the fine wool of a dark blue coat. Why hadn't he worn this to the wedding?

At the back of the cupboard, a scarlet military tunic glowed, a hero's coat, just as Gardiner had said. Hector had said there was more to Temberlay than salacious gossip. Meg only knew him as the Devil of Temberlay, rake, gambler, and lover. Which was the real Temberlay?

She opened the door to his bedroom. His bed was even larger than hers, and the ducal crest had been carved in oak in his room, a reminder of duty, responsibility, and power.

There was another shelf of books here, and still more volumes on a battered campaign table that stood in the corner. She ran a finger over a divot in the wood. Was that a bullet hole, or the careless mark left by a booted foot propped on the mahogany surface?

She glanced at the books, wondering what a man like Temberlay liked to read. There was a treatise on artillery, an atlas, and a tome on astronomy, among others.

She picked up a book with an exotic blue leather cover, embossed with swirls and arabesques and set with gems. It had no title, so she opened it.

Her eyes widened in surprise.

Every page had drawings of naked men and women, together, embracing, caressing. She stared at a sketch of a woman on her back, her face slack, her eyes closed, as a dark-haired man kissed her throat, his hand on her breast. The woman's fingers were tangled in his hair, white on black. Was it Temberlay? She couldn't tell. She tilted the book and looked closer.

The latch rattled in his sitting room, and she heard the door open. Footsteps came toward the bedroom, and she raced for her own rooms, still clutching the book. She shut the door and froze, her ears pricked for sounds of pursuit. Was it Temberlay, returning? After a few moments, all was quiet.

She opened the book again. Was this how it was between men and women? Is this what Temberlay would do to her, here, tonight, in this very bed? She stared at the smooth satin counterpane and swallowed.

In some of the paintings, sloe-eyed women draped in exotic garments of colorful silk lay with their lovers in lush gardens under crystal stars. Each lady reclined serenely as he knelt between her thighs, or caressed her from behind. The male member was as large as a stallion's. Surely there couldn't be room for such a thing in the tight trousers English gentlemen favored. The women did not appear to be distressed. In fact they looked as placid as mares.

It seemed there was a vast number of ways to accomplish the deed. Legs, arms, mouths twined together in endless variations.

She shut the book with a snap, and paced the floor, thinking. Her heart was pounding, her skin hot. The paintings made her feel warm, restless, tingling.

Her mother had said to lie still. Temberlay had insisted that innocence was an inconvenience and a hindrance to pleasure. She was mystified.

She shut her eyes and fled to the safety of the sitting room, and tried to concentrate on the sober book on travel, but the images of Temberlay, and bed, refused to leave her alone.

Chapter 13

Nicholas was shown into the drawing room of Ives House to see his friend and comrade in arms, Major Lord Stephen Ives.

"Hartley! I heard you were about to get married. Actually, you're Temberlay now, aren't you? Should I bow?" Stephen asked.

Nicholas didn't answer. "I've come to ask a favor," he said.

"Do you wish me to stand as best man, perhaps? Come and sit down. Whisky or tea?"

Nicholas set his hat on the table and followed Stephen into the drawing room. "Neither, and the wedding was this morning. Other than the requisite witnesses, there were no guests."

Stephen's smile faded. "I see," he said, and Nicholas wondered if he did.

"I understand you will be going to Vienna with Lord Castlereagh for the peace conference, Stephen."

"They seem to think I'll make a suitable aide to the ambassador," Stephen replied, taking a seat across from Nicholas. "Do you wish to come as well? We could use an officer of your particular talents. Talleyrand will be there, and that's one Frenchman who is even more slippery and dangerous than Napoleon. We'll have our hands full making sure he doesn't negotiate us into allowing France to keep half of Europe."

"I have responsibilities here, I'm afraid," Nicholas said, wishing again he was free. "Do you remember Lady Julia Leighton?"

Stephen's brow furrowed momentarily. "Of course. She was betrothed to your brother, wasn't she? My sister knew her slightly as well, and they spoke at parties when they met, since you and I served in the same regiment as her brother James. Dorothea hasn't heard from Julia for some time, though she sent her condolences after David's death. Have you word of her?"

"She is under my protection for the time being, but she wishes to leave England," Nicholas said.

Stephen's face clouded. "Ruined?"

Nicholas nodded. "I don't have the full details, since she will not reveal them. My brother died in a duel shortly after she admitted she was with child. Her parents declared her dead, and I put her up in a house nearby, but her father insists she must leave London, or better still, the country."

"And the child?"

Nicholas tried to read his friend's face, searching for an indication of scorn or disgust, but there was only vague interest.

"A boy," Nicholas said. "Not David's, though. She named him James, after her brother."

He could tell by the flush of Stephen's skin that he remembered James Leighton. "A thousand men would have died if James Leighton had not sounded that alarm, and I would have been the first of them. It cost him his life, and he died a hero." He looked at Nicholas. "You knew him better than I did, since his sister was betrothed to David."

"Since childhood. I was wondering if you would consider taking Julia with you and Dorothea to Vienna. She could be a companion to your sister."

Stephen looked thoughtful. He rose and poured two tumblers of whisky and sat down. "What about her son?"

"She has said she will not give him up. There is a nurse, of course."

Stephen sighed. "Dorothea was brokenhearted when she lost her husband, and then her child. She has not been the same since Matthew's death, and I'm not certain how she would react to having another woman's baby near her." He shook his head. "Nor am I sure the ambassador will approve of having a fallen woman among the British contingent."

"Julia's smart. I daresay she'll make herself useful."

"Is she likely to, um, commit any future indiscretions?"

"It was a surprise to everyone that she committed the first. She is hardly likely to trust another handsome face. I proposed to her, Stephen, and she refused."

"Are you in love with her?" Stephen asked in surprise. Nicholas thought of his bride. Would he have been happier to find Julia under the veil instead?

"No," he replied. "It was a gesture for David's sake, and for hers. I wanted to protect her and the child. We grew up together, and she's like a sister to me. Julia made a mistake, and she will pay for it for the rest of her life. The bastard who seduced her won't face such scorn."

"I'll broach the subject with my sister. Company might do her good, especially a friend like Julia. She's refused every invitation for months. I can't leave her here alone, and I'm hoping this trip to Vienna will revive her spirits, but I can't force Julia and her child on Dorothea if she isn't ready. Will that do?"

"For now." Nicholas picked up his hat. "Thank you."

Stephen followed him to the door. "When will we meet your bride?"

Nicholas shook his head. "I only just met her myself this morning, at the wedding. I plan to banish her to Temberlay Castle first thing tomorrow."

Stephen folded his arms. "You surprise me. You show Julia such compassion, yet you have no regard at all for your bride? You were always most chivalrous with women in Spain, whether they were ladies or camp followers."

"This isn't Spain. I have no idea if she deserves my compassion or not. She's a complete stranger, and my grandmother has paid her well for the honor of becoming a duchess. I, in return, have one more responsibility I do not want."

"I've never known you to run from a challenge, Nick. In Spain, the bigger the danger, the faster you'd go toward it. You never took the easy way in my recollection. I know the field you're facing now may not be optimum, but this is simply another battle to be won. Perhaps you'll find your bride to your liking. She was brave enough to marry you, and that alone speaks well of her."

Nicholas remembered the kiss, the way she handled Sebastian. "She shall get as good as she gives."

Stephen shook his head. "I shall wish you happy anyway, old friend. You deserve it."

Nicholas climbed into his coach. "Pulteney Street," he ordered the coachman. Was Stephen right? He'd imagined a wife would be one more burden, another dull duty. Was she?

Tonight he would bed her, a virgin stranger, and Stephen was right about one thing. He had the same feeling in his gut he always got before a battle.

Chapter 14

"**W**hat will you wear for dinner tonight, Your Grace?" Anna asked, and Meg realized that the magnificent wardrobe that had been purchased for Rose was now hers. She hoped again that Rose was safe. If her sister was here, preparing for her wedding night, would she be as afraid as Meg was?

Her stomach quivered again. "I'll wear the gray silk." It was demure and unassuming, and even if she was the bride, she hoped the other guests would outshine her, draw attention away from her.

"How many people are coming for dinner?" she asked.

"There will be six, I believe, or possibly seven. Her Grace—the dowager duchess, that is—thought your sister might attend."

Meg looked up in surprise, then realized that Anna meant her, Meg, not Rose.

"No. She is—out of Town."

"There are some lovely diamond earrings and a matching necklace that would go with this gown if you'd like to wear them tonight," Anna suggested, fastening the buttons.

Rose would leap at the chance to wear diamonds. They'd have difficulty getting her to take them off again at the end of the evening. But Meg was an imposter, the paste jewel and not the priceless gem. She imagined the duchess tearing the diamonds from her neck in a rage when she realized, and she most certainly would without the veil. Meg sat at the dressing table. "No jewels tonight. Since there was no breakfast, I shall wear my wedding veil to dinner. Tuck my hair up under it."

If Anna was surprised she didn't let it show. Meg picked up a red silk fan and unfolded it. It was the kind of toy Rose would have loved, if she didn't have diamonds to hold her attention. In low light, with the veil hiding her hair, and the fan hiding everything but her eyes, Meg hoped the duchess wouldn't recognize her.

She descended the stairs slowly, half expecting Temberlay to be waiting for her at the bottom, but he wasn't. Gardiner glided out of the shadows instead.

"The Countess of Wycliffe, Viscount St. James, and Lord Bryant have arrived, Your Grace."

They were in the salon. Viscount St. James was pressed to the wall, and Flora was holding him there with her own fan, which was pointed at his throat like a weapon.

"'Pon my honor, I vow I was not with him this afternoon!" St. James pleaded. "I have every confidence that he will be here. He must have been del—"

He caught sight of Meg in the doorway and fell into guilty silence. "Good evening, Your Grace. Forgive me for not bowing."

Flora released him and rushed at her. "*He* isn't here!"

There was no need to ask whom she meant. Temberlay was quite obviously, dramatically absent. The room seemed bare without him. Meg felt her heart skip. Had he found out somehow that she was an imposter? She glanced at Gardiner, but his bland face gave nothing away. "Is His Grace at home?" she asked.

"No, Your Grace, he is not."

Meg's hand tightened on the fan. "And Her Grace?"

"Her Grace sends her regrets," Gardiner said. "She is still suffering from headache."

"A dozen Your Graces in this place and none of them here for supper!" Flora hissed. "This is an insult!"

"Not at all," Meg said, feeling relief flow through her. It was a reprieve, not an insult. She snapped the fan shut and set it on a table. She wouldn't need it now. "Perhaps it is as the viscount said, and he is only delayed," she soothed her mother, though St. James's smirk told her Temberlay had no intention of attending his wedding supper. Another lesson, no doubt. Well, she would teach him one of her own.

"We are ready to dine now, Gardiner." Sebastian St. James's grin faltered. "Viscount, since you likely know the way to the dining room and I do not, perhaps I may prevail upon you to escort me to dinner?"

He looked uneasy, trapped, but unless he had even fewer manners than Temberlay, there was little he could do but bow and offer his arm.

She laid her hand on his sleeve, winced at the hard glitter of the diamond and sapphire ring Temberlay had placed on her finger that morning. St. James stared at it as well.

"Truly, Your Grace, I have no idea where Nick is tonight," he murmured. She glanced at him, read the lie in his eyes. He knew exactly where her husband was, or at the very least, he suspected. She tossed her head as if it didn't matter. "He could not be anywhere more important, or in lovelier company than yours—" he said, but she cut him off with a cold glare. He swallowed, and tried to smile reassuringly.

Lovelier company. She felt her stomach contract.

Would he be here if she were Rose? She took her place at the head of the table, and nodded to Gardiner to begin.

The food was lavish, even if the conversation was sparse. Meg barely tasted what she ate. Gardiner introduced each dish with a flourish as a parade of footmen entered, far outnumbering the guests. The salmon had been brought specially from His Grace's Scottish estates. The hip of beef had come from Temberlay's farm, while the strawberries were from his manor in Kent. The pheasant and grouse had come from yet another property, this one in Cumbria, and the vegetables were grown in the glasshouses at Temberlay Castle.

"Please give my compliments to Cook, Gardiner. Everything is delicious," Meg said graciously.

"Tell me where he is!" Flora hissed at Sebastian again when the servants departed.

"Don't badger the poor viscount, Mama. Apparently Temberlay has secrets even Viscount St. James doesn't know, and I would prefer he be allowed to keep the details to himself. I don't wish to hear them. In fact, if there is somewhere *you'd* rather be this evening, my lord, then please don't let us keep you."

St. James blinked in surprise at his dismissal. His jaw dropped, and he shut it again with a snap. He rose, and bowed stiffly. "I shall bid you good night, then, Duchess. No doubt you'll sleep well tonight."

Meg felt the barb hit home, felt her skin heat as he turned on his heel and left. His meaning couldn't have been plainer.

Chapter 15

Nicholas spent the afternoon with Mr. Dodd, David's man of affairs, going over his brother's finances. There were still a number of vowels and bills unpaid, signed for by David, yet not brought to Mr. Dodd's attention until Nicholas had returned to assume the title.

His brother had invested heavily in a private shipping venture, the voyage of a vessel called *Orion*, which promised rich dividends that never appeared. David had lost a fortune. The contracts did not name the other investors, and their identities were buried in layers of secrecy and complications that had proven impossible to decipher thus far.

"I would have advised him it was a poor investment, had he brought it to me, Your Grace, but he did not," Dodd said.

Once the *Orion* venture had failed, David had turned to gambling to win back his losses, hoping to avoid ruin, but he had failed there as well, and lost almost everything that wasn't entailed.

Dodd pleaded for Nicholas's understanding as he laid the account books before him. It wasn't until the bills could no longer be paid that Dodd had realized the extent of the disaster, and that was after David's death when the creditors closed in. "Temberlay credit was always good before then. No one *ever* demanded payment."

With Nicholas out of the country, there was little Dodd could do but see the duchess. She had provided the necessary moneys to keep the various Temberlay properties functioning, but she hadn't wanted to know the details. In fact, she refused to hear them.

She had instead let David's final words convince her that the ruin of the dukedom was Nicholas's fault, although he'd been in Spain for three years, at war.

Nicholas barely looked at the contract his grandmother had ordered drawn up, before he signed it. In return for marrying her choice of bride, she would continue to support Temberlay properties. All past bills, however, including David's gambling debts, would fall to Nicholas to settle however he could. He wondered how much his grandmother had paid his bride to marry him.

Granddame's money came from rum and sugar, a fortune made by her French grandfather before the Revolution. When power shifted, he'd wisely married his children into noble English families, and ensured his Caribbean plantations supported British interests. He dowered his only granddaughter generously, and left her a vast fortune under the stipulation that it be held in her own name.

Upon his return to England, Nicholas had used the money from the sale of his commission to support Julia, and to make several small investments in secure bonds that were beginning to show a profit. He gambled as well, usually successfully, since he knew when to quit, unlike David.

He authorized Dodd to make several payments and more investments now, including necessary improvements at Temberlay. He gripped the pen with crushing force as he signed as Duke of Temberlay. Would he ever get used to the title? At least his investments were earning, and the harvest at the various Temberlay estates promised to be good. He looked at the balance sheet, and realized if he'd been able to delay his grandmother for another few months, he would not have had to marry Rose Lynton at all. Her incredible hazel eyes flashed in his mind, the taste of her lips. He pushed the erotic thoughts away, concentrated on what Dodd was saying.

It wasn't until the clock in Dodd's office struck ten that Nicholas realized he was late for his wedding supper. He pictured his bride sobbing while her mother lay prostrate in a nervous fit. Granddame was probably threatening to have him publicly horsewhipped.

He climbed into his coach, tempted to order the driver to take him to White's for the evening. He raised his hand to knock on the roof of the coach, and hesitated.

He thought of that tempting, teasing, delectable little mouth.

He could go to the theater, wait for Angelique.

But the memory of his bride's perfume lingered, the way she'd melted in his arms.

He knocked. "Take me to the—"

The way she blushed . . .

"Home," he ordered the coachman and sat back. The possibilities intrigued him. Would she ambush him with angry accusations, or dissolve in a flood of tears like sugar in the rain? Tears were more likely, he decided.

He hated women who cried. He raised his hand to knock again.

She had wrapped her arms around his neck, tangled her fingers in his hair, and sighed when he kissed her.

His hand fell to his lap.

If she failed to please him, and even if she did, getting the bedding over and done with would give him a reason to send her off to Temberlay Castle in the morning. He wouldn't have to look at her again, or be tempted by that mouth, those eyes.

He stared out the window at the lights of Mayfair. He raised his hand yet again to tell the coachman to hurry, and stopped himself.

There was no point in being too eager. More likely than not, his bride would still turn out to be a disappointment.

Strangely, he was nervous—he, the man who could charm any woman alive.

But he had never been able to *reason* with one.

He considered telling the coachman to take the long way through the park. He tried to replace his trepidation with anger at finding himself in the position of having to bed a sobbing virgin. At last he ran a hand through his hair, and tried to think of anything but his bride, and bed.

He braced himself as Gardiner opened the front door.

The house was quiet. There was no crying, or screaming. He released the breath he was holding.

"Is my wife at home?" he asked the butler, then wondered if she'd fled home to her mama. "Here, I mean, at Hartley Place?"

"Of course, sir. Her Grace has retired," Gardiner replied. The butler was calm, obviously unscathed by any unpleasantness that had taken place this evening. Gardiner would have made a steady soldier under fire.

"And my grandmother?"

"She is also abed," Gardiner replied pleasantly. "Can I bring you anything, Your Grace?"

He considered asking for a meal, but he had no appetite. Was she sleeping? Would she pretend to be asleep while he—

He ran a finger under his cravat.

"No. I think I shall retire as well." Gardiner would probably think that odd, given the fact that it was only ten-thirty and Nicholas usually did not go to bed until well after dawn. He watched the butler cast a subtle glance at the clock.

He could still go out, still go to the club. He hesitated at the foot of the stairs, and the butler waited too. Nicholas squared his shoulders.

"Good night, Gardiner."

He marched up the stairs, hearing the cadence of battle drums in his mind, seeing her eyes before him, wishing for the hundredth time that day that he was safely back at war.

Chapter 16

Nicholas went through the dressing room. Her door would be locked, of course, and she would be sobbing into her pillow. He paused in the dark like a spy on a mission, and listened.

He heard laughter in her room, and the soft murmur of voices raised in pleasant conversation.

Was her mother here with her? He'd rather face Napoleon's Imperial Guards than an angry mama. Perhaps it was his grandmother.

But that was impossible. Granddame never laughed.

He didn't bother to knock. He opened the door. It was his house, and she was his wife.

And it was his wedding night.

His brows shot up. There were two women in the room. He recognized the shorter of the two as one of the maids. The other, the beauty, must be his bride. He drew a sharp breath. She was tall and graceful, clad in a gown of gray silk. The heavy veil was gone, and her hair cascaded down her back in a shimmering curtain of silk.

Red.

He hadn't imagined her hair would be red. He preferred blondes. Or at least he thought he had.

Both women had books balanced on their heads, and were walking around the rug.

"That's better, Anna. Don't let the book fall. Keep your back straight and your knees bent a little."

The maid took three tottering steps and whooped with laughter, catching the book as it slid off her head.

His bride laughed. She hadn't noticed him, and didn't appear to be missing him in the least.

"Try again—watch me." She placed the book on her head. Her hair shone in the candlelight. His hand curled on the door latch. Was it as soft as it looked? He supposed he'd find out when it brushed his naked skin in bed. He swallowed a groan.

Her gown rustled as she walked gracefully forward.

She curtsied to her maid, and rose to spin in place, the book never moving. "My father insisted that perfect posture was the hallmark of a la—"

She came to a stop in a swirl of silk and hair as her eyes met his. She let out a cry of surprise and the book tumbled. He stepped forward and caught it.

He stared at it in surprise.

He knew by his bride's deep blush that she'd already seen what lay between the covers. It had been a wedding gift from Sebastian, a book from the erotic collection of a famous traitor who had a penchant for such things. The man's widow had sold his collection to men like Sebastian for a fortune to rival Granddame's own.

Anna set the other book on the table and curtsied. "Forgive me, Your Grace. I didn't see you there. I meant no disrespect. Were we too loud? Did we disturb you?" She blushed, and put a hand to her mouth, suddenly realizing why he was there. His bride was staring at him, apparently tongue-tied.

Anna bobbed another curtsy. "Um, if it would please

you to wait in your own rooms, I'll advise Mr. Partridge when Her Grace is ready—" Anna bobbed another curtsy, reddening further.

The blushing bride looked every inch the frightened virgin now.

A gentleman would leave the room, apologize for intruding.

His feet were rooted to the floor. Something about this woman brought out the devil in him indeed. Perhaps it was her beauty, perhaps her boldness. Perhaps it was the fact that she was his wife, and he didn't want a wife.

He pulled up a chair instead. "I think I'll wait right here."

Both lady and maid regarded him with identical expressions of horror. "You may proceed," he ordered Anna, but she remained frozen to the spot.

It was so quiet he could hear the clock in the sitting room ticking.

"We could dismiss Anna altogether and I could assist you out of your gown, Duchess," he said at last. "I daresay I am as proficient with tiny buttons as any lady's maid in London."

Her eyes narrowed as she assessed whether he meant it or not. He rose to the challenge and crossed the room. She held his gaze fiercely, and he stepped behind her, lifted her hair over her shoulder—it *was* as soft as it looked— and reached for the first button.

She shot forward out of reach. "Anna, you can go!" she said in a breathless rush, and the maid ran for the door.

She turned on him. "Anna didn't deserve to be treated like that, Your Grace. She's a respectable girl," she rebuked him.

He gave her a guileless look. "I said nothing inappropriate. I simply offered to help you out of your gown. I am your husband, am I not? And you are my wife, bought and paid for. That gives me certain privileges. Wherever are you getting your ideas?" He picked up the wicked blue book. "Here, perhaps?"

She colored, and her throat bobbed as she swallowed, but she held his gaze. "Tell me, did you see anything you liked? Anything titillating?"

She made a small, strangled sound and shut her eyes. He tossed the book on the bed and prowled toward her like a wolf. Her hands were white knots, and he wondered if she intended to fight him. She was trembling.

"Were you taught that bedding is shameful? Did your mama tell you what would happen when I came to your bed tonight?"

The delicate scent of her perfume drew him closer, like a moth to a flame. "She told you I would hurt you, didn't she?"

He stepped behind her, and continued to open the buttons on her gown. She drew a ragged breath as he traced his fingertip down the vee of exposed flesh between her shoulders. "Did she tell you about the pleasure I can give you?"

He swept the silk off her shoulders, and the gown billowed around her ankles, leaving her in her chemise and stays, Venus on a cloud.

He had seen beautiful women before, wearing far less than the prim undergarments his bride had on, but there was something infinitely enticing about this woman. Was it her innocence? He stepped back, frowning. This was supposed to be duty. He hadn't expected to feel desire.

Her breasts were pressed upward by her stays, and the silk revealed the shadow of her nipples. She folded her arms over her body and studied his boots.

"Look at me," he commanded softly.

She raised her eyes to his. He expected fear, hoped for nascent desire, but he met fierce determination instead.

She lowered her arms to her sides and let him look, color rising in her cheeks.

He reached to undo the ribbon ties that held her stays closed, but she put her hand over his, stopping him.

"The light, Your Grace. Please blow out the candles," she said, her voice husky.

"I prefer them lit." He stroked the petal-soft skin of her arms, felt goose bumps rise.

"Why?" she demanded. "What difference can it make to you? Surely you've seen—"

He laid a finger on her lips. "I told you you're not what I expected. Perhaps if you had been, then I'd want it dark. But I want to see you, learn what you like, teach you—"

She frowned, oblivious that the slippery ties of her bodice were loosening every second, revealing tantalizing flesh. "I am not a toy! Nor am I one of your women," she snapped.

He leaned on the bedpost, drank in the sight of her. "Ah, but you are my woman. You're my wife. I've never had a wife before. Well, not my own, at least. You will share my bed, bear my children . . ." He stepped closer, holding her gaze with his. He let his fingers glide over her shoulders, down her arms. Her eyes glazed at his touch. He grasped the ends of the ribbons between thumb and fingers. "And you're beautiful."

He saw disbelief in her eyes, and she pulled away from him. The ribbons unfurled, and the garment parted, revealing her breasts to his hungry eyes.

Her gasp of dismay and his groan of desire came out at the same moment.

She was naked—well, as naked as she'd ever been outside the privacy of the bath. Meg felt her body heat, but it wasn't just mortification. It was the look in Temberlay's eyes. She didn't understand it, but it started a tingle low in her belly, made her naked breasts swell under his gaze as if he'd touched her. She tugged the edges of the bodice together, but her fingers had forgotten how to tie a knot. She held the garment closed. He was still fully clothed. It made her feel all the more exposed.

"Can we please get this over with?" she demanded, but he seemed to be having trouble lifting his gaze from her breasts. His eyes were heavy-lidded and shiny. The gray was gone, faded into black as dark as the sea at night. Her mouth went dry.

"No, we'll do this properly," he muttered. "I want—" He stopped and grinned foolishly at her.

"What does that mean? It is impossible for me to 'do this properly.' I will require instructions!"

"Instructions," he murmured, his voice husky, but he didn't move.

"Tell me how to proceed," she insisted.

He gave her another foolish grin. He looked younger, sweeter, and infinitely more dangerous when he smiled like that. The tingle in her belly intensified.

"It would be much easier, and much more pleasurable, to show you." He loosened his cravat and tossed it aside, opened the buttons of his shirt with one hand without taking his eyes off her.

His naked chest was broad and muscular. She curled her hands more tightly around the edges of her stays, her armor. His body carried a dozen small silver scars, but they didn't detract from his masculine beauty. She wanted to push the shirt off his shoulders, see them all, touch them, explore each little mark. She could see his heart beating under his skin.

She waited for him to come to her, but he didn't move. He just stood by the bed with one hand on his hip, staring at her every bit as intently as she was staring at him. He looked like he was pondering a question.

"Please get on with it!"

"I was considering where to begin. This could take all night."

She gaped at him. "All night? Why? It is a simple act. It doesn't take that long from what I've seen. A few minutes at most—"

His brows shot up, and she could have bitten her tongue.

"And just what did you see?" he asked, grinning. "Who have you been watching? A stable lad with one of your maids, perhaps?" his tone was teasing.

She didn't reply.

"Tell me," he coaxed.

She swallowed the knot in her throat. "Horses!" she managed at last. "My father bred horses at Wycliffe!" His jaw dropped, and she knew at once she'd said the wrong thing.

All hints of amusement fell away as Nicholas stared at his bride. "You think that this is like—that I, um—" he spluttered. He found the chair and sat down. "I think we'd better go more slowly."

She picked up the discarded gown at her ankles, and clutched it to her chest. "Why?"

"Because I am not a stallion, and you are not a mare, for one thing."

She strode past him and snatched up the blue book. She opened it and flipped through the pages with one hand until she found what she was looking for. Still holding her gown with one hand, she thrust the book under his nose. "There!" she said.

He stared at the drawing for a moment, a painting of an exotic Eastern couple lying together on a patterned rug under the stars. Although the man was several feet from his partner, he was buried within her.

He swallowed, and took the book from her. "As difficult as it is for any man to admit, I am not built like that. This drawing is not anatomically correct. Look, he's bigger than the tree next to him!"

She took the book back and studied the painting again, ignoring him. "Is this what I'm supposed to do, lie on my back? Or should I lie on my side like this?" she asked, choosing another illustration.

He grabbed the book and snapped it shut. "Do you learn a lot of things from books?"

She frowned. "Of course. Wycliffe had an excellent library. There were books on every topic." She bit her lower lip. "But not this. Nothing like this."

He rose to his feet, untangled her grip on the gown, and took it from her, dropping it on the floor with his shirt. "There are some things you can't learn by reading, Duchess. This is one of them."

"Then how am I to begin?"

There was fire in her eyes, but the wrong kind entirely. He was also wondering where to begin to turn her determination to passion. She was still clutching the fastenings of her stays in her fist. He cupped her shoulders, stroking her skin with his thumbs.

"Did you like it when I kissed you?"

She held his gaze. "Yes."

He picked up a long lock of her hair and ran it through his fingers. He used it like a paintbrush, drawing it over her throat, across the slope of her breasts. Her eyes drifted shut, and her lips parted. How could a woman be so damned arousing just standing still, letting him play with her hair? He wondered what she was thinking, *if* she was thinking.

He lowered his head until his mouth was an inch from hers. "Kiss me."

She raised her face to his, tilted her head, and met his lips. Her mouth was soft and warm. He sipped at her lips, letting her get used to the intimacy, the feel of him.

The tentative touch of her tongue surprised him. She was testing him, trying what he'd taught her in that single, ravishing kiss he'd given her in the salon.

She learned fast.

Desire surged like wild horses.

He pulled away and looked at her. Her eyes were glazed, her cheeks flushed, her lips parted. She ran her tongue over them, an invitation for more that he couldn't resist.

This time her lips parted as their mouths met, and he pressed his tongue inside. She sighed, and the sound shot straight to his groin. He groaned, and pulled her closer. She didn't resist, but her hands still clutched her bodice between their bodies. He ignored that little impediment and tangled his hands in her glorious hair, angled his mouth over hers. He trailed his mouth over her cheek, her jaw, the hollows at the base of her throat. She tipped her head back and allowed it all. If he spoke now, he'd break the spell, so he kissed her again. Her tongue found his immediately, hungry.

He wanted her naked, writhing under him. He wanted to plunge inside her. The need to go slowly was making him sweat.

He stroked her back through her stays, and she arched

closer, her hips against his, sweet pressure that drove him wild. He concentrated on learning the delicate curve of her shoulder blades, the hollow of her waist, the swell of her hips. She made soft, sweet sounds that told him she liked his hands on her.

He skimmed his fingertips over her collarbones, along the silken column of her neck, and then back, sweeping aside the straps of her stays. She didn't stop him. She probably didn't even realize that he was stripping her.

He followed the swell of her breast until his hand found hers, clutching the edge of her garment. He opened it, laid her palm on his naked chest. Her other hand loosened of its own accord, joined the first, and curled against his skin. Her bodice parted, dropped away, and caught at her elbows. He pulled her against him, and pressed the naked heat of her breasts against his body. She made a low sound of pleasure, and her nipples pebbled against his chest. She wrapped her arms around his neck, tangling them in his hair, claiming his mouth.

Meg didn't want to stop kissing. She liked the taste of him, the feel of his hands on her. She reveled in the scent of his male body, the sensation of her skin on his, the heat. Perhaps she was drunk. His tongue did taste faintly of whisky.

Her mind tried to take control, to bring her back to a place where she could think clearly, manage things, but her body wouldn't allow it. She wanted more of the heady, exquisite pleasure.

She barely felt him lift her. There was only the softness of the mattress beneath her, the hardness of the man on top of her, and she arched against him, rolled her hips, wanting him nearer still. She touched him where he touched her, caressed him, traced the little scars with her fingertips, then her lips. She let her hands tangle in the softness of his hair, marveled at the roughness of his stubbled jaw, the flex of hard muscles under velvet skin. She ran her hand over his chest, across the flat plane of his hard belly, and reached the waistband of his breeches. She frowned at the barrier, tugged, and he pulled back, staring down at her, his face shadowed and unreadable.

"You want this, don't you?" he said, his voice husky.

Wasn't it obvious? She didn't want to talk. She kissed him again, and his hand cupped her breast, and she sighed, realizing she wanted that most of all—until he rolled his thumb over her nipple, and it felt even better. She arched against his hand like a cat.

Then his mouth found her nipple and she gasped at that too, and all sensible thoughts were forgotten. His mouth was so hot, so wet, so delicious. She moved against him, rolled her hips restively. "Slowly," he whispered, but she didn't want to go slowly.

She reached for his nipple, pinched it the way he'd pinched hers. He shot backward with a cry of surprise, and sat on his heels at the bottom of the bed with his eyes closed.

She raised herself on her elbows and stared at him. He appeared to be counting. She waited until he finished.

"Is something wrong, Your Grace?" She braced herself. She couldn't bear it if he told her she was too plain, or worse, that he simply couldn't bring himself to— She swallowed, waited for him to laugh, to reject her, to turn away and wish aloud that she was blond, sweet, and pretty, like . . .

Rose.

Bitterness filled her mouth, and she hugged her arms over her breasts, but he held up a hand.

"Nothing wrong. I just need a moment. Call me Nicholas in bed, sweetheart, never Your Grace," he said breathlessly.

Sweetheart. No one had ever called her that before.

"Nicholas," she said on a sigh, reaching for him. "Kiss me again."

Nicholas looked down at her. She was propped on her elbows, watching him intently with her incredible eyes. Her hair was an erotic tangle, her lips swollen from his kisses. Her stays were still tangled in the crooks of her arms, the lace a frothy foam around her breasts. Her shift was bunched around her thighs, exposing the slim, shapely length of her legs. He searched for a flaw, hoping it would slow his desire, but there wasn't one. His famous control was threatening to desert. How long had it been since he felt like this with a woman? He couldn't remember. Her tentative touches were erotic, born of honest desire. She was too innocent to make a pretense of her arousal.

She shifted, and kissed his nipple, then let her tongue circle, doing to him what he'd done to her, showing him what she liked by copying him, her eyes on his, gauging his response. It was torment, and heaven.

He slid his hand over her calf, pinched the soft skin behind her knee, caressed the silk of her thighs. He raised her shift and cupped her bottom.

She slid her hand under the waistband of his breeches, tried to do the same. He brushed his hand over the nest of curls between her thighs, and her hands stilled, unsure of how to proceed.

But he knew. He let his fingers find the moist heat of her body. She gasped, and her nails dug into the hard flesh of his buttocks as her hips moved in wordless, unwitting invitation.

Her lashes fluttered on pink cheeks. She caught her lip between white teeth and moaned, arching against his hand, demanding more.

Meg felt the world drop away. She was floating, the whole world centered on this moment, this man, and what he was doing to her. She told herself that he was a practiced rake, and he'd probably done this with dozens— hundreds—of women, but it didn't matter. Right now he was *her* rake, intent on pleasing only her. She couldn't think. There wasn't room in her mind with all the sensations, the feelings she'd never even known existed until now, with him.

She felt his mouth at her breast again. His caresses grew more urgent, demanded a response, and she cried out as the most exquisite sensation of all burst over her.

He kissed her tenderly as she drifted back to earth. She opened her eyes and looked at him.

"Is it over?" she asked. She did not want it to be over.

He shook his head and rose from the bed, fumbling with the flies on his breeches.

"No, sweetheart, it's hardly begun." He peeled away his breeches and stepped out of them.

Her mouth went dry.

She had seen perfect male statues carved in marble, though they'd been modestly draped in togas. She'd spent the afternoon studying the paintings and illustrations in the blue book, but none compared to Nicholas. He was powerful, beautiful, magnificent. She let her eyes roam over him, and met his eyes boldly. She held out her arms in a wordless plea, and he tumbled into them, pressed her back against the mattress, kissed her again.

His skin melted against hers, his male angles fitting perfectly against her feminine curves. This was how it worked, she thought, marveling. It was a dance, and the steps were instinctive.

She closed her hand on the hardness that jutted against her hip, and he gasped, and put his hand over hers in an iron grip, keeping her still.

"Slowly, sweetheart. In fact, don't move at all," he said, his voice hoarse.

Had she lost the steps, mistaken the rhythm? "Tell me what to do," she whispered.

"Lie back," he said. She felt his fingers upon her again, arousing her all over again. As she cried out, he knelt between her thighs, and she felt the blunt tip of his erection where his fingers had been.

"Now it will hurt, won't it?" she said.

He winced apologetically. Sweat beaded on his forehead, and his teeth were gritted. "A little," he said, trying to sound reassuring. "I'll go very slowl—"

She put her hand on his shoulders, closed her eyes and tilted her hips to meet his.

He swore as he plunged into her. She stifled a cry against his shoulder and dug her nails into his flesh as he filled her, withdrew and filled her again. The pain ebbed.

She was his, married, bedded, consummated.

He cried out, and she felt him shudder, his body thrusting powerfully into hers one last time before he collapsed against her, his heart pounding against hers. She held him to her.

After a long moment he raised his head to look at her, still buried within her body.

"Did I hurt you?"

Reality returned. "Yes. A little." He rolled away, and she felt the cool air rush to touch her skin. She missed him at once. She sat up and hugged her knees to her chest.

He lay on his side, propped on his elbow, regarding her with pride clear in his eyes. "It won't hurt again. It's only painful the first time. After that, the pleasure is—"

She looked at him in astonishment. "The only time, Your Grace," she said. Surely she was with child already. He was so powerful, so vital, so *ready*.

He chuckled. "For tonight, certainly," he said, and stroked her arm. She leaped off the bed, and picked up his shirt, the first piece of clothing that came to hand, and shrugged into it, wrapping it around her body.

Nicholas's heart was still pounding. He wondered if his wife had any idea how fetching she looked in his shirt. She was tousled, her breasts heaving.

He patted the mattress beside him. "Come back to bed, Rose."

Instead she fled for the dressing room, and returned wrapped from chin to ankle in a thick woolen robe.

Oblivious to his own nakedness, he rose and set about picking up his clothes and untangling his boots from his breeches. He laid the garments carefully over the back of the chair. He turned to find her watching him. His body responded to her gaze, and he grinned at her.

She stared at him in horror as he crossed to the bed and began loosening the bedclothes.

"What are you doing?" she asked.

"Don't worry, I think we both need some sleep."

"You can't sleep here!" she squeaked, and he stood by the bed with his hands on his naked hips.

"Why the hell not? This is our wedding night."

She turned her back. "You can't stay."

"Why not? Look, Rose, I don't intend to—"

"Don't call me that!" she snapped.

He leaned on the bedpost and crossed his arms over his chest, regarding her as if he were fully dressed and they were having this conversation in the drawing room. "Do you wish to be called something else?" he asked.

"Yes!" she said. "No."

She wasn't making any sense. Any moment, she'd burst into tears and demand he send for her mother. He felt a sharp stab of disappointment after all.

He picked up his clothes. "Never mind. I'll sleep in my own bed. It's been a very long day, and you obviously need some sleep to calm your nerves."

He strode through the dressing room to his own bed-chamber. Behind him, he heard the lock turn on her side. He stared at the door in astonishment. Never, ever, had a woman thrown him out of her bed. Usually they begged him to stay. This was a completely new situation, and Nicholas didn't like it at all.

He regarded his bed sourly, and tossed his clothes on the floor and kicked them. He yanked back the covers and got in. The sheets were cold. He shut his eyes, but he could still smell her on his skin, still taste her on his tongue and his fingers. He ground his teeth, willing away his renewed erection.

They were still essentially strangers, of course. He had time. He had never failed to win a woman he wanted, and he wouldn't this time either.

He would have his fill of his unexpectedly delicious, stubborn, infuriating little wife, and then he would move on.

Chapter 17

The fragrance of toast and chocolate woke Meg the next morning.

"Good morning, Your Grace. I apologize for waking you so early, but I was unsure of your usual habits," Anna said. "The dowager is already up, and has asked to see you once you've breakfasted."

Meg sat up. "She wishes to see me?" But of course she did, and she was expecting Rose. She ran a nervous hand through her hair, a nest of tangles. She licked her lips, still swollen from his kisses, and glanced around the room, her eyes falling on the door that connected their rooms, now standing open as Anna bustled in and out of the dressing room.

Had it really happened, or had she dreamed it? Other than the thick woolen robe she was still wearing, there was no sign that anything remotely interesting had occurred in this room last night. She got up, and winced. Well, there was that—a little soreness, but it was a mere shadow compared to the pleasure.

"I would like a bath," she said to Anna, surprised that her voice was even, calm. She thought of Temberlay— Nicholas in bed—and drew a ragged breath.

She crossed to the mirror and stared at her face. Did she look more knowing, more wanton than she had yesterday, more married? Her lips were red as cherries, her eyes bright, and her cheeks were pink. She looked much more like Rose this morning, almost pretty.

She picked up a comb and began to work at the knots in her hair. Anna quickly came forward. "Allow me, Your Grace."

Meg surrendered the comb and met her own eyes in the mirror again. She swallowed a smile and the urge to giggle. Her toes curled into the carpet. The way he touched her made her feel like the most beautiful woman in the world.

The faint fragrance of his soap rose up from his robe, and she resisted the urge to bury her nose in the sleeve.

She hadn't imagined she'd sleep last night after he'd left her. She had lain in bed clutching her robe to her throat, marveling at what had just happened, and staring at the locked door, half dreading, half hoping he'd come back. He hadn't. Nor had the nightmares that often plagued her. She hadn't wanted him to see those—she pushed the thought away. She didn't wish to think about her fears now. There were other, more important things to face.

She looked at the door yet again, and felt her heart flutter. Was he asleep in his own bed, or awake and thinking of her?

"Has His Grace risen yet?" she asked, and winced at the fiery blush that rose over her face in the mirror. Her voice was husky, the seductive purr of a woman who had been bedded by a lover. Anna didn't seem to notice.

"Hours ago, ma'am. He likes to ride in the park before the sun is scarcely up."

"I see." The flutter fizzled. Something as trifling as a wedding night hadn't interrupted *his* routine. Anna finished combing her hair and looped it up in a ribbon for the bath.

She drew a screen around the tub and Meg sank into the warm water with a sigh, unable to think of anything, or anyone but Temberlay. The sweet painted face of a nymph smiled knowingly at her from the screen. Meg smiled back. A second nymph sat on a bench by a pond, combing her hair placidly, her diaphanous robe open, looking out at Meg as if she knew exactly what she'd experienced last night, had experienced it herself, and felt the same sense of wonder.

Meg frowned. He'd admitted that he'd bedded dozens of women—hundreds, even, if the scandal sheets were to be believed—she was simply one more.

But for her, one night, one man, and she would never be the same.

She picked up the soap and reminded herself that this was no time to be silly. She had done her duty, married Temberlay, and consummated the match. Her family was safe, and Wycliffe would remain their home. She might be carrying the required heir even now. She ran a hand over her flat stomach under the water. Of course, if she *were* pregnant, then there would be no need to repeat the experiences of last night. Disappointment curled in her chest. The soap slipped out of her hand. She watched it sink.

She still had to face the duchess this morning. Would she be angry, disappointed that her grandson had married the plain Lynton sister instead of the beauty?

She glanced at the nymphs, but they had no advice to offer, or even reassurance. The deception was all Meg's, and so would be the consequences.

She reached for a sponge, ran it over her shoulders, shoulders he'd caressed last night. Whatever the duchess thought of her actions, surely it was too late to change things.

Unless they publicly denounced her, of course, rejected her as an imposter and sent her away in disgrace. Her face flamed. She'd be the laughingstock of London, the chit who thought she could deceive the Devil and get away with it. She imagined the fun the scandal sheets would have with *that*.

She sat up, let the cool air chill her wet skin, splashed away the burn of shame in her cheeks. Surely the dowager would not wish to face a scandal. She would have to accept the fact that Meg, not Rose, was married to Temberlay.

Temberlay. She sighed as the image of his face came to mind, flushed from kisses, sex.

The small crescent-shaped marks she'd left on his skin when he—

She shut her eyes tight, willing him away so she could think clearly. This was not a love match. It was a business arrangement. He had already gone on with his life, and she must do the same.

She got out of the bath. She would face the dowager bravely. She was a duchess herself now.

She would tell the dowager she intended to leave for Wycliffe today, to wait to see if she was indeed with child.

If not, she would have to share her husband's bed again. Her toes curled again in anticipation, and she uncurled them at once, and reminded herself that she must be practical.

She would also have to face Temberlay today, tell him the truth. She clutched the towel tighter. He had, in her untutored opinion, lived up to his reported prowess as a lover. What if he lived up to the rest of his wicked reputation as well?

"You're shivering, Your Grace. Was the water too cold?" Anna asked.

Meg forced a smile. "Not at all. Would you please tell Her Grace I will be there within the hour?"

There was no point in delaying the inevitable.

Chapter 18

Nicholas rode through Hyde Park in the buttery morning sun, his mind fixed on the pleasures of his wedding night. He shifted in the saddle, easing a very inconvenient erection, and nodded out of habit to a passing rider without even noticing who it was. He thought of her lips parted with desire, her long legs tangled with his, the sweet sounds she made that left him in no doubt that she liked what he'd done to her. He'd certainly liked what she did to him.

He groaned, and the other rider cleared his throat and spurred his horse onward.

He watched him go, whoever he was, and mentally listed the pleasures he planned to show Rose tonight.

He smiled absently at a carriage full of fashionable ladies of the *ton*, but did not stop to flirt.

It wasn't until Hannibal snorted that he realized he was on the verge of directing the stallion home, toward his bride, before they'd even begun their morning's exercise. Hannibal missed the heat of battle as much as Nicholas did, and he let it show in his boredom with ladies and London parks, but he objected to missing any ride at all with a toss of his head. Nicholas curbed him, made him walk sedately.

The horse obeyed instantly. Why couldn't his wife do the same? She'd thrown him out of her room. If it had happened to any other gentleman of his acquaintance, he would have laughed till his sides ached, but it was different now.

He supposed he should have demanded an explanation, or set out some rules. When he'd woken this morning, he'd considered having his valet tell her maid that he wished to see her at once, but he'd decided against it. He wasn't ready to face her just yet, not without wanting to touch her, kiss her—he sighed like a lovesick boy.

Hannibal snorted a warning, and Nicholas looked up and winced. Lady Fiona Barry's carriage slid to a stop beside him.

"Devil! I know you wouldn't dare ride past me without bidding me good morning," Fiona chirped, her eyes roaming over him hungrily.

Nicholas gritted his teeth, pulled Hannibal to a standstill. "Good morning, Lady Fiona. Fine weather for a ride."

Fiona could smell gossip a mile off, and dined on scandal for breakfast. "There's a dreadful rumor afoot that you've taken a wife. Tell me it isn't true! Every female heart in London would be broken by such terrible news, including mine."

"Alas, Lady Fiona, it is true indeed," Sebastian said, riding up with his sister Delphine in tow.

My, but it was crowded in the park this morning, Nicholas thought, imagining pulling Sebastian's tongue out, but it kept flapping. "I stood as his groomsman at the wedding yesterday. The official notice is in the *Morning Post* today."

Nicholas turned his attention to Delphine, and tried to divert the conversation. "Hello, Delphie. That's a fetching hat." But Fiona put a gloved hand to her cheek, her eyes glowing with delight.

"Poor, poor Devil! She must be positively dreadful if you are already up and out so early on the very morning after your wedding. Who is she? Come to breakfast and tell me all. I am a sympathetic listener, and the soul of discretion."

Sebastian stifled a laugh, damn him, and Delphie made a small sound of indignation at Fiona's audacity. Nicholas realized he was about to become the laughingstock of London. It infuriated him, made him incautious.

"On the contrary. My bride is sleeping late for obvious reasons, but I, poor mortal that I am, can hardly stay away from her. I had to leave lest I found myself too tempted by her charms to show her due consideration."

Delphie gasped in maidenly shock. Sebastian's jaw dropped. Fiona looked stunned. Even Hannibal rolled his eyes.

Nicholas felt his neck grow hot under his cravat. Now whose tongue should be plucked out? Why the hell had he said such a thing, and to Fiona of all people? Was it chivalry, coming to the defense of his wife, or idiotic male pride?

Fiona slid her eyes to Sebastian. "Who is she, St. James?"

It was like offering candy to a wide-eyed child. Sebastian liked to gossip almost as much as his sisters, but even Delphie winced as her brother leaned in to share his knowledge.

Short of shooting Sebastian, there was little Nicholas could do but watch the disaster unfold. By lunch, half of London would know every detail about his wedding. He regretted the green coat now. By tea, the other half of the *ton* would be making up stories of their own about the ceremony, the bride, even the wedding night.

"She's a beauty," Sebastian drawled. "The daughter of the late Earl of Wycliffe, blond like her mother. She was beset by wedding nerves yesterday, of course, having to marry Temberlay sight unseen, but she is renowned throughout her native Somerset for her beauty, sweet nature, and gentle ways." He had the nerve to wink at Nicholas.

Blond like her mother. The words hit Nicholas like grapeshot.

He tightened his hands on the reins and stared at his friend.

"You should be glad you didn't wed her sister," Sebastian rambled on. "They say that one is a wild hoyden, complete with the devil's own red hair. She has a sharp tongue and a bold manner. I think your sweet Rose has just a touch of her sister's temper, perhaps."

A red-haired hoyden with a sharp tongue.

There was no mistaking which sister he'd married.

"You'd do well to curb that streak of temper early, Devil," Fiona said with acid sweetness. Anger welled in his gut, churned upward.

Red, not blond.

"Perhaps your husband could advise me," he said coldly, ignoring her gasp at the set-down. Without another word, he tipped his hat and nudged Hannibal to a trot.

Sebastian caught up with him. "No one could have gotten away with that but you, Nick. Fiona's ears will be stinging for a week."

Nicholas ignored him, stared at the track ahead, seeing his wife's glorious red hair.

"So how'd it go last night?" Sebastian asked. "We missed you at dinner. Or at least some of us did. Your bride seemed quite content without you, though I feared her mama was going to carve me like the roast! Where were you, anyway? With Angelique?"

Nicholas reined Hannibal to a sudden stop. He hadn't even thought of Angelique.

Sebastian fought to halt his own mount, turn him to face his friend. "What the devil is the matter with you? You're acting strange this morning, even for you. Did something go wrong after I left?"

Nicholas's hands tightened on the reins so hard the leather of his gloves squeaked.

"How do you know Rose is blond?"

Sebastian's grin shone again. "There are times when having sisters is quite useful. Delphie asked Eleanor, and Eleanor's maid just happens to be from Somerset, from quite near Wycliffe Park, in fact. Wycliffe had four daughters. Despite his own ugly face, he managed to breed three beauties that resemble their mother, all of them blond and sweet-tempered. The fourth girl is an odd duck, to put it politely. Apparently Rose left a lot of broken hearts in Somerset when she married you. Your grandmother did you a favor after all."

There was a curious buzzing in Nicholas's head. He sat very still, his jaw tight, his eyes forward.

"Nick? What's wrong with you?" Sebastian asked. "D'you fancy going to the club for a drink? We could celebrate—"

Celebrate?

Nicholas kicked Hannibal to a gallop and left Sebastian coughing dust.

Redheaded hoyden. Liar.

She'd tricked him.

No one had ever duped him. Not his wily French enemies in Spain, not the hardened gamblers he met in the clubs and gaming hells, and certainly never a woman. He was—or at least he *used* to be—smarter than that.

At home, he tossed Hannibal's reins to a waiting groom

and climbed the steps two at a time. Gardiner stood in the hall, in the way, or Nicholas would have gone straight upstairs to find the odd duck, redheaded hoyden.

"Where is my . . ." He paused. What was she? Not his wife, surely. Not his duchess.

His deceiver.

He watched the butler's imperturbable smile slip a little at the harshness of his tone.

"Her Grace is with the dowager, sir. Is there anything I can get for you?"

Nicholas stared at the staircase, wondering what Granddame was saying to the treacherous little—

He didn't even know her name.

Shame warred with anger in his breast. Had she said it yesterday when she spoke her vows? He hadn't bothered to listen, only thinking how unfortunate the whole situation was. If only he'd known the truth of that! But he'd been so busy giving his own performance that he hadn't even suspected she was giving one of her own. His mouth dried. Was her response in bed yet another deception?

"Send for Mr. Dodd, Gardiner. I want to see all the marriage documents, the contract, the license, everything. Send it all up to—her—apartments."

Gardiner hurried to obey, and Nicholas went to his wife's rooms to wait.

Once Granddame was through with the little imposter, it was his turn.

Chapter 19

The dowager duchess was seated at her desk by the window when Meg arrived in her study, her black-clad back to the door.

"Good morning, Marguerite," she said without turning.

Meg let out the breath she was holding. "How did you know it was me?" She'd been ready to fight this morning, but the dowager's smile as she rose was—well, pleasant, almost welcoming.

"I knew the day I saw you at the modiste's. Or rather, I suspected it would come to this."

"But I didn't—" Meg began, but the dowager waved her to silence.

"Come now! When I did not see your sister, I had inquiries made. I was hardly surprised she'd run away, given her reluctance to marry Nicholas. I wondered what your mother would do, what you would do, so I simply waited. Do sit down. We have a lot to discuss."

Meg obediently sank into the straight-backed chair the dowager indicated. "Why didn't you stop the wedding?"

The dowager's laugh was filled with icy triumph. "That would have caused quite a scandal. Nicholas would have undoubtedly enjoyed the fiasco, given his behavior yesterday, but neither you nor I would have liked it, and it would not have done the Temberlay name any good. I arranged this marriage to tie him to a lady of impeccable respectability. Imagine how it would have looked if I'd denounced you as an imposter?"

Meg swallowed. She was simply a female of suitable pedigree, interchangeable with any other lady of her class. Emotions were never meant to enter into this match. But after last night—she shut her eyes, feeling shame, regret, and longing.

The dowager mistook her frown. "There's no need to feel guilty. You're a clever girl. Your sister was unavailable and you took her place. I applaud your daring. I knew it was you the moment I saw that hideous veil. Why else would a bride wear such a thing? To be truthful, I prefer you to your sister. You have the spine to stand up to Nicholas, and I have hopes that you will truly reform him. Your sister would not have managed such a feat."

Meg felt her skin flush. "I have no interest in reforming him, Your Grace. I married him, and the marriage is consummated. I intend to return to Wycliffe."

The dowager cackled. "Running away already? Perhaps you are not as brave as I thought. Did the wedding night frighten you? Was he rough with you? He is angry, but it's done now. Next time I daresay it won't be as difficult for you."

Meg felt her skin heat from her toes to her hairline. She raised her chin. "That may not be necessary. There is much to do at Wycliffe. I will send word if I prove to be with child. Or not."

The old lady's gray brows rose. "You are not Wycliffe's daughter any longer. You are Temberlay's duchess. You have social obligations, and you will remain in Town. You must be presented at court. If and when you are indeed with child, you will retire to Temberlay Castle. The heir to the dukedom must be born there. Your mama will have to do without you from now on."

Meg raised her chin. "This is a marriage of convenience, Your Grace, not a love match. No one will expect us to appear together in public."

"On the contrary, Marguerite. You were chosen to give Nicholas the appearance of respectability. You will be seen at every ball, every soiree, every opera as his wife, the virtuous daughter of the Earl of Wycliffe. That is your duty, as much as producing an heir."

It meant more nights in his arms, days in his dangerous, seductive company. Was he the hero Hector and Gardiner believed he was, or the rogue of the scandal sheets? Tempting as he was in print, he was overwhelming in the flesh.

"What is it, child?" the dowager said with mocking pity. "Surely you realize it's too late to be unhappy now. You married Temberlay to save your family, didn't you?"

Meg's temper prickled. "I married him because I wanted to be rich again."

The dowager laughed again. "Then why would you wish to return to Wycliffe? If you want to enjoy his money, then London is the place to do so—the jewels, the parties, the pretty clothes are all here, not in Somerset. But you don't really care about that—you sold yourself to the devil for your family's sake." She paced the room, leaning on her stick. "Of course, I suspect there's more to your choice than family or money isn't there? You wanted *him*."

Meg shook her head, felt her skin heat.

"Come now. Let us be honest now it's done. I saw your face that day at the modiste's. And why not? He's a handsome man, has a certain reputation for—"

Meg shot to her feet, aghast. "No!"

The dowager raised her brows. "Oh? You said the marriage had been successfully consummated. He enjoys almost legendary status as a lover. Did you enjoy it?"

Meg didn't answer. She felt her flesh heat as her body remembered every caress, every kiss.

"Well?" the dowager demanded.

Fury made her bold. "He was magnificent, Your Grace, everything they say, and more," she snapped, trying to shock the old harridan into silence. Instead she grinned and thumped her walking stick on the floor with glee.

"See? I knew you'd make him a fine match! You've got the fire your sister lacks."

Meg stared at the dowager. She didn't care a whit for anyone's happiness. She had arranged this match to get a child of her blood. The feelings of the parents of that child didn't matter in the least. She wondered what would happen if she dared to disappoint the dowager hopes, and produced a girl. She remembered the disappointment in her father's eyes every time he looked at her. Surely the dowager would be even colder, crueler.

"You'd best go and prepare yourself to receive afternoon callers," the old duchess said, dismissing her. "Once word gets out, and since Sebastian St. James is as much a gossip as his sisters, I don't doubt it already has, the *ton* will want to get a look at you." She pursed her lips and regarded Meg. "Wear something fetching. You should also plan to introduce yourself to Temberlay. We can't have him calling you Rose any longer. It would be irksome as well as awkward, should she choose to reappear now the wedding is done." She nodded a crisp dismissal. "You may go."

Marguerite was speechless. She stumbled toward the

door, her stomach in knots. This was not how she imagined it would be.

She walked back along the corridor to her apartments, watching her slippered feet appear and disappear under the frothy hem of her morning gown.

Facing the *ton* was almost as terrifying as facing Temberlay.

The finest ladies in London, the richest, most noble, most dangerous females, would arrive to scrutinize Devil's bride, and to judge her suitability to number among them. Or not. A trickle of sweat rolled between her shoulder blades. Surely they'd cut her to pieces. Every country flaw, every little mistake would be magnified in the retelling, whispered about behind fans and kid gloves in fashionable salons all over London. She imagined the scandal sheets—the plain stick of a woman the handsome Duke of Temberlay had shackled himself to, and quite by mistake. She had saved her family, and ruined herself.

She gritted her teeth, and clasped her hands together, feeling the weight of the wedding band on her finger.

She must start today as she meant to go on, yet again. She couldn't afford to set a foot wrong, and the rules of etiquette were complicated. How *should* she begin? She would start by asking Cook to make extra cakes and biscuits, she decided. Her heart quailed at the task of choosing the perfect gown.

Her wardrobe included dozens of morning gowns, day dresses, walking ensembles, riding habits, and evening gowns. The selection of tea gowns alone was endless. As the Duchess of Temberlay she would be expected to know the intricacies of fashion and good manners, even if her duke considered himself exempt.

And conversation . . . there would be questions about

the wedding, about Temberlay, about her pedigree. How on earth was she to answer?

The footmen stationed outside her apartments swung the doors open as she approached, and she walked across the room to the window. She needed air, time to think of what she would say. She tugged at the sticky latch. Why wouldn't it open?

"Do you plan to jump?"

Meg spun to find Temberlay seated in the wing chair by the fireplace, his legs crossed, his hands tented before his chest, his eyes as cold as ice. Her knees turned to water.

"I didn't notice you there," she managed.

He knew.

She put a hand to her throat. "I—" she began, but her explanation died on her lips as he got to his feet, and prowled silently across the carpet toward her with the lithe grace of a panther. She took an involuntary step backward.

He was still dressed for riding, hadn't bothered to change. Today his coat was dark blue, his breeches buff, his top boots still coated with dust.

She was glad to see he didn't have a riding crop.

Another step back and she was against the wall. He stopped and regarded her from a scant few feet away, his eyes gray chips of fury.

She forced herself to push away from the wall and stand on her own two feet, to look him in the eye. "I—" She cleared the frog from her throat. "I was hoping to see you today, Your Grace. I need to speak to you."

"Ah, so it's back to 'Your Grace' this morning, is it? Not Nicholas?" He slid an insolent gaze over her body. She curled her hands at her sides, resisted the urge to fold them across her breasts. "Why did you wish to see me?

Do you wish to relive the delights of last night? I've a mind to do so myself."

She felt hot blood fill her cheeks, and she dropped her gaze.

He came closer still. She could smell the wool of his coat, the slight tang of his horse, the now-familiar scent of his skin. He leaned in and blew softly in her ear. She flinched in surprise.

"There's just one thing I'd like to know," he whispered.

The timber of his voice vibrated through her, and she turned to meet his eyes, just inches from her own. "Yes?"

"When I come, and I feel inclined to cry out someone's name, what in hell should I call you?"

Mortified, she would have turned away, but he grasped her chin, held her eyes with his own. "I can't call you Rose, because you're not Rose, are you? I hear that Rose is sweet, pretty, kind, and gentle. Her sister, however, is described as a redheaded hoyden." He cast a disdainful glance over Meg's careful coiffure. "That, I assume, would be you."

The insult put steel into her spine. She pulled away, met his eyes boldly. "Marguerite," she said bluntly.

He barked a laugh, spread his arms wide, and began to sing.

"Oh Maggie mine, with your sweet tits divine, you are a delight in the dark of the night, but oh what a sight in the light!"

Meg flushed to her hairline.

"There are more verses, if you'd like to hear them, each one cruder than the last," he offered. She shook her head, unable to speak.

"Then perhaps you'll be good enough to tell me where my real bride is so we can end this charade."

Meg's anger flared like a torch. He wanted Rose now,

after— "Sorry to disappoint, Your Grace, but *I* am your wife."

He sneered. "I've sent for the contracts, the marriage license, even the *Morning Post*. I have no doubt my solicitors will prove otherwise. Within the week, this farce of a marriage will be annulled and all London will be laughing about the chit who tried to sneak into a duke's bed to claim a fortune."

Meg's eyes widened. "You wouldn't dare!"

"Do you think I have any less daring than you, my lady?"

Meg was far less certain of her position now. Shame heated her cheeks.

"And just where is your delectable blond sister? How intriguing to have the virginity of sisters!"

Meg raised her chin. "Rose ran away the day she was told she would have to marry you. She *is* sweet and gentle. Why would she want a man like you? You're disgusting!"

"You weren't so disgusted in bed last night, Maggie."

"Don't call me that!" she snapped.

"Why not? It suits you. Maggie has the sound of the gutter to it, perfect for a sneak thief and a harlot."

"Get out," she managed through gritted teeth. It came out as a croak instead of a roar.

"This is my house. You get out," he shot back.

She blinked at him for a moment. She could feel tears stinging the back of her eyes, and she would not, could not, allow herself to cry in front of him. He had a right to be angry, but his insults stung, especially after he'd made her feel so—

She reminded herself she wasn't Rose, wasn't beautiful. What man wouldn't be disappointed?

She turned on her heel and made for the door, opening it and slamming it behind her, ignoring the shocked footmen. Temberlay didn't follow.

She hurried down the stairs, her head held high, unshed tears blurring her vision. She prayed Gardiner would not appear now.

She did not stop until she'd reached Bryant House, and the front door closed behind her. The heavy oak panels shut out the sound of London traffic, and sealed her inside the quiet sanctuary. She breathed in the familiar scent of beeswax polish and her mother's perfume. Shame made her shiver, but she was safe.

For now.

Chapter 20

"*M*arguerite Lynton!" Nicholas growled as he looked at the marriage contract. The license also bore her name, as did the announcement in the *Morning Post*. Mr. Dodd also sent a lad running to the church to check the registry. She'd signed her own name in a clear, elegant hand.

He shoved the documents away, and rubbed his eyes. She'd duped him completely, and he'd been too much of a fool to even notice.

"Everything is quite in order, Your Grace. All legal and binding, though you may wish to amend your will now you're a married man," Dodd advised.

Nicholas rose. "Thank you, Dodd, we'll discuss that another time."

He stared at Marguerite's signature. He was certain he had heard Sebastian call her Rose.

There was no way of getting around the truth. It was his own fault. He'd been too busy playing the rake, trying to frighten her away, to give a damn. *He* was the one who should have been frightened. She was a bold, seductive, clever little liar.

The door of the library opened and Granddame entered. "There you are, Nicholas. I wish to speak to you.

Will you ring for tea?" She settled herself on the settee and regarded him like a cat with a prized bird hidden between her sharp little teeth. He ignored her request.

"How did you get that woman's name into the marriage contract without my knowing?" He kept his tone calm.

She swallowed the canary whole. "I had it changed a week before the ceremony. It was quite plain, written in bold, black ink if you'd cared enough to look."

"You might have told me."

She waved her hand. "Oh pooh. You should be glad things turned out as they did. Hector Bryant insisted I offer for the eldest girl, but I knew Marguerite would be a better match as soon as I met her. She'll make a fine duchess." She rose and pulled the bell herself. "Did you know Rose Lynton ran away rather than face the prospect of being tied to you for the rest of her life? I merely waited to see what the Lyntons would do. Marguerite solved the problem beautifully. I like her—she has fire and spirit. Tea, Gardiner, and don't be all day about it," she ordered when he appeared, and waited for the door to close behind him. "She said you were a magnificent lover."

He looked at her in surprise.

"Come now. That expression doesn't suit a man of your reputation. I've heard the stories about you. There's no part of you left that could be shocked by anything I might say. You must have found her worth the effort. Men need not go to the trouble of seducing their wives."

He raised an eyebrow at her frankness and decided to match it. "She was a virgin, Granddame. What did you expect me to do?"

She pursed her lips. "Given your behavior at the wedding yesterday, I expected that you'd do what most men would do. I am pleased in this case—only in this case— that you are not most men."

"You mean I'm not David," he said.

She smoothed a hand over the black taffeta mourning gown. "No, you are not. If not for you, your brother would still be alive, but you are duke in his place. Marguerite is your last chance to redeem yourself, to honor your brother and your title. It's time to grow up."

He glared at the ducal ring he wore. So she'd heard all the stories, and it didn't matter one whit to her that none of them were true. She wanted to believe the worst. She had never asked about his years at war, or how he spent his days now he was home. She saw him as she wanted to, a scapegoat for David's failings. His blood made him suitable for bearing an heir, but otherwise she had no love for him.

He stared at her marble profile. It would destroy her if she knew her beloved David was the gambler, the liar, the wastrel. He could never be so cruel—as cruel as she was—and tell her. Nor would he give her another child to misshape into another David. He'd rather have the unhappiness, the title—all of it—end with him.

Gardiner arrived with the tea tray.

"Would you ask Her Grace to join us?" his grandmother asked.

"I'm afraid she's gone out, Your Grace. She left some time ago, on foot." Gardiner calmly poured the tea, apparently unaware of the tension in the room. Granddame's face reddened dangerously as she pinned Nicholas with a malevolent glare.

"That will be all, Gardiner." She waited until he'd left the room. "Damn you, what did you say to her?"

"I told her she was an imposter and invited her to leave."

For once Granddame looked stunned. "You did what? You fool! Go and get her back this instant!"

He crossed the room and poured himself a drink. "She was eager enough to go, and I don't particularly want her back."

Granddame gaped at him. "Think of the scandal! Your wife has walked out on you, left you the very morning after the wedding. What will people think?"

"I suppose they'll think I'm like most men after all."

She thumped her stick on the carpet, glaring at him, but she was powerless to control him now, to force him to do her bidding. Nor would he allow it any longer. He would have to call upon his wife at some point, and soon, but he needed time to decide what he would say. It would do her good to cool her heels with her mama for a while.

"Go and get her back!" Granddame ordered again.

Nicholas left the drink untouched and strode to the door. "Perhaps tomorrow," he said, and left the room.

When he saw his duplicitous little wife again, the upper hand would belong to him.

Chapter 21

Hector watched Flora circle the rug in his sitting room like a caged lioness. She was twisting yet another lace handkerchief to shreds between angry fingers. He cast a sad glance at the remnants of three others that already lay on the carpet. Between the wedding ceremony and this unexpected turn of events, Meg's marriage to Temberlay had cost a fortune in Belgian lace handkerchiefs.

It had taken only a single look at Meg as she stood in the entry hall to send Flora into a torrent of tears to rival Noah's flood. She had been alternately crying and cursing Temberlay all afternoon. He'd been watching the clock, expecting—hoping—Temberlay would arrive to fetch his wife. He hadn't come, and Meg was certain he would not.

His goddaughter was calmly sipping tea and nibbling on raisin cake as if nothing at all was amiss, but there were two spots of vivid color in her cheeks, a sure sign that she was furious. She drew calm around her like a cloak when she was most upset. It came from the necessity of having to keep her mother and sisters from falling into hysterics when things went awry. Meg had arrived at the door flushed with anger that she tried her best to hide from her mother. She blushed every time Temberlay's name was mentioned.

"Do sit down and have your tea, Mama. There's nothing at all to worry about," Meg soothed. "We can go home to Wycliffe tomorrow. I'd rather not be in London when the marriage is annulled. I have met no one at all, and no one has met me, so the scandal will blow over all the faster if I am not here."

She set her cup back in the saucer with exquisite care, but Hector noticed that her hands shook slightly. Her control was cracking. Her jaw was set hard as she fought to control her emotions. He held his breath, wishing she would fly into a rage, or soak the room in a flood of tears to rival Flora's. Either would do her a world of good.

"What exactly did Temberlay say?" he began, but Flora turned on her daughter.

"Go home? Annulment? We'll be ruined!" Flora interrupted. Another handkerchief shrieked as she tore it in half.

The sodden lace landed on the toe of his boot, and Hector regarded it sadly. It would mean far more than ruin. The Lynton ladies would be back where they started, and Meg's notoriety would make it difficult for her to find a job now. But this was hardly the time to bring that up. And there was the possibility that Meg might be with child. What then?

Flora was muttering insults upon the absent Temberlay as she paced. She was making him dizzy, and Hector caught her hand. "I'm sure it's all a misunderstanding. We expected there'd be some anger—"

"He was most insulting," Meg licked icing off her fingers. Her face flamed again.

How insulting?

"Even so, I think it best if we send a note telling Temberlay that you are here. We can put it all down to a case of bridal nerves."

"I'm not in the least nervous," Meg said sweetly. "There's no need of a note. He'll know exactly where I am. The footman who saw me leave will report to Gardiner, who will report to the dowager. Temberlay will no doubt have informed his solicitors by now where they can find me. Can I pour anyone more tea?"

Hector squeezed Flora's hand to keep her from shrieking.

"We must hope it doesn't come to that. Perhaps if an apology was made," he suggested.

"Men like Temberlay never apologize!" Flora growled.

Hector looked at her patiently. "That's not what I meant—" but Meg was already on her feet.

"Then why wait? Since I have nothing to pack, I see no reason why I cannot leave for Wycliffe immediately."

Flora shook his arm. "Hector, do something!"

He blinked at her. "Such as? I could order my coachman to take Meg back to Hartley Place immediately, willing or not, or perhaps you'd prefer I find Temberlay and call him out."

Flora looked at him thoughtfully. "On what charge?"

Irritation pooled between his eyes. Three short weeks ago, his home had been a sanctuary, blissfully free of feminine hysterics. "Oh, for pity's sake, Flora, I meant it as a joke. It's too late to do anything today. Meg can stay here tonight, and we'll sort it out tomorrow."

"Perhaps I don't want it sorted out," Meg grumbled, but he sent her a sharp look, and she subsided back into simmering silence.

Flora sat down, and looked at him. "I do hope you're

right, Hector." Her hopeful expression suggested she thought he could fix anything, even this. The earnestness in her blue eyes almost made him believe it too.

He smiled reassuringly, praying it would deflect another noisy flood of tears. "Of course I am. Everything will be just fine."

Even Meg looked half hopeful when he glanced at her, though she turned away quickly. Perhaps, with a few apologies, and some delicate negotiations, things might work out after all.

Chapter 22

~~~ ∞ ~~~

The next morning Flora sailed into the breakfast room waving a handful of paper. "Marguerite, this is dreadful! Look what I caught the maids giggling over in the kitchen."

Meg looked. They were the latest scandal sheets. She braced herself and leafed through them. The first showed a caricature of Nicholas being dragged to the altar by a buxom bride—herself, presumably—while a crowd of London beauties sobbed in the background. Nicholas was watching them with lascivious eyes. "Fear not, ladies, I'll be back to play tomorrow" read the caption.

The second scandal sheet showed Nicholas clad in the shocking green coat with a half-naked woman under each arm, while his bride cried in the background, and her mama, who looked surprisingly like Flora, chased him down the street with a cleaver in her hand.

"I've never handled an axe in my life!" Flora said. "And I would never wear such a hideous gown!"

Aside from those details, Meg felt her gut tighten at the cruelty and remarkable accuracy of the drawings. The artist portrayed her predicament almost as if he'd been present, like a fly on the wall.

Or a bedbug.

She ground her heel into the carpet as if the vermin was lurking under the table. Still, there was nothing she could do about any of it. She would go back to the country, and Temberlay would go back to his women.

Her mother was watching her, waiting for a reaction. Meg forced herself to pick up her fork and eat, as if it didn't matter to her in the least. She swallowed something that might have been sawdust, since it only added to the lump in her throat. She forced a smile. "There's no point in getting upset, since there's nothing we can do about it," she said soothingly.

She made herself glance casually at the last cheaply printed page on the table as she set her fork down.

She couldn't believe her eyes. This caricature was cruel beyond measure. How could anyone have known to draw such a thing unless—?

She shot to her feet, and her chair crashed backward as if it had fainted in horror.

"What is it?" Flora asked.

"How *dare* he!" The illustration, daubed with vivid color, showed Nicholas riding a lace-veiled mare with shapely human legs, long lashes and full breasts. Three other female horses stood placidly in a nearby paddock, gazing upon her grinning rider. "The Temberlay stud and the Wycliffe mare" read the caption.

Meg recalled all too well how she had made a fool of herself on her wedding night, comparing men to stallions.

He'd told the world. He must have. He had gossiped about the most intimate moment of her life. She crumpled the sheet, not stopping until it was a tight ball in her fists, and hurled it into the fireplace. Heat flared against her cheeks as the flames consigned the paper to hell where it belonged. Even after the fire fell back, sated, the burn remained.

Obviously, the wedding night had meant less than nothing to him. He had plenty of prettier bedmates to choose from, *experienced* women who did not compare men with animals.

Fury churned in her belly as she imagined Temberlay telling the tale, keeping his audience rolling on the floor with laughter as he described the hilarity of his wedding night in ribald detail.

She cursed Temberlay with all her might, wishing she knew darker, stronger words to describe him.

"Marguerite! Such language! Remember you are a duchess. Well, I suppose there's some doubt about that, isn't there?" Flora admonished unhelpfully.

Meg turned a tongue-stopping glare on her mother. She shut her lips on a tart reply when she saw the dismay on her mother's face.

None of this was Flora's fault. Meg had no one to blame but herself. She'd dared to wonder what it would be like to kiss the Devil of Temberlay, to marry him, to bed him. Now she knew.

"I'm going home." Did that make her as cowardly as Rose? She didn't care. "I will ask Hector to make the arrangements immediately." There was no reason to remain in London. Hector could sign anything that needed signing, and send her word when her marriage had officially been dissolved.

She marched across the hall and opened the door of Hector's study without knocking. She didn't even bother to say good morning, since there was nothing good about it.

"I want to go home, Hector. Today, if you please."

He was sitting at his desk with a strange, flat expression on his face. He rose slowly to his feet.

"Meg, my dear, I think you should—"

Someone else in the room cleared his throat. Horror dragged her stomach to her shoes. She read the apology in her godfather's eyes as he nodded toward a chair hidden from her view by the door. Her hand tightened on the latch as she peered around the edge of the oak panel.

Temberlay was seated in a leather chair by the fireplace, his long legs crossed as if he hadn't a care in the world.

Meg's heart leaped at the sight of him, even now. She'd forgotten how elementally male he was, how devastatingly handsome. How very tempting.

"Good morning, Maggie," he said smoothly, rising.

With a growl of fury, she strode across the room and slapped him. "How dare you gossip about me?" She clenched her fists, ready to hit him again, but in one fluid motion, he swept her off her feet and dumped her into the chair. She backed into the corner of the still-warm leather as he leaned over her, blocking any hope of escape, his eyes granite chips of fury.

"I don't know what you're talking about, but if you strike me again, I'll put you over my knee, no matter who's watching.

Meg glanced around Temberlay at Hector. He was standing behind his desk in stunned silence, gaping at them. He shook his head in response to her silent plea.

"Your travel plans are canceled," Temberlay said. "It appears our marriage is legal after all. You are my wife whether I like it or not, and you're coming back to Hartley Place, where you will learn to act like a proper duchess."

Meg flinched. What kind of marriage would that be? A match filled with cold hatred, anger, and distrust. The shame of a quick annulment would be better.

She glared at him mutinously. "No."

There was no quarter in his hard stare. "You can leave here on your own two feet, or I will carry you out to the coach over my shoulder."

"You wouldn't dare!" she hissed, her fury clashing with his.

There was a subtle shift in his expression, something dangerous she didn't notice until it was too late. He hauled her off the chair and over his shoulder with remarkable ease. "I've warned you before, there's very little I haven't dared, Maggie."

She shrieked as the room spun. She stared down at the heels of his boots in utter disbelief as he strode across the carpet with her. He paused only briefly by the door.

"Good day, Bryant," he said, and Meg twisted to regard her godfather, who was watching in stunned silence.

"Hector!" she cried. Temberlay's shoulder was pressed into her midsection, and it was hard to speak at all. "Surely you won't allow this—this barbaric abduction!" she panted. She used her fists to pummel his back, and kicked him. A sharp, unexpected swat on her upturned bottom stopped her cold.

"You'll only create more gossip if you scream. Behave yourself and I'll let you walk to the coach."

They were nearing the front door, and in a moment the footman would open it. Heaven only knew what *he* was thinking, what he'd tell the maids in the kitchen, and how it would sound when they spread the story to the staff next door. She did *not* want to appear in the scandal sheets with her bottom in the air.

She went limp. "Release me!"

"So you'll behave," he said, and let her slide down the hard length of his body until her feet touched the floor.

One look at the triumph in his eyes and she changed her mind.

She bolted for the stairs, heading for the safety of her room, and a locked door.

He caught her before she'd reached the third step. "You really are a hellion, aren't you?" he asked as he put her back over his shoulder.

She could hear her mother nearby, her wailing muffled, pounding on something. Hector had probably locked her in the breakfast room to keep her from seeing this—or interfering.

Meg thrashed, but his grip only tightened. Her hair came loose in the struggle and floated around her like a red flag, obscuring her vision. She heard the front door open, smelled the dust of the street, felt the cool morning air on her silk-clad rump. She could hear voices and carriages going by. She could *feel* people staring at her. Was that laughter she heard? She couldn't bear it.

Mortified, she began to struggle again, yelling every epithet she could think of, none of them very effective given her position, but he held her easily, and didn't stop until he'd deposited her in the coach, dizzy and breathless.

"Hartley Place, Rogers," he ordered calmly.

Meg caught a glimpse of her mother's anxious face peering out the window of the breakfast room as the coach pulled away from the curb. Hector tugged her away and closed the curtains.

Heaven help her, there would be no rescue, no reprieve. She truly belonged to the devil. She wondered what further punishments he had in store for her. Bread and water? The torments of hell?

She sent up another desperate plea to St. George.

Chapter 23

Nicholas studied her. Her magnificent hair was tangled around her, and feathered over the velvet squabs like a spider's web, glinting copper fire. He remembered the feel of it wrapped around his naked flesh, and the way her anger had melted to passion in bed. The rowdy reclamation of his bride had been arousing.

What should he say? Should he threaten to lock her up, tie her to the bed, send her away? He would walk away from any other woman, but this woman was his wife. Every time they'd spoken so far, they'd argued. There was only one place they agreed, it appeared. He couldn't let her off the hook for her treachery so easily. He would have to teach her who was in command. She was staring out the window, refusing to look at him.

"There was a bet at White's last night as to what color your hair was," he said. "St. James reported that it was blond, like spun gold. I said it was red, and I was roundly accused of bedding you in the dark." Her eyes swung to him at last, unwilling curiosity mixed with anger in their hazel depths.

"The betting went against red, since most people know I like blondes."

She looked away. "Then go find one!"

He leaned forward, closing the distance between them.

"I had a blonde lined up, but you took her place. Now I've discovered I have a penchant for redheads after all."

She swallowed and looked out the window again. Did she imagine she could shut him out so easily? He wanted her eyes on him, her full attention. He captured a long lock of her hair and wound it slowly around his hand, reeling himself toward her until he had to come and sit next to her. She edged away along the seat, glaring at him like a cornered cat.

She was beautiful when she was angry. He kissed the hair around his hand and looked into her eyes, silently reminding her of everything he'd done to her on their wedding night.

She drew a sharp breath.

"I've a mind to take you to the theater tonight. Once people see your glorious hair, I stand to win a great deal of money." He kissed her hair again as if it were a gambler's charm. "Perhaps I'll buy you a bauble." He kissed her cheek, her earlobe. She smelled sweet.

Her breath hitched.

"What would you like, Maggie?" he whispered in her ear and felt her shiver, saw goose bumps rise on her skin in the wake of his kiss. She shut her eyes, a futile effort to block him out. "A diamond? A jewel to match your eyes? Maybe a ruby to symbolize a drop of virgin's blood."

Her eyes flew open and met his. With a cry of fury, she pushed him with all her strength. He slid off the seat onto the floor of the coach, but she was obliged to follow, since her hair was still coiled around his hand. She landed on top of him in an ungainly sprawl. He freed his hand and brought his arms around her, holding her in place, keeping her fists in control. She wriggled like a hooked fish, muttering much more inventive curses now, ones that surprised even him for their originality. He'd never been called a poxy, dog-bitten, louse-raddled horse thief before.

He laughed. He couldn't help it.

"Oh, Maggie, the more you squirm, the better it feels!"

She went completely still, and stared down at him in horror.

He grinned at her. "I think I may even have missed you last night, wife."

"I'm sure you found a willing substitute."

He gave her his most devilish, irresistible grin, and shifted his hips, letting her feel what she did to him. Color filled her cheeks.

"I had plenty of offers, but alas, they were all blondes, and I was in the mood for a redhead. I like redheads." He lifted his mouth to catch her lips. "Saucy—" He kissed her again. "Spicy."

She looked down at him as if she did not quite believe him, and he remembered that she had never played lovers' games before. One more thing he'd teach her, after obedience.

She tried to rise, perhaps understanding at last the danger she was in, what his intention was, but he held her in place.

"Perhaps I won't give you a jewel. Perhaps I'll give you the blue book you so enjoyed, further your education."

She swung at him again and he caught her wrist.

She fought him. "How dare you tell everyone—"

The coach hit a rut, and drove her body against his, knocking whatever she was about to say out of her head. He nipped her earlobe.

She gasped, tried to pull away. "Really, Your Grace, I think—" she objected.

"I told you never to call me that in bed." He didn't miss the way she tilted her head to give him better access to her throat.

"But we're not in bed," she murmured. He smiled against the hammering pulse point. She really did think too much. He'd have to break her of that habit, and this was as good a time as any to start.

But another jolt brought her back to reality. She was even stronger of mind than he thought. He really would have to speak to Rogers about his driving. His seductive spell broke, and he felt her stiffen, renewing her struggles. "You gossiped about me!" she accused him. "You told everyone what I said about horses!" she panted.

He had no idea what she was talking about. "I never gossip, Maggie."

"Then who—" she began, and he captured her lips again to silence her.

"I never listen to gossip either. Nor should you. Most of it isn't true." He started the process of seduction again, licking at the seam of her stubborn lips, nibbling at the fullness of them, tasting the corners until she relented and opened to him, kissing him back with a hunger that rivaled his own.

Neither of them felt the coach come to a stop.

Footman Rob Vale's jaw dropped as he opened the door of the coach and found the Duke of Temberlay and his bride tangled on the floor, completely unaware that he was standing there gaping at them. Rob didn't quite know what to do. He'd only been in service for a month.

He knew all about the duke's reputation, of course. Who didn't? The man was a proper tomcat, but this was his *wife*. No matter how long he stayed in service, he'd never understand the upper classes. They didn't marry for love, or for whatever this was. They kept mistresses for that. Strings of 'em, in His Grace's case.

Thinking quickly, Rob supposed privacy was in order. It wouldn't do to lose his place because he'd seen his master a-kissin' his missus, so he shut the door again and knocked loudly on the gleaming ducal crest that gave the coach grace and dignity, even if what was going on inside did not. He listened to the commotion, and waited for the thumping to stop.

When he opened the door again, he was relieved to find the duke seated on his own side of the coach. Her Grace was in her place as well, looking perfectly normal, though her pretty face was flushed, and her hair unbound. Rob lowered the step to help her out of the coach. She picked up her skirts and fled as soon as her feet hit the cobbles, scooting up the steps as if the devil was on her heels. He wasn't. He was standing next to Rob, watching her go, looking rather bemused.

"Not a word, Robert," His Grace murmured. Rob couldn't help it. He grinned back like a conspirator.

"'Course not, Your Grace."

The duke didn't follow his wife into the house. He got back into the coach and drove away.

"Was that His Grace?" Tom, another footman asked, watching the coach depart.

"Aye," Rob replied. "As long as I live, I'll never understand the upper classes."

"Are we supposed to?" Tom asked.

Nicholas smiled to himself as the coach pulled away. He'd been tempted to follow her, to take her upstairs and finish what they'd started. He'd spend all day in her bed, and the whole of the night as well. There he'd stopped cold. She'd have him wrapped around her finger.

He couldn't have that. He'd made his point, shown her he was in charge, proven he could seduce her any time he wished, and she was powerless to resist him, or herself. He decided it would do more good to leave her alone to mull over her lesson.

He ran a finger under his cravat. To be honest, he'd been as seduced as she, and that put him on dangerous ground.

He *wanted* the damned duplicitous, stubborn little hellcat.

He shook his head, trying to dismiss her from his thoughts. He wasn't a green lad. He was in full control. He told himself that he'd won this round in the game, and smiled smugly at the seat she'd so recently occupied.

A long strand of red hair clung to the squabs, glowing like lust in the morning sun. The sight of it, the taste of her on his lips, the faint hint of her perfume lingering in the coach, had him hard as a rock.

Chapter 24

The fact that Temberlay didn't bother to follow her upstairs after he'd taken the trouble to abduct her and seduce her in the coach didn't bother her in the least, Meg told herself.

She sat at her desk, and pretended to write letters, but she was watching the door, waiting for him. Hoping.

The clock ticked the morning away, and half the afternoon, and he did not come.

She dressed for tea in an embroidered gown of ochre silk, and entertained a dozen ladies who came to stare at her. If they were surprised that her hair was red, or that she was introduced as Marguerite and not Rose, they were too polite to show it, especially with the dowager duchess seated by her side.

Meg hardly noticed if there were snide comments or indelicate glances. Her eyes were on the door, still expecting Temberlay to walk through it. She imagined the stir it would cause if he were to hoist her over his shoulder now and carry her off, but he did not come.

She forced a placid smile when Lady Emmett commented on the weather, even as she fumed silently. Why bother to drag her away from Bryant House just to ignore her? Perhaps this was her punishment.

"Would you care to join me at the opera tonight, Your Grace? There's a chance the Russian tsar and his sister will be in attendance," Delphine St. James, Sebastian's sister asked.

Lady Clive rolled her eyes. "The tsar! How dull a topic he is becoming. Every glittering monarch and commander who defeated Napoleon is in Town, and there are only two things anyone can talk about—the tsar, and Devil's marriage!" She put a hand over her mouth, and colored at her gaff. "Oh, I do beg your pardon, Your Grace!"

Meg smiled sweetly. "I hear the tsar is very handsome, and his sister is a beauty. I am quite looking forward to seeing them myself." She glanced at the door again.

"You're quite right, Lady Clive. No one will notice if the tsar attends. Everyone will be looking at the new Duchess of Temberlay," the dowager said, sipping her tea. "Yes, you should attend the opera this evening, Marguerite, let them see the Devil's wife."

A flurry of invitations from the other guests followed Delphine's, to balls, parties, teas, races, and breakfast routs. Meg wondered how she'd keep such a hectic schedule straight, especially with such distraction as Nicholas.

As she dressed for the evening, Meg listened for sounds of Nicholas's return, but beyond the connecting door, his suite was quiet. She chose a dress of sea green silk with delicate puffed sleeves.

"I have brought you the Temberlay pearls to wear, Marguerite," the dowager duchess said, arriving with her maid, who carried the box. At a wave of the dowager's hand, the maid opened it with a flourish. Meg gasped. The collar was magnificent, set with a large yellow diamond in the center.

"Should I not wait for an occasion when I am with Temberlay?" she murmured as the cold pearls touched her skin.

"He is no doubt busy with some male pursuit tonight," the dowager said, looking at the necklace in the mirror and avoiding Meg's eyes. "Like buying a racehorse, or dining at one of his damnable clubs."

"Or perhaps he's with one of his mistresses," Meg said tartly. Lavish jewels could never make up for a lack of love or even regard from her husband.

"Don't be impertinent, Marguerite. It is equally important to be seen in public with someone like Delphine St. James. She and her sister are quite influential. Win her, and you'll win the *ton*."

Pride and position—it was all that mattered to the dowager, while Nicholas flouted both. Where exactly did Meg fit in? How was she to act if the *ton* imagined her husband was disappointed with her? She supposed the pearls were meant to be a sign of her acceptance, his ownership of her.

She turned away from the mirror and rose, letting Anna settle her cloak around her shoulders.

The dowager looked her over and nodded her approval. "Remember who you are, and keep your chin high."

Meg took her place in the St. Jameses' box at the opera. Delphine leaned in. "No one is watching the opera. Every pair of opera glasses in the house is trained on you, Meg."

"No doubt they're surprised I am not blond," Meg murmured.

Delphine laughed. "Not at all. Nicholas never did the expected thing in his life. They are all scrambling to say they were the first to know all about you." She regarded Meg. "Are you concerned there will be awkward questions?"

"Our marriage was—hasty," Meg said.

"It was arranged. No one expects it to be a grand romance," Delphine replied. "There are plenty of women who envy you, foolish debutantes mostly, who imagined that they would be the one to capture him. He's never been the marrying kind."

"You seem to know him well," Meg said.

"He and Sebastian have been friends since school. Nicholas was every bit as bad as Seb once, but that was before he went to war. He came back a different man."

"How so?" Meg asked.

"Harder, more circumspect. He's not the man he used to be, the one in the scandal sheets. Perhaps it was David's death, or inheriting the title. And now he's married." She sighed. "I must admit I quite admired him myself for a time, had hopes . . . I wish Sebastian had gone to war. He must grow up sometime, and I despair of that ever happening."

Delphine raised her opera glasses and scanned the crowds with as much eagerness as they were scanning her. She lowered them again. "It appears the tsar has not come tonight after all. Or the grand duchess, but look, Claire Howard has made a rare appearance."

Meg looked at a lady sitting with an older woman in the box across from them. She looked very young, and very pale. She wore a magnificent necklace as well. She nodded to Meg.

"Wasn't she at tea today?" Meg asked.

"Yes, with her dreadful companion, Miss Phipps. Her husband is Augustus Howard. He adores Claire, can't bear to let her out of his sight for fear she'll run off with the man she loved before her parents insisted she marry him. Augustus is old enough to be her grandfather. Claire only appears in public with her husband or her companion, and no one has ever seen Claire Howard smile."

"How sad," Meg said.

"Uh oh—Fiona Barry is looking this way—smile!" Delphine chirped. Meg felt her skin heat under the unaccustomed scrutiny of the audience.

They were probably wondering where her husband was, and why she was here alone. She searched the crowds for a friendly face. Claire Howard gave her a shy smile. Meg smiled back. Delphine caught her arm.

"Look, there's Major Lord Ives," Delphine sighed. "I have quite set my cap for him. My sister is married to a colonel, and I think it would please me to marry an officer like Major Ives if I can't have—well, Stephen Ives is almost as heroic as Nicholas, I hear. I daresay Nicholas would still be in uniform if he hadn't inherited the title."

The handsome officer nodded to Delphine, and regarded Meg for a long moment before he looked away. Did Nicholas look as magnificent in his scarlet tunic?

"Delphine, why did Nicholas inherit the title? What happened to his brother?"

She tore her eyes away from Major Ives. "David? He died in an accident. No one really knows the circumstances, since the dowager refused to say. His death was simply announced in the papers without explanation. There were rumors of a duel over a lady, but it was a year ago now. Nicholas came home from war months later to take the title, and now everyone would rather talk about him."

A year ago. The same time her father had died. Meg wondered if Nicholas had been close to his brother, had suffered when he died, felt grief, as she had. She studied the diamond wedding band. She knew nothing about her husband.

At intermission, there was a rush of people wanting an introduction to the new Duchess of Temberlay. Delphine was quite right. No one seemed to find it odd that she had red hair, or that her husband of three days was not by her side. She smiled and exchanged pleasantries.

"You're a natural at this, Meg. You'll be busy tomorrow, beset with callers who wish to know you," Delphine predicted. "And poor Gardiner will be awash in invitations."

Whatever tomorrow brought, tonight Meg would go home and offer an apology to her husband for her deception. Perhaps he was indeed more than he appeared.

Start as you mean to go on. The words haunted her.

It was time to start again.

Chapter 25

He should go and see Angelique.

But Nicholas had no interest in visiting his mistress. When he thought of sex, only one woman came to mind.

His wife.

She'd tricked him, seduced him, insulted him, and still he wanted her—and he wanted her as he'd never wanted any other woman. And he didn't want to think about it.

He was by nature chivalrous to women, kind and honorable, but he did not involve his emotions when dealing with them. How was this any different? He should hate her.

But she was bold, clever, passionate, and beautiful.

So were a lot of women of his acquaintance. Just not in a single package.

He slumped miserably in the leather chair, looking around the club at other men in other chairs, also drinking, and no doubt avoiding their own wives.

"I'm surprised to find you here, Temberlay, newly married as you are."

Nicholas shut his eyes, willing whoever it was away, not wanting to discuss the fact that he'd stupidly married the wrong sister, which was probably the hottest bit of gossip in the *ton* by now.

"May I join you? I have a bit of news I think you might wish to hear." He opened his eyes and found Stephen Ives staring down at him.

"Does it involve redheads or weddings?" Nicholas asked.

Stephen frowned, and glanced at Nicholas's half-empty glass. "I saw your lovely wife at the theater not an hour ago with Delphine St. James, but I came to see you about a duel."

"And why would that interest me, unless my wife—or her mother—has called me out?" Nicholas asked.

"Another officer asked me to stand as his second this morning. Some silly affair over a woman."

"Shall we make a pact, my friend, never to shoot each other over a woman?"

"Agreed," Stephen said as the waiter set a pint of ale in front of him.

"So what's this duel got to do with me?"

Stephen shrugged. "Everything, or perhaps nothing. There was a doctor present, just in case he was needed. It seems he regularly offers his services at dawn in Hyde Park, and makes a pretty penny tending the injured and dying. They pay him to keep his silence, since dueling is illegal."

"Was he at David's duel?" Nicholas asked leaning forward.

Stephen shrugged. "I don't know. It's a place to start, Nick. He might have some information, if he's paid well enough."

"His name?" Nicholas asked. The prospect of finding a witness, someone who knew who David's opponent was, the details of his death, made him sharp, despite the amount of drink he'd consumed.

"He didn't give one. Kept his face covered as well.

I had someone follow him." He fished in his pocket. "Here's his direction."

Nicholas read the scrawl on the scrap of paper. It was the first link to discovering just what had happened to his brother.

"Thank you." He took out his purse and laid money on the table to pay for their drinks. Stephen pushed the coin back across the table. "Keep it. You'll need it to pay the good doctor."

An hour later, Nicholas knocked at the door of a house that squatted in a neighborhood that was firmly in the shade of respectability. It was the perfect place for a man with secrets, since his neighbors likely had dark dealings of their own, and knew not to ask questions.

He bribed the maid who opened the door, and was shown into the foyer to wait.

The doctor appeared a few minutes later, a shabby man of middle years, with sharp eyes and a bland face. "Your Grace, this is most unexpected," he said, pulling on his coat at the same time he tried to remove his spectacles. "Do come in. Sadie, bring the port at once."

He opened the doors on a sitting room that was as dowdy as he was himself, the worn furniture many decades out of date. Stacks of books served as perches for empty wineglasses, papers, and clothing. A dead cat floating in a glass jar filled with yellow liquid regarded Nicholas in dull surprise. Other similar specimens stood on the bookcases, taking the rightful places of the books.

"Is there a matter I can help you with? I am not used to such esteemed company as a military hero like yourself. I read of your exploits in Spain, sir." When Nicholas failed to smile, his own grin faded.

"My surgery is closed at the moment, of course, but if you come back tomorrow, or allow me to come to you in the morning, then I can certainly offer my medical opinion."

"You attended a duel a year ago. The late Duke of Temberlay, my brother. Do you recall it?"

The doctor's eyes shifted to the floor. "Dueling is against the law here in England, Your Grace. I understand you have been away at war for some time. Perhaps you are mistaken—"

Nicholas tossed a purse on the dusty table, and watched the doctor's eyes widen as the guineas clinked.

"Tell me what happened to my brother." He made it an order.

The doctor made a low sound in his throat and pushed the books off the settee and indicated the seat, but Nicholas remained standing.

The surgeon shook his head, and his jowls wobbled. "Please, Your Grace, there was nothing I could do to save him. He was wounded by all three of his opponents."

Nicholas felt his brows shoot up in surprise. "He was fighting with *three* men?"

The doctor looked grim. "He challenged them all at the same time. It was, I believe, something about the honor of a young lady, and His Grace—your brother—seemed to feel he'd been swindled in some way."

Nicholas shut his eyes.

"I trust he fought them one at a time, and was wounded by each?" The David he remembered was not much of a swordsman.

The doctor fished a handkerchief out of his pocket and mopped his florid face. "No, he fought them all at once. They declared that since the challenge had insulted all three of them, that your brother must meet them at the same time."

Nicholas imagined David beset, desperate. He had lost the entire Temberlay fortune through a foolish investment. Then Julia had come to break their betrothal, telling him she was with child. David had died just two days after her visit.

Nicholas felt sick to his stomach. Duels were affairs of honor. There had been nothing honorable about the match that ended David's life.

"Who were the gentlemen who fought my brother?"

The surgeon shrugged uneasily. "Men of rank, Your Grace, but I don't recall their names."

Nicholas drew his sword, and pointed it at the doctor's throat, dimpling the second and third chins that hung over his wrinkled cravat. "Now do you recall?" he asked.

The doctor swallowed carefully. "I seem to remember Lord Charles Wilton being present," he said.

Wilton? He had no idea that David even knew him.

"And the others?" The doctor tried to step backward, but Nicholas followed. "I assure you, I am far better with a blade than my brother."

"Lord Augustus Howard!" the surgeon squeaked. "And the Earl of Wycliffe."

Wycliffe? The doctor whimpered as the blade slipped.

"That's all I know, Your Grace, I swear! I did my best to save him, but Lord Wilton's blade pierced his lung, and Lord Howard skewered his liver!"

Nicholas lowered his sword an inch.

"And where did Wycliffe's blade land?"

"He merely grazed His Grace's hand, and refused to do more. He was sick, there in the grass, and was crying like a babe when they led him away."

"Who was my brother's second?" Nicholas asked.

"He was a gray-haired man, Your Grace, short of stature, older. He was quite dismayed when your brother was struck down. I didn't catch his name, but I make it my business to avoid introductions."

The maid appeared in the doorway bearing a tray of port. She gaped at the sight of the weapon poised at her master's throat.

Nicholas sheathed his sword. He took the tray from her shivering hands and set it on the table. "Thank you, Doctor. You've been most helpful. I won't stay for the port, but do have a glass yourself."

The doctor put a hand to his throat. "Oh, I will, Your Grace. I do believe I will."

Nicholas let himself out.

He got into the coach and shut his eyes. "Home, Rogers," he ordered.

The Earl of Wycliffe. Marguerite's father.

Did she know? His chest tightened at the thought that this was one more part of her deception.

Granddame would never forgive anyone who had a part in the death of her beloved grandson. Wycliffe had deloped, turned away, refused to lay a killing blow. And he had died soon after. Of what? Guilt? Or had Wilton and Howard taken deadly exception to his cowardice?

He knew the names of the investors now, and possibly one of them had been Julia's seducer, but what concerned him most was how much his wife knew. Was it enough to win him an end to their sham marriage?

He needed more information, something solid to base any accusations upon, something even Granddame couldn't refute.

He pondered what the doctor had said about David's second. Tobias Simmons, David's valet, fit the description. He would have done anything for David, was more like a second father to him, a beloved uncle. Simmons had been there at the end, holding David's hand. Granddame had granted him a pension, given him a cottage at Temberlay for his services.

Nicholas ordered Hannibal saddled as soon as he arrived home. He stood in the shadow of the stable and looked up at his wife's bedroom window. It was dark. Was she there, lying in her bed, waiting for him to come to her?

Until he had answers, he could not face her, or his grandmother.

"Please advise Mr. Gardiner I will be at Temberlay Castle," he told the groom, and rode out into the darkness.

Chapter 26

"**G**ood evening, Gardiner," Meg greeted the butler when he came to collect the pearl necklace to return it to the safe. "Is His Grace at home?"

"He left earlier this evening for Temberlay Castle," he said.

"Temberlay?" she murmured. "Did he say how long he'd be gone?"

"No, Your Grace." He took the jewels and left the room.

Meg went to bed, and lay in the dark, listening to the silence.

He'd gone without leaving word for her.

What did that mean?

He hadn't forgiven her after all. Kisses didn't make anything right. They just made things more confusing.

Chapter 27

Temberlay Castle sat on several hundred prime acres of Derbyshire countryside. Each duke since the sixteenth century had added to the original keep, until red stone towers dominated the horizon for miles.

The marble hall rang with footsteps as the staff hurried to greet Nicholas.

"Lord Nicholas—rather, Your Grace!" the housekeeper said, looking fondly at him as if he were still the child she'd known. "It is lovely to see you home at last."

"Hello, Mrs. Dunne. I apologize for arriving unannounced."

She looked over his shoulder. "Is your new bride with you? We read the announcements, and of course Her Grace sent us word. I'll have your mother's apartments ready in no time at all—"

"I came alone. Just for a few days."

"I see," Mrs. Dunne said, masking her disappointment behind a wan smile.

He looked around the grand entry hall, at the carved wood, painted plaster, and marble. Two staircases twined upward toward the glorious ceiling his father had commissioned. The goddess of the dawn bore his mother's gentle face. The naughty cherub teasing a dove at her feet was himself at the age of three. Cupid had David's eight-year-old face, and was gazing at the painted Derbyshire landscape that would someday be his inheritance, while his father as Zeus pointed out a distant copse of trees. The perfect family—until his parents had died the following year in a carriage accident and Granddame had stepped in as guardian and decided that her grandsons needed a stricter upbringing.

He knew Mrs. Dunne was hoping for those dulcet days of family happiness back again at Temberlay Castle, especially now he was married.

"All in good time," he promised her.

She searched his face, no doubt about to ask him about his bride.

He changed the subject. "Have you any treacle tarts, by chance? I'm starving."

She puffed proudly. "Of course. Go through to the library and I'll bring you tea, and something to eat. Some good beef stew first, mind you, before treacle tarts."

He smiled his thanks. "I understand Tobias Simmons retired to Temberlay. Is his cottage nearby?"

"Oh yes—at the end of the village, near the river. He comes up to visit us in the kitchen on occasion, but he mostly keeps to himself, does a bit of gardening. He'll be glad to see you, sir. He was dreadfully upset by Lord David's death. Cried like a babe at the funeral. We all did."

"I'll visit him tomorrow," he said.

He went into the library. David's portrait regarded him soberly from above the fireplace, a new addition since he'd last been here, painted while he was at war. His grandmother had probably placed it here instead of the gallery. David never liked the library or books, but she knew that when Nicholas returned to Temberlay, this would be the first room he'd come to. No doubt she'd wanted him to look into the sad, gentle face of the brother he'd betrayed and feel shame.

He studied his brother's face for a long moment. He felt sorrow, resentment, and confusion, in that order.

He left the library and explored the empty castle, taking the long way to his boyhood rooms, listening for ghosts as he passed the portraits of nine generations of earls and dukes of Temberlay. His own ducal portrait would hang here one day, and the children he sired would add their likenesses. Would they be happy with the title, and the life that went with it? He stared into his grandmother's proud painted eyes, felt his lips twist bitterly. Happiness was not important to her. She had raised her grandsons to believe that duty, power, and tradition were the only things that mattered. To her, a child of his would be simply another portrait to hang on the wall.

Nicholas had been fortunate. Since he'd never expected to be the Duke of Temberlay, he'd been allowed to make his own happiness. He looked at the childhood portrait of himself and his brother. He was a smiling imp while David was dull and sober even then. Had David ever been happy?

He'd never know. He hadn't exchanged a single letter with his brother while he was in Spain. His quarterly allowance had been paid regularly, but there'd been no news from his family until he received his grandmother's terse letter informing him of David's death and demanding that he return at once to take up his responsibilities.

Responsibilities. How he hated that word.

He opened the doors to the ducal apartments. The room stood in shadow, the furnishings draped as if mourning for David. Time stood still. Even the clock on the mantel had stopped. Were his brother's clothes still in the wardrobe?

He shuddered. The room was a tomb. He remembered how David had cried when Granddame insisted he move out of the nursery and into these rooms just days after their parents' death.

Nicholas backed out and shut the doors. He could not sleep here. He tried to imagine Marguerite in his grandmother's rooms, or their children in the nursery upstairs. That room too had been a silent, lonely place after David had been moved downstairs. He hadn't been alone long. Granddame sent him away to school.

When—if—he had children, they could fill the whole castle with noise. He would not allow them to be raised as David had been. They would know joy as well as pride, he decided as he opened the door to his old rooms, still filled with books and boyhood collections. He opened the drapes and looked out over the magnificent fells. He'd always loved this view. It had reminded him that there was another world beyond these walls, freedom.

He shut his eyes. Now everything he could see was his *responsibility*, and he didn't want it.

Turning on his heel he made his way down to the kitchens where there was life and laughter.

Chapter 28

Breakfast with the dowager became a daily ritual so the old lady could go over Meg's schedule for the day, relay instructions, remind her of the rules, and discuss the invitations that came in the post.

"Won't people think it odd if I never appear with Temberlay?" Meg asked bluntly after he'd been gone for three days with no explanation. She was beginning to wonder if he really was at Temberlay, and if he was alone.

"It can't be helped. He has a great many responsibilities as duke. That is what you will tell anyone who asks where he is," the old lady said bluntly.

Meg took a careful bite of toast. "He's left Town in the middle of the Season, right after his wedding, and without his bride."

The dowager waited until the footman refilled her teacup. "If he doesn't return, you will join him at Temberlay Castle at the end of the Season. If he has left because he is angry at your deception, he will be over it by then. Let him sulk, and don't discuss it with anyone."

"And if he is not alone?"

The dowager glanced pointedly at the untouched sausages on Meg's plate and changed the subject. "You aren't eating. Are you, perhaps, with child?"

Meg shook her head.

The dowager turned to the post, which sat by her elbow. "There are a dozen invitations here for you, regardless of his presence. I will advise my secretary which ones to accept on your behalf. Tell me, do you miss him?"

Meg swallowed. She couldn't sleep. She lay in bed watching the connecting door, hoping he'd walk in. By day, she scanned the crowds on Bond Street and in Hyde Park, looking for him.

"Not at all," she said.

The dowager smirked. "Good. Then he will likely return all the sooner. You might as well enjoy yourself without him. There's an invitation here from Fiona Barry. Best to accept it, I think. Her opinion can make you or destroy you." Her lips pursed as she surveyed Meg. "Fiona looks for flaws, but you have acquitted yourself well thus far."

Meg's stomach churned. And the dowager wondered why she couldn't eat.

She attended Fiona Barry's ball wearing yellow diamonds in her hair. She looked for Temberlay among the guests, held her breath in anticipation of seeing him there. She learned to smile through a churning mixture of emotions—shame, pride, and disappointment.

Fiona did indeed examine every inch of her before she wondered aloud where Nicholas was.

"May I beg an introduction?" an officer in a scarlet tunic interrupted, and Meg turned to him thankfully, and recognized Major Lord Stephen Ives from the theater.

Fiona swatted him with her fan. "I hadn't imagined

there was anyone left in Town that had not met Marguerite. Where have you been, Stephen?"

He bowed over his hostess's hand, but his eyes remained on Meg. "Alas, Lady Fiona, I am part of the diplomatic corps now. We have been quite busy welcoming the crowned heads of the alliance to London."

Fiona's eyes widened. "Including the tsar and his sister? Why did you not bring them this evening? I am the premier hostess of the *ton*! I would have welcomed them with open arms."

"I'm afraid my duties lie in more mundane circles than their highnesses' social schedules. And their attendance would have caused a dreadful crush. Their entire entourage would have to come too—food tasters, ladies-in-waiting, page boys, interpreters, and protocol officers." He smiled at Meg. "In such a crowd I might have missed my opportunity to be introduced to Her Grace of Temberlay."

Meg smiled at the subtle reminder that Fiona had forgotten the requested introduction.

"Her Grace, the Duchess of Temberlay, recently wed to the Devil himself, may I present Major Lord Stephen Ives?"

He bowed over her hand with a smile.

"There. My duty as a hostess is done here, and since you appear to have no interesting tales to tell me about the tsar, I shall go and do my duty elsewhere, if you'll excuse me." She sailed away.

"I am an old friend of Nicholas's, Your Grace. I wanted to offer my congratulations on your recent wedding. Please blame my belated felicitations on duty, rather than lack of manners or interest. I've heard quite a lot about you." He did not ask where Temberlay was, Meg noted with relief. She looked at his uniform.

"From Nicholas?" she asked breathlessly.

He shook his head. "I have not seen him recently. Mostly, I have been listening to Delphine St. James, who sings your praises as the perfect bride for Nick, being both clever and beautiful. Under those circumstances, I could hardly wait for an introduction. I had not thought there *was* a match for Nicholas, and I am pleased to be wrong about it."

Meg felt her cheeks heat at the flattery. "Did you know my husband in Spain, Major Lord Ives?"

"I did indeed. We served in the same regiment, the Royal Dragoons."

Meg tried to imagine Nicholas in uniform. "I know little about the war, I'm afraid. My father did not believe young ladies should know about such things." She hesitated. "Could I impose upon you to tell me about it?"

His expression grew careful. "You could ask Nicholas."

"But he is not here. He is at Temberlay Castle."

She saw the understanding in his eyes before he looked away. "I see. Then you want to know about Nicholas as much as the war. Has he been away for long?"

She raised her chin. "Do you feel I'm prying?"

He held out his hand. "They're starting a waltz. Perhaps you'd care to dance?"

She let him lead her onto the floor. "What would you like to know?"

She swallowed. "Anything. Everything."

He laughed. "That would take much longer than the span of a single waltz, Your Grace. Nicholas Hartley is a fine man, and a respected officer."

"Please, Major, call me Marguerite, or Meg. I am still not used to 'Your Grace.'"

"Makes you think of Nicholas's grandmother, I daresay," he said, leading her through the steps. "Then you must call me Stephen."

She felt the warmth of the connection between them, and smiled.

"If he's not here with you, his absence must be essential indeed," Stephen murmured, and Meg met his eyes in surprise, and he colored slightly and looked away. What had Delphine told him about her? "I mean running a dukedom is certainly a battle in its own right, especially if you weren't raised to it. But you wanted to talk about Spain. I'll tell you what I can. Some men—Nicholas among them, apparently—prefer not to discuss their military service. Some feel that those conversations do not belong in polite society, and should remain on the battlefield." He scanned the crowded room as he moved her through the steps. "Some simply wouldn't understand or believe what we've seen, and others still might imagine a man like Nick was bragging."

She thought of his reputation, the rake, the rogue, the devil.

"I promise to believe every word," she said eagerly. "If it's true."

He laughed. "I am a diplomat, Meg, forbidden to lie. I must tell the truth at all times, as graciously as possible."

"Sugared almonds," she murmured.

"Pardon?"

"Whenever my father had to tell my mother anything difficult, which might have been something as simple as being unable to get the exact kind of lace she ordered from London, he brought her sugared almonds to sweeten the bad news."

"Exactly so," he said, and hesitated. "Do you wish me to sweeten my stories, leave out the harsher realities of war?"

She raised her brows. "I dislike sugared almonds intensely. I want to know everything."

"That might take some time. Nicholas had a very distinguished career. Would you care to ride with me tomorrow morning? I can begin the tale then. Tonight is for dancing."

Meg smiled, let him charm her. No one had ever flirted with her before. It was exciting, and fun. "I would like that very much indeed."

Chapter 29

Nicholas found Tobias Simmons gazing at the portrait of David the next morning, his cap clutched in his hand.

"I was going to send a carriage for you, Toby," Nicholas said quietly.

The old servant turned, and wiped his tears on his sleeve, but it wasn't sorrow in his eyes, Nicholas realized. It was anger.

"Pardon me, *Your Grace*, I didn't see you there," he said stiffly.

Nicholas felt his gut clench. Did Toby blame him as well? The man had been like a father to him and David after their parents died, had loved them both. Nicholas didn't care what the rest of the world thought, but this was Toby, the man who'd dried his tears, taught him to fish, told him stories. To see hatred in this man's eyes was worse than seeing it in Granddame's.

"Come and sit down," he said. "I expect you know why I've come to Temberlay."

Simmons remained where he was. "I'll stand."

Nicholas took a seat under the portrait, feeling David's bland eyes on the back of his neck.

"You were at the duel."

The old man's lips twisted bitterly. "I was."

"You're an unusual choice of second, Toby."

Tobias glanced up with fire in his eyes, then lowered them, remembering his place. "Lord David didn't want to involve anyone else. He was too ashamed."

"For Lady Julia's sake?"

Simmons shook his head and slid his eyes to the portrait above Nicholas's head. "He made me swear not to tell anyone. With his last breath, he did."

"Was it Lord Wilton who ruined Lady Julia? Or Lord Howard? Or the Earl of Wycliffe, perhaps?" Nicholas persisted.

Tobias looked surprised, then indignant. "So you know them all, do you? It wasn't any of them. *That* gentleman did not arrive. His Grace challenged the men you mentioned for quite another reason."

Nicholas clenched his fist, felt the ducal ring press into his flesh.

"Even if it breaks my word, I will speak," Tobias said. "His Grace wouldn't have been there at all that morning—wouldn't have died—if it weren't for what you did. You as good as killed him!"

Nicholas sat very still. Granddame had said the same thing. "I was in Spain, Toby, at war. How could I have caused any of it?"

"I heard Lord Wilton say it. He told David everything you did. You took his wife in adultery. Lady Wilton said that his child wasn't his at all, but yours, gotten in wicked sin. Yes, you were out of the country when it was all found out, but what were you up to before you left? Since you were out of reach, Wilton decided that Lord Davy must be punished in your stead." He choked on the nickname he'd had for David as a boy, and wiped his eyes angrily.

Nicholas's heart froze in his chest. He'd never even met her. "That's not possible."

"I heard them say it!" Tobias insisted. "And you cheated Lord Howard at cards. He wanted revenge too, and joined Lord Wilton to ruin poor Lord David."

Nicholas braced himself. "And Wycliffe? What is it I did to him, Toby?"

"Nothing *I* know of. Only you know the truth of that. Lord Wilton and Lord Howard tricked David to investing everything he had. I gave him my life savings too. So did Mrs. Dunne, since he promised it was a sure thing. Lord Wycliffe put his fortune in as well, and since he was a righteous, upright man, it made it all look right and proper."

Nicholas's stomach twisted like the cap in Tobias's angry hands.

The servant's mouth quivered. "The scheme was always meant to fail, I know that now. Davy told me he lost everything. It was cruel enough to ruin a man for something he didn't do, and his servants along with him, but they told Lord Wycliffe that it was all David's fault, that he stole the money. Lord Wycliffe was ruined, penniless. He was the one who accused David of cheating him, and in public too. What else could David do but challenge him for the insult? Lord David was drunk, you see, still upset over Lady Julia coming to tell him she was calling off the wedding. All three men were there, and he challenged them all."

Toby took a step closer, and Nicholas wondered if Toby intended to hit him, or try. He'd let him, allow him to shed some of the terrible pain they both felt, but Toby stopped, standing like a bantam cock.

"They told him about your part in it, at the duel, as he lay on the grass, wounded—" He swallowed tears, his throat bobbing. "And that was the worst wound of all. Your wicked ways got your own brother killed!"

Nicholas's chest ached. He got to his feet, tried to speak, to tell Toby he was wrong, David was wrong, that it had all started because of a woman's lie he had no part of, but his tongue stuck to the roof of his mouth.

Toby turned away in disgust when Nicholas remained silent. He reached into his pocket. "Here. He told me to burn this, that last day, but I couldn't do it. It's a journal he kept. I haven't read it, since it's not my place." He tossed it on the table. "I'm going now. And even if you revoke my pension and take the cottage back again, I will not bow to you. Not ever again."

Nicholas looked at the book. It was the kind that gentlemen recorded their vowels in, or wrote notes regarding appointments and assignations.

Simmons was halfway to the door.

"Lady Wilton lied, Toby. So did Lord Howard."

The servant turned, his expression hard, unbelieving. "Your reputation says otherwise."

There was nothing more for Nicholas to say without proof. He watched the old servant leave without a backward glance.

Nicholas stared up at his brother's portrait. He'd died thinking Nicholas had betrayed him. Nicholas clenched his fist and leaned his forehead on it.

Did no one believe that he was a man of honor? He lived by his own rules, but he was never cruel, or wanton, or dishonest.

He had never so much as *danced* with Wilton's wife. She was the wife of a rich baron, and he was a young rascal who preferred whores to ladies, especially married ones.

And he didn't recall ever playing cards with Augustus Howard.

It's all Nicholas's fault. David's dying words echoed through the room.

He looked up at the portrait again. "What now? Another duel, more death?" he demanded, but there was no reply. Helpless fury filled him, and he drove his fist into the stone mantel under the painting. The pain did little to relieve his anger, and he stared at the blood on his broken knuckles.

He wanted revenge.

Chapter 30

"We were lost in the hills above Burgos, you see, had no idea we'd crossed enemy lines. The French were on the march, and we were in great danger of being cut off and slaughtered." Meg's eyes widened as she listened to Stephen Ives. He laughed.

"What?" she asked.

"You look exactly like the poor young soldiers, terrified, listening to the French drums. They got closer and closer—"

"What did you do?"

"I?" He laid a hand on his chest. "I advised the lads to load their muskets, fix bayonets, and pray."

She blinked at him, picturing the flash of the steel, tasting the fear and the rising dust. Hyde Park, the other riders, the lovely morning, all fell away.

"Nicholas, however, mounted Hannibal with his sword drawn. He burst out of cover scant yards in front of the French column, yelling insults in French that would make a whore blush." She blushed herself, but he was staring off into space, as if he were watching the scene. She could almost see it herself. Nicholas riding low over his saddle, galloping across the field, his dark hair blowing back, his thighs gripping the horse.

"He drew them away from us. They followed him, and we were able to slip away."

"How remarkable," Meg murmured, her heart pounding.

"Yes. Hannibal is a fine horse indeed," he teased.

"Was he—" She remembered the scars on his body, the fine white lines and deeper marks.

"Shot in the shoulder and captured," Stephen said. "We feared we'd never see him again."

Meg bit her lip, her hands tightening on the reins. She'd kissed that scar.

"That was the first time he was captured. He escaped, of course, and he brought back three maps and a French captain willing to tell tales if only he might be spared the fate his countrymen had planned for Nick. That's where he earned the nickname Devil, you see. The poor Frenchman kept calling him that, over and over. Our lads picked it up, and Nick was Captain Devil Hartley thereafter."

Meg felt a frisson of astonishment in the pit of her stomach. "Then it's not because of—"

A peal of feminine laughter filled the park, and Meg looked up.

Temberlay, her husband, the Devil himself, was chatting with a carriage full of ladies.

She hadn't known he was back in London, hadn't asked, or been told, yet here he was, a living caricature from a scandal sheet, kissing the hand of a giggling debutante, looking at her with that rogue's grin that turned a lady's insides to jelly. Meg knew that feeling well. She took a fortifying breath and straightened in the saddle.

"Now I know why they call you Devil!" the chit cried, setting a hand to a flushed cheek. The rest of her companions twittered and preened like a nest of noisy birds.

Meg felt her own face heat, and she shot Stephen a

sharp look. His story was suddenly far less believable.

He held up a hand. "No sugared almonds, Meg, I swear."

"Shall we ride on?" she asked tartly.

Nicholas's head came up as if he'd heard a siren's call, and he met Meg's eyes across the grass. His smile faded. Anger made her sweat, despite the chill in the morning air.

Every woman in the open carriage gaped at her for a moment before they fell to whispering and casting speculative glances at husband and wife.

Meg's stomach knotted. More gossip.

She watched her husband's eyes slide to her companion, and narrow.

"Nick! You're back!" Stephen said, riding forward.

"I thought you had a Russian grand duchess to chaperone," Temberlay said coolly.

Stephen's smile faded at the rebuke. "And who were those lovely ladies you were flirting with?" he countered.

Meg started at them. It looked, even to her inexperienced eye, like they were *jealous* of her. She'd once seen two of Rose's beaux come to blows over which lad would have the pleasure of helping her across a mud puddle on a country walk. They'd circled each other like dogs fighting over a bone until Meg had aided her sister herself.

She pressed her horse between the two men now. "Good morning, Your Grace." She stared after the departing ladies. "Please don't let us delay you. Your companions are escaping."

"Good morning indeed, Maggie. Did you miss me?" he asked.

"Not at all. If I wish to see you, I need only look at the scandal sheets," she said. She turned to Stephen with a sweet smile. "Is this the hero you've been telling me of, Stephen?"

"I—" Stephen began, but Meg inclined her head to the big white stallion under her husband's rump.

"You're quite right, he is a magnificent horse!"

She urged her own horse on, ignoring the stunned silence from Nicholas, the bark of laughter from Stephen.

"Stephen?" she heard Nicholas ask. "She calls you Stephen?"

"I am pleased to say she does. Many people do, don't they, Meg?"

"Meg?" Nicholas demanded through gritted teeth.

"Everyone calls me Meg, Your Grace. Except you," she said tartly.

"And just what have you been doing in my absence, Duchess?"

"Well, I met her at Fiona Barry's ball," Stephen said, falling in to ride on Meg's other side.

"Fiona?" Nicholas muttered, and looked sharply at his wife. "You met Fiona, and survived?"

She studied her gloves and didn't bother to reply.

"Meg has charmed half the *ton* in your absence, old friend, and only half because the rest haven't had the pleasure of an introduction yet." Stephen sighed. "I am among the fortunate."

She gave him a gracious smile, just to annoy Nicholas.

"Just what have you been doing to charm these poor mortals so, Maggie?" he asked.

Meg felt her face flame anew at the innuendo. Her hands were shaking simply because he was riding at her side.

"She waltzes divinely, for one thing," Stephen said. "Almost as well as she rides."

"Indeed," Nicholas said, and she felt his eyes slide over her. "Do you ride often?" he asked her, nudging his horse closer. She knew he was judging the way she sat her horse, the set of her gloved hands on the reins.

"She's an excellent rider," Stephen said.

"Still here, Lord Ives?" Nicholas asked, looking at him with irritation.

He laughed. "Perhaps I should take my leave, Meg."

"Don't feel you must," Meg said sweetly as he picked up her hand, and kissed it.

"I'll see you this evening at Lady Hilliard's ball. Save me a waltz?" Stephen said.

Nicholas plucked her hand out of Stephen's grip. "Apologies, Ives, but *my wife* will be unable to attend the party tonight. She's dining with me, at home, alone."

They both turned to gape at him in surprise. Stephen recovered first. "Then no doubt I shall see you at another time, so we might continue our conversation, Meg."

She watched him ride away, her heart sinking. She was alone with Nicholas. "That really wasn't necessary, Your Grace."

"Shall we continue to ride?" he asked. She nudged the stallion on. She wondered how long he'd been back, what he'd been doing, but she was afraid she knew. Trills of feminine laughter still followed them.

"You sit a horse well," he said. "And that habit you're wearing is quite fetching. Tell me, do you ever ride astride?"

She sent him a scathing look. They were back to meaningless flirtation. How had Rose borne it? She scanned the park, ignoring him. She wanted to ask him to finish Stephen's story, but her tongue stuck to her teeth in his presence.

"I ask because the stallion you're riding is named Devil's Whim. He needs a strong rider, yet you handle him as if you're quite used to having a stallion clasped between your thighs."

Meg nodded graciously to a passing rider, and didn't bother to reply. She felt a bead of sweat slip between her shoulder blades.

"You've tamed him, I suppose, like the *ton*. He likes you. I almost envy him his position under your sweet—"

With a gasp, she kicked the stallion to a gallop, felt his powerful muscles tense in a burst of speed that carried her away from Nicholas's merciless teasing. She gave the stallion his head, and leaned over his neck, and let the wind cool her flaming cheeks. Had he come back simply to torment her? She almost wished he hadn't come back at all. Almost. She let a smile tug on her lips, and spurred the stallion on. Let him catch her if he could.

Chapter 31

For a moment, Nicholas thought Devil's Whim had bolted. He hadn't planned to tease her. He'd been—what?—*jealous* of Stephen Ives? He looked again at his wife, and wondered if he had reason to be. Stephen *talked* to women. Nicholas either charmed them or seduced them, but he didn't hold conversations with them.

He spurred Hannibal in pursuit. There were few riders in her path, and she flew down Rotten Row unimpeded. Hannibal caught up easily, and he rode alongside her. She kept her eyes fixed on the track ahead, a look of utter exhilaration on her face. It caught him in the gut like a punch. He wondered if she was aware of his presence, and now he really did envy the damned horse. She rode like an extension of the animal's powerful body, neck-or-nothing.

Her fetching little hat flew off and sailed away, and she barely noticed. A lock of hair was coming loose from the prim coif, floating behind her. He swallowed, remembering how it felt to be wrapped in her hair, kissing her.

Obviously she wasn't recalling any such intimacy, though her expression was almost as blissful as it had been when he made love to her. Today it was all for the damned horse—and bloody Stephen Ives.

He'd been surprised to see his friend this morning, surprised to see Meg laughing with him, smiling at him. *Talking* to him.

He'd spent a week brooding at Temberlay. All he could think about was Meg. He'd read David's journal. Wycliffe had been as much a victim as David had been, had left his family penniless. Had it contributed to his death? He understood why Meg had played the desperate gambit, and taken her sister's place. He almost admired her, though it didn't change the fact that he knew almost nothing about her. Would she make a good wife, a loving mother?

He'd returned to Town yesterday, and hadn't been able to think of how to begin a conversation with her. He'd stayed at his club, and risen early to ride and think.

Then he looked across the park and met her eyes. And Stephen Ives's.

She was so innocent, so inexperienced, so ripe for seduction, especially from a charming, intelligent man of excellent character like Stephen. No doubt she would have chosen to marry a man like him if she'd had the chance. Would she, the daughter of a righteous champion of female virtue, take a lover? Surely Stephen wouldn't betray him that way, but he remembered the admiration in his friend's eyes as he'd looked at Meg, the regret when he'd left her.

Nicholas had had enough. He leaned over and grabbed the reins of her horse, checking her wild ride. His grip was iron, and Devil's Whim obediently slowed and came to a halt, breathing hard.

She glared at him, her chest heaving, her eyes glowing. She looked like a woman who had just been bedded, or should be.

Without a word, he dismounted and reached up to haul her out of the saddle. Before she could protest, he pulled her into his arms and kissed her.

Her resistance was token at best before she melted against him, kissing him back with a hunger of her own. She'd missed him. He felt a surge of pride. He could take her home, have her now, but that wouldn't fix anything but the damned inconvenient erection he was sporting. He pulled back.

"We have to talk," he said. Unable to resist, he kissed her neck above the high collar of her riding habit. "This isn't the place. To talk." She sighed and leaned up to kiss him again, but he stepped back and brushed his fingers across her lush lips.

"We need to have a conversation, Maggie, get things straight between us."

She blinked. "Then you were in earnest about our dining together this evening?"

He hadn't actually planned to insist on dinner. It had been a spur-of-the-moment thing, to lay claim to her and take her back from Stephen, but he nodded. "At eight-thirty." He promised himself that he wouldn't touch her, wouldn't kiss her between courses, wouldn't ravish her on the dining table.

"To talk," he repeated.

"To talk," she panted, and he swallowed a groan.

Chapter 32

Meg ate supper all the time. It was an ordinary thing. At balls and parties she talked and laughed and flirted between bites and sips, and so did her companions. Why was it so difficult now?

Meg glanced at her husband. Nicholas was concentrating on the soup, a delicious cream of cauliflower. She stifled the urge to get up and race down to the kitchen to thank the cook, not just because the soup was excellent, but to get out of his company, where she could think.

"Please thank Mrs. Parry for the soup," she murmured to Gardiner as he refilled their wineglasses.

Nicholas looked up at her expectantly, as if she'd made a comment of unusual complexity. "How was your visit to Temberlay, Your Grace?" she asked.

"What would you like to know?"

"Crop yields, the number of acres under hay, corn, and barley, and how many sheep there are on the estate."

"Really?" he asked.

She smiled at him. "No. The dowager said it was your first visit there in several years. How did you find it?"

"Right where I left it," he quipped, and her smile slipped.

"You said you wished to talk, Your Grace. I am trying to make conversation. Is there a topic you prefer? We could discuss the weather or the latest fashion in ladies' hats, or we could simply wait for the next course and lavish it with comments and comparisons."

"It's probably fish," he said. "There's a limit on what you can say about something that's staring up at you, listening to every word."

She laughed. "Shall we ask Gardiner to lay a penny on its eye?"

"Or you could ask the fish his opinion of Temberlay. He likely came from the river there."

"Did you catch it and bring it back?"

"I haven't been fishing since I was a boy."

"With your brother," she said, and he looked at her sharply, searched her face, and she could have bitten her tongue. "I'm sorry. I understand his death was recent."

He ran his hand over the spiral stem of the Venetian wineglass. "It was a year ago. David and I didn't spend much time together after our parents died. I was sent away to school when I was eight. Granddame thought it would be better for David not to have a younger child underfoot, disrupting his tutors."

Gardiner carried in the fish and served it. Nicholas sent her a conspirator's grin and laid a sliced almond over the eye on his plate, then hers. Gardiner looked at them with his brows raised.

"This looks delicious, Gardiner. Compliments once again to Mrs. P.," Nicholas said. They waited until he'd glided out and shut the door before bursting into laughter.

"Do you recognize him?" she asked, pointing at the fish.

"No, but I probably dined on his great-great-grandfather at some point."

"Did you miss home?" she asked. "When you went away to school?"

He sobered. "At first. But the education of a duke is different than what is expected for a second son. David had the finest tutors, and stayed at Temberlay to be raised by my grandmother."

"It sounds lonely," she murmured. "For both of you. Yet men are fortunate, being able to receive such a wide education. My father believed girls need only know enough to be gentle wives and mothers and passable hostesses, which I believe is the reason your grandmother asked Rose to marry you."

"What *did* you study?"

She concentrated on her fish. "Oh, the usual things—manners, embroidery, watercolors, French."

He narrowed his eyes. "Ah, but your education is broader than that, I suspect. I cannot imagine you contentedly embroidering a sampler."

She felt her cheeks heat. "I was very, very bad at embroidery."

"Watercolors?" he asked.

"Dreadful."

"French?"

"Passable."

"And Rose?"

"She excelled at singing and playing the pianoforte, and she embroiders like an angel."

"Then thankfully you are here, and not Rose. I hate warbling sopranos, lady pianists, and embroidered anything."

"Oh" was all she could manage in response to the compliment, if that's what it was.

She searched his face to see if he meant it, and their eyes locked. She felt heat rise, fill her limbs, and her mouth watered. "I like—" he began, leaning closer, and she shut her eyes in anticipation of the kiss, but the door opened and Gardiner entered with a parade of footmen bearing dishes, and she sat back at once.

"Chicken," Nicholas murmured. She frowned at the insult.

"I meant the next course."

"With cream sauce and assorted French dishes, each in its own sauce," Gardiner added brightly, and served out.

"If you did not sing or embroider, what did you do?" he asked once the servants had departed.

She sipped her wine. "Oh, I was a governess's worst nightmare. I asked questions she could not answer. She would banish me from the schoolroom for impudence, send me down to see my father in the library. He wasn't often there, so I spent my time reading."

"What did you read?" He reached out with his napkin and wiped a bit of sauce from her lip. His eyes were on hers, interested, serious.

"Everything. History, science, botany. I tried to learn Latin as well."

He rolled his eyes. "I detested Latin. But when *I* misbehaved and they sent me to see the headmaster for a thrashing, I went to the local pub instead."

She pursed her lips. "I'm not surprised."

"Ah, but it was a useful education. "I learned to gamble, so when Granddame cut off my allowance for failing Latin, I had money."

"For women?"

"For pork pies and cider. Growing boys are always hungry." He took a healthy bite of roast chicken. "Women came later."

"Why did you join the army?"

He shrugged. "Second sons must do something. I had no interest in the church."

She laughed out loud, and he looked at her, his brows raised. She put a hand over her mouth. "Forgive me, but I cannot imagine you as a churchman."

"Nor could I," he said. "And you? What did you imagine your life would be?"

"Marriage to a churchman," she quipped, and he chuckled.

"You would have been a dreadful minister's wife."

"Too much of a hoyden," she said, and he shook his head.

"You'd kill him in bed."

She felt hot blood fill her cheeks, and had no idea how to respond to that.

He changed the subject. "Your father bred horses, didn't he? Is that where you learned to ride?"

"My father kept dainty palfreys for us, and we were not allowed to go faster than a trot over smooth ground."

"You don't ride like a lady used to palfreys."

She toyed with her green beans. "I did not always do as I was bidden."

"Why am I not surprised?"

She sent him a sharp look, but there was no rebuke in his eyes. "My father sold the horses before his death to pay his debts, and it still wasn't enough." She shook off the memory. "That's why I enjoy riding Devil's Whim. He reminds me of the Wycliffe hot bloods."

"Who bought them?" he asked.

She frowned. "I don't know. A friend of Papa's I understand."

"You needn't have suffered as you did. You could have come to London once your mourning was done, married well."

"Rose might have. She's pretty, but we didn't have the money or the connections to give her a debut season."

"So Lord Bryant arranged for Rose to marry privately?"

"Hector? Not at all. He's a bachelor. He knows nothing about debuts or matchmaking. Your grandmother's visit was quite unexpected."

"Who suggested you take Rose's place, Maggie?"

She lowered her hands to her lap. "I'm afraid I'm to blame. It was entirely my idea."

"Why?" he asked.

"For Wycliffe, for my family." She raised her chin. "And I did not want to become a governess."

"You would have been a terrible governess."

"No worse a governess than you would have made a churchman."

He lifted his glass in salute to her wit.

"It took courage, I'll give you that."

"I must apologize. I had no thought of how my deception would affect you. I thought you would not care, since we had not met. You made no effort to see Rose."

She watched his hand tighten on the delicate stem of his glass, and winced, waiting for it to snap. He let go slowly, and met her eyes. "We are still essentially strangers. This time I will make my own proposal."

Her throat closed. "What do you mean?" she whispered.

"I propose that we take the time to get to know each other."

"Start again," she agreed. "What if it turns out that we simply do not suit?"

His mouth twisted. "Then we shall live like most other married couples of the *ton*, I suppose. At least we have one thing in common."

"What's that?" she breathed, her heart beating faster at the look in his eyes.

"Desire." He cupped her chin when she lowered her gaze. "No, don't look away. You know it's true. And yet . . ." He stroked her skin, leaned closer. "I think we must live without it for a time, until we know each other."

Did knowing a person, loving their thoughts and ideas before anything else, make a bond stronger? Her father had disliked her boldness, her intellect, as much as he despised her looks. Meg swallowed, searched his eyes. "When do you wish to begin?"

He withdrew his hand from her face and shifted in his seat, closing his eyes. He was counting again. "Now," he said. "At least, I think we just have." He couldn't recall enjoying a conversation more with anyone, man or woman.

As the clock struck midnight, he led her to the bottom of the staircase. He kissed her forehead. She shut her eyes, turned her face up for a better kiss than that, but he stepped back. "Good night, Maggie," he murmured. "Meg."

He stood at the bottom of the stairs and watched her go up alone.

Chapter 33

The theater glittered with jewels and silks as Nicholas escorted her to the Temberlay box. Meg's stomach knotted as a hundred pairs of opera glasses snapped open and turned upon them like birds of prey.

First, shocked silence descended at the incredible sight of the Devil Duke of Temberlay actually sitting with *his wife*.

Then a whisper began, rose, and made its way around the theater like fire. She opened the program, pretended to study it. Her heart melted.

Angelique Encore, Temberlay's famous mistress, was playing the lead.

She slid her eyes to her husband, but he was studying the crowd and looking bored in the extreme. Did he know? Surely he must.

She gazed around the boxes, filled to capacity since it was the height of the Season, and searched for a friendly face. Delphine waved her fan and grinned. Flora fluttered her handkerchief.

There was nothing to do but smile as if the whole world wasn't waiting for her reaction to being in the same room with her husband's lover. She closed the program and folded her hands over it, resisting the urge to tear it into pieces.

Nicholas swore silently. If he'd known Angelique was performing tonight, he would have taken Meg to the opera, or stayed home. He hadn't seen Angelique in weeks, not since the wedding. He hadn't even thought of her. He supposed he should have ended it officially before it came to this. He wanted to lean over and tell Meg, but she was staring out into space, her expression placid under the scrutiny of the *ton*, but he was close enough to see the pulse point hammering in her throat, making the Temberlay sapphires glint. A slow blush rose from somewhere beneath the low bodice of her ice blue gown and crept upward over her breast and face to disappear under her hair.

He would explain later. He had a gift for her—a diamond bracelet set with rubies. He'd planned to give it to her this evening, in the coach on the way home, before he took her to bed. He'd discovered he liked his wife. He enjoyed talking with her almost as much as he liked talking to Stephen, and infinitely more than any kind of conversation with Sebastian.

Perhaps conversation with Meg would be even more enjoyable if he wasn't constantly thinking how much he wanted to make love to her. He supposed they were facing a conversation of a different kind tonight, and his mistress was going to be the topic of discussion.

He reached for her hand, but her fist was clenched, her fingers icy. She refused to look at him.

The sapphires winked at him as she drew a shaky breath. When she appeared at the top of the stairs, the fabulous necklace was the last thing he noticed. He felt like the most fortunate man in the world as she floated down the steps to his side. If this is what it felt like to be a duke, he was content at last, as long as Meg was his duchess.

The theater darkened and the curtain rose, and Angelique took the stage. The play was a clever Italian comedy. No one paid attention to the story. Every eye in the house swiveled between the blond actress, her lover, and his wife. Nicholas did his best to look bored.

He usually enjoyed watching Angelique perform, since her talents on stage were as mesmerizing as her skills in bed. She caught his eye now, winked, and eyed Meg coolly as she performed a bawdy little song. She performed it for him. Every gesture, every roll of her hips emphasized the double meanings, was meant to entice him. A mistress could hardly demand her protector's attention. She could not call on him, or demand his presence. She could only wait for him to come to her. He really should have ended it when he knew—knew what? That he preferred his wife to any other woman, actually liked her?

He glanced at Meg. She was smiling serenely, laughing in the right places, but the program was crumpled in her gloved hands.

He shifted again. Was the damned song not over yet? Angelique wouldn't be lonely long. After this performance, there'd be a dozen men willing to take his place as her lover. The audience applauded wildly as the last suggestive trill died away, but she took her bow for him, giving him a long look down her bodice.

Meg made a small strangled sound.

At long last, the curtain came down for the interval.

"Meg—" he began, reaching into his coat for the bracelet, but Delphine rushed into the box.

"Wasn't that positively decadent?" she asked, grinning. "Nicholas, how wicked she is!" She slid into the seat beside Meg, and looked at the crowd. "Everyone is here tonight—Augustus Howard even brought his wife. And look, she's wearing the necklace." She leaned closer. "They say that's how he got her to marry him, by promising to wrap her in jewels!"

Nicholas stared across at the young girl by Howard's side. She looked like she belonged in the schoolroom. The lavish jewels detracted from her beauty, rather than enhancing it. While Meg carried the magnificent sapphires, Claire Howard wore her jewels like a shackle.

A footman entered, bearing a tray of champagne. "Miss Encore's compliments, Your Grace."

Meg reddened, her eyes narrowing as she glared at the golden liquid.

Delphine tittered.

Nicholas rose. It was time to put a stop to Angelique's hopes that he would return to her. He'd found someone else, someone whose charms would never pale in his eyes as Angelique's had.

And all because of a deception, and the art of conversation.

He had to speak to his mistress now, stop her from making fools of both of them, or the second half would be more torment for Meg.

"Would you excuse me?" he said stiffly, and left the box.

Chapter 34

"Oh, the boldness of her!" Delphine said. "I daresay she means to fight you for him, Meg!"

It wouldn't be much of a contest, Meg thought. She'd managed to keep her expression flat throughout the breathtaking blond actress's performance. Angelique Encore's bountiful curves put her own willowy body to shame. The actress had a seductive way of moving that ensured every eye was riveted to her lush hips. Her eyes were so brilliantly blue they put the Temberlay sapphires firmly in the shade. Meg wanted to tear them off her neck.

She smiled at Delphine as if it didn't matter, but the pain in her chest was awful.

"Of course, she's already lost him," Delphine purred. "Nicholas wasn't watching her. His eyes were on you."

"He was probably wondering if I'd make a scene," Meg said. She smiled brightly, forced a laugh, and looked around the room as if none of this mattered.

Delphine sobered. "There's no doubt the *ton* is waiting to see if you'll throw a tantrum in public. But you won't, will you?"

Meg raised her chin. "Never." She had her pride, though Angelique had infinitely more than pride to keep her warm. Did men love their mistresses? Perhaps they did, if they were more beautiful than their wives, more talented.

The lights dipped, and the curtain rose, Nicholas hadn't returned yet. She studied her gloves, willing away tears. Was he with her?

A cry rose from the audience and she looked up at the stage.

Her heart dropped to her slippers.

Chapter 35

Nicholas made his way backstage. He nodded to the cast and crew, all of whom knew him well, from other nights, other visits to Angelique's dressing room. They moved aside to let him pass. He knocked on the familiar blue door and entered.

Angelique was waiting for him, as he knew she would be.

"Devil!" She lit up with a seductive smile. She was changing her costume, and she let the half-buttoned garment fall open to reveal her breasts. "How naughty you are. I haven't seen you for weeks. You'll have to hurry. The curtain is going up in a few minutes."

He stayed where he was, leaning on the door. After a moment she pulled her gown together and fastened it. "Has your wife got you on a short leash?" She turned to the mirror to fix her makeup. "She's pretty."

She looked at him in the glass, then rose to put her arms around his neck, pressing her body against his. "Break free and come play with me after the performance!"

He looked down at her. She wore brilliant rouge on her cheeks and lips, dark kohl around her eyes. He'd once found her fascinating. Now he felt nothing.

"No, Angel. I only came to tell you that I won't be back."

She gave him a teasing look of disbelief.

"Places!" the stage manager called, and Angelique, ever the professional, slipped her arm through his and moved toward the wings.

"You know you don't mean that, Nick," she said, her tone seductive, playful. "You'll be back."

She took a breath, making note of her mark, already distracted. He took her shoulders and turned her to face him.

"I do mean it. It's time this rake reformed."

The smug confidence in her eyes dropped away. A few tears, real ones, perhaps, sprang up, and he quickly reached for his handkerchief before her makeup ran. She took it and dabbed her eyes.

He reached into his pocket again. It was customary for a man to give his mistress a parting gift. He hadn't considered that. He held up the bracelet. Her eyes lit up. Angelique loved the perks of sex.

"Oh, Nick, it's beautiful!" He watched as she quickly estimated the bracelet's value. "It *is* good-bye then." She sighed.

She stood on her toes and kissed him. "I'll miss you. There's no one else like you." She put her arms around his neck. "Change your mind, Devil. Stay with me." His eyes flicked to her lush cleavage, now pressed to his shirtfront. She noticed the glance, of course. "Change your mind," she murmured again, an octave lower.

"Curtain up!" the stage manager called.

"Good-bye, Angel," he said, kissing her forehead as he reached up to untangle himself from her arms.

He saw the harsh gleam of the footlights as they caught her bright blond hair, watched the light race toward them.

He heard the gasps, the titters, then the roar of the audience.

He looked up across the width of the stage, right into the Temberlay box, and straight into Meg's eyes.

Angelique shoved him out of the way without missing a beat, and moved upstage to say her first line. Meg was retreating, scrambling backward into the shadows. The crowd was on its feet, hooting.

He had to get to her. To go around backstage would take too long. The shortest route would take him straight across the stage. Of course, that would cause even more scandal.

He didn't care.

Angelique stepped aside as Temberlay raced across the stage, his eyes on the empty Temberlay box. The old Nicholas might have paused, taken a bow, stolen a kiss. Her heart sank at the loss of him. She had never had a better lover, or a more handsome one, but she reminded herself of who she was, and where she was—and the house was filled with potential protectors to take his place.

As Nicholas bolted offstage, she waved his own handkerchief after him, let the bracelet sparkle as she blew him a kiss, and gave her delighted audience a saucy wink.

Chapter 36

Meg heard the laughter, saw Angelique in Nicholas's arms in front of the whole theater.

She had to get away, find some air to breathe before she choked. She picked up her skirts and ran headlong down the marble steps, with no idea where she was going.

Hands caught her sleeve, gripped her shoulder, and she struggled, pulled away.

"Take your hands off me!" The words rang through the marble foyer.

"Meg, for heaven's sake, it's me, Hector!"

She scanned his face, read the angry concern. She collapsed into his embrace. "You saw?"

He nodded against her hair, and put his cloak around her. "Let me take you home. I sent your mother out to the coach already. She wanted to climb out of the box and challenge Miss Encore to a duel. Hat pins at dawn!" he tried to joke.

Meg felt her lips tremble, and tears stung the backs of her eyes, but she refused to let them fall.

In the coach, Flora alternated between sobs and fury. "A curse upon his adulterous, lecherous, misshapen head!"

"It's not misshapen, Mama," Meg murmured.

"It will be when I get through with him. You will come home to Bryant House tonight, Marguerite. Hector, you will arrange an annulment first thing in the morning. That may have been impossible before now, and would have caused our shame, but now the shame will be entirely on him. How dare that man do this to me—not to mention Marguerite—in public, with that strumpet of an actress! Marguerite, did we sell your father's dueling pistols?" She dissolved into tears, and Hector pressed his handkerchief into her hand.

"What do you want to do, Meg? Shall we take you to Bryant House for tonight?"

Meg thought of what had happened the last time she'd gone home to Bryant House. This time, everyone would be watching to see what she would do.

She shut her eyes against the pain that went beyond scandal this time. He'd spent time with her, talked to her, smiled at her. She was beginning to think he was content to have her for a wife after all, that someone at last wanted plain Marguerite. How foolish she was. Men like Temberlay might *talk* to ugly women, but they made love to beauties. Her father's philosophy had tried to make that clear, but she'd failed to listen. The lesson was clear enough now. Shame heated her cheeks in the darkness.

"There are rumors of other women as well as the actress," Flora hissed. "They say he's been visiting a young woman with a baby."

Meg looked up.

"Flora!" Hector warned.

"Take me to Hartley Place," she said. "I'm very tired. I need to think, need to sleep. He likely won't be home tonight." Or tomorrow night, or the night after that. She clenched her fists, hating Nicholas.

"Are you sure that's what you want?" Hector asked.

She stared out the window into the darkness. "Everyone expects me to run away. Perhaps that's what he expects. I will decide tomorrow what I will do, when I am calmer."

"Calmer? You barely seem upset at all! Surely you don't have *feelings* for him?" Flora asked.

"He's my husband, Mother. I had—hopes."

Flora sniffed. "Hopes. You've always had hopes. Your father never paid you any attention, and you tried to be smarter and better than your sisters so he'd notice you, didn't you? I suppose you hoped Nicholas would notice you too, not give all his attention to actresses. It's not that your father didn't love you, Marguerite. He didn't know how to deal with strong, clever women."

"He'd be proud if he could see you now," Hector said.

"Would he?" Meg asked softly. "Married to a man who doesn't—couldn't—love me?"

"It was your father's shortcomings that brought us to this, not yours, in my opinion," Flora said. "You are the best of us all, and you make a magnificent duchess. If Temberlay can't see that . . ." She paused. "I suppose that doesn't ease the shock and hurt you're feeling now."

She opened her reticule and pressed a small vial into Meg's hand. "Take this. It's laudanum. It will help you sleep without dreams, and without any pain at all."

"Flora, I'm not sure that's a good idea," Hector said.

"Don't be ridiculous, Hector! There are times a mother knows what's best." She held up the glass bottle and stared at it. "I used it after your father died to help me sleep. His death was a terrible shock. He simply abandoned me to face what was quite unfaceable. Sleep made it bearable."

"Meg made it bearable, Flora, not the drug. Meg, Laudanum is dangerous. Too much can make you completely unconscious, or worse," Hector said.

"Oh, for heaven's sake—" Flora interrupted.

"For how long?" Meg asked. She took the vial and looked at her mother.

But Hector put his hand over Meg's. "You'd be out for hours, and you'd wake feeling awful, and want more."

"I see." Meg stared at the vial in her palm, and closed her fingers over it. "I'll be careful," she said.

"Just a drop in a glass of water," Flora advised. "Or two, perhaps. Certainly no more than three or four. Five at the most."

At Hartley Place, Hector escorted her up the steps and asked Gardiner to fetch some warmed wine.

When the butler looked past Meg's shoulder for signs of Nicholas, Hector's face hardened. "See to Her Grace! I doubt your master will be home tonight."

Gardiner bowed.

"You can still come back to Bryant House for a few days until this blows over, Meg," he said. "At least give me the laudanum."

She kissed his cheek. "I'll be fine. You'd better get Mama home before she faints."

She went upstairs and sat down at her dressing table, too exhausted to do anything but stare into the mirror.

The dowager entered. "Gardiner told me you were unwell," she said. "Good Lord, you're as white as linen!"

"Why would Gardiner come for you?" Meg asked, unfastening the sapphires herself.

"I told him to alert me if you were unwell. Are you with child?" she asked bluntly.

Meg's stomach coiled. "I am ill for quite another reason. I saw Angelique Encore in Nicholas's arms. In fact, everyone in attendance at the theater tonight saw them. It was far more entertaining than the play."

The dowager sat in the wing chair. "Damn him."

Meg began to pull the pins out of her hair. "Have you seen her? She's beautiful, everything a man could want." She felt tears sting her eyes, and she blinked them away.

"You are not so innocent that you don't know that men keep mistresses, Marguerite. But for him to be so indiscreet is unforgivable."

"There is little I can do," Meg said.

"On the contrary—you must do your duty, give him an heir," the old lady said.

Meg felt her face heat. Other than on their wedding night, he had not done more than kiss her. She shut her eyes. She'd believed him when he said he wished to talk, to start over. Now the truth was plain. He didn't want her. Shame burned as she looked at the dowager.

"You yourself said these things take time," she hedged.

"You're not trying hard enough." The old lady's voice dripped with ice.

Meg met her hard, cold eyes. "I am not Angelique Encore. I am not sweet and pretty like Rose. I am the one woman in the world it appears that he does not want. Perhaps if he's very drunk and the room is very dark, and every other female in London is otherwise occupied, he might be willing to bed me."

The dowager rose and walked toward Meg. "This is not the time to feel sorry for yourself. If you wish to be complimented, petted, then I'll tell you plainly that you're more beautiful than either your sister or that strumpet. Miss Encore's talent is all between her thighs. He'll tire of that soon enough. You have wit and brains. Surely you can think of a way to seduce him. You may be innocent, Marguerite, but you are not a fool."

Laughter bubbled up and spilled out of Meg. "I'm sorry, Your Grace, but Nicholas has his clubs, his mistresses, and his own life. He has no time left for me."

The dowager gripped Meg's chin. "The whole purpose of this marriage is to get an heir of Temberlay blood. Nicholas is the only Hartley left. If you cannot do that, then you are of no use to me, and neither is he."

Meg stared at the hatred glittering in the old lady's eyes. No wonder she didn't care which sister her grandson married. Better the plain sister after all, to make Temberlay's punishment worse.

"You think I'm cruel, no doubt," the dowager said. "I'm merely practical, no different than you. You married Temberlay to save your family. I arranged it to save mine. I want an heir. Perhaps your sister would have been a better choice after all, but it's too late now. You have chosen this course, Marguerite, and you will do as I say. I want an heir. Even if your family is safe now, that could easily change."

Meg's throat closed. "What do you mean?"

The old lady smirked. "I could destroy the prospects of your sisters forever. If the details of your father's death were made known, for instance—"

She knew? Not even Mama or Hector knew the truth. Meg had made sure . . .

"You wouldn't," Meg croaked around the lump of dread that filled her throat, threatened to choke her.

The dowager smiled unpleasantly. "Wouldn't I? I made Nicholas marry against his will. I control him because I control the purse strings. His blood, his seed is all I have. I want a child to raise to be duke in his place—a decent, honorable man who deserves the title. Once I have an heir, Nicholas can swive himself to death with a whole chorus of actresses for all I care."

Meg paled. And she would no longer be necessary to anyone. The dowager reached out and grasped Meg's chin again, and her fingers dug into her flesh like claws. Meg held her eyes, refused to flinch.

"Seduce him, Marguerite. Find a way. If you are not with child within three months, I will reveal what I know about your father's death, and expose your mother as his brother's whore. Is that clear? You would all end up in the gutter."

Meg looked away first.

The dowager released her, then picked up a long lock of her hair and stroked it through her bony fingers. "Good girl." She left the room.

Meg went to the basin and scrubbed the old witch's touch from her skin, and stared at her blotched face in the mirror.

Seduce him? With a lover like Angelique a short carriage ride away? She turned away from the glass. *Impossible.*

But the safety of everyone she held dear depended on it.

Chapter 37

By the time Nicholas reached the staircase that led to the foyer, there were a hundred people in his way. Men slapped him on the back. Women turned away to whisper behind their fans.

He was in too much of a hurry to catch his wife to stop and explain, or to plant a fist in anyone's face. He shoved his way through the crowd, but Hector's coach was gone by the time he reached the street.

He clenched his fist and drove it into the stone wall of the building, feeling his knuckles split. The pain didn't erase the image of Meg's face, the stark horror, the betrayal in her eyes. He felt hot shame flood him at who he'd allowed the *ton* to make him.

He found his coach and climbed in. The ghost of her perfume rebuked him. "Bryant House," he commanded.

He'd look there first.

Chapter 38

Meg wasn't sure how long she sat at her dressing table. The soft knock on the connecting door startled her. She stared at the shadowed panels, her heart in her throat, unable to speak.

The latch rattled and she cast a quick glance at the key on her dressing table. She picked it up and clutched it in her hand, squeezing until the metal dug into her palm.

"Go away."

"Open the door, Meg," he commanded.

She stayed where she was. She couldn't look at him tonight, fresh from the arms of another woman, her perfume on his shirt, her touch still on his skin.

She stood in the center of the room, and glowered at the portal. "What do you want? To gloat?"

"I won't have this conversation through a locked door."

The word "conversation" made her lips twist bitterly. "You want to talk?" she hissed. "I think we've said everything. Go back to your mistress!"

She flinched as his fist hit the door. At least she thought it was his fist until the door crashed inward and landed at her feet. He stood in the opening, shattered wood at his feet, more pirate than duke.

A shiver of fear coursed through her.

"Never lock me out again, Maggie. This is the only time I will warn you."

She folded her arms over her chest and glared back, meeting the anger in his eyes with her own fury. "Oh, is that the way to tempt you into my bower? To challenge you? That door has been locked for weeks, and you've shown no interest in opening it. Why tonight? Was my public humiliation not revenge enough? Have you come to laugh, to point out that I can now see why I am not good enough for you?"

Nicholas regarded his wife, saw the pain in her eyes. She was trembling. He felt shame fill his chest at the hurt he had caused her, even if it had been unintentional. She wore only her shift and a silk dressing gown that she'd forgotten to fasten. Her skin was flushed pink, her breasts heaving with anger. There was no paint, no jewels, no artifice. She was more beautiful than any woman, especially Angelique.

He had planned a very different ending to this evening. He had no idea how to fix this. Should he apologize, fall to one knee and beg? He didn't beg. Nor could he bring himself to tell her that he'd dismissed Angelique because he couldn't even think of any woman but his wife. He sensed even saying Angelique's name would make things worse, not better.

"Perhaps I came to claim my husbandly rights," he said instead.

It was the wrong thing to say. He saw that at once. She flushed scarlet, and her chin rose. She clenched her fist, and he thought for a moment she'd punch him. She threw a key at him instead. It hit him in the chest, and fell to the carpet.

"You dare to come to me from the arms of another woman and talk of rights and privileges? You have her makeup on your mouth! What of my right to respect as Duchess of Temberlay, *your wife*, or does that apply to everyone but the Duke of Temberlay?"

His gut tightened. "It seems you've forgotten the fortune you earned as your reward for marrying me. You want my respect as well? You'll have to earn that, Maggie."

She made a strangled sound of fury. "How, on my back, while you compare me to *her*?" she demanded. "Please leave, Your Grace. You have shown me that I am repugnant to you—"

She drew a breath as he advanced on her. "Shall I take you to bed and show you how far from repugnant I find you?"

She stared at him, and he watched anger warring with indecision in her eyes. She turned away. "No. I cannot do this. Not tonight, not now."

For a long moment he stared at her silk-clad back, her bare feet.

"I have no interest in bedding an unwilling woman. Go to bed, Maggie. Alone. I wish you joy of it."

He ignored her gasp of indignation as he stepped over the broken door and went to his own room. He crawled into his cold bed and pulled the pillow over his head and shut his eyes against the image of Meg's tormented face, the ghostly sound of David's final words. *It's all Nicholas's fault.*

This time at least, it was true.

Chapter 39

"The Countess of Wycliffe is here to see—"

Marguerite watched as her mother barreled poor Gardiner out of her way and entered the breakfast room the next morning.

"I have brought the scandal sheets," Flora said, brandishing a sheaf of papers.

Meg turned to Gardiner. "Would you burn those, please, Gardiner? The dowager sent the morning papers to my rooms this morning, Mother. I did not read a word, and I do not wish to read them. In fact, I have banned them from being brought into my presence ever again."

Flora frowned and sat down, helping herself to tea. "You sound very regal this morning. I trust the laudanum helped?"

Meg focused on stirring her tea. "I didn't take any."

She had stared at the vial after Nicholas left her, and put it away. She had lain awake half the night, thinking of the dowager's threat. What would Flora do if she were publicly disgraced? She had retreated into a dangerous half world induced by drugs when her husband died.

The only thing to do was to find a way to make Nicholas sire a child to protect the ones she loved. Poor, poor child. It was an impossible choice, but perhaps it would be possible to find a way to protect her son.

"I came to ask which invitations you'll be accepting this next week or two. I'll arrange my schedule to match yours. The old cats may hiss behind your back in the face of this dreadful scandal, but they won't claw at me!" her mother bungled.

"That's kind of you, Mama, but I will be staying in this week."

Flora's eyes popped. "Staying in? Do you think that's wise? You should be everywhere, seeing everyone, proving that it does not matter one whit to you what he gets up to."

She raised her chin. "But it does matter. I must start again, come to an agreement with Nicholas if this marriage is to be bearable for the short time necessary to get an heir."

"Get an heir? You still mean to allow him husbandly privileges?"

Meg felt her skin grow hot. What would her mother say if she knew it wasn't a case of allowing him, but rather forcing him to bed her?

Meg got to her feet, breakfast rolling in her belly like an uneasy sea. "I must speak to him before he leaves for the day." She hooked her arm through Flora's, and led her firmly toward the door. "I trust you'll be able to enjoy the parties and hold your head high without me?"

"Of course," Flora said, and kissed her daughter's cheek. "I shall tell everyone . . ." She paused. "What shall I tell everyone?"

"Not a thing. Let them think what they want," Meg advised.

When her mother had gone she went along the hall toward the library, steeling herself, thinking of just how she would insist that he must—

"You are too good to me. I could not have a better, dearer, more loving—" a woman's voice murmured, and dissolved into tears. Meg froze in the hallway.

"I'm glad this has worked out, Julia," Nicholas replied.

"I must thank you for the little house, and for all the gifts. You have quite spoiled us both."

Meg peered around the door. A young woman with dark hair sat on the settee. Nicholas sat beside her, gazing at her with a gentle smile and love in his eyes. Her heart twisted.

"How is the child?" Nicholas asked.

"I think he's excited about the trip. He'll miss you."

He looked dubious. "Can a lad his age miss a dreadful old man like me?"

Meg's heart stopped beating. *A child?* Hadn't her mother heard a rumor that he had been visiting a woman with a child? His child? Her heart sank to her shoes.

She watched the young beauty lean forward and kiss his cheek. "I am grateful for all you've done, Nick."

They rose, and the woman looked around. "I might have been duchess here," she murmured. "How different things might have been, if only . . ."

Meg fled. She didn't stop until she was safely back in her room. She put her back against the door. Someone else might have been duchess, if not for Meg. And there was a child.

She wrapped her arms around her own empty womb and let out a panicked cry of pure agony. No wonder he didn't love her, couldn't love her. He'd had hopes of marrying someone else.

She thought of the duchess's threat. How would she ever get his attention now, lure him into her bed? She'd have to be the only woman on earth.

She crossed to open the trinket box that sat on her

dressing table. The vial of laudanum lay amid the earrings and pins and ribbons. She picked it up, held it to the light. The liquid was as dark as sin, as dangerous as—

"Good morning."

She closed her hand on the vial and hid it behind her back at the sound of Nicholas's voice.

He stood in the doorway regarding her soberly. "We need to talk, I believe."

Meg swallowed. There was no indication in his expression of what he might wish to say. His gaze held none of the love he'd shown the dark-haired woman in the library. For her, there was only wariness in his eyes. Her heart sank. Talking wasn't going to help. She desperately needed him to do much more than that if her family was to be safe.

"Yes," she said, her voice hoarse. Could she drag him to her bed, make him—

"I was thinking we might take luncheon together."

Luncheon?

She squeezed the vial in her hand. "I have a better idea. Let's take a picnic outdoors somewhere." She forced a smile.

He smiled, relaxing. "I know a lovely spot a few miles outside London, by the river. Will that do?"

She nodded. "Perfectly."

Chapter 40

 ⌒⌒⌒

"This outing was a nice idea," Nicholas said. "I wasn't sure what to expect, after last night."

Meg was staring out the window, her hands clasped in her lap. She'd barely looked at him as he'd handed her into the coach, and there were two bright spots of color in her otherwise pale cheeks. Was she still angry, afraid, nervous? He reached out to touch her hand, found it icy. He let go. "I thought it would be easier to talk away from the servants, and—others."

The color spread briefly. She met his eyes at last, her expression guarded. "Tell me, how do you know of this perfect picnicking spot?"

She assumed he took other women there. He could tell by the skyward tilt of her chin, the ice in her eyes. "I used to come here to fish—alone—before I left for Spain. I haven't had time to come since my return. This is my first visit to the place in years. I hope you'll forgive me if it isn't quite as I remember it."

"Oh," she murmured.

"Did you imagine I intended to take you out into the wilds to seduce you? This may surprise you, but I prefer the comfort of a bed."

"Then I must assume you haven't found one that's just right, since you have tried most of the mattresses in Mayfair," she quipped.

He let it pass. He'd carefully planned what he would say. If she wished to quash the gossip about what happened at the theater, the best way was to live as if it didn't matter. They could leave London if she wished, go to Temberlay. He had no idea how the conversation would go from there. Accusations, tears, threats . . . he was ready for anything.

He hoped. He was as nervous as a bridegroom.

He pulled a flask of wine out of the basket she'd arranged, and two glasses as well. "Mrs. Parry has done well," he said, examining the contents. "There's chicken, duck, fruit, cheese, and even cakes. We'll be well fed."

He handed her the glasses, and took the stopper out of the bottle. She watched the wine flow into the glass, her lower lip caught in her teeth. It sparkled like rubies.

"To a new beginning?" he toasted.

Her eyes were sharp, but she nodded.

He sipped, hoping the wine would lend him courage to tell her he'd dismissed Angelique, but her name stuck in his throat, as if speaking it aloud would sully the air between them, shatter the fragile truce. He sipped again and again, seeking courage, until he'd emptied the glass. "Do you fish? I could teach you," he said.

"No, Your Grace," she said, staring at him with odd intensity.

"Nicholas," he said, pleasantly warm from the wine. "Say my name, Maggie."

"Nicholas," she said. "More wine?"

He sipped again. He frowned and looked into the glass. "This tastes a touch bitter. I'll have Gardiner check the stores in the cellar. Perhaps it's a little—"

He felt dizzy, and suddenly sleepy. He rubbed a hand over his eyes. It wouldn't do if he fell asleep now. He tried smiling at Meg, but there seemed to be two of her.

"What the hell is happening?" he said, and shook his head to clear it. Meg was sitting very still, her glass still full. She tossed it out the window.

"God in heaven, Maggie, what have you done?" he asked. Poison. She'd put poison in the wine. He dropped his glass from nerveless fingers, and watched the dregs spill across the floor like blood, crawling toward the door. She reached for the glass, and he grabbed her hand, held it tight.

"What have you done?" he demanded again, his words slurring. She pulled away, broke his grip easily.

"It's only a little laudanum," she said from a long way off.

"Laudanum? How bloody much?" he mumbled. "You can't—" His tongue wouldn't work. His eyes drifted shut, and he couldn't force them open again. Oblivion rushed up to claim him.

Chapter 41

Nicholas had a feeling that opening his eyes would be a bad idea. His head was pounding and his mouth tasted vile. He rolled his head to one side on the pillow and wished he hadn't.

He tried to remember where he'd been and how he'd come to be so roaring drunk, but even thinking seemed more complicated than it was worth. He swallowed, but his tongue was thick and dry, too big for his mouth.

He heard the unmistakable rustle of taffeta, painfully loud in the silence.

"He's awake," a gruff male voice said, and Nicholas tried to reconcile the sound of taffeta with a man's voice.

"He'll need a drink of water. Laudanum makes you thirsty, and fuzzy in the head," a woman replied.

Laudanum? Where in the hell had he gotten that? He forced his eyes open, the edge of memory tantalizingly close in the fog that filled his brain.

A pair of blue eyes stared into his own.

While he was no stranger to waking up next to a pair of blue eyes, they usually came with an attractive female attached. This pair had thick dark brows above them and a bulbous nose and a bushy brown beard beneath.

He drew a sharp breath and instantly wished he hadn't. Onions.

"I've got some water for ye," the man said gruffly, but not unkindly. Nicholas shut his eyes, and opened them again. He was still there, hovering over him.

"Who are you?" he asked, his voice thick and sticky.

"John Ramsbottom," the man answered in a thick country accent.

It meant nothing.

Ramsbottom chuckled. "Don't fret, Yer Grace. Meg will be here soon. Amy's gone to get her."

"Meg?" he said, trying his tongue again. "She drugged me—"

John Ramsbottom cupped a beefy hand behind Nicholas's head, raising him like a sick child. Nicholas gritted his teeth against the lip of a cup and swallowed obediently. John Ramsbottom smelled of horses in addition to onions.

He dropped Nicholas's head back on the pillow none too gently, rattling his brains.

"There. That's better, eh?"

Nicholas looked around the room. It was sparsely furnished and somewhat shabby. There were dark squares on the faded wallpaper where pictures had once hung. The fireplace squatted like a ghost in the dim light. The window was shuttered, the drapes drawn. He couldn't tell if it was night or day.

"Where am I?" he croaked.

"Welcome to Wycliffe Park, Yer Grace," Ramsbottom said brightly, as if this was the usual way guests were greeted.

"How the devil?" Nicholas looked around again. "Why? How long have I been here?" He rubbed a hand over his stubbled jaw. He might have been here for days, weeks even, in a drugged stupor.

"Since yesterday evening."

The door opened, and Meg came in. She wore a plain blue gown, and her hair was tied at the back of her neck with a bit of ribbon, a country lass today, instead of a duchess.

She had the grace to blush when she looked down into his angry eyes. It took almost Herculean strength to reach out and grab her wrist.

"I'll call you if I need you, John," she said calmly, and waited until he'd left the room.

She plucked her hand loose. "Would you like more water?"

"I'd like an explanation."

She stepped back out of reach and folded her hands at her waist. "I needed your undivided attention, away from—distractions. I promised that I would provide an heir. That seems impossible in London. You may leave once I am with child."

Anger swept through his butter-weak limbs, gave him the strength to sit up. "You mean I'm your prisoner? Not only a prisoner, but a sex slave?" He forced a laugh, though it hurt.

She blushed scarlet. "Is it truly that difficult? Doesn't every gentleman want a legitimate heir?"

Right now, he only wanted to wring her neck. "Eventually. May I point out we barely know each other?"

"Know," she repeated bitterly. "In the five weeks we've been married you've only managed to 'know' me once. I cannot compete with Angelique Encore and your other lovers. If I am the only woman available, and there is no one better, then perhaps it might be easier for you."

He stared at her, wondering if he was still under the influence of the drug, and this was a dream or a hallucination. "So you intend to wait until I'm so desperate that anything in skirts looks good, and then just throw yourself in my way, is that it? By God you hold yourself cheaply! What if I decide to walk out that door right now?"

There were tears sparkling in her eyes, and her fingers twined together into knots. This was not Meg's choice, and he wondered what was driving her to such foolish, desperate measures.

"John will ensure you stay," she said.

He glanced at the door, wondered how close by the burly manservant was. No doubt his grandmother was right behind him.

He gave Meg one of his best go-to-hell grins. "And will John stand by and ensure that I perform to your satisfaction?"

She raised her chin. "He will lock us in this room together at night, and let me out again in the morning."

"You've thought of everything, haven't you, Maggie? I could choose not to play."

She frowned, confronted with something she hadn't considered. "Your appetite is well known, and I am the only woman here."

She looked more like a child, wide-eyed, pink-cheeked. "You are even more innocent than I imagined," he said.

"You have made no secret of the fact that you do not wish to bed me, Your Grace, though we have established that I am indeed your wife. I promised to marry you and provide an heir. I have done the first. Once the second is accomplished, and I am with child, you may go back to—her, or them."

Anger rose. He'd tried to be considerate, to woo her and win her, despite the circumstances of their marriage. Once they knew each other, felt some regard . . . oh, he'd made a dreadful mistake! Was there a more complicated woman alive than Marguerite? "Just like that?" he asked. "I play stud, and then we are rid of each other for good?"

She met his eyes, and he read fierce determination, and a touch of sadness. "Yes."

He called her bluff. He tossed back the coverlet and patted the mattress. Someone had done him the service of undressing him down to his smallclothes. "Then take off that dress and get into bed. I have a busy social schedule in Town. Ladies are lined up around the block, in fact."

She shot a look at the door, and colored. "But it's the middle of the afternoon!"

"Some of my most memorable moments in bed were in the middle of the day. In fact, I do my best, most potent work by day," he dared her.

"No!" She darted forward to flick the cover over him again. "Tonight."

"Not so easy as you thought, Maggie?"

She blushed. "You need more rest, and a meal, and, um, a bath!"

He lay back. "As you wish. If I am to be up all night, so to speak, I suppose I'd better rest while I can. Will you be the one giving me my bath, or did you kidnap Partridge as well?"

She colored again, and opened the door. John Ramsbottom nearly fell into the room. He quickly righted himself.

"Everything all right, Meg, er, Your Grace?"

"I'm going to get His Grace some soup. Perhaps you could assist him with what is, um, necessary," she said.

"I object! If anyone should handle my intimate needs it should be you, Maggie. In fact, I insist on it. John is not my type."

John stepped forward with a frown. "Now see here, Your Grace, I mean no disrespect, but no one's going to speak to our Meg that way. You'll mind your manners, if you please."

"*Our* Meg? She's my wife, Ramsbottom," he said with all the haughty authority his title afforded.

John wasn't impressed. "Maybe so, but she's been our Meg since she was a babe. There'll be none of the kind of thing here that you get up to in London. There are children in this house."

"With more to come, I understand," he muttered, glancing at Meg, who still hovered in the doorway.

"Let him bathe, John, and keep an eye on him."

"You heard her, Your Grace," John said equably. "Up ye get." He crossed the room and lifted Nicholas bodily out of bed.

Nicholas wasn't a small man. He was taller than most, and strong, but not as powerful as John Ramsbottom. "Put me down!" he commanded.

"Don't worry, Your Grace, John won't drop you." Meg laughed. "I've seen him lift colts heavier than you. He'll be as gentle as a lamb as long as you are."

Damn her, he thought as her manservant dumped him in a chair, rattling his brains again. She had no idea how dangerous this game was. Or how easy it would be for him to win.

It was an intriguing situation.

He wouldn't make it easy for her to seduce him. He had his pride.

He was anticipating the night already.

Chapter 42

Meg returned to Nicholas's room at dusk. She helped Amy carry up trays of food and drink for two.

If she expected her husband to be angry, or eager to see her, she was mistaken. He was sitting at the table playing cards with John. He got to his feet as she entered.

"That looks heavy—let me help you," he said, and brushed past her to take Amy's tray. He left Meg holding her tray while he grinned at her housekeeper. "Something smells wonderful."

"Nick, this is Amy, cook and housekeeper," John said amiably. "Amy, Nick's been telling me stories about the war, and I've been telling him about your jam tarts. Can ye make him some?"

"*Nick?*" Meg muttered. She set the tray down with a thump that rattled the dishes. She narrowed her eyes at her husband, but he was kissing Amy's hand as if she were the duchess. And Amy, damn her, was as charmed as John. She was blushing, and nothing had made Amy blush in years.

"I was just about to make a batch," Amy simpered. "I'll bring you some hot from the oven, Your Grace. They're best when they're warm."

"In the kitchen you swore he'd get nothing from you but bread and water," Meg said. Amy sent her a look.

"Please, Amy, call me Nick. Only Meg calls me Your Grace."

He crossed the room to her at last, and her heart tensed, waiting for him to greet her. Instead he untied the napkin on the basket of rolls, took one, and turned back to Amy.

"Delicious," he said.

"The little lasses can't decide which they like best, my jam tarts or hot bread rolls with fresh butter," Amy said.

"Little lasses?" Nicholas asked.

Amy giggled. "Oh, they're charming creatures, both of 'em. They take after their mother. They've been asking all day when they could see you, but Meg said—"

"Why not now?" Nicholas said. "I'd love to meet them."

Meg folded her arms. "They're in bed."

Amy shook her head. "No, they aren't. They're too excited to sleep. I'll go and fetch them."

She was out the door before Meg could stop her. Nicholas had the audacity to wink as she glared at him.

"Another hand while we wait, John?" he asked.

"The food will get cold," she said.

"Amy won't like that," John said. "She can be a trifle sharp if things aren't done properly."

"A family trait perhaps?" Nicholas asked giving Meg a sideways glance as he rose to uncover the dishes. "Would you like some, John? Looks like there's enough for two."

He fed her manservant her supper, without even a by-your-leave. He poured wine for John as well, and sat down to deal the cards. They appeared to have forgotten she existed.

Amy returned with the girls. Their blond curls bounced

as they bobbed curtsies to Nicholas, two more of Papa's perfect daughters.

He dropped to one knee and kissed their hands as Amy introduced them, making them giggle. "I am honored to meet you, Lady Lily, Lady Mignonette. How are you this evening?" he asked, as if they were meeting in a ballroom. Even Minnie, who was only seven, sighed.

Was there a woman born Nicholas couldn't charm? Except her, of course. She knew exactly what kind of wicked, wanton, vile—

"You didn't tell me he was so charming," Amy whispered, her eyes on Nicholas. "Or so handsome."

"Handsome is as handsome does," Meg said tartly. "He ought to be locked up somewhere away from anything female." Or male, for that matter, she thought, glaring at John Ramsbottom's besotted expression.

Somehow, he'd managed to turn a kidnapping into a party.

Meg was starving. She snatched the last roll from the basket. Amy looked at her expectantly, as if she expected Meg to go and fetch more from the kitchen.

Meg glared back. Minnie was sitting on Nicholas's lap, and Lily was leaning against his knee. Both girls were beaming at him. How many times had she seen older women looking at him the same way? He was telling her sisters a story about when he was a child, something about learning to ride a pony and falling into a pond.

Lily sighed. "Meg promised to teach me to ride before she left for London. Perhaps now you're here, you could teach me instead."

"Me too!" piped Minnie. "But Meg said I was too small for her mare, and I haven't a pony."

"Then we'll get one for you," Nicholas promised, pinching her nose.

Minnie squealed and threw her arms around his waist as if he'd offered her diamonds. "Thank you, Your Grace. I love you!"

Was it that easy?

"You must promise me one thing, though. Call me Nicholas, not Your Grace."

"Meg said we had to call you Your Grace and be polite, no matter how angry you were," Lily said, casting an eye on her sister.

Nicholas ignored her, but John and Amy cast accusing glances at her, as if she'd lied about him.

"Let me show you a card trick," he said to the girls, and Amy and John crowded in to watch. One big, happy wholesome family. And Meg was once again the outsider.

"Amy, it's past time the girls were in bed," she said sharply.

Five pairs of eyes turned to stare at her. "Now! You can visit with His Grace tomorrow."

"Nick," they all reminded her in unison. He had the nerve to give her a devil's grin.

Amy led the girls away, frowning at Meg as she passed. John gave no sign of rising.

"Another hand, Nick?" he asked.

"John?" Meg said.

He looked up, his blue eyes wide and innocent. "Yes, Meg?"

"Do you have the key?"

John stared at her uncomprehending for a moment. "Oh," he said at last. "I suppose it's *everyone's* bedtime." He patted his pockets for the key.

"Allow me," Nicholas said, and made a show of pulling the key from behind John's ear with a flourish.

John laughed heartily. "Now how'd ye do that, Nick?" he asked.

"It's simply a matter of—" Nicholas began to show him.

Meg snatched the key out of his hand, and pressed it into John's.

"Good night, John," she said firmly.

John looked hurt. "Ye don't have to tell me twice, Meg. I'm not dense. Good night then, Nick."

Meg shut the door and leaned on it, and waited until the key turned in the lock, and John's heavy footsteps retreated down the hall.

She turned to look at her husband, sprawled in the chair, his legs crossed, a glass of wine held loosely in his hand. Even in yesterday's clothes, unshaven, he looked every inch the duke, formidable, devastatingly handsome, and completely in command.

She forced herself to stand away from the door, but her feet refused to carry her toward him. She was still out of her depth where he was concerned, besotted and terrified. She smoothed her hands over her skirts anxiously, hoping he would make the first move.

He drained his glass in a single swallow, and she resented even the false courage the wine might offer, but there was none left. He set the empty glass on the table and met her eyes with a heavy-lidded, expectant gaze that made butterflies swoop through her body.

"Well, Duchess, I'm waiting. Are you going to seduce me or not?"

Chapter 43

Nicholas wasn't going to make it easy for her. She stood where she was, rooted to the floor, uncertain, despite the determined tilt of her chin.

It was harder than he'd imagined to resist getting up and taking her in his arms, carrying her to the bed. She looked like a flame in the shadows, her hair bright, her figure delicate. He remembered what she tasted like, felt like, the sounds she'd made on their wedding night.

It was an intriguing situation, having a woman kidnap him and demand sex, but this wasn't a casual tumble in the hay, this was his wife, and somehow their marriage had become a contest of wills, and he did not intend to lose.

She just stood in the shadows watching him.

He crossed to stretch out on the bed, propped on one elbow. "Is this better?"

She lay down beside him, still wearing her clothes, right down to her shoes. Her toes pointed toward the canopy, and she clasped her hands at her waist like a corpse ready for burial.

He studied her profile. "Do let me know when you plan to begin." He yawned and began to undo the buttons on his shirt. "It's been a busy day, being drugged, kidnapped, and imprisoned. Wears a man out, even without the added burden of stud duty."

She turned her head, her lips opening to deliver an angry rebuke. But her eyes fell to his naked chest, and her breath caught.

"If you aren't in the mood, there are other things we could do to pass the time," he suggested.

"Like what?" she snapped. "Card tricks? No thank you. You've proven quite convincingly that you can be charming to everyone else in the world except me." She rolled her eyes. "Must be your penchant for blondes again."

He chuckled. "John's not blond."

"Just thickheaded."

He lay back. "Nice chap, actually. He reminds me of a sergeant I knew in Spain."

"I'm sure you told him so."

"I did, actually," he said, and she shot him a hard look. He grinned at her.

"And you knew exactly what Amy and the girls wanted to hear too."

He resisted the urge to turn, to take her in his arms. He traced his finger along her cheek instead. "And what do you want to hear, Maggie?" he asked. "I have something for everyone. I could tell you about the last ball I went to, what we had for supper, what every woman wore—"

"Tell me about Spain."

His gut tightened. "Why?"

"Because that's what I want to hear."

"Blood and gore? That's why you brought me here?" he quipped, but her eyes remained serious.

He lay back and stared at the faded damask canopy above them. He'd never spoken to anyone about Spain.

None of the ladies he knew, or men like Sebastian, wanted to know.

But she did. He felt a surge of something akin to relief.

"I bought a captain's commission in the Royal Dragoons when Stephen did, spur of the moment, because I was tired of drink and women and cards. I wanted an adventure."

"Adventurers make poor heroes, I understand."

He glanced at her, but there was no mockery in her eyes.

"Stephen told me a little about your time in the army."

"Then why ask me?" he demanded, suddenly angry.

"Because I want to hear it from you," she insisted. "He said you were captured."

"Twice," he said, and the damask faded, became the plains of Spain. "The second time I was an intelligence officer, and that was much more dangerous, since men on both sides hate intelligence officers. We're sneak thieves and spies, but our information saves lives when it comes down to it." He glanced at her. "Does that fit what you think of me, Maggie? A sneak thief and a rogue?"

She reached out and touched his chest, pulling his shirt back. Her touch was gentle, unintentionally sensual. He clenched his teeth. "The scars," she said. "Where did you get them?"

He closed his hand on hers, removed it from his chest, but didn't let go. "A dozen places. Shrapnel, sword cuts, musket balls. A French lancer nearly finished me once."

"Still, you would have stayed, wouldn't you?" she asked. "If you had the choice."

He glanced at her, felt his heart skip a beat. Had any woman looked at him like that before? With interest in what he had to say? Curiosity in who he was, what he thought? He resisted the urge to touch her. She put her hand on his, bidding him to continue.

"There was no choice. My brother died. I inherited the title and had to resign my commission and come home."

Her fingers curled, tightened. "What happened to him?"

It was a strange way to seduce a man, even for her. He got up off the bed, and looked around the room. "Whose room is this? Not yours, surely. There's nothing feminine about it. If I open that closet, I doubt your clothes will be there."

She sat up and curled her legs under her. "It was my father's room. Mama insisted this wing of the house be locked when he died. It's the first time I've been here in over a year." She looked at the walls, the books, as if she expected the dead earl to appear.

He stood on the other side of the room and watched her. "Who took care of things when he died? Was it Hector?" he asked.

She shrugged. "He helped where he could."

"But not enough. So you took your sister's place."

She looked at him fiercely. "Can you imagine what would have become of my mother, or Lily and Minnie, without money or connections?"

"You might have told me who you were, been honest."

"What would you have done?"

He would have canceled the wedding. He could not say it aloud, but he knew she read the answer in his eyes. She looked away.

"You have not been honest either. Even if our vows are legal, you have no intention of honoring them, do you? You have other, more desirable women . . ."

She thought the worst of him. It stung his pride, though he'd done nothing to make her believe he was anything else but a worthless fool. "Do you honestly believe I spend my days whoring and gambling?" he asked.

"How can I not?" she asked. "I've seen you with other women!"

"And you think this is the way to get my attention?"

"I promised your grandmother I would provide an heir. There is too much at stake if I fail in that duty."

"My grandmother?" He frowned. "Our children would belong to us, not her, Maggie."

"Of course," she said quickly. Too quickly.

He came around the bed and gripped her shoulders. "My grandmother raised my brother to be Duke of Temberlay. He did exactly what she wanted, didn't dare stray. He was miserable, but he did his duty. Granddame never intended me to take his place. She ignored me as a boy, left me to do as I pleased. She would do anything to bring David back. But I won't let her, is that clear?"

She looked at him fiercely, with pain in the golden depths of her eyes, determination to see this through. He let her go and moved away, his mouth twisting bitterly.

"I will not give her another child to warp and twist. You married me to protect your family, what of our child? Would he deserve anything less?" She didn't answer, but her eyes dropped. He shut his eyes, rubbed them with his thumb and forefinger. "You might as well go, Meg. Your plan won't work."

Her face flared scarlet. "We're locked in until morning," she said. "I can't leave."

"How disappointing for both of us, then."

Her fierce determination faded behind a blush of shame. She was an innocent indeed, confused by his refusal, unsure of how to proceed, what to do to seduce him. She could, he thought, just by looking at him. Instead she turned away. She knew he was right, or she believed even more strongly now that he didn't want her. He wanted to take her in his arms, soothe her fears, prove just how desirable he found her, but they'd both lose if he gave in now. Only Granddame would win. He stayed where he was.

"I shall sleep in the chair," she said at last, stiffly.

"As you wish." He didn't bother to argue. "I have no night attire," he said, tossing his shirt aside, stripping off his breeches, not caring if his naked body enticed or offended her. She turned away, blushing.

"I sent word back with Rogers, asking Partridge to send clothing and necessaries for your stay here. They should arrive tomorrow."

"Then I can hope for rescue?" he asked. She pursed her lips.

"Don't tell me you're determined to keep this up, Meg." Her shoulders sagged. "I'm afraid I must."

She took off her dress, folded it neatly, and left on her shift and curled up in the wing chair by the fireplace. She looked like a child seeking shelter. He noted the dark circles under her eyes as she closed them and pretended to sleep.

He could go now, pick the lock and be gone before she woke, but he stayed where he was, watching her.

Kidnapping him was a desperate act. Like marrying him. He'd lived by his wits in Spain, learned to read the subtle signs of trouble. She was hiding something—a secret she couldn't or wouldn't share. He wondered what it was. He watched her fall into an uneasy sleep.

He covered her with a blanket.

Trust. It came down to that. No marriage could work without it. She was lovely, smart, loyal, and resourceful. If they could find a way to deal with each other, get to honesty, they might fit well together, even be happy.

But there were ghosts to lay to rest. Escaping in the night wouldn't make her trust him. Proving that he could protect her from the demons she feared most just might.

Chapter 44

An eerie cry woke Nicholas. The last candle had met its end, and the room was cold and very dark.

"Oh no, Papa, breathe! Please breathe!" Meg whimpered.

He groped for the chair by the fireplace, and found it empty. "Maggie? Meg?"

He found her in the corner, scrabbling at the wall with her nails, crying. Her skin was icy under his hand. He lifted her into his arms, and she clung to him, shivering, still whimpering in the throes of her nightmare.

He carried her to the bed and lay down beside her and pulled her into his arms, warming her, soothing her until her cries subsided and she slept.

He'd had his own nightmares after his parents died, and after David's death. He'd used whisky and women to chase them away. He wondered what comfort there'd been for Meg. He kissed her forehead and she nestled into his neck, and he fell asleep feeling safer than he had in years.

Meg tugged at the covers. Her sister had more than her fair share of the bed again. Her arm was draped over Meg's shoulder, and her leg was tucked between Meg's feet, keeping them warm. She wiggled her toes. Rose's legs were hairy.

Her eyes popped open as she remembered where she was.

With a gasp, she tried to move, to slide out from under Nicholas.

"Don't move," he muttered, his mouth against her ear. "You're letting cold air under the covers. I'd forgotten how cold it gets in the country at night, even in the summer."

"How did I get here?" she whispered, lying still. Her back was curled against his chest, and she focused on the only part of him she could see without moving, his arm. It was tanned, muscular, and sprinkled with dark hair and the now-familiar scar running up his thumb and wrist.

"You had a nightmare," he said. "I carried you to bed."

She stiffened, tried to move away, but his grip tightened.

"Did you, um, did we—?"

"No," he growled. "If I'd made love to you, you wouldn't have slept through it, I promise you." She lay still.

"I'm sorry. I still have nightmares about my father from time to time. I didn't mean to disturb you." She plucked at the hair on his arm, traced the scar with her fingertip.

"I assume that's why you threw me out of your bed on our wedding night?"

"Yes," she admitted, embarrassed.

He kissed her hair.

She turned to face him. His hair was sleep-tousled, his eyes heavy lidded, his jaw stubbled. Her body tingled.

Perhaps it wouldn't be so difficult to seduce him after all.

"Thank you for keeping me warm," she murmured, her eyes on his mouth, wondering if she dared to kiss him. She put her hand on his sleep-warm chest.

He grabbed her fingers, kept them still. "I wish I could say it had been my pleasure, but I haven't actually had the pleasure, so to speak."

She met his eyes. "You can," she whispered. "Have the pleasure, I mean."

His eyes narrowed, fixed on her mouth, and she parted her lips in anticipation of his kiss.

Instead he turned away and sat up, his feet dangling over the edge of the bed. He tugged the sheet around his naked hips, leaving her the blanket.

"Not here, not this way."

"Then how? I couldn't think of another way," she murmured, feeling desperation war with shame. How was she to tempt him? How did other women do it?

She sat up, and her shift drooped from one shoulder as the blanket drifted to her waist. It was cold, and the nipple of her bare breast peaked.

"Then you should have—" He turned to face her, his breeches half buttoned. His jaw dropped. She resisted the urge to straighten her clothing. It wasn't revulsion on his face. It was desire. It gave her courage.

"Come back to bed," she pleaded.

He swallowed. "God, Maggie, what did my grand-mother promise you?"

"I—" she began. She couldn't admit the truth. Not here in this room, of all places. Her family was more riddled with scandal than he was.

The key rattled in the lock and John knocked loudly.

She dove under the blanket as Nicholas shouted "Come!" John had a trunk balanced on his shoulder. "Good morning, Nick. Look 'ere, I have a Mr. Partridge who's just arrived from London with some things for ye."

Nicholas picked up Meg's gown and tossed it to her. She put it on under the covers and got up.

Partridge entered, carrying a small leather case. "Good morning, Your Grace. I came as soon as I heard you were lost in the country without so much as a fresh cravat." He winced at Nicholas's disheveled appearance. "Good heavens, it looks like you slept in that shirt, sir! I had no idea how long you'd be rusticating here in the country, so I brought several trunks, with clothing for every possibility. Will you be hunting, sir? Rogers insisted you'd want Hannibal."

"Several trunks?" Meg gasped. Partridge's eyes widened in surprise as he noticed her.

"Your Grace!" His eyes flicked over her before he bowed. "Your pardon, I didn't see you there, I thought you were—" He swallowed. "Anna insisted I bring a trunk for you as well."

He thought she was what? A servant? One of Temberlay's strumpets? She drew herself up. "Thank you for coming so promptly, Partridge. John will see you have a room in the servants' quarters."

He looked horrified, and Nicholas laughed. "Not to worry, Partridge. I will only be here for a day or two. I plan to return to London before the end of the week."

Meg read the determination in his eyes.

Partridge sighed in relief. "Shall we see about making you ready for the day, Your Grace?" He looked at John. "Is there hot water?"

"Plenty in the kitchen," John said.

"For a bath?" the valet asked.

"What's wrong with a cold wash?" John nodded at the pitcher in the corner.

Partridge's brows rose. "Primitive surroundings, I must say, Your Grace."

Nicholas sat at the table. "I'm sure you'll do your best, Partridge, as always."

"Amy is laying out breakfast in the dining room, Meg. She doesn't think Nick is going to be a threat to anyone. She says she won't carry a hot meal all the way up here just to have it get cold. She wants Nick to have a proper breakfast." He grinned at Nicholas. "She's made sweet rolls."

"Partridge, you must try one of Amy's rolls. They are an unparalleled taste of heaven."

"I'm sure Mrs. Parry would be most distressed to hear you say so, sir," Partridge said mildly, laying out the tools and equipment necessary to prepare a gentleman for the day.

There was no point in remaining. He had dismissed her from his thoughts. Meg slipped away, her face burning, and went to her own room and made herself ready for the day. She chose an elegant day dress that made her look every inch a duchess.

Then she went downstairs to take control of the situation back into her own hands.

Chapter 45

"**H**ector!"

At Flora's panicked scream, he dropped his pen and ran from his study to the breakfast room. Flora's sobs were loud enough to be heard all over the house. He passed a footman in the hall.

"I swear, sir, all I did was take Her Ladyship the post!"

"Never mind. Summon her maid, and fetch the harts-horn."

He burst into the breakfast room to find Flora holding a letter. She waved it at him like a flag.

"It's a letter from Rose! She's in Scotland of all places. She's married herself to a sailor and now she wants to come home."

"A sailor?" Hector took the letter and scanned it.

"My daughters will be the death of me yet, Hector. My poor nerves cannot stand much more of this, and I still have two at home to marry off. A sailor! It couldn't be worse. He's a cabin boy or something. How can he hope to support her, an earl's daughter, the family beauty? Now he's abandoned her and taken ship for who knows where."

Hector finished the letter and set it on the table. "It's not as bad as all that, Flora." He crossed to the sideboard and poured her a small sherry. "He's hardly a cabin boy. He's just made lieutenant, and his father is an admiral. Admiral Winters."

Flora blinked. "An admiral?" She swallowed the sherry at a gulp.

"It says his family has an estate near Glasgow. Rose is there with Edward's mother and sisters, but they're planning to come south for a visit. Won't that be nice?"

"Edward?" Flora asked. "Is that his name?" She folded her hands. "She married without me there. My eldest child. And Marguerite's marriage is a disaster, one scandal after the other. My nerves are worn out. Perhaps I should go home to the peace and quiet of Wycliffe Park."

"Probably a very good idea. You can get some rest," he said sympathetically, hoping he didn't sound eager.

"But that would be cowardice, wouldn't it?" she mused. "Leaving you to face the scandals alone. Marguerite and Rose will need me nearby." She refilled her sherry. "No, I cannot leave. We must face this together. Lady Emerson's musicale is tonight, and I know she invited me in hopes of winkling out the latest details of Nicholas and Meg's marriage, and if we don't attend the musicale, any tales that *are* told would be all the worse. Do you see?"

"Not at all," he murmured. "Why don't I send Lady Emerson your regrets, and arrange for you to leave for Wycliffe this afternoon?"

The footman entered with another note on a tray. "It's another note for Her Ladyship," he whispered nervously.

Flora put a hand to her cheek. "Oh, Hector, you read it. I cannot stand the shock of more news of any kind today."

Hector opened the letter and scanned it. "Good God!" He shot to his feet.

"What now?" Flora cried.

Hector took out his handkerchief and mopped his

brow. "It's from Meg. She drugged Nicholas with the laudanum you gave her and carried him off to Wycliffe. According to her letter, she intends to keep him prisoner until he does his husbandly duty and gets her with ch—"

"Does this mean an annulment is a possibility yet again?" Flora asked. "Only now he could annul her, and the scandal would be ours once again, doesn't it?"

"I can't think Temberlay will take kindly to being kidnapped. Meg may have gone too far."

Flora folded her arms. "Yet if he did such a thing, drugged her and carried her off, it would be viewed as romantic and quite acceptable! If not for that actress—"

"The fact remains that polite people do not kidnap their spouses and carry them off at all." Hector interrupted what promised to be a long tirade. "Especially ladies."

"Why?" Flora demanded.

"Because ladies are meek and gentle and—"

"I meant why did Marguerite kidnap Temberlay?"

"The letter says she wishes to be rid of him for good."

"Rid of him? No she doesn't. If she wanted to be rid of him she should have drugged him, locked him in a trunk, and sent him to sea. But to take him to Wycliffe?" She rose from her seat. "If you'll excuse me, I have a lot to do."

"Do you wish to go home after all?" he asked. "Shall I order the coach?"

"And invade a honeymoon? Of course not! I must remain in London. I'll need to see the modiste at once, order a new wardrobe if Rose is coming to visit. I can't have her relatives thinking I'm a bumpkin!"

She sailed out and Hector sighed. Rose was back, Meg had abducted her husband, and Flora was planning a new wardrobe to meet the results of both in style.

The Lynton ladies never ceased to surprise him.

Chapter 46

"**H**is Grace and I will be breakfasting alone," Meg announced, entering the dining room moments behind Nicholas. She looked every inch a duchess to be reckoned with, but he noted that she avoided looking at him as she issued instructions. He took a seat at the head of the table and waited.

"Amy, you may leave the food on the sideboard and take the girls into the kitchen for their meal."

"But Meg, they've been looking forward to eating with Nick, and I—"

She sent the housekeeper a quelling look. "You will call him Your Grace."

"He said not to," John said. Everyone turned to look at Nicholas, awaiting confirmation, but he held his tongue, kept his eyes on his wife.

"He is a guest here. I am in charge," she said calmly.

He gave her a disarming smile, watched her color, though her firm expression didn't change."

"John, you have my word I won't try to escape. And Amy, I promise to eat every bite on my plate."

"I'll be right outside if you need me." John grumbled as he closed the door.

"Who do you think he was talking to, you or me?" Nicholas asked. The chair creaked under him, in need of glue. The room was spotless, but nearly bare of furnishings and decoration. She crossed to the sideboard and began to fill two plates. In her London finery, she was as out of place here as he was. Looking around, he realized he might have done exactly the same thing she had to stop the slow and dreadful slide into poverty.

"Yes, everyone is on your side," Meg said bitterly. Her hands were shaking as she set the plates down.

"This is hardly about sides, Maggie. You look lovely this morning, by the way," he complimented her.

To his surprise she set her hands on the arms of his chair and leaned down to kiss him. He drew a sharp breath and met her lips. She was tentative, careful, as she let her tongue dart in to touch his, before she backed away.

"That's not how I taught you to kiss. I know you can do better than that." He caressed her cheek, and she turned her face into his palm, let her eyes drift shut.

"Show me again," she said, her voice husky. He dragged her into his lap, ignoring the groan of protest from the chair. He tangled his hand in her hair, loosened the careful coiffure, intent on giving her the kind of kiss that she'd never, ever forget. One that proved to her that she was beautiful, desirable, his.

It wasn't that he was any more willing to play her game now than he was last night, but what could possibly happen here in the dining room?

But he was as intoxicated as she was. He groaned at the sweetness of her mouth, her eagerness. He nipped at her lips, sucked them, tickled the sensitive inner surfaces with his tongue. She wrapped her arms around him, pressed closer, her hands in his hair, on his face, sliding into his shirt.

He wanted to shove the breakfast dishes off the table and lay her down, devour her like one of those damned sweet rolls, tease her, taste her, and sate the insatiable desire he felt for this stubborn, difficult, incomparable woman. She wriggled in his lap, and he felt her hands on the buttons of his breeches.

His resolve cracked. He began to work at the delicate shell buttons that closed the bodice of her gown. He slipped his hand in to cup the heat of her breast, and she sighed.

But then she shifted again, trying to put her leg over the arm of the chair. The old joints squealed a warning, bringing him back to his senses.

"Maggie, what are you doing?" he asked. She was panting, but only because her foot was tangled in the chair.

"The book showed a man sitting and a woman on top," she muttered. "How does—"

He untangled her foot, lifted her, and set her on her feet. He rose himself and stepped away from her. She stared at him, her lips kiss swollen, her bodice open, her hair in loose curls around her face. He clenched his hands behind his back to keep from reaching for her.

"The chair has arms, sweetheart. It wouldn't be impossible, of course, but difficult for a novice like you. It was a very nice try, though, but may I suggest you start with something simpler, like apologizing and coming back to London with me?"

She lifted her chin. "To watch you with other women?"

He buttoned his breeches and went to the door. John was waiting outside.

"Lock me up, my friend," he said.

Meg slumped into the chair he'd just vacated. She'd almost had him. It hadn't been difficult at all. Her body had been on fire for him the moment she'd walked into the room and set eyes on him, handsome, freshly shaved, devastating to her firm determination to insist that he follow her upstairs as soon as he'd eaten and do his duty. She remembered how it felt to wake up next to him in bed, touching him.

Mortification prickled her skin. She was a fool. He didn't love her, could never love her, and still she wanted him. Her desire for him went beyond the dowager's ultimatum, though she couldn't afford to ignore that.

She knew what would happen if they returned to London. He'd proven he could charm anyone. Unfortunately, it didn't include her, and she could not stand by and watch him . . . She fought back tears. Her mind whirled with thoughts, erotic, naughty, petty, jealous little thoughts.

Things she'd never felt before. But she'd imagined them, when she'd looked at the caricatures of his handsome face. But this wasn't love. It was supposed to be a business arrangement. Had she truly thought this marriage would be that easy?

She had to think of another way, and start again.

Chapter 47

"**I** hate to have to lock you up, Nick—Your Grace—but Meg will have my guts for stockings if I don't," John said as he led Nicholas back upstairs. "If you left her in a temper, then she'll probably clean the whole house this morning, if I know our Meg."

Nicholas glanced at him. "Meg does the housework?"

"She does everything since His Lordship died. She calmed the rest of 'em, dried their tears, buried her da, and took over running the place, and under the circumstances, you might have expected her to fall to grief first, and harder than the others. She's a strong lass, and a smart one—"

"Under what circumstances? Nicholas asked, pausing on the landing where the three wings of the house joined.

John frowned. "She found him. The day after His Lordship sold the horses. She went out to the stable to talk to him, and there he was. He hanged himself in one of the stalls."

Nicholas felt his stomach cave in.

"She cut him down, even though she was just a lass. I found her trying to revive him." He wiped away a tear. "Saddest thing I ever saw. She told me not to let the others see him, not to tell what had happened. She told her mother that he'd fallen, hit his head." He sighed. "She was different after that, not a girl anymore. She grew up overnight, took charge, got the rest of 'em through it, with no one at all to comfort her."

He looked fiercely at Nicholas. "Ye'll take good care of her, won't you? God knows she needs someone to do it, and ye seem like a good man. Don't let her down, Nick. The others are silly, vain creatures, but Meg is the best of 'em."

Numb with shock, Nicholas climbed the rest of the stairs. He let John unlock the door to the earl's bedchamber, and walked in. He stood in the center of the room and stared at the empty walls, at the last miserable vestiges of Wycliffe's life.

"I swear she'll never want for anything, John."

"She doesn't need pretty gowns or money or rings, Nick. She needs someone to love her. The earl was a fool, if you'll forgive my being so bold—she'd never let me say such a thing about him—but he never saw the worth in her, called her his ugly duck while he petted the others."

How could any man alive think Meg was worthless or ugly?

"She's safe with me, John."

John got out the key. "I'd better lock you in, Nick. No doubt the lasses and Amy will be up to see you before long. You've given a bit of life to the old place again. It's a nice thing to see."

The key turned in the lock, leaving him in silence.

Chapter 48

Nicholas cursed Wycliffe. How could a man do such a thing to his family, to Meg? He preached the sanctity of womanhood, the need for women to be protected and honored, and he'd ruined Meg's young life, left his burdens on her shoulders, with no training, no knowledge of the world.

And she had borne it.

He shut his eyes, ashamed of himself. She didn't need him to teach her lessons. She could teach him a thing or two.

His wedding day had been the luckiest day of his life.

He crossed to the bookshelves, glanced at the titles, thinking of what he'd say to her when next she came to him.

Every book on the shelf was about morality, manners, and self-denial. He pulled out the only book that didn't make him feel ill at the man's hypocrisy, a folio of paintings of Thoroughbred horses.

The watercolors were magnificent. The Wycliffe Arabian was a stallion with rolling eyes, pulling against the groom who held him. Another portrait titled *Lady Arabella and Foal* showed a beautiful mare with soft dark eyes, her face maternal. A young girl in pink held the foal's bridle, her hair a mass of blond curls. Another child held the mare, and he could see that the artist had changed the hair, painted over the russet locks, tried to make them as golden as her sister's. He cursed Wycliffe again.

A sheet of paper fluttered from between the leaves of the book, landed at his feet. He picked it up.

It was a bill of sale for the three horses, describing them as prime Arab hot bloods. Such horses were usually worth a king's ransom, and the price they should have fetched would have made Wycliffe rich, but he'd sold them for a pittance, a quarter of their true worth.

Nicholas looked at the signatures at the bottom of the page.

Wycliffe's was a shaky scrawl.

The buyer's signature was crisp, clear, and purposeful.

Lord Charles Wilton.

Nicholas used a fork he'd purloined from last night's dinner to pull the nails out of the shutters, rage burning in his chest. Did Meg know? Was Hector Bryant aware that his stepbrother had been cheated by Wilton? The answers lay in London, along with the chance to revenge yet another sin Wilton was guilty of.

He pulled open the shutters, stared out at the facade of Wycliffe as he donned a riding cloak before climbing out the window. He tossed his hat down to the lawn and followed it, descending by windowsills and broad lips of stone to the ground.

He peered around the edge of the building, wondering where the stables were, and followed a low stone wall to a kitchen garden and a small orchard. From there, a gravel path led to the stables.

The stables were in better condition than the house itself and more modern. The earl's pride in his horses was evident.

He hoped they'd stabled Hannibal inside, and he wasn't out in some distant pasture, filling his belly with country clover.

He was also concerned he'd meet John out here somewhere and have to explain himself, but there wasn't a soul in the garden, not even a dog to bark a warning as he entered the cool dimness of the stable.

He imagined Meg coming through this door and finding her father. He could see the scars on the oak beam above one of the stalls where the rope had bitten into the wood. An engraved brass plaque labeled the stall as the former home of the Wycliffe Arabian.

Hannibal stood in the luxurious space now.

His stallion was ignoring him, his eyes on the mare across the cobbles. She was a healthy, well-kept bay meant for ordinary duty. She regarded Nicholas with cool suspicion. Another mare was stabled next to her.

At the sound of footsteps on the gravel outside, he ducked into the stall next to Hannibal's and crouched.

"Hello, my beauties," Meg greeted the horses softly. "And Hannibal too of course. I'm sure you've got the girls all a-twitter like your master, don't you?"

He heard the crunch of an apple. Hannibal liked apples.

She crossed and took a saddle off the wall, and opened the first mare's stall. "You like him, don't you? He *is* a handsome devil," she whispered to the mare, and Hannibal snorted proudly. "But he's not for the likes of you. He's used to a finer type of lass." She sighed. "Only a London beauty—or two or three—will do for him."

Nicholas shut his eyes, his stomach sinking at the bitterness in her voice. How could she honestly believe he didn't want her? He stared up at the scarred beam.

He'd never told her.

He couldn't now. Not until he could right some of the wrongs in her life, prove himself worthy of her.

He waited while she saddled the mare, and led her out to the yard. He watched as she swung up onto the horse and rode out.

He saddled Hannibal quickly. The stallion didn't need coaxing. As soon as Nicholas mounted, he set off at a gallop after Meg and the mare.

The road to London lay on his right. He only needed to point Hannibal in that direction, leap the hedge and be gone.

But Meg had taken the path to the left, toward the woods. He could see her galloping across an open field, riding low over the horse's neck. She slipped her leg astride the mare, and the wind caught her hair, unfurled it like a battle flag. Desire caught him in the chest, made him gasp.

He turned Hannibal to chase her.

Chapter 49

Meg let the soft air flow over her, wishing it could blow away heartache and confusion and fear. Without a child, the dowager would ruin her. Her mother would be destroyed when she learned the truth about her husband's death. Nicholas was right. She did not want to give a child to such a woman.

Being back at Wycliffe simply reminded her of her father's disappointment in her. He'd always said she'd make a dreadful wife.

And he'd been right.

She let the wind take her tears. The only reason she was married at all was that she had tricked Temberlay. He must fear that any child he sired upon her would turn out like her. Imagine, the handsome Devil of Temberlay, lover of beautiful women, with an ugly wife and an equally unattractive child. The scandal sheets would have a field day.

It was easier to tease her, tempt her until she was half out of her mind with longing, and walk away.

The pain of that brought tears of self-pity to her eyes, and she slowed the mare by the river and dismounted. When the news came out, would the disgrace of her father's suicide provide enough grounds to end their marriage? And then what? She leaned on the mare's strong shoulder, and swiped away her tears. She stared at the dark smear on the buff leather of her glove. She would never be the same after Temberlay, but she would go on, somehow.

"Is this land part of Wycliffe?" he asked, and she turned to find Nicholas seated on Hannibal and dressed for travel. He looked as cool and elegant as if he were out for a ride in Hyde Park. She brushed a lock of hair out of her face.

"I suppose I shouldn't be surprised to see you," she said, hating the fact that he'd found her crying over him like a ninny.

"I did escape from much sterner prisons during the war," he said, and swung down from Hannibal's back.

"How kind of you to bid me farewell, or did you come to gloat?"

He stood beside her and looked out across the broad surface of the river. "Wycliffe is beautiful. No wonder you didn't want to lose it."

"I'm not sorry I married you. I did it for my family, but I owe you an apology for this, at least. It was a—mistake," she managed.

"We're not so different, Maggie. I agreed to marry for my family too. I believed my grandmother was heartbroken when David died. I wanted to make her happy. Since my brother left Temberlay bankrupt, I married you for money as well. My grandmother offered to provide the money to run my estates if I married where she wished." He brushed another lock of hair over her shoulder. "I will always protect my family—you, and eventually if we are so fortunate, our children."

She pursed her lips. "Perhaps it would have been different—better—if you'd married Rose."

"I wouldn't know. I haven't met your sister, but from everything I've heard, I got the best of the whole garden of Wycliffe beauties."

She met his eyes with a final plea. "Couldn't you just—pretend—I'm what you want?"

"God, Maggie, I don't have to pretend. I know what I want."

She turned away. "Yes, but she's in London."

"That isn't it, but I can't stay. I have to go back. There are things I must see to that can't wait. Will you come back with me?"

She imagined the pain, the agony and pretense of balls and parties and gossip, looking the other way every time he went to his lover, or took a new one. "I can't."

"Amy told me you spent hours reading about me in the scandal sheets. Every word. I think you were smitten with me before you even met me, curious to see if I was really as wicked as you'd heard, and if you could tame a rake like me."

She tossed her head. "How vain you are!"

He rubbed his thumb along the curve of her lower lip. "You melted the first time I kissed you. You turn to flame in my arms." He leaned closer and she stared at his mouth, inches above her own. "Why else would you be so jealous of other women, women who mean nothing to me?"

"I'm not—" she began. But she was.

"You won't share me," he murmured against her lips.

"No," she agreed on a sigh, curling her hands into his lapels, pulling him closer.

"I won't share you either," he said, and she looked into his eyes. "This marriage is for two. There isn't room for anyone else. Do you understand?"

"I have no other lovers," she said. "If that's what you mean."

"I mean anyone who tries to dictate how things will be with us, Maggie. Not your mama, not the gossips, and especially not my grandmother." He nuzzled the skin beneath her ear, nipped her earlobe. She kissed his jaw, wound her arms around his waist under his cloak.

"When we have children, they will be our children, is that clear? I won't give them over to my grandmother. They will be raised with all the love we can give them. You have to trust me, Maggie."

He kissed her deeply, gathering her into his arms. "How the hell can you think I don't want you?"

Meg gasped wordlessly as he closed his hand on her breast, and teased the nipple through the thin muslin of her gown. "Come back to London," he murmured against her ear.

She let him ravish her mouth as his hands roamed over her. She wanted him, and not for anything other than sheer desire. He picked her up, leaned her back against Hannibal, and she hooked her leg over his hip when he reached for her hem.

"Oh, praise the Lord, there you are, Nick!" John called out from the other side of Hannibal's broad back. "I've been looking everywhere for you. I was afraid you'd left us. You decided to come outside for some fresh air, did you?"

Meg looked at John through glazed eyes. He was grinning as if he'd found Temberlay sitting in a tavern with a glass of ale instead of draped over his wife on the riverbank. She met Nicholas's eyes, read the plea there to send

John away. She looked away. She couldn't deceive him anymore. She needed to think, needed to find another way to protect her family from the dowager's threats. Perhaps that would be easier if he wasn't here. She let her hands drop away from his shoulders and turned to John.

"He *is* leaving, John. He was just saying good-bye."

"Meg?" Nicholas murmured, still ignoring John, confusion in his eyes. Did he think it was so easy to fix everything? She had secrets she could not reveal, people to protect, if that was possible. She had to make it possible. She pushed him away.

"Please guide him back to the road, make sure he has what he needs," she instructed her servant.

She mounted her mare. "I wish you a safe journey, Your Grace," she managed, and set her heels to the horse before she dissolved into tears.

Nicholas stood with John and watched her ride away, and wondered what the hell had happened.

"Sorry if I interrupted anything, Nick. I thought I'd catch hell from Meg if I lost you."

"Have you ever been in love, John?" he asked as they rode back toward the road.

The big man blushed like a girl. "I'm not the kind of man lasses fancy. Too big and awkward." Nicholas smiled sadly at him, and John's jaw dropped. "You weren't—that is, you weren't asking for *advice*, were you? From *me*?"

He scanned the green fields of Wycliffe. He understood sex and seduction well enough. Marriage was something entirely different, especially if one had *feelings* for his wife. He might have asked Stephen, but he'd gone to Vienna, and he was a bachelor. So was Sebastian, and he was the last place to look for sensible council. Nicholas realized that he did not actually know any happily married men.

He was on his own, and he'd never been so utterly confused in his life.

He turned Hannibal toward the road. Fixing the situation lay in London. First, he needed to speak to his grandmother.

Next, he wanted revenge for his brother's senseless death, and for the tragedies that had befallen Meg's family.

Perhaps it was better if Meg remained here, till he'd worked that out.

He couldn't imagine being in Town, or anywhere, without her.

He tipped his hat and forced a smile when they reached the London road. "Come to Town, John, soon. Bring Meg home."

He set his heels to the stallion and rode hard.

Chapter 50

"**M**ama!" Rose rushed into Hector's sitting room and threw her arms around her mother. To his eyes, the two were so much alike it was hard to tell where one blond head ended and the other began.

He was glad to see Rose safe, married, and apparently happy, if the tears filling his home were anything to go by. Mother and daughter soaked each other's gowns before they exchanged handkerchiefs, as if a small square of lace could stop the deluge.

He edged toward the door.

"Hector, where are you going?" Flora demanded. "Rose has only just arrived. Don't you want to hear her news?"

Hector pasted on a fond smile and kissed Rose's damp cheek. "Of course I do. It is good to have you back, and looking so well. I was just going to arrange for tea. You both look like you could use a cup."

Flora sniffled. "Don't be silly, Hector. What we need is a glass of sherry. Then tea."

He crossed to the decanter and set out three small glasses. He poured sherry for the ladies, and filled his own with good strong brandy.

"None for me, Hector. I am unable to take sherry at the moment," Rose hinted, giving her mother a meaningful glance.

"I can well imagine you're out of sorts after such a long trip. Jouncing over those dreadful roads all the way from Scotland is enough to put anyone out of countenance," Flora sniffed.

"No, Mama, I meant—" Rose began, but Flora hadn't finished.

"I myself cannot bear being in a coach for more than an hour at the most, and that's on smooth roads. You must be exhausted."

"Actually, we arrived yesterday evening, and I had an excellent sleep at Admiral Winters's London home. It wasn't the journey, Mama. I'm—"

"He has a London home as well? Where? How big is it?" Flora asked.

"Oh, it's quite fine and elegant indeed. Edward's aunt and sister traveled down with me, and they insisted I rest before visiting you because I'm—"

"His aunt and sister?" Flora said. "You should have brought them with you. We must have a dinner party for them, Hector, or perhaps even a ball."

Hector frowned. His largest reception room seated ten, and only if everyone sat very close together.

Flora crossed to the desk for a sheet of paper. "We'll make a list," she said.

Rose got to her feet. "I'm afraid that won't do at all, Mama."

Flora set the pen down. "Why? Don't these new relations of yours like parties?"

"Of course they do, but—"

"We'll bring everything back to a simple dinner party, then."

Hector snatched the pen out of her hand. "For pity's sake, Flora, hold your tongue. Rose is trying to tell you she's pregnant!"

Flora stared at him balefully and snatched the pen back again. "There's no need to yell, Hector. I could see right off that Rose is in a delicate condition."

"Well, aren't you pleased?" he asked.

"Of course I'm pleased! How could I not be pleased? Look at her, she's radiant, the very picture of loveliness!" She gave her daughter a look of pure maternal pride. "I was only thinking of poor Marguerite. Marriage has not agreed with her at all."

"Oh?" Rose's eyes widened with curiosity.

"We don't know that," Hector said. "We haven't seen her in almost a fortnight. Things could be going quite well by now. She might even be —"

"I suppose it's all my fault," Rose said, and helped herself to a cream bun as the maid brought in the tea tray. "I don't regret not marrying that dreadful man. It is unfortunate that Meg married him in my place, but if she is unhappy, then she only has herself to blame. She should not have stolen my bridegroom." She popped the cake into her mouth.

Hector tried to make sense of her logic. Even Flora was frowning at her daughter.

"Still, to be so miserable, must be—miserable," Rose finished.

"Well!" Flora said indignantly, and got up from Rose's side and crossed the room to sit next to Hector. Rose helped herself to another cream cake.

"Meg and Temberlay are at Wycliffe, on their wedding trip. I'm sure they are quite happy."

"No they aren't," Rose said.

"Aren't happy?" Flora asked.

"Aren't at Wycliffe. At least he isn't. The *London News* said this morning that he was back in Town. I met him at the opera last night."

"Did he make any mention of Marguerite, or her family?" Flora asked.

Rose shook her head. "No, but I've read there's a certain actress who is very glad to see him. Are there more cakes?"

"Was he alone?" Flora asked. "At the opera?"

"Not at all! He was surrounded by people!" Rose said, and Hector clenched his jaw and refrained from rolling his eyes.

"Was he escorting anyone?" Flora asked.

"A Lady Delphine St. James, I believe. Is she one of his mistresses?"

"No," Hector said, feeling relief. "The St. Jameses are old friends of Temberlay's."

"I should write to Marguerite at once," Flora said, rising to go to the desk again. "I am surprised she hasn't sent word to us herself."

"Perhaps Devil murdered her on the way to Town, or left her to die among strangers. Perhaps she sent a note, but the messenger met with a terrible accident, and the letter was lost," Rose said.

"You've been reading those dreadful novels, haven't you, Rose?" Flora asked.

Rose pouted. "It was a very long trip from Scotland to London. They helped pass the time."

Hector looked longingly at the brandy decanter across the room.

Flora looked worried. "I must write to Marguerite at once," she said, and picked up the pen again.

"Surely you don't think—" Hector began, but she shook her head.

"Of course not, but there must be some reason she hasn't returned to Town, or come to see me if she has."

Rose got to her feet. "If there are no more buns, I really must be getting back. Emma and Charlotte will fuss. They don't want me overdoing it in my delicate state, but I just had to come to Town for at least part of the Season."

Hector smiled at her. "It's good to see they are taking such good care of you, my dear."

Rose laid a hand on her little belly. "Yes, they are. We have a party to attend this evening, but they've insisted that I must not even consider taxing myself by attending Lady Samson's supper party before it. We're going to the Kendalls' ball instead, and I am strictly forbidden to remain there past three! I believe Temberlay will also be there."

Hector's smile crumpled.

Flora handed him the note. "Take this to Hartley Place for me, if you would, Hector, see if Marguerite is there."

He made good his escape as Rose began to chatter about the latest London fashions.

Chapter 51

⟨◦◦⟩

"**G**ood afternoon, Gardiner, is Temberlay at home?" Hector asked, looking around the cavernous hall of Hartley Place.

"I'll inquire, if you'd like to wait in the salon, my lord."

Nicholas entered a few moments later, looking none the worse for his kidnapping.

"I was planning to call on you this afternoon, Bryant. You've beaten me to it."

"Flora heard rumors that you were back in Town, and wants news of Meg," he said.

Nicholas crossed and poured two tumblers of whisky and handed one to him. "Are you wondering if she's still alive after kidnapping me and dragging me to Wycliffe?"

Hector scanned his face. "Yes, as a matter of fact. We expected you'd be away for some time."

"I had things to see to here in London. Meg chose to stay at Wycliffe for the moment."

Hector felt alarm. "Is she—"

"Too bruised to appear in public? Broken in body and spirit? She's perfectly well, I assure you. I asked her to return with me, and she declined. I think that might be better, for the moment."

"I see," Hector said, though he didn't. "I have a note for her from her mother."

Temberlay dropped it on the table. "I'll see she gets it." He reached into his pocket, and handed over a piece of paper. "Have you seen this?"

Hector read the contents of the bill of sale, and looked up at Temberlay in surprise.

"Did Meg—"

"She imprisoned me in the earl's apartments. I found that tucked in a book. I assume she hasn't seen it. Did you know of it?"

"I knew he'd sold the horses before his death, but—" He felt fury gather in his chest. "They were the finest horses in England, worth ten times this amount!"

"Did you know of his other business dealings with Charles Wilton?"

"Wilton? No. Marcus asked me to invest in a new scheme he was entering into with several other gentlemen, told me it was a sure thing. My fortune is modest, and my capital was—and is—tied up in navy bills and the three percent consolidated annuities. That's why I couldn't be of more help to Marcus's family after his death."

"My brother was involved in that sure thing as well—" Nicholas began.

The door opened and the dowager duchess entered. She fixed her gaze on Hector and raised her brows.

"I'd hoped you'd brought Marguerite home at last. Do you at least have word of her?"

Hector glanced at Nicholas. "I understand she's still at Wycliffe Park, Your Grace."

She glared at Nicholas. "What have you done?"

Hector bowed. "Perhaps I should be going. The countess will be waiting for news."

"No, stay, Bryant. I wish to discuss things with my

grandmother that concern Meg. I think you should hear them as well," Nicholas said.

"Oh?" the dowager said. "I do hope the news is good. Is Marguerite with child, perhaps?"

"Did you make having a child a condition of our marriage contract? I did not see that clause included," Nicholas said mildly.

The dowager pursed her lips. "Isn't producing legitimate heirs the usual reason for marriage?"

"In time, if the match is fruitful. Meg seems to be under the impression that something dreadful will happen if she does not have a child immediately."

Hector watched the old woman smile. She looked like a cat with prey in her paws, and since Temberlay didn't look afraid in the least, it meant Meg was the prey. He swallowed bile.

"You are the last of the Hartley line. You need an heir, just in case something should happen to you. Marguerite—" She shot a sharp glance at Hector. "—and her family have profited from this match. She has a responsibility."

"What did you threaten her with?" Nicholas asked. "To leave her penniless again? I won't let that happen, Granddame."

The dowager sneered. "You? You have the money I give you and nothing more. I can still cut off every penny, and you will be as poor as your wife. I want an heir. It is your duty. I don't believe that's too much to expect even from you."

"Do you intend to raise my son as you raised David?" Nicholas asked.

"As a decent man, a good duke, rather than a rake and a wastrel? Of course. That child is my hope for the future, and I will not trust you with such a precious thing. You destroy everything you touch!"

"I don't need your money, Granddame," Nicholas said flatly.

"What?" the dowager said, her jaw dropping.

"For the first time in five years, the Temberlay estates are showing a profit. Good management, a few improvements. The dukedom—my dukedom—will be solvent again by the end of the year."

She glared at him. "You make it sound as if your brother mismanaged things. If it hadn't been for you—"

"We both know that isn't true," Nicholas said.

She raised her chin. "I can still destroy you. If you refuse to give me a child, I shall expose what I know, ruin the Lyntons, and they will never rise from the disgrace!"

"What can you possibly know?" Hector dared to ask. "There is nothing—"

The old lady glared at him. "Your stepbrother didn't die accidentally, did he?"

Hector felt his skin heat. "I understand he fell from a horse . . ."

She looked smug. "Nonsense. He hanged himself when he sold his pretty horses. He took the coward's way out and left his family to face his shame."

Hector felt his guts turn to water.

The old harridan cackled. "You didn't know? Even you? It was in the doctor's report, plain as day. I can direct you to him if you'd like to speak to him yourself. For a small fee he's happy to tell what he knows of the matter."

Hector stared at her, too stunned to speak.

She swung her obsidian eyes on Nicholas. "You don't look surprised. I assume you know, then. Did she tell you, beg you to make me keep my silence?"

Temberlay knew? That meant Meg knew. Hector shut his eyes. He didn't want to think of what that meant. He was certain Flora had no idea. It would kill her to hear that Marcus had taken his own life, left her alone and destitute.

"Yes, I know the truth," Nicholas said calmly. "And if you say one word about it, I will tell the world how David died, Granddame."

Hector gaped. Another secret? He'd heard the last duke's death was an accident as well, a broken wheel on a carriage. A bead of sweat crawled down his face, and he mopped it away. He had feared Meg would be marrying into perpetual scandal and misery, but not like this.

"You wouldn't dare!" the dowager said, and thumped her stick on the ground. "It's your fault, your sins that killed him! You took money, invested badly, and the scandal with the Leighton chit—"

"It had nothing to do with Julia. David died in a duel with three men."

Hector gaped again, and she made a strangled sound.

Nicholas's eyes flicked to Hector. He blinked. "The men involved lied to him, cheated him, used my name to do it. You could easily have discovered that, if you wanted to, Granddame. You found out about Lord Wycliffe easily enough."

The dowager paled. "You wouldn't expose such a secret. Think of the scandal!"

Nicholas smiled, and crossed to pull the bell. "Indeed. It would be devastating to you and to David. I believe it would exonerate me of a number of imagined crimes if the truth came out. You wouldn't want that, would you, Granddame? That would make David—"

"No!" she croaked. "I will never believe that!"

"Then you will leave Wycliffe's ghost at peace as well."

Gardiner entered. "Tea for the dowager, if you please, and sherry," Nicholas ordered. When the butler had gone, he turned back to her.

"I thank you for Marguerite. She will make a fine duchess, and a good wife, and in time and with luck, an excellent mother, but not on your terms. I won't have three people in my marriage bed."

The dowager glared up at her grandson with such malevolent hatred that Hector shivered.

"Care to join me in the library, Bryant? I believe we have further matters to discuss. We'll leave you to your tea, Granddame."

Hector bowed stiffly to the old lady, but her face remained cold and impassive. She didn't acknowledge him. He followed Temberlay down the hall to the library.

The dowager took her tea up to her study. This wasn't over. She wasn't ready to retire to the dower house at Temberlay and live out her dotage while Nicholas ran the duchy into the ground again. If it was making a profit, surely it was due to her money, her influence. It had nothing to do with him. He was the second son, the spare. He had no idea how to run the vast Temberlay holdings.

She had loved David, spent her life training him, molding him into everything a duke should be. He depended on her, needed her, trusted her. *Were* there things she didn't know?

Impossible.

She stared at the bloodstain on the rug, the place where David had died in her arms.

It's all Nicholas's fault.

Nicholas had been in Spain, at war, David had taken large amounts of money out of the estate. Dodd had shown her. He hadn't known where the funds had gone, but she knew. He must have sent it all to Nicholas. There were surely as many harlots in Spain as England, as many men to gamble with. She had heard rumors that he'd been careless enough to get himself captured by the enemy, not once, but twice. David had probably paid to ransom his brother.

He should have left Nicholas to rot in prison.

She could no longer control Nicholas, that was clear. She'd never been able to control him. She thought she had him when he agreed to marry the Lynton girl sight unseen. But he no longer needed her money, and he would never ask her for advice.

She sipped her tea. She still had Marguerite.

"When the cat's away, who knows what the mice get up to?" she murmured, and smiled.

Chapter 52

"Is it true? About Marcus's death?"

Nicholas nodded, and watched Hector Bryant run a hand through his hair. "And Meg? Meg knew? She told you?"

"John Ramsbottom did."

Hector sank into a chair, and got up again. "She didn't even tell me. She handled even that on her own. I wasn't close to my brother. I didn't agree with his philosophies. But Meg—my God, she was barely nineteen! How did she endure that?"

Hector scanned the bill of sale again. "Arabella was her mare. She was the one thing that gave Meg pleasure," he said. "Marcus didn't deserve a daughter as fine as Meg. I hope you understand how very fortunate you are that she decided to take Rose's place, Temberlay."

"I'm beginning to."

"If the truth comes out, it will destroy Flora," Hector said, pacing the rug.

"Why do you think Meg drugged me, kidnapped me, and dragged me off to make me do her bidding? She's protecting everyone but herself."

"Shall I apologize on her behalf?" Hector asked. "You

removed yourself from the situation quickly enough. May I ask what you said to her?"

"I invited her to return to London with me, but it's probably better that she isn't here. I intend to deal with Wilton and Howard first. It's time someone took care of things for her."

Hector swallowed. "I'd hate to be the man who crossed you, Temberlay. I almost—only almost, mind you—pity Wilton and Howard. Who was the third man involved in the duel?"

"Wycliffe," Nicholas said.

Hector gaped. "How is that possible?" he whispered. "Marcus was a moral crusader, a fool, but he wasn't a killer. He didn't believe in duels."

"He deloped. Wilton and Howard delivered the killing blows."

"Over horses?" Hector said.

"Over money and lies."

"What can I do to help?" Hector asked.

Nicholas looked at the dapper, middle-aged lord. He was of small stature, medium weight, and kind, not ruthless. "I want to do what I can now, for Meg's sake," Hector said. "For Flora, and for Marcus. I should have been there to protect them. I would have been if I'd known." He drew himself up to full height. "I know now."

"A duel," Nicholas said. "After I do to them what they've done to us—take away what they love most."

Chapter 53

∽◦◦◦∾

"There's mail for you, Meg," Amy said, bringing several letters into the library where Meg was reading to Minnie and Lily. "And no, before you ask, there isn't one from Nick. They're all from the dowager."

Meg gritted her teeth. The old harridan had been inundating her with daily deliveries of the latest scandal sheets, London newspapers, and letters filled with gossip about Nicholas.

She read the newspapers, since Napoleon had escaped from the island of Elba and was once again gathering an army, but avoided the society news.

Amy waved a scandal sheet that showed Nicholas with a dozen of the Season's prettiest debutantes on his arms, grinning lustfully above a caption that read "Fresh Spring Blossoms."

Other notes linked him with several actresses, and one very notorious widow. There was a drawing of Angelique Encore wearing Nicholas on one arm and a magnificent diamond bracelet on the other, with the words, "Will the famous sapphires be next?"

The dowager wrote emphatic letters insisting that Meg

must return to London at once. She would have to go eventually. When her pride healed.

She hid her hot cheeks behind the newspaper, pretended to read it.

She had scrubbed Nicholas's presence out of the house. She hadn't heard a word from him directly. She found one of Nicholas's shirts that Mr. Partridge had left behind in his haste to return to the conveniences and comforts of London, and slept with it under her pillow. The scent of his skin rose around her like a ghost, tormenting her.

She was all too aware that time was running out.

She found a dusty pile of old London papers in her father's study, and searched them for old news of the war, and of Nicholas. He was a hero indeed. How sheltered her life had been. Her father's philosophy had been worse than wrong. A wife should be a partner, a helpmeet to her husband, not a mere ornament. She searched out the books on French, history, and science and set about giving her sisters a proper education.

One morning a notice in the newspaper caught her eye, advertising the auction of several horses, to take place in London within the week. Out of habit she looked for her father's hot bloods on the list.

"Look, it's a picture of Rose!" Lily interrupted, putting aside her history lesson to point at one of the scandal sheets.

Meg peered around the newspaper.

Amy took it. "Why, so it is! She looks radiant, doesn't she?"

Her mother had sent word that Rose was safe, happily married, and living in Scotland. "Since when do the scandal sheets report social news from Scotland?" Meg asked.

"Didn't you read your mother's latest letter? Rose is

in London. Her husband has gone to sea, and she's come south to visit."

Meg put her nose back in the newspaper. She scanned the list. "Arabella's Glory."

Her heart stopped as she read the name of the foal. She hadn't seen her mare or the foal since the day her father had sold them.

"Look, Rose was at a party with Nick!" Minnie cried, waving another drawing.

Meg's stomach clenched as she looked at the drawing. Rose was gazing adoringly up at Nicholas—*her* Nicholas—wearing a fetching smile and a very low bodice. Nicholas was smiling back at her, that seductive, charming devil's grin of his. "Would a wife by any other name smell as sweet?" the caption read. The delectable Mrs. Winters was described as his latest companion in another drawing, and she appeared with him in yet another caricature as "A Rose Without a Thorn."

Meg snatched them all out of her little sisters' hands. "Girls, go into the kitchen and get some tarts."

"He wouldn't dare," Meg muttered to Amy when they were gone. "*She* wouldn't dare! Angelique Encore is one thing, but Rose is my own sister! She's *married*!"

"So is he. To you," Amy said. "It might all be quite innocent, you know."

"I don't care," Meg said.

"Yes, you do."

She left the room and swept up the stairs. Amy followed her.

Meg stopped on the stairs and spun to face the housekeeper. "How dare he take advantage of someone as thickheaded as Rose? Doesn't she see it's all an act, that he is only interested in—?"

She couldn't say it. She continued on and Amy hurried

after her. "And what's that, Lady High and Mighty? If you were there, she wouldn't stand a chance. I saw how he looked at you, and you looked at him!"

Meg entered her own room and dragged a valise out of the wardrobe. "Don't be ridiculous, Amy. He does not want me. I must find a way to live my own life. Once I've produced an heir, of course." There was always that, and the dowager's threats to consider before she could decide how to live with Nicholas, or without him.

Amy began folding gowns to put into the bag. "You're wrong. He asked John to bring you back to him. John's been packed to go for a fortnight, waiting on you."

Meg added a handful of stockings, shifts, and nightgowns. "He hasn't even written!"

She crossed to the desk and found a sheet of paper in her mother's stationery, wrote a note, folded it, and sealed it.

"He has his pride," Amy said mildly. "And don't tell me you don't want him. You're as thin as a rail. You don't eat, you don't sleep. It's about time you did something about it. Are you ready to go?"

Meg tucked the letter into her pocket and looked around the room. She hadn't intended to go back to London today, or even been aware that she'd been packing to do so, but it couldn't wait any longer.

"Yes," she said.

Amy reached under the pillow and pulled out the shirt. "Then you won't want to forget this," she said, and smiled knowingly.

Meg's skin heated. She snatched the shirt. "Please ask John to get the coach ready," she said with all the dignity a duchess could muster.

Amy grinned. "It's been ready for days. You need only get in it and go back to Nicholas. If you take my advice, you'll use your heart this once, lass, not your head. That'll get you what you want." She brushed her fingers over Meg's cheek. "You deserve to be happy."

Meg lifted her chin. "I'm not going to him."

"Then what are you going to do?" Amy asked, her hands on her hips.

"I'm going to buy a horse."

"What about Nicholas, and Rose?"

Meg turned to go. "I will see what the situation calls for."

Chapter 54

Nicholas watched Augustus Howard gambling and losing.

"I hear that Howard's afraid of losing his pretty young wife," Sebastian said, following the direction of his friend's gaze. "He promised her a fortune, a lavish and luxurious life, and other than the necklace he gave her as a wedding present, he has failed to present her with anything else since. Augustus needs to win tonight."

The old man was sweating as he placed his bets. He could barely conceal his panic when he lost. Nicholas had no doubt the money to woo the lovely and very young Lady Claire had come from cheating David, and had just as quickly been gambled away again.

"Do you know Daniel Napier?" Sebastian asked. "He's a baron's son from Cheshire. Hasn't got a farthing. I hear Claire was set to marry him when Augustus made her father a rich offer for her. Delphine and Eleanor think it's romantic. Napier was brokenhearted when she married, and tried to join the army, but it was too late. The war ended. I suppose he'll have better luck now Napoleon has escaped and is back to terrify Europe once more."

Nicholas watched Howard lose another hand. He

mopped his brow and pasted on a wan smile as he wrote out yet another vowel. The man was at the lowest point he could reach.

Nicholas strode forward, and Howard looked up and saw him coming. He watched fear kindle in his eyes, and guilt. He took a step backward, and cried out as Nicholas slapped him with his glove.

"Dawn tomorrow," he muttered.

Sebastian grabbed his arm. "What the devil are you doing, Nick, what's the challenge?"

"Honor," Nicholas said, his eyes boring into Augustus's as he held a trembling hand to his slapped cheek and cowered. "And lies, and murder."

The crowd muttered in surprise. Those holding Howard's vowels moved in. The old roué blanched, and Nicholas turned away.

"I'll stand as your second," Sebastian said, scrambling after him.

"Agreed," Nicholas said. "Excuse me, Seb, but I've another errand to see to."

"**W**ilton doesn't race the Wycliffe Arabian?" Nicholas asked Hector at the racetrack, as they watched one of Lord Wilton's horses lose. The animal was high-strung and skittish, and poorly trained. Definitely not one of the hot bloods from Wycliffe's stable.

"I was able to find out that he lost the Arabian some time ago to Lord Eldridge," Hector noted. They watched Wilton make good on his losses with a handful of vowels and a sick smile. "Looks like he'll have to sell the rest of his stable too."

"What do you know of Wilton's wife?" Nicholas asked as Wilton walked toward them.

"Even less than I know about his horses. They are estranged, and she stays in the country," Hector said. "What of *your* wife, Temberlay? Have you heard from Meg? It's been a fortnight."

"She's safer in the country. Once this business is sorted out, I'll go and fetch her."

Wilton frowned as Nicholas stepped into his path.

"Temberlay," he said, looking smug, still imagining Nicholas didn't know.

He flinched as Nicholas issued the challenge, the glove cracking against his face. "How dare you!" he cried.

"No, Wilton, how dare you? But I suppose we'll find out at dawn tomorrow. Have your second see Lord Bryant."

Chapter 55

Charles Wilton looked at the suspicion in the eyes of the gentlemen around him as they watched Temberlay's retreating back. Wilton felt his gorge rise and swallowed hard, tried to still the panic in his breast. Nicholas Temberlay was an officer, a crack shot, and a far better swordsman than his brother.

There was a very good chance Charles would die tomorrow.

If he showed up.

He got into his coach and ordered his coachman home. He had estates all over the country. He'd leave London and go to ground. He made a mental list of valuables to take with him, now, in a hurry. He cursed Temberlay as he climbed the steps of his house. Within hours, men would come to demand he honor his vowels, pay his debts. He didn't even have time to sell the last of his wife's jewels, or the few works of art that remained.

He was ruined.

And Temberlay, the man he'd painted as a villain, as dishonorable, had honor after all.

He went into his study and poured a drink, quaffed it at a gulp, and poured another. His butler entered the room behind him and cleared his throat, and Charles turned on him.

"What do you want?"

The man held out a letter on a tray. "This just arrived, my lord."

Charles took it. The cream envelope bore the Wycliffe crest. What the devil could Wycliffe's widow want with him? Did she mean to challenge him as well, or had her husband's shade risen from the grave to take his revenge?

He broke the seal and read it. Then he read it again, and smiled.

It wasn't from the Countess of Wycliffe.

It was from Temberlay's lovely duchess.

Chapter 56

It was nearly midnight when Meg arrived at Bryant House. Her mother was attending a party, and was not at home, but Hector was in his study.

"Surprise!" she said with brittle brightness.

He embraced her, then held her at arm's length to look at her.

"You look tired," he said. "Are you on your way to Hartley Place?"

"If you'll have me, I'd like to stay here for a day or two," she said. "I've only come to run an errand."

"Perhaps that's a good idea. You can visit with your mother."

He looked away, refused to meet her eyes, and Meg's heart lurched, suspecting the worst.

"She must be delighted Rose is back, and safe," she said, forcing a light tone. "Though she's hardly written a word about what Rose is doing in Town. Have they been busy?"

He led her into the sitting room. "Your mother is a whirlwind of activity. If you're hoping for even a brief word, you'll have to catch her between social engagements. You've found me on one of my rare evenings at home. Your mother usually insists I accompany her to whatever party she's attending, but I begged off with a headache tonight. I sent her out with Rose and her relations."

"Then I've come at a bad time," Meg said, biting her lip.

Hector smiled. "Not at all. I haven't really got a headache. I just couldn't bear to attend one more soiree. *That* gives me a headache. I simply anticipated it a little—and I have an early appointment in the morning."

"Do you?" She imagined Flora dragging him to a breakfast rout at noon. "Tell me all the latest gossip. I feel like I've been rusticating in the country forever," Meg said, but he rose to pull the bell.

"Gossip is more your mother's department, but I can see you get a meal. You look as if a strong wind could blow you away. We can talk while you eat, and you can tell me why you've chosen to arrive in the dead of night."

She studied her fingertips, and her wedding ring. "I'm here for two reasons, actually. I lied, Hector—I hear plenty of news from Town. The dowager sends me the *London Times* and the scandal sheets, so I know every *on dit* and wicked story about Nicholas."

"And?" he prompted.

"Is he having an affair with Rose?" She braced herself for the answer.

Hector's brows shot up. "What? Why on earth would you think that?"

"The scandal sheets, the dowager—it's been more than hinted at."

He frowned. "Nicholas has been rather busy of late. I suppose he may have met Rose through your mother, but I doubt she knows him well. Those infernal relations of Edward's keep Rose under close watch. She's with child, so they don't allow her to stray very far. Certainly not *that* far."

"Then what has he been so busy with?" she asked. He looked away.

"You're tired, my dear," Hector said. "Why don't you get a good night's rest, and we'll talk tomorrow."

She looked at him sharply. "Don't brush me off, Hector. You're the one person I can trust to be honest with me."

"Then I am certain Rose is not having an affair with Nicholas."

"Have you seen him?"

"We attended the races yesterday." He shifted his gaze to the floor.

Meg felt suspicion rise. She felt tears prick behind her eyes, even as anger flared, hot and thick. "Then I assume there's another reason why he has not written?"

He took her hands with a soft sound of sympathy. "Meg, you have nothing to worry about. He's a good man. You must trust him. I can't tell you any more than that. You've been brave, but you're not on guard anymore. It's time to let him take care of things for you." He led her toward the stairs.

"What does that mean?" she asked.

He kissed her forehead without replying. "Go and get some rest."

She climbed the stairs, her feet like lead, even more uncertain now.

"Meg?"

She turned to look at her godfather, standing at the bottom of the steps.

"You said you came for two reasons. What's the second?"

She smiled wanly. "Arabella's Glory has come up for sale. I came to buy him back."

He paled. "You what? Have you spoken to Nicholas about this?"

"No. Arabella was my horse. I can manage this on my own."

"Who is selling the foal?" he asked, his face tight.

"Lord Charles Wilton. Do you know him?"

He gripped the banister. "Unfortunately I do. Meg, stay away from him. Let Nicholas handle this for you. You can't imagine—" He swallowed. "I can't say more than that now. We'll talk tomorrow, find a way . . ."

Hadn't she proven she could manage perfectly well on her own in the past year? He made it sound like there was something sinister about simply buying a horse.

"Yes, tomorrow," she said vaguely and turned to go up.

By the time they spoke again, the deal would be done.

Chapter 57

There was a letter from Stephen Ives waiting for him. Nicholas read it, and stared out the window, not seeing the green square, or the budding trees. He saw the dry Spanish hills, the lines of red-coated soldiers, and heard the beat of distant drums as a French column came into view, marched closer.

Napoleon was once again threatening the peace of Europe. The armies of Britain, Prussia, and Russia were gathering in Brussels to meet the threat. They needed intelligence officers to find out just what Napoleon intended to do. Stephen had recommended Nicholas, the best spy he knew.

It was tempting. Nicholas had been certain in war, good at his job. He shut his eyes. But he had responsibilities and duties here. Men without heirs did not go to war. Nor did someone about to fight a pair of duels within the hour make such grand plans, though he fully expected to survive the encounters.

Once it was all over, he was going to Wycliffe to bring his wife home.

He picked up his pen and stared at the blank paper, at the ducal crest at the top of the page. His crest. He wrote his refusal of the commission.

Chapter 58

The morning mist hid the illicit activities of gentlemen intent on proving their honor in Hyde Park. Somber figures gathered under the trees, anonymous in dark cloaks, their hats pulled low over their faces, sinister against the silver fog.

Nicholas watched a coach pull up. Had Wilton and Howard chosen to arrive together?

Howard leaped from the coach almost before it had stopped moving, hurried over the grass.

"You took her!" he screamed. "Where is my wife, you devil?"

Sebastian looked at Nicholas. "Did you?"

"No," Nicholas said.

"Claire is gone. What have you done with her?" Howard sobbed, and gripped Nicholas's lapels. His eyes were wild and bloodshot, desperate. He pulled a dueling pistol out of his belt and waved it. "Tell me!"

"If you have—interfered—with His Lordship's wife, Your Grace, it changes this affair completely," Howard's second said.

"He hasn't seen Lady Claire," Sebastian replied in his best lord-of-the-manor tone. "Perhaps she ran off with

Daniel Napier after all. It was common knowledge she was unhappy."

"Common to whom?" Howard cried, pointing the pistol at Sebastian.

"Everyone with eyes." Sebastian shrugged. Augustus sagged to the grass, blubbering. Nicholas stepped forward and took the gun before Howard shot somebody, and gave it to his second.

The gentleman looked uncomfortable. Augustus resisted all attempts to raise him to his feet. The gathered group looked at him with a mixture of pity and disgust.

"Are you still going to shoot him?" Sebastian asked.

"No." He'd lost what mattered most, more than his life. That was revenge enough.

Another coach pulled up.

"What the devil? We've got quite a crowd," Sebastian said as Hector Bryant hurried across the grass.

"Wilton's late," Nicholas told Hector.

Sebastian gaped. "You challenged Wilton as well?"

"Temberlay, he isn't coming. I think Meg is with him," Hector said, his face pale.

"Does anyone know where their wife is?" Sebastian quipped.

Nicholas's stomach rose. "Meg is at Wycliffe," he said, but Hector shook his head, his eyes frantic. "She arrived at Bryant House last night. Wilton is selling one of Wycliffe's hot bloods. She came to buy it back. I told her to wait, told her to speak to you, but she was gone this morning. She doesn't know about the duel. She doesn't know about Wilton at all!"

"Where did she go?" Nicholas asked, taking his coat from Sebastian, shrugging into it. He took the dueling pistol and tucked it into his belt.

"I don't know. She said there's an auction today. Tatter-sall's perhaps? It's no place for a lady, but that won't stop Meg," Hector babbled, distraught.

"I'll find her." Nicholas vaulted onto Hannibal's back and kicked him to a gallop.

Chapter 59

"What a stroke of luck finding the foal for sale," John said as he handed Meg down from the coach. "It'll be good to have him back at Wycliffe where he belongs. Any chance the others are for sale?"

Meg smiled at him. "Anything is for sale at the right price, John. I would love to get all three of them back again. Perhaps if Lord Wilton bought Arabella and the Arabian as well, we can come to an agreement. I handled the sale of our paintings and furnishings and silver. I can do this too."

"I don't think buying hot-blood horses is the same, Meg," he began, but she grasped his arm and pointed.

"There he is!"

Most of the paddocks of the auction house were filled with carriage horses, matched teams, and leggy colts. Only Arabella's Glory had a pen of his own.

He'd grown, John saw, and bore the fine lines of both his dam and his sire. His ears pricked as they approached him. Meg ignored the mud and the stares of the gentlemen around her, but John didn't. No one should be looking at Meg that way but Nick. She'd been evasive when he'd asked if her husband was coming with them today.

"You seem to be the only lady here," John said, moving closer to her.

She stroked the horse's velvet nose with a cry of joy that warmed his heart. He hadn't seen her this happy since the night the foal was born.

"Ladies do not usually come to horse sales," a smooth voice said. "But Her Grace is a lovely flower among the usual thorns of this place, and most welcome."

He bowed over her hand. "Lord Charles Wilton. I don't believe we've had the pleasure of an introduction."

The man was whip-thin, dark and dangerous, and he was staring straight down Meg's bodice. He held her hand far longer than necessary in John's opinion. "D'you know her husband, perhaps, the Duke of Temberlay?" he asked.

Lord Wilton's eyes narrowed. "I can escort you from here, Your Grace. Your servant would no doubt be more comfortable with the other stable hands in the barn."

He was far more than a stable hand, but Meg didn't bother to correct the gentleman. Instead, she smiled at the gent. It was the kind of smile Rose bestowed on besotted lads. He winced as she tilted her head like a true Lynton coquette. John scowled and stepped closer to her.

"I was delighted to see Arabella's Glory listed in the sale today, my lord. I have not seen him since my father sold him a year ago."

"Fine lines to him. Good breeding," Wilton said, barely glancing at the colt, his eyes still on Meg.

"Do you, by chance, know of his dam, Arabella, or his sire, the Wycliffe Arabian?"

His gaze slid sideways, like a snake slithering over smooth ground, John thought. He smiled like a snake too, without any warmth at all. There was something calculating about him that John didn't like. He felt sure Nick wouldn't like him either.

"Why, I hear of them constantly—my stable master sends me reports on a weekly basis. They are at my stud farm."

"Oh," Meg breathed, leaning toward him. John laid a hand on her shoulder, pulled her back.

Lord Wilton was still holding on to her hand, and John plucked it free. "Let's start with the foal. How much d'you want for him?"

Wilton frowned, kept his eyes on Meg. "This is not the kind of negotiation one conducts with stable hands, Your Grace. It is usually a matter between gentlemen, or in this case, people of breeding."

"I'm the duchess's horse master, among other things." John gave his bona fides to the man, towering over him.

Meg sent him a sharp look, then turned back to Wilton. "John helped birth this foal," she said. "He knows horses as well as my father did. Did you know my father, the late Earl of Wycliffe?"

The man reddened. "I . . ." He hesitated. "Actually, the business of purchasing Wycliffe's horses was handled by my man of affairs."

"Consider me Her Grace's man of affairs, then, in His Grace's absence," John said.

Wilton shifted his gaze from Meg to John and back, obviously waiting for Meg to rebuke her servant. When she didn't, he stepped back with a sigh.

"I must tell you that there have been a number of offers for Arabella's Glory, and for the other Wycliffe hot bloods."

"I will double the highest bid!"

"Meg!" John warned. "Shouldn't Nick—"

She shot him a look of furious desperation. "Any price, John."

He would have told her she couldn't buy back the past,

could only go forward in life, should walk away, talk to Nick, but Wilton spoke first.

"Done. My man is in the stable offices, over there." He waved John toward a distant building. "You may make arrangements with him."

John didn't want to leave her alone with the shifty-looking lord, but she looked at him expectantly, her brows raised, making it a command. There was nothing he could do but go. She turned her attention back to Wilton immediately.

"Might we discuss Arabella and the Arabian, Your Lordship? Would it be possible to purchase them as well?"

He smiled at her. "Something might be arranged, my dear duchess. But only if you call me Charles."

"Charles," John growled as he made his way across the muddy field, out of earshot. It would serve Meg right if Nick turned her over his knee for this.

Charles Wilton looked at Temberlay's wife. She was a beauty, and though she was doing her best to charm him, she only had eyes for the damned foal.

"Would you, perhaps, like to come see the horses?" he asked. "My farm is nearby. We could be there in time for luncheon, and back in London for tea if we left now."

"Well, I hadn't planned—" she began, and shot a glance toward her servant, who was out of earshot, but still throwing baleful glances over his massive shoulders at Charles as he went to arrange payment.

"I fully understand if you have unassailable plans to see your modiste or take tea with friends. I must go either way. There is another gentleman coming to see the horses this very afternoon, you see. He is also quite interested in purchasing them," he pressed.

She bit her lush lower lip in dismay. Did Temberlay enjoy kissing his wife? he wondered. Would he want her after she'd been with another man? He shivered. "This is going to be a pleasure," he murmured.

"Pardon?" she asked, and he realized he'd spoken aloud.

He snapped his fingers and a groom rushed over.

"Tell—" He glanced at the lovely duchess with his brows raised, waiting for her decision.

She raised her chin. "Tell John Ramsbottom, my stable master, to take the foal and the coach home. I will be lunching with Lord Wilton at—?"

She was waiting for the name of his estate. "Orion," he said smoothly. Let them tell Temberlay that when he came for his wife.

"Orion," she repeated, smiling, relaxing, and Wilton watched the man march gingerly across the muddy field to deliver the message. Could it have been any easier?

He took her hand and set it on his sleeve. "Shall we go?" he asked.

She smiled and let him lead the way.

Nicholas arrived at the auction house to find John Ramsbottom holding one of the groom's two feet off the ground and threatening to throttle him. Meg was nowhere to be seen.

He grabbed the big man's arm. The fury in his eyes faded instantly, and he dropped the groom like a doll and grinned. "Nick! It's good to see you."

"John, where's Meg?"

His frown returned. "She bought a horse, that foal there, from a lord named Wilton. He told her he had Arabella and the Arabian as well, and she's gone to see 'em, and this dunderhead won't tell me where!" He glared at the groom, who was still staring at John in horror.

"Orange. He said orange," the lad panted. "Or onion, perhaps. I *did* say so."

"But where is it?" John demanded. "You didn't tell me that."

Dread prickled the back of Nicholas's neck. "Orion?" he asked.

The groom rubbed his neck. "Oh, aye, that was it. Sounds like Orange, though. Thought he might mean the inn nearby, called the Coach and Angel. The gentry use it for trysts in the country. Maybe that's where they went."

Nick stopped John's fist before he hit the man.

"D'you know it, Nick?" John asked.

"I'm afraid so," Nicholas said. Would he find her there? She could be anywhere, since *Orion* was the name of the imaginary ship that David and Wycliffe had invested in. It was a message from Wilton. Meg was in trouble, and she probably didn't even realize it.

"Take the coach home, John. I'll see to it." He strode back toward Hannibal.

John caught up with him before he'd gone a dozen steps. "She'd never do anything like what that fool suggested."

"I know," Nicholas said, his teeth clenched. "But Wilton would. Meg is an innocent, like her father, like—" *David, or Julia Leighton.*

"She's smart, Nick. She'll figure it out, come to no harm," John said, but there was worry in his eyes. "Ye'll find her, won't ye?"

He mounted Hannibal. "John, go back to Bryant House and wait for her. Tell Lord Bryant, but don't say anything to the countess."

He kicked Hannibal to a gallop, and headed toward the

ton's favorite illicit trysting spot, and prayed he wouldn't find her there in Wilton's arms.

He'd be obliged to kill Charles Wilton.

And Meg?

He shut his eyes and spurred Hannibal harder. He didn't want to think about that.

Chapter 60

Lord Wilton's high sporting curricle made for a windy ride. Meg held tight to her bonnet as they left London behind and set out on the open road.

"Where did you say your estate was, my lord?" she asked. He had no idea how to handle horses. His hands were hard on the reins, and the horses were suffering.

"Oh, it's not far now. The turn is not more than ten miles ahead."

"I had no idea that it was you who purchased my father's horses," she said, hoping they had not been as mistreated as the cattle that pulled his curricle. Their ears were plastered flat against their manes as he sawed on their mouths.

He snapped the reins against their backs and grinned at her. "Your father's horses were famous. Pity he didn't make it known his daughters were so lovely. You could have had your pick of husbands. God knows, Temberlay has had his pick of enough wives. I'm sure you know the stories."

"Have you raced the Arabian?" Meg said, trying to change the subject.

He ignored her. "There's an inn ahead. I thought we might stop, take luncheon there."

She felt her stomach shift uneasily. "I would prefer to go straight through to—Orion, did you say it was called, my lord?"

"Do call me Charles," he said. "And I will call you Meg. Try to relax and enjoy yourself." He put his hand on her knee and squeezed. "Tell me, does Temberlay have a pet name for you, something he whispers in bed?"

She gasped and tried to shake his hand off, but his grip was like iron. She dug her nails into his flesh, and he let go.

"Now don't be like that," he said. He pulled on the reins and the horses shied, and the curricle swayed. Meg gripped the edge of the seat and held on.

"You should know that Temberlay and I share our wives. Well, at least he had the pleasure of mine. Fathered a child on her, abandoned her, and went off to play soldier."

She felt her skin chill from more than the breeze. Was Lady Wilton the woman in the library?

"You didn't know?" he asked. "It's quite true."

"Take me back to London," she commanded.

"Oh, we've come too far for that. Another hour or two, and it will be my word against yours that I've had the pleasure, so to speak. You may as well enjoy the afternoon. I will feed you well, and do my best to seduce you. Whatever happens, I intend to tell your husband that we—"

Meg grabbed for the reins. "Stop this contraption at once!"

The horses veered over the road in panic.

Wilton cuffed her, making her head ring. "Don't be a damned fool!" He tugged the horses to a stop by the side of the road, and gripped her shoulders, pulled her close, forced a wet mockery of a kiss on her mouth. She twisted away with a cry of disgust.

"Look, I said I'd *try* to seduce you, but if you don't cooperate—"

Meg shoved him away, tried to leap off the carriage, but he grabbed her arm painfully. Her fashionable spencer tore with a shriek. He pinned her beneath him, pressing her backward, his hand on her breasts, his mouth against her neck.

She screamed, and he slapped her and laughed.

"Now, now, this isn't the time to go all missish on me. You're just like your father, aren't you? Bold and full of airs until it comes down to being useful."

She turned her head away from his grip. "What are you talking about?"

"I knew your father rather well. He was a fool!" Surprised, she went limp for an instant, and he shifted. "That's better."

She twisted and clouted him in the mouth, a punch, not a ladylike slap, screaming with rage.

"Damn you!" he said as her wedding ring cut into his lip and blood spurted. He grabbed her collar, and tore at her clothes, ripping the buttons away. She gathered breath to scream again as he pushed her backward, forced his knee between her thighs. He clamped his fist in her hair, and pushed his mouth against hers in a hard, sour kiss as he crushed his body against hers, grunting as he tried to raise her skirts.

She shoved him away, left him with a handful of hair. Her shriek of fury and pain made the horses jerk and dance. Wilton lost his balance, slid off the seat. Meg kicked him, and the toe of her boot caught him hard under the chin.

He stared at her in dull surprise as he flew backward over the high edge of the vehicle. The horses bolted, and she grabbed for the reins, pulled them to a stop. She backed up, found the place where Charles Wilton had landed. He wasn't moving.

She stared down at him for a long moment, trying to pull her clothes together, to still the trembling. She rubbed a hand over her face, felt tears. They were more from anger and shame than injury, though her lip was bleeding, and her jaw hurt. There was a scratch on her shoulder, visible through the hopelessly torn muslin of her gown.

"How dare you?" she began, but he stayed still. Panic gripped her. Had she killed him?

She climbed down and nudged him with her foot, then put a finger against his throat. He was still alive, just unconscious. She turned away and threw up in the ditch.

He stirred, groaning, but she didn't wait. She climbed back into the curricle, and turned the contraption back toward London.

Chapter 61

Nicholas reached the Coach and Angel Inn, but no one had seen Meg or Wilton. A generous bribe still produced no results. A search of stables and private dining rooms also resulted in nothing but threats from the innkeeper and the couples he interrupted.

He rode out of the inn yard, wondering which direction to take. Wilton would want somewhere secluded where Nicholas wouldn't find them too quickly. There were other villages to the west and north, other inns. He could hardly check them all. Nor could he go back and wait, and simply hope that no harm would come to Meg at Wilton's hands. He knew Charles better than that.

He shut his eyes. He'd been a spy in Spain, the man they trusted to find what was impossible to find. Orion. Why would he choose that name?

He'd only just begun to study Wilton. Wilton, on the other hand, was an old hand at harming those Nicholas loved. He rubbed a hand over his face. He couldn't allow his feelings to cloud his judgment.

Orion was a mythical swordsman, and a hunter. Wilton had insisted on swords at the duel with David. He also had an estate east of London that had once been a royal hunt-

ing lodge, the place where he'd banished his wife. What
better place to take Meg, to let her hear Lady Wilton's lies
for herself? He turned Hannibal east.

It was late afternoon when he found her. He was almost
two hours from London when he saw a distant plume of
dust on the road ahead of him. He pulled Hannibal to a
stop and watched it come toward him. It was too fast to
be a farm cart, too small to be the mail coach, or a stage.

His gut clenched, half in dread, half in hope. He took
the pistol from his belt and laid it across the saddle.

He saw the telltale flag of red hair as the curricle drew
closer. She was the vehicle's only occupant, driving Wilton's high-strung bays like a warrior queen. He moved
Hannibal into the middle of the road and waited for her
to reach him.

She pulled the horses to a stop.

His heart climbed into his throat at the sight of her. She'd
been through a battle. Her clothes were torn and stained
with dust and blood. There was a bruise on her cheek,
scratches on her neck. Fear warred with anger in her eyes.

She brushed a long lock of hair out of her eyes with
shaking fingers. One of her gloves was gone too.

"Are you hurt?" he asked, bracing for the worst.

She shut her eyes. "No," she managed the single word
with effort.

"Where's Wilton?" he asked.

She looked at the pistol in his lap. "I left him by the
side of the road. He isn't dead, but he'll have a dreadful
headache when he wakes up."

"I wouldn't have been so kind." He put the pistol away.

Hot blood replaced the pallor in her cheeks. "He told
me he had Papa's horses."

"You might have let me handle it, Maggie."

She raised her chin. "I wanted to do it myself."

"What would you have done to get them back?" he asked harshly. "Would you have allowed Wilton to—" He flicked his eyes over her torn dress.

"Never," she hissed.

"So what do we do now?" he asked. "You're a mess. We could go to the nearest inn, and I could send for your mother—"

"No," she said quickly.

"Then I will take you home."

"Home?" she asked warily.

"Hartley Place."

She nodded. It was her home, as his duchess, and yet he read doubt in her eyes. His gut clenched. She had trusted Wilton over him, chosen to believe every word, every lie from him, though she would not trust him.

He dismounted, tied Hannibal to the back of the curricle, and got up beside her. He took off his coat, put it around her shoulders to cover her torn dress. "You have dust on your face, Duchess," he said, and brushed it away, examining the bruise on her cheek. "You must have fought like a tigress."

She sagged for a moment, lost inside his coat. "If I'd known—"

"You would have, if you'd asked me."

"I don't know what to believe."

"Believe your own eyes, for a start."

She stared at him. "I see smoke and sugared almonds, conjurer's tricks. You tell me what you think I want to hear. What do you tell Rose, and L-Lady Wilton?"

"Ah, so Wilton told you I knew his wife, did he? Actually, I've never met the lady." He looked at her cuts and bruises again. "Damn him. If I'd found him with you, if he'd hurt you, I wouldn't have bothered to call him out."

"And what about my sister? Do you 'know' her? And Angelique Encore, and—all the other women?" She ticked them off on her fingers. "If I keep going, I'll run out of fingers to name them on."

He grabbed her left hand, touched her wedding ring. "That's the only finger that matters, Maggie. "Your sister—" He stopped. *She is the silliest woman I have ever met* hovered on his tongue. Meeting Rose Winters had made him very glad that Meg had taken her sister's place. He wondered how any man could stand in a room with both sisters and prefer Rose. He could never fall in love with a woman like Rose. "I—" he started, but his tongue glued itself to his tonsils.

He snapped the reins, and the curricle moved forward. In the short weeks of their marriage, he'd come to admire his wife as much as he desired her. He had never loved a woman before. If this was what it felt like, it was damned unpleasant. He'd rather take a bullet.

She sat up straight as they entered London, the perfect duchess, out for a drive with nothing amiss, ignoring the curious eyes that followed them through Mayfair. Torn gowns might have been the new fashion, worn with poise and grace, but her knuckles were white as she clenched her hands in her lap.

"If I'm the Devil Duke, surely you will now be forever known as the Disheveled Duchess," he murmured.

She looked at him with tears in her eyes. "What do we do now?" she asked.

"A bath, perhaps, a glass of brandy, a meal. And then—" He'd tell her, or try to, what he felt.

He felt panic creep up his spine. What if she didn't feel the same?

They'd reached Hartley Place and Gardiner was rushing down the steps at the sight of her. "Your Grace!" he cried, ruffled for once.

"I'm all right, Gardiner. Just a fall." She let him help her out of the curricle.

Gardiner was issuing orders to summon her maid, to send for the doctor, and to fetch hot water.

Nicholas's staff loved her as much as he did. She was in good hands. He willed her to look back at him as they bore her up the steps, but she didn't. He climbed down and untied Hannibal, and handed the reins to a waiting groom. "See Hannibal is rubbed down," he said. He went into the library to write a note to Hector to let him know Meg was safe.

Chapter 62

Meg hid in the bath until her fingers pruned, cursing her foolishness. She hadn't thought she was so gullible. She had wanted to prove to him that she didn't need him.

But she did.

He had been there, on the road, a hero on a white horse, his eyes filled with concern, and she had wanted to fall into his arms and cry, let him comfort her.

But she was the strong one. There had been no one to cosset her when her father died, or when Rose ran away. She was the brave one, forever calm, in control.

She didn't feel in control now. She didn't want to believe what Charles Wilton had told her, but she'd seen the woman in the library, heard her speak of her child and Nicholas's generosity. She'd seen the evasive look in Hector's eyes when she asked him what her husband had been up to.

She loved him. The pain she felt went beyond jealousy or fear of the dowager. She would not trick him, or beg him. She had lived with the crumbs of her father's affection while he lavished his attention on her sisters. It was never enough.

Tomorrow, after she'd slept, and she could say it without crying, she would set him free, retire to Wycliffe, let him live the life he wished. She would comfort and protect her family as best she could.

She looked at herself in the mirror. She had a scratch on her shoulder, a bruise on her cheek, a cut on her lip, but the worst hurts were on the inside, the pain of a broken heart, the sting of her own stupidity.

His coat still lay on the bed, and she crossed and picked it up, held it to her face, breathed in the familiar scent of him. Now, more than ever, she had to be brave.

Nicholas stared down at the envelope on the desk, addressed to British army headquarters in Brussels. It should have gone out with the post, but it had somehow been forgotten. He crossed to the bell, intending to get Gardiner to send it now, but he hesitated.

His time in Spain was the last time anything had made sense. He was a respected officer, trusted by his fellow officers and men. He was only "devil" to the enemy.

As a boy, he had learned that tales of his misbehavior made his brother smile. Granddame kept her favorite grandson on a short, tight leash of dull duty and discipline. David lived through Nicholas. The stories of his misadventures made David smile, and it gave Nicholas perverse pleasure that Granddame hated every scandalous, shocking, naughty thing he did. But she held up his sins to David like a corpse in a gibbet, a warning that he must never, ever stray from ducal perfection. Nicholas had never bothered to tell either of them that the tales about him were only half true at best.

He got even further out of the habit of explaining himself in the army. His missions had been secret.

And now, with Meg, he had no idea where to begin.

Should he admit that he was in love with her? How could she love him if she believed him guilty of every sin he was accused of? How long before she sought the comfort of a man like Stephen Ives, or worse, someone like Wilton?

He couldn't bear that.

She turned to flame every time he touched her, but desire burned out eventually. Lust alone did not make a relationship. And love . . . unreciprocated, it was the worst agony on earth. Revenge too had proven a hollow victory. It brought nothing back. It simply destroyed more lives.

Meg would make a wonderful mother. She protected her family like a tigress, wouldn't let any harm come to them. He could give her that at least, or try.

He tossed the letter into the fireplace and wrote another.

Chapter 63

Meg watched the long strokes of the brush as Anna combed her hair.

The dowager had sent a new pile of scandal sheets to her rooms that afternoon, and Meg had burned them without looking. Other images of her husband burned in her mind as the fire devoured the paper—Nicholas at the altar on their wedding day, Nicholas in Angelique Encore's arms, Nicholas's face as he rode away from her at Wycliffe, and riding toward her on Hannibal on the London road.

She had gambled and lost. She'd married him to save her family, to give them a future. What of her future? If she were honest, she'd married him because she'd wanted love, children, and a home of her own, a family that would adore her as much as she did them, and a man who looked at her with the kind of admiration that Rose got, or Flora had seen in her husband's eyes.

"May I?"

She opened her eyes. She hadn't heard him enter the room. He took the brush from Anna, and took up where the maid had left off.

"You have beautiful hair," he said softly. He stroked

his hand over it in a slow, sensuous caress, and raised a lock of it to his lips, meeting her eyes in the glass.

"I don't want any other woman, Meg."

She swallowed the knot in her throat. "I thought, that is, I was afraid—"

He put the brush down on the table. "It doesn't matter now."

She could feel the warmth of his body, smell the scent of his soap.

She saw the desire in his eyes, the sadness. He touched her face, and she pressed her cheek into his palm and shut her eyes.

"I am sorry," she said. "For everything. More than you can know."

She rose and laid her cheek on his chest. His arms came around her, held her, and she felt safe next to the sound of his heart.

"Nicholas—"

He put a finger against her lips. "I know. I'm not the man you imagined, the one from the scandal sheets."

She looked up at him. "No. You're much . . ." She hesitated.

"Worse?" he joked.

"No, not at all," she said, her voice husky. "Different." Where was her courage now? Her boldness had deserted her when she needed it most.

He rested his chin on the top of her head. "The chances of this match succeeding came with very long odds, I'm afraid."

She curled her fingers against his shirtfront, her heart rising in her throat. Would he say good-bye now, walk away? He stroked her back through the silk of her robe.

"Perhaps if Rose had stayed . . ." She couldn't bear to think of that. This man belonged to her. And yet he did not.

"Meeting your sister made me glad fate took her in a different direction," he said dryly. He looked down into her eyes, his own dark with desire, and stroked her lower lip with his thumb. He lowered his face to hers. "Perhaps we've done enough talking for tonight," he whispered against her lips.

His kiss was gentle, teasing, seductive.

She stood on tiptoe, deepened the kiss as she slid her hands up and clasped them behind his neck.

He undressed her, untying the sash of her dressing gown, pushing it off her shoulders to drop at her feet. He unbuttoned her high-necked nightgown, let it fall too, leaving her naked before him.

"So beautiful," he murmured. "Wife."

She fumbled at the buttons of his shirt, caressed the hard warmth of his muscles. His hands were on her hips, pulling her against the jut of his erection. She fumbled with the flies of his breeches, wanting his flesh against hers, no barriers between them.

When they were both naked, she rubbed her body against his, reveling in the heat, the sensation of his flesh on hers. There were no titles, no others, just Meg and Nick.

He carried her to bed, their lips still joined, and laid her down, sinking into the mattress with her.

"You're beautiful," he told her again.

She felt beautiful. He touched her as if she were the most enticing woman on earth, caressing her limbs, kissing her lips, her breasts, her hips, her legs.

She ran her hand over his body, memorizing every inch. He caressed the curls between her thighs, dipped between, stroked her until she cried out, and slid into her body as if they were old hands at this, knew each other well. She welcomed him, wrapped her legs around his hips, savored the sensation of their two bodies joined, lost in the terrible sweetness, her eyes on his as he made love to her. If she never experienced this again, she had this night, this moment.

She gripped his shoulders, held on as he increased his pace, heightening the pleasure, until they both cried out. She felt tears sting as he poured himself into her in one last deep thrust.

They lay together for a long time, their hearts pounding, their bodies still joined.

He kissed her gently and moved away, got up from the bed.

"Stay," she said.

He looked at her from the shadows for a long moment, and she reached for him, drew him back to bed, held him tight as he loved her again and again until the dawn rose and she fell asleep in his arms.

Chapter 64

Nicholas watched dawn creep into the room, and turn her skin to gold.

Meg was fast asleep in his arms, her hair covering both of them like a blanket.

He kissed her forehead, and she sighed as he slid out from underneath her. One last look, and he covered her with the blankets.

An hour later, he was at the docks with Hannibal, boarding the ship that would take them back to a world he understood, to honor and respect.

He watched the sun rise on the city as the ship slipped her moorings and headed out into the Channel, seeing the blaze of her glorious hair in the sunrise.

Chapter 65

Meg woke when Anna opened the curtains to let the sun into the room.

"Good morning, Your Grace," she said. "Lovely day. The troops are marching through the streets this morning, taking ship for the continent. They do look handsome in their scarlet coats!"

Meg touched the empty bed beside her. The sheets were cold. She missed him. In the night, she had only had to turn, and he was there. He'd held her, murmured against her hair, but she was too sleepy to listen.

She loved him. She smiled. She would find him and tell him.

"Has His Grace gone riding already?" she asked eagerly, getting up.

"I'll go and inquire of Mr. Partridge," Anna said. "All is quiet in his rooms."

Meg hummed as she went to the wardrobe and took out the blue-gray riding habit, and went to bathe.

She would start the day with an apology, and admit how much she loved him.

She spun in a circle, grinning.

They would go riding, and—how many hours before

they could return to bed? They'd made a new start last
night, and she was eager to go . . .

"Your Grace, Mr. Partridge says that His Grace has
gone," Anna said.

Meg smiled at her. "No matter. Ask one of the grooms
to saddle my horse, and I'll catch him up."

Anna shook her head, her eyes wide. "There's a room-
ful of folk downstairs to see you. Mr. Gardiner is quite
beside himself. It's not the hour for callers, but he could
not keep them out. The Countess of Wycliffe is threatening to come upstairs to find you if you don't appear at
once."

"My mother is here?" Meg asked.

"With Lord Bryant."

"Is something wrong? My sister? Is His Grace with
them?" Anna helped her dress quickly, choosing a morning gown instead of the riding habit.

"Gardiner didn't say. He only asked—respectfully—if
you would hurry."

Flora leaped off the settee when Meg entered the salon
scarcely ten minutes later. "There you are at last! Did you
intend to lie in bed all day?" she demanded.

Meg glanced at the clock on the mantel. It was barely
eight o'clock. "I am surprised you are up this early," she
said. "Is something wrong?"

"Is that a bruise?" Flora asked, grasping Meg's chin
and turning it to the light. "Did Temberlay—"

"Of course not. I had a slight accident yesterday in a
curricle," Meg murmured. Hector frowned at the lie. "I'm
glad you're safe. Nicholas sent me a note to say you were.
He also sent some other documents, Meg." He held up
a thick file. Meg felt her stomach drop to the floor. She
clasped her hands together.

"It's bad news?" she asked.

Hector nodded gravely. "He asked me to give it to you this afternoon, to advise you that he—"

"No," she said, and sat down heavily on the settee, shutting her eyes.

"I came as soon as they arrived, Meg. I was hoping to change his mind, but Gardiner tells me it's already too late."

"Too late? How can it be too late?" Meg whispered. "Is he sending me away? Is it to be divorce?" she asked.

"Divorce?" Flora said. "As if this isn't scandalous enough!"

"He's provided for you very generously," Hector said. "But only in the event that he—"

The door opened again and the dowager entered, her eyes fiery. She too was waving a letter. "How could you allow this to happen?" she demanded.

"I—" Meg began. Her head was buzzing. She wanted to run to him, find him, beg for an explanation. How could he make love to her with such passion, only to dismiss her in the morning? She had made dreadful mistakes, but she had thought—hoped—he had forgiven her.

"I have not yet spoken to Nicholas this morning," she said to the dowager.

"Spoken to him?" the dowager snapped. "He's gone!"

"Meg, Nicholas has gone to Brussels," Hector said gently.

"Brussels?" she murmured.

"You mean he did not even tell you?" the old lady demanded. "He must detest the sight of you!"

Shock vibrated through her.

Flora rose to her feet. "I will not have you speaking to my daughter that way, Your Grace."

"Why did he go to Brussels?" Meg asked, her heart rising in her throat.

"Your daughter had a duty to me, Countess, and to her title. She was to marry my grandson and get an heir. Now it's too late." She glared at Meg. "You've failed, and you know my price." Meg scarcely saw, scarcely heard. He was upstairs in his rooms, or in the library, or out riding. He would stride through the door in a moment, and grin at her. There was only one reason to go to Brussels now.

War.

Meg put a hand to her throat. The dowager was yelling at Flora, who was screeching back. Hector was trying to calm them both.

Meg picked up her skirts and raced up the stairs. She went through her chamber, past the bed where he'd lain with her, loved her, kissed her.

It could not have been good-bye.

She opened the door to his room. It was neat, tidy, and silent. She couldn't breathe. She crossed to the wardrobe and flung it open. She scrabbled through his coats. The bottle green one was there. So were a half dozen other, more sober coats.

The scarlet tunic was gone.

She turned to find Partridge standing behind her. "I wanted to go with him, Your Grace, but he would not hear of it. Other officers took their valets. Some even took their wives and their families," he said. He straightened the coats on their hangers. "Should I simply wait for him to return?" he asked, bewildered.

She looked up at him. "They took their wives?"

"And evening wear and hunting clothes. It's been in all the papers. The *ton* is flocking to Belgium to see the final battle with Napoleon. Everyone who can find passage has gone. No one knows when it will be, but there will be grand parties while they wait. There's hardly anyone left in London." He sighed. "He won't be properly dressed."

She hadn't read the papers, didn't want to see her sister on Nicholas's arm.

She was as blind to what was happening as she'd been under her father's rule.

"Who else is going, Partridge?" she asked, and crossed to the desk.

"Everyone. Captain Lord Reed sailed two days ago. Colonel Lord Fairlie has been gone for a fortnight. They say the Prince Regent himself had to be prevented—"

"Lord Fairlie, Lord St. James's brother-in-law?"

She opened the desk, searched for paper and ink.

"Marguerite! What are you doing?" Flora asked, bursting in through Meg's apartments. "You must come home with me this instant!"

The dowager came in through the sitting room. "Partridge, I assume you helped him prepare for this fool's errand?"

"I did, Your Grace."

"And did you not think to advise me of his plans?" she demanded. "Did you think it was yet another idiotic prank, some kind of holiday? You are dismissed without reference."

"No, I have need of Mr. Partridge," Meg said. She took out a sheet of paper and scrawled a note. "Take this to Viscount St. James. If he isn't at home, give it to Lady Delphine."

He took the note and bowed.

She pulled out another sheet of paper. "What do you think you're doing?" the old woman demanded.

"I am going to Brussels," Meg replied.

The dowager laughed. "You mean to follow him to war? Is this some grand gesture of love? I warned you not to be so foolish as to fall in love with him. He destroys everyone who loves him."

"Come to Bryant House, Marguerite," Flora said, putting an arm around her daughter's shoulders, but Meg had no need of comfort. She loved Nicholas. She had thought that he might even love her, but he had gone. It didn't matter. She would go to him, tell him, before it was too late. She hadn't dared to tell her father.

"Bryant House?" the old duchess said. "She must go to Temberlay Castle. Is there any chance you are with child?"

Flora gasped at her bluntness, but every eye in the room turned to regard her with interest.

Meg resisted the urge to lay her hand on her stomach. Was that why he'd come to her last night? It was too soon to tell. "If I am, this is my child, and Nicholas's."

The dowager thumped her walking stick. "How dare you play games with me? Do you expect more money from me? You won't get it. You will leave for Temberlay Castle at once, this very day, and remain there until it can be determined if—"

"I'm going to Brussels," Meg replied, meeting the old lady's cold stare.

"To war?" Flora gasped, and the harridan sneered.

"Meg, this isn't a game. It might be dangerous," Hector began. "Won't you read his letter?"

She crossed and kissed his cheek, and looked at the papers under his arm. "Is there anything I need do? Papers I must sign, any arrangements for Mama and the girls?"

"I will remind you that if you are carrying Temberlay's heir, and he is killed, the child will be the next duke," the old lady objected.

"If it's a boy," Flora said. "Wycliffe had four girls."

"If it is a girl, or if she fails to be with child at all, I will destroy you."

Flora raised her brows. "Destroy us? Because a bride fails to produce a child in a few short months of marriage?

Rose took three years to make an appearance. There is no scandal you can threaten us with, Your Grace. Marguerite has done her part, played the role you wanted. No one can fault her if your grandson—"

"No scandal?" the old lady said, advancing on Flora. "There are rotten apples in every tree, Countess. There's the fact that your husband died by—"

"No!" Meg cried, and stepped between the dowager and her mother. "Leave it. I will go to Temberlay Castle," she said.

Flora set her hands on her shoulders and moved her aside. "Nonsense. You will go where you please, Marguerite. Just because we do not speak of family tragedies, it does not mean they are unknown to us. If you spill your venom, then your grandchild must live with the consequences. Have you considered that, Your Grace? I doubt you'll jeopardize the reputation of Temberlay while there is a chance Nicholas will return."

"He *did* come back from war the first time," Hector said. "And he came back a hero."

Meg glanced at him. He regarded her steadily. Somehow, the secret she had buried, kept hidden to save her family the pain of knowing the truth, wasn't a secret at all. She thought of the comfort they might have given each other if they'd talked about it.

"Mama?" she whispered the question. "You knew?"

"The doctor told me, Marguerite. I insisted. How could I tell you I knew when you were trying so hard to protect us? I didn't want to think of it, and what the future would bring. You managed the thinking and doing for all of us, and I am sorry I was not more—capable, but I never have been. Until now." She sent the dowager a warning glance. "I'll help you pack."

There was doubt in the old duchess's eyes, defeat. "You

will bring him back, insist that he does his duty," she commanded, but it was feeble in the face of Meg's own determination. "A man with no heir has no business going to war at all," she said. "D'you hear me, Marguerite?"

Meg turned. "I will find my husband. I will give him sons if he wants them—"

"Or daughters," Flora put in.

"—and I will spend my life showing him that I love him. I am through with lies and deceit."

She left the old lady standing in the ducal bedchamber, and went to pack.

"**M**eg, I have something to tell you. I should have told you sooner. Please come and sit down for just a moment," Hector said, and led her into her sitting room while Flora directed Anna on what to pack.

He opened the folio of documents. "This first."

She took the bill of sale and looked at it. "Papa was cheated! Arabella alone was worth five times this much!"

"Nicholas found that in your father's room, at Wycliffe. It's one of the reasons why he was in such a hurry to return to London." He handed her another bill. This one was for much more, signed by Temberlay and the Earl of Eldridge, for the sale of two horses.

"Nicholas bought Papa's horses?" she asked, tears stinging her eyes.

"Wilton forfeited them months ago. Gambling debts. John told Nicholas how much the horses meant to you. They cost him a fortune, since Eldridge didn't want to part with them."

"He did that for me?"

"A wedding gift," Hector confirmed. He handed her a small notebook. "This is David Hartley's journal, kept during the last year of his life. It explains how your father lost his fortune, why he—" He swallowed. "Meg, I should have been there to protect you. Nicholas challenged Wilton and Augustus Howard to a duel yesterday morning. I was his second. Wilton didn't arrive, and I told Nicholas you'd gone to buy the foal, sent him after you." He looked at her with love in his eyes. "Even in such a situation, against such a man, you managed, didn't you?"

"I shouldn't have been there. I should have trusted Nicholas."

"Everything he's done in past weeks was for you. I believe he loves you, Meg, though I'm a bachelor and I know nothing of such things." He studied his hands. "I thought I might find out though. Would you mind if I proposed to your mother?"

Happy tears sprang to her eyes. "Are you sure? There's still Lily and Minnie to raise and marry."

He looked through the door of her bedroom at Flora, who was selecting a dozen evening gowns and wondering if it would be enough. "Yes, I'm sure," he said fondly. "I've grown used to her way of thinking, you see. I don't think I could live without it."

Delphine arrived an hour later with Sebastian in tow. "Delphie, I'm going to Brussels. Do you think I could stay with your sister Eleanor and Colonel Lord Fairlie?" Meg asked.

"Get me pen and paper," Delphine instructed the nearest footman. "I'll write to her at once, and I'll go with you."

Sebastian glared at both women. "Don't be a fool, Del! Everyone thinks they are off on a grand adventure. You'll all be back in a few weeks, sunburned and complaining about how rude the Belgians are and never having seen Napoleon at all."

"Sebastian is lily-livered," Delphine told Meg. "I can be ready to leave when you wish. Sebastian, make yourself useful and go and arrange our passage."

Sebastian reddened. "I most certainly will not take any part in this fool's errand! This is all your fault," he said to Meg. "He had no thought of going back to war until you took up with Wilton. The news is all over Town. And I'm not lily-livered. I am Father's heir. He's forbidden me to join a regiment."

Delphine laughed. "Wilton is a cad. Everyone knows that. No one believes a word he says. He owes money everywhere, while Meg has never given anyone cause to gossip. Why shouldn't a woman buy horses? There are currently a dozen ladies of my acquaintance planning sorties to Tattersall's."

"She broke Nicholas's heart!" Sebastian pointed at her. "I didn't think any woman could, but why else would he do such a damned fool thing as going back to war?"

Delphine kissed her brother's cheek. "I didn't think you had a romantic bone in your body, but you do, don't you?" She smiled at Meg. "Nicholas loves you," she gushed. "And you love him."

"How do you know that?" Sebastian demanded. "Going off with Wilton hardly suggests—"

"She is going all the way to Brussels for Nicholas," Delphine explained. "Come now, Sebastian, be a good brother and arrange passage, and we'll let you stand on the pier and wave your handkerchief as we go off to find Meg's brave soldier."

"If we weren't twins, I'd call you out and shoot you for that remark," Sebastian pouted, pulling on his gloves to go.

"If you wish, dear heart, but I'm a better shot than you," Delphine retorted.

Chapter 66

Brussels was filled with an air of frantic gaiety, as if everyone who had gathered for the impending battle felt they must live life to the fullest before the end. The sultry promise of an early summer made it difficult to think of war at all.

Every day, thousands of uniformed men poured into the city in preparation for the coming event, but Napoleon's armies didn't appear, and sightseers and ladies began to think the whole exercise was mere spectacle and pageantry.

Meg hadn't found Nicholas. He was out of the city on military business, but no one would say more. He wasn't Captain Lord Hartley as he'd been in Spain, but simply Temberlay, and a major. To the men who had known him in Spain, he was still Devil, the man who outsmarted the French.

Delphine's older sister Eleanor and her husband, Colonel Lord Fairlie, welcomed them. By day, the ladies strolled and lunched and had tea just as if they were still in England. Meg searched every face, every group of officers for Nicholas, but he wasn't among them. With every disappointment, the longing grew worse.

The Fairlies had rented a small estate on the edge of the city, surrounded by orchards and gardens. Eleanor turned the salon on the ground floor into a workroom for ladies who wished to do more for the cause than simply look pretty and provide officers with dance partners.

"We might as well roll bandages and gather supplies," Eleanor said. "The parks are full of soldiers in tents, since there is nowhere else to house them, and we cannot walk there. Fairlie says we shall be forced to give up our orchard next. The outbuildings have already been commandeered by the army, but I suppose being surrounded by troops makes us safe."

Meg threw herself eagerly into the tasks. The ladies gossiped while they worked, and just as in London, there was plenty of gossip to be had.

"D'you know what I heard today?" Delphine asked as they climbed into bed. Meg had given up her own room to a captain's wife, and shared a bed with Delphine the way she'd once shared with Rose. "Claire Howard is here in Brussels. She came here to the house to help and they turned her away. Can you imagine? She left old Augustus for Daniel Napier, and followed him here when he bought a commission. They say she sold her famous necklace to pay for it too, and she is quite in love with him, and fears he will be killed and she'll have to go back to Augustus after all. No one has seen them together, though. It appears Daniel is out on patrol somewhere, like Nicholas."

Poor lady, Meg thought. David's journal had said that Augustus had used the money he gained from cheating her father to buy the necklace to convince Claire to marry him.

"Why would they turn her away? Surely an extra pair of hands would be useful."

Delphine looked at her with delighted shock. "She

is not respectable! She abandoned her husband, and ran away with her lover, Meg. Surely you can't imagine Countess Huntley or Lady Aimes allowing her to become part of their circle of good works."

"Yet isn't Lord Wellington escorting the wife of one of his own officers while her husband is away on duty? No one would dare exclude *her* if she decided to roll bandages of an afternoon," Meg said.

Delphine grinned. "I suppose not. What d'you suppose she *does* get up to in the afternoons?" she asked wickedly.

Meg blew out the candle. She could imagine the duke's mistress whiling away the sultry afternoons in the arms of her lover. Did she wonder where her husband was, if he was safe?

She shut her eyes, and saw Nicholas's face as he made love to her. She could never want another man.

"I think I shall go and see her," she murmured.

The rope frame of the bed creaked. "The duke's paramour?" Delphine gasped.

"No, Claire Howard."

"How bold you are! Eleanor will never allow me to accompany you."

"Then I will go alone."

"**Y**our Grace!" Claire Howard dipped a curtsy when Meg arrived at her humble lodgings. "Will you take tea? I will understand if—"

Meg smiled. "I never had the chance to meet you in London. I came to see how you are. I didn't know until yesterday that you were here in Brussels, or I would have come to visit sooner. Please call me Meg."

Claire led the way to a small sitting room that overlooked the main road. "I am guessing this is more than a social call. You must know you are courting scandal by coming here. Is it because of my brother-in-law, Charles Wilton, that you've come?" Meg felt a frisson of surprise climb her back at Claire's frankness.

"No. I came because you are alone, and no doubt worried about . . . Lieutenant Napier. My husband is also away from town, you see."

Claire's face crumpled. "Daniel said he must prove himself. We cannot marry, since I am still Augustus's wife. Daniel is out on a scouting mission. I am very afraid. If he does not come back, what will I do? I love him. I don't think I can live without him. I have no money—the necklace everyone envied was made of paste. Augustus gambled away every penny. I sold my wedding ring to buy my passage here. If Daniel is killed—"

Meg swallowed her own knot of fear. "He must come back," she whispered, speaking of both Daniel Napier and Nicholas.

"You are afraid for Temberlay too," Claire said.

Meg nodded. "He doesn't even know I'm here."

"I'm glad you are, and that you came today." Claire rose and went to the window, and parted the lace curtains to gaze out into the street. "You must forgive me. I find myself checking the road for signs of Daniel a hundred times a day."

Meg studied dappled shadows of the lace on Claire's pale cheek. "I came to ask you something, Claire. A favor."

Claire turned. "A favor?"

"Your sister, Lady Wilton. I understand she had a child with Nicholas." She raised her chin as she felt her cheeks heat.

"Oh. You've heard that bit of gossip," Claire said. "You should know—"

"I don't wish to cause trouble. Please don't imagine I

would do such a thing. I only wished to ask if I might visit her, meet her son. You see, if Temberlay does not—" She squeezed her eyes shut. "The dukedom will need an heir, and I thought that possibly . . ." The words, the idea that she would never see Nicholas again stuck in her throat.

Claire came and sat beside her. "Oh, Meg. There are things you need to know. My sister and Wilton had an argument. He had a mistress, and Lavinia was jealous. When he refused to give the woman up, Lavinia told him that their daughter was not Wilton's. It was an unforgivable lie. She chose the first name that came into her head when he demanded to know who the father was. There was a copy of the *London Times* on Charles's desk, and she saw the name of an officer who had left London some months before. She told him Captain Lord Nicholas Hartley had been her lover."

Claire went to a small desk in the corner of the room and ran her hand over the lid. Meg watched her, her heart in her throat.

"Lavinia never even met Nicholas. I think even Wilton knew that it was a lie, but Lavinia had borne him only a daughter, and he was tired of her. Her thoughtless lie gave him a way to be rid of her. Wilton swore he'd have revenge. He sent Lavinia to the country, separated her from Charlotte, their daughter. He sent his own daughter to a foundling home that very day, wouldn't even allow Lavinia to see her child."

She opened the desk and took out a packet of letters tied with a blue ribbon. "Nor would he let my sister write to her family, or have friends near. My mother pleaded with him to tell us where she was, but he refused, and under the law there was little we could do. We feared she was dead by his hand."

She untied the ribbon, pulled out one envelope. "Then

I received a letter from her, smuggled out somehow. I went to see Wilton, demanded that he let me see her." She reddened. "He insisted I do something for him first." She shut her eyes.

"What did he make you do?" Meg asked. Her skin prickled, remembering Wilton's hands on her in the curricle.

"He insisted I marry a friend of his, Augustus Howard. I was in love with Daniel, planned to marry him, but my sister had begged for my help. What could I do? Wilton encouraged Augustus to pay a large debt my father owed, and then my parents forced me to marry him. When I returned from the wedding trip, my sister was dead."

She looked at the letters. "A few weeks ago, a servant who had been with her at her death brought me the letters she'd written me in those long months. She said my sister died of guilt and grief."

She handed Meg one of the yellowed letters. "There is one she meant for Nicholas, a warning that Wilton meant to harm him, or to destroy his family if he could not reach Nicholas in person. Forgive me. I should have given it to Nicholas the moment I read it, but it was nearly two years old by then. I decided to leave Augustus, go away with Daniel the next day. When I return to London, I will look for Charlotte, try and find her, but she is not Nicholas's child, and could never be heir to Temberlay."

Meg stared at the letter in her hand. It explained many of the accusations in David's journal. A single lie, and a ruthless man had destroyed so many lives. She also knew of Julia Leighton from the pages of the journal, David's fiancée. She understood now the kindness Nicholas had shown the frightened young woman, realized her child was not Nicholas's son.

He must come home, Meg sent up a prayer. *He has to live, if only so I can tell him I love him.*

Chapter 67

"Hold on, Napier," Nicholas murmured. The young lieutenant lay on the floor of a barn, bleeding from a bullet wound that had just missed shattering his knee. He had no time to spare Napier more than a quick glance. They were surrounded by French soldiers, and under fire. They'd be lucky to make it out alive.

"If I don't make it, please tell Claire that I love her," Napier said. "She's waiting for me in Brussels."

"You can tell her yourself," Nicholas said with more confidence than he felt. He wondered who would tell Meg that he'd been killed and what they'd say of his final moments. He'd kissed her forehead as he'd left the warmth of her bed, whispered that he loved her. He licked the dust from his lips now, wishing he could kiss her once more.

In his pocket he had information that Wellington would need, maps of Napoleon's planned route from Paris to the Belgian border. The wily French emperor had set a trap for the allies, sending a small number of troops west, in hopes they'd race to meet them while he crossed the border at Charleroi, an easy march from Brussels.

It had been luck that he'd found the maps at all. He'd stumbled across Napier, separated from his patrol and wandering in the countryside, a sitting duck. They'd found shelter in a stable, and a French courier had chanced upon the same haven, with a pretty French milkmaid to tumble. When the man shed his clothes, Nicholas went through his pocket and took the maps.

"Are they regular soldiers?" Napier asked now. He reloaded his pistol and passed it to Nicholas. A musket ball came through the window and buried itself in the wall beside Nicholas. The splinters stung his cheek.

"They're too clever to be regular French troops," Nicholas replied. They'd found him only hours after the maps went missing. He waited for the next shot to tell him where to aim, and fired. A man screamed and fell from behind a hayrick and lay still in the dust of the farmyard. "One more down," he said to Napier, as he passed back the empty pistol.

"We're running out of shot, Temberlay. How many more are there?"

Nicholas scanned the farmyard, the outbuildings and the house. There were a dozen hiding places, most of them empty now. "Three or four, I'd say. Possibly fewer." He shot again, heard a grunt, and smiled. "Fewer still."

Screams broke his concentration. A man dragged a woman out of the farmhouse with his pistol pointed at her head. "Is that you, Hartley?" her captor asked in French, scanning the barn. "Come out, or I'll shoot the woman. You should know there are children inside, and I'm quite willing to kill—" The woman's tearful pleas cut him off. He cuffed her to silence, and Nicholas's eyes narrowed.

"D'you know him, Temberlay?" Napier whispered.

"Ferrau." Nicholas growled the name. "I thought he was dead." Judging by the terrible scar on the side of his face, he almost had been. Nicholas had left him bleeding the last time they'd met, before his second escape from

French custody. He wasn't usually so careless with enemies of Ferrau's caliber, but he'd been in a hurry.

"Can you hit him without harming the woman?" Napier asked.

"Not with a killing shot," Nicholas said.

Ferrau moved into the middle of the farmyard as if the outcome was already in his favor. Nicholas had always hated the French spy's arrogance. "I have men pointing pistols at the heads of the little ones inside, Hartley. I seem to recall you had a weakness for protecting women and children. It's how I captured the first time, *n'est-ce pas*? I have heard rumors that you inherited a title. Has it made you so jaded you're willing to take innocent souls to hell with you now?"

"What makes you so sure I will be the one to die, Ferrau?" Nicholas called.

The Frenchman smiled, the grin twisting the ugly scar. "How many men do you have in there with you? As I recall, you prefer to work alone. I have a dozen soldiers on my side. Come out and I'll shoot you cleanly, give you a good death. You've stolen something that belongs to me. You need only return it and admit that I have won. You are a poor spy, Hartley, and a terrible thief."

"Now what could I possibly have that belongs to you? Last time I saw you, you were blubbering over that scratch I gave you."

Ferrau pointed the gun at the woman and fired into her arm. She screamed as her striped apron turned crimson and blood sprayed Ferrau's face. He held her up, refusing to let her fall. "The next bullet kills her if you do not come out, *mon ami*."

Nicholas's gut tightened. He had only minutes before she bled to death. He kept his face impassive as he studied his old adversary.

Ferrau took a second pistol out of his belt and pointed it at her head. "Shall I blow her head off?"

Nicholas took the map out of his pocket and hid it under the straw where Napier could reach it. "Let her go. I'm coming out," he called out to Ferrau. Lieutenant Napier was pale and sweating. "Stay quiet," he told Napier. "Take the map and ride out at nightfall if I don't win this round."

"You can't go out there—he'll kill you!"

"No he won't," Nicholas said. "Not right away. We have a history, you see. He'll want to torture me awhile before he kills me."

He tucked a loaded pistol into Napier's hand. The gun shook. The young lieutenant would need help soon.

He lifted the heavy bar and the door swung open. He tossed the empty pistol in the yellow dust at Ferrau's feet. In Spain the dust had been red.

"Let her go."

Ferrau instantly dropped the woman into the dirt and turned his pistol on Nicholas. She crawled away, whimpering.

"Now return what you stole."

Nicholas frowned. "I have no idea what you're talking about."

Ferrau reddened. "You were seen leaving that stable. You are not as clever as you think. You seem to have lost your touch after so many years of dissipation. I shot the courier for his stupidity. Imagine what I will do to you."

Nicholas looked over his old enemy. Like Nicholas, he usually wore civilian clothes while out on a mission, yet today he had on the same style of military greatcoat that Napoleon favored. It suggested the French army was close by, and he was on his way to join them. Ferrau wore a glittering military decoration over the place where his heart would have been if he'd had one.

"I regret my offer to kill you quickly, but I am in a hurry." He pointed his pistol at Nicholas's heart. "But I can spare a few minutes to hear you beg for your life."

Nicholas stared into the barrel of the gun. He had come to war not caring what happened to him. He intended to acquit himself bravely and honorably on the field of battle and leave this life a hero. But he realized now that he didn't want to die. He wanted to go home to his wife.

"Check my pockets, Ferrau—there's nothing in them but my watch."

Ferrau suddenly changed his aim and fired at someone behind Nicholas. Napier slumped against the barn door. "I thought you were alone. Are the maps in his pocket? The next bullet goes through your knee, *mon ami*. Then I'll shoot your fingers off, one at a time, then your ears . . ."

Napier was screaming, rolling in agony on the straw. It was impossible to tell how badly he was hurt.

Nicholas turned back to Ferrau and shrugged. "Now how can we discuss things with all this screaming? Let me get one of the others in the barn to help him, and I'll see what I can remember about—maps, was it? I've been drinking rather a lot in the past few days." His eyes bored into the Frenchman's. "Dissipation."

A flicker passed through Ferrau's eyes as he quickly glanced into the dark interior of the barn, and Nicholas knew. His men were dead, and Ferrau was alone.

"Temberlay, move!" Napier croaked, and Nicholas dove. Daniel's shot went wide, but it gave him time to draw his own gun, and his shot hit the Frenchman in the eye, and he dropped without a sound. The dust darkened under his head, a black halo. This time Nicholas leaned over the corpse, making certain he was dead.

Nicholas went to Napier. He had a second wound in the arm, a mere scratch, but his leg was bleeding again. "Is he dead?" he whispered, his white face sheened with sweat.

"Yes, at last," Nicholas said. He retrieved the maps.

"Will you tell Claire that I did my duty?" Napier sighed. "She's with child—"

Nicholas unpinned Ferrau's gaudy medal and put it in the lieutenant's tunic. "Something to show her when you see her. Those look like real diamonds," he murmured.

He thought of Meg, wondered if possibly— He shook the thought away. He wanted to be there, see her face when—if—

But that pleasure would have to wait.

He bandaged Napier's wounds as best he could, dosed him with rum, and pulled the lieutenant up behind him on Hannibal and rode north.

Blessedly, Napier fainted after a few miles. When Nicholas reached British lines, he tucked the maps into Napier's tunic. "Get him to headquarters in Brussels as quickly as possible, he has information Wellington will need to see."

He turned Hannibal's head.

"Where the devil are you going?" the major asked.

"Charleroi. That's where Napoleon will cross the border," he said.

Nicholas spurred Hannibal along the road. It was nearly dusk. Lives were at stake, including his own. He looked down at the ducal signet ring on his finger. He had a duty, to his wife, his country, and Temberlay.

If his luck held, he'd see them all again.

Chapter 68

❧

"**W**hat a crush!" Delphine said as they took the Fairlies' coach to the Duchess of Richmond's ball. "It is becoming a dreadful inconvenience to have all those soldiers in the streets. It is impossible to go anywhere at all! We're sure to be late."

Meg looked out the window. White faces passed the coach, torchlight gleaming on gunmetal and bayonets.

"William, this is hardly the time for a parade," Eleanor said to her husband. "What's happening?"

"There's nothing to worry about, my dear. The duchess herself asked Lord Wellington if it would be safe to hold her ball tonight. He assured her it would indeed, and if he believes—"

"Will." Eleanor insisted on the truth. "These men are not out for an evening stroll. They are on the march. I have been an army wife for eight years."

The colonel glanced at Meg and Delphine and sighed. "We had word this afternoon. Napoleon has crossed into Belgium."

Delphine gave a shriek and put a gloved hand to her mouth. "Is he coming here, tonight?"

"Calm yourself. We are merely on alert. There's no

danger. It may be days yet before anything happens. Would Wellington be dancing the night away otherwise?" Fairlie soothed.

Meg searched the crowds. She watched as a soldier fell out of line to kiss his sweetheart as the sergeants bawled. *Be safe*, she wished him, and hoped wherever Nicholas was, he was safe too.

The Duke and Duchess of Richmond had rented the grand home of a coach maker as their Brussels residence. The ball was being held in the workshop, a fine open space for a party, which the duchess had decorated with trellises, flowers, and thousands of candles.

"Listen," Meg said as they climbed the steps. The sound of marching feet kept macabre time with the gay dance music that spilled out the open windows. She shivered.

The duchess's daughter met them at the door. "Georgiana, the streets are filled with soldiers! Aren't you afraid?" Delphine asked.

Georgiana laughed. "You look as if Napoleon himself is going to march up to these doors and invade the party. Lord Wellington has assured Mother a dozen times there's nothing to fear. Have you ever seen anything so grand as this? So many handsome gentlemen—I plan to dance with all of them."

The gay atmosphere inside stood out in stark contrast to the scene outside. If anyone was fearful, it didn't show. The candlelight here glinted off nothing more threatening than gold braid and diamond necklaces. Meg supposed she should feel relieved, but her chest knotted.

"Do you think Temberlay is here?" Eleanor asked.

Meg shook her head. She'd spoken to soldiers who had known him in Spain, heard more of the stories that Stephen Ives had begun telling her. She knew now that the soldier, the man of honor, was the real Nicholas. The rake, the rogue—those were the false images. If battle was imminent, he was near the fray.

Delphine pressed a glass of champagne into her hand, but the sparkling wine tasted bitter. Georgiana dragged Delphine off to meet a group of grinning officers.

"Would you excuse me, my dear?" Fairlie said, and took his leave. Meg stood with Eleanor and watched him cross the room.

"I suppose that leaves us to join the matrons. Shall we do so, or would you like to dance?"

"I don't think I could," Meg replied.

Eleanor squeezed her arm. "I'm a soldier's wife too. Fairlie may be a colonel, but he sees limited action now he's inherited his title. Nicholas is a duke. They won't put him in harm's way. He will stand well back if there's to be a battle, with Wellington, out of danger."

"He isn't that kind of soldier," Meg murmured. "He wouldn't want that."

Eleanor pointed. "Look, there's Lord Wellington. Would he be here tonight at all if there was any danger? Come, I'll introduce you."

The commander swept a bow as the ladies greeted him, his dark eyes assessing Meg. "Is it true that Napoleon has crossed the border, Your Grace?" Eleanor asked.

Wellington raised his brows. "Yes, Lady Fairlie, the rumors are true. We are off tomorrow."

Eleanor gasped. "As soon as that?"

Meg's limbs turned to water. She read the truth in Wellington's eyes. There was little time left for gaiety and parties. War was upon them yet again.

"Your Grace, might I ask after my husband? Have you any word of him?" she asked breathlessly.

His eyes traveled over her with male appreciation. He

held out an arm. "Dance with me, Your Grace." It was an order, and she laid her hand on his sleeve and let him lead her out.

"Do you have any idea what your husband does, madam?"

She studied the braid on the front of his uniform for a moment, the medals and honors on the blue silk sash, and swept her gaze back up to meet his. "I believe I do, Your Grace."

"Then you should know that there are gentlemen here tonight who perform similar services for the enemy."

Meg looked around, but the duke squeezed her hand. "Smile, if you would, Your Grace, as if I've said something amusing. This is a party. It wouldn't do to give the impression that we are in the least worried about the outcome of the battle."

A young officer swept up to him and bowed. "Your Grace, I must interrupt. A courier just arrived."

Wellington bowed over her hand. "Please excuse me—duty calls, Your Grace." He paused. "Wherever Temberlay might be, I pray that he is safe, both for your sake and for the sake of my army."

He asked his aide to escort her back to Eleanor, and she watched as he disappeared into a small withdrawing room and shut the door.

An officer emerged moments later, and waved the orchestra to silence.

"Gentlemen, finish your dances, and return to your regiments as quickly as possible."

Eleanor clutched her arm. "It's begun!"

Fairlie pressed through the crowds toward them. "It's time to go. I will see you to the coach, and go and join my men."

Delphine leaned out the window of the coach and

waved the regiments off with her handkerchief as they made slow progress through the streets.

As they passed Claire Howard's rooms, Meg turned to Eleanor. "I'm going to see Claire. She might not know what's happening. She'll be worried about Daniel."

Eleanor laid a hand on her arm. "I cannot let you do that! If things go badly, Fairlie has ordered us to go north at once. By morning, possibly."

Delphine frowned. "Are we in danger?"

Eleanor took her sister's hand. "This isn't the time to go missish! We must be brave. I'm simply to keep the horses in harness, be prepared."

Meg opened the door. "Then it is all the more important that I speak to Claire."

Eleanor pursed her lips a moment. "Yes, fine, but hurry. Napoleon is advancing far faster than they imagined he would. I can't send the coach back for you."

"We'll find a way," Meg said, and got out of the vehicle.

Whatever happened, she was not leaving without Nicholas.

Chapter 69

Claire was pacing the floor when Meg arrived. She burst into anxious tears when Meg told her the news.

They sat in the window throughout the night and watched the soldiers march toward the city's south gate. The Royal Dragoons, Nicholas's regiment, rode past, each man tall in the saddle, ready to fight, but he and Hannibal were not among them.

At dawn, low rumbling peals of thunder rolled across the Belgian farmland. "We're in for a storm," Claire said.

"I think that's artillery. Colonel Fairlie said we'd be able to hear it," Meg replied with tears in her eyes. "The battle has begun."

Chapter 70

{ornamental divider}

The Belgian army came through the city in a disordered retreat as the sun rose, causing panic. Behind them, carts filled with wounded men began pouring into town.

"I can't sit here and wait," Meg said, worry choking her. "I'm going to see if—" She couldn't say it.

"I'm going with you," Claire said, and picked up her cloak.

The two women went to the Richmonds' lodgings, where the carts were unloading their grim passengers in the same courtyard where coaches had let down ladies in silk and lace only hours before. The carefully swept cobbles were slick with blood.

Claire began to search among the wounded for Daniel. Meg felt her stomach shrivel at the sheer number of men here. The sound of their cries rose like a dirge.

Georgiana, still in her evening gown, stood staring down at one mangled body. The young man was still wearing his dancing shoes and his dress uniform.

Meg took her hand. "I danced with him last night, Meg! He can't be dead." Meg bent and placed two fingers on his neck, seeking a pulse, but his heart was still, his flesh cold. She closed his eyes and looked around for something to cover him. Georgiana burst into tears. "Go and find your mother, Georgiana. Ask her for some blankets, something we can use as bandages," Meg told her.

Someone caught at her skirts. "Water, miss, if you please." Meg crossed to the pump and filled the bucket. She held the dipper to the man's lips.

"What happened?" she asked.

"The French are pushing us back," he grunted. "We're trying to stop them at a place called Quatre Bras, south of here. The line won't hold. I was hit in the first volley. Am I going to die?" He clutched at her hand, leaving bloody streaks on her skin. Meg resisted the urge to pull away.

She looked for a surgeon, anyone who could help. The courtyard was full now, and still men were pouring through the gates, some walking, some being carried. They slumped against the walls, exhausted. She looked back at the soldier still clinging to her hand and saw Nicholas's face in his homely features.

"No," she said firmly. "You are not going to die."

Meg carried water until her arms ached. She asked every man who could speak for news of Temberlay, but no one had seen him. She offered what comfort she could, hoping some other woman would do the same for Nicholas if he came to her.

"There's more wounded in the park," a soldier told her. "Women are looking for their men there."

She found Claire, working with the wounded as she was, and they hurried through the chaos of the streets. The park was crowded with bodies, and women tiptoed from man to man, looking into each battered face.

Claire cried out, and bent over a wounded man. "Daniel!" His arm came around her, the fingers filthy as they caressed her hair. Meg felt her heart swell, then break with disappointment.

"Are you well?" he asked, caressing Claire's face. "Are you even real?"

Claire began to touch his limbs with shaking hands, searching for his wounds. "Temberlay bandaged me as best he could, got me back to our lines."

Meg dropped to her knees. "You've seen Nicholas?"

He focused on her slowly. "Two days ago, Your Grace."

"Was he—unhurt?" she asked.

Daniel smiled tiredly. "He saved my life," he said.

"That man next," a surgeon directed, pushing her aside. "Carry him over to the taproom."

"Please, I have rooms, just there." Claire pointed. "I can care for him."

The surgeon wiped his hands on his apron. "There are many men needing care, many that have a better chance than he does."

"He's her husband," Meg said fiercely. "Surely he stands the best chance of all in her care."

The surgeon stared at her for a moment, then nodded to the stretcher bearers to carry Daniel where Claire directed. He caught Meg's arm as she tried to follow. "I need help here. Can you stitch wounds?"

Meg looked around her. It appeared the whole city was filled with blood and misery. She straightened her shoulders. She had managed to cope with death before.

She turned to the surgeon. "Show me what to do."

It was dark when Nicholas rode toward Wellington's lines at a full gallop. The fields were high with ripening grain, and he stayed low, hoping it would shield him.

Too late, he stumbled on a line of French infantry

squatting in the dark, probably lost. With a shout of surprise, they opened fire as Nicholas turned Hannibal to avoid them.

A shot whistled past his ear, and the night lit up in a blinding white flash. The pain was instant, and searing. He felt the ground slam his teeth together as he fell, thought of Meg and how she'd looked the first time he'd lifted her veil and seen her, blushing, beautiful. How could he have imagined he didn't want her? He was a fool.

And then he felt nothing at all.

Chapter 71

"**Y**ou—the lady there. Come here," the surgeon commanded, and the russet-haired beauty looked up. She was still wearing a cream satin ball gown trimmed with gold lace, and if it weren't for the bloodstains, she'd look like an angel. She didn't bother to pick up her skirts to keep them from brushing the wounded as she moved toward him between the tables of the tavern. She smiled at them, touched their hands, offered comfort. An angel indeed. She'd been here nearly as long as he had. He noted the fragile slimness of her figure, and the exhaustion in her face, at odds with the determination in her eyes. He felt a surge of admiration. Three other ladies had come to help some hours ago, and had departed again almost at once, two of them bearing away the third after she fainted at the sight of a man's naked thigh.

This woman was different, stronger.

"You've proven you can sew. Can you dig a ball out of a man's flesh?" he asked bluntly. She paled slightly but raised her chin.

"If I'm shown how."

"There's no shortage of men to practice on." He led

the way between the tables to a man with a ball buried in his shoulder. "By the way, what's your name?"

"Meg," she replied simply, her eyes already on the patient.

"Just Meg?" She was pretty and he smiled at her, but her brows rose aristocratically in mild rebuke that he should dare to flirt here, now.

"You'd best be careful, Major. This is Devil Hartley's missus," the patient said, eyeing the tools the surgeon laid out.

She looked at the soldier in surprise. "You know my husband?"

"I was camped in Colonel Lord Fairlie's orchard, ma'am. You spoke to me when you came looking for word of him. I'm Sergeant Bird. Have you found him yet?"

The surgeon dug into the wound with his tweezers, and the sergeant grimaced. She caught his hand and squeezed, giving him her fragile strength.

"And just who is Devil Hartley?" the major asked, half jealous as he probed for the ball. The sergeant swayed, and she propped him up with her delicate frame.

"Devil Hartley . . . was a captain in Spain with the Royal Dragoons . . . a hero," the sergeant panted. "Now he's a major, and a duke. Temberlay, isn't that right, my lady?"

The surgeon found the ball and plucked it free, and dropped it to the floor. The sergeant fainted, and she pressed a cloth to the wound to stop the blood, so she could bandage it.

"You're a duchess?"

She ignored him, kept at her task.

"Yet you're a natural at this," he said.

"No," she said. "I could never get used to this. Not ever."

"But you do, you see," he said. "When you've seen enough of it, it doesn't matter anymore. It doesn't make you sick, it doesn't move you to tears. You grow too tired to care." He cleaned the wound with a splash of rum and the patient woke with a hiss, making her jump.

"It will always matter. Someone loves each and every one of these men," she said fiercely. She began to bandage the sergeant's arm with deft precision.

"If it helps, I haven't seen many cavalry officers come in yet. Either they've been lucky or they're beyond need of my help," he said. He met the pain in her eyes and instantly regretted his glib choice of words.

"Come, Your Grace. Take a shot of the sergeant's rum and buck up." He looked around. The room was filled with the wounded and dying, and most said the fighting was still underway at a village called Waterloo, the last bastion between Napoleon and Brussels. The air reeked of blood and death, and the distant roar of the guns went on, and the carts continued rumbling into Brussels with their grim cargo.

Orderlies helped the sergeant off the table, and another man took his place. "Your next patient, Your Grace." He indicated the bullet wound in the thigh as he tore the man's breeches open. She took the tweezers and poured the proffered rum on them like a surgeon.

"Call me Meg," she insisted again, and set to dig the ball out.

It was light again when Nicholas woke to the boom of distant artillery, with the rain chilling him and Hannibal nibbling at his hair. He had a blinding headache. He touched his scalp gingerly, felt the gash where the bullet had grazed him.

"How bad is it, old boy?" he asked the horse. "It could have been worse, I suppose, if it had been an inch to the left. I suppose I have you to thank for getting me out of harm's way."

The horse snorted, and Nicholas rose, leaned on him. Hannibal was wet, caked with mud, and Nicholas wondered if he looked as bedraggled as his horse.

He looked around for a few moments, getting his bearings, fighting the dizziness. The land reminded him of Wycliffe. He was thankful that Meg was safe in England. He'd been away from her for over a month, and the yearning was still as fresh and painful as the cut on his head.

Another blast of gunfire made Hannibal prick his ears. The crackle of musket fire made the horse's nostrils flare.

Nicholas opened his saddlebag, pulled out a flask of whisky and took a sip, then poured some on the cut, cursing the sting.

The ground shook as the battle intensified. Nicholas took his coat off and put on his uniform, bright red against the gray mist.

He mounted Hannibal gingerly, and put his heels to him.

Sending up a prayer that he wasn't behind enemy lines, he followed the sounds of the guns and headed north.

The Royal Dragoons were making ready to charge when he reached the battlefield. Everything was in chaos, the battle joined on a hundred fronts. The familiar fog of smoke and powder filled the air, and the wind carried the stench of blood and death.

He shut his eyes for a moment, felt the familiar buzz fill him, eliminating fear and pain. As the Dragoons reached them, he spurred Hannibal to a gallop and joined their ranks, racing across the wet ground, the hoofbeats pounding through his legs, his chest, becoming his heartbeat.

He opened his throat and screamed as he rode down upon the French guns, seeing fire burst from the black muzzles. In front of him, beside him, men fell, horses were cut down and shrieked in pain. It was a lost cause. Too many were dying, yet they were almost there. Shots whistled past him, and he leaned low over Hannibal's neck.

The bastion was ahead.

On the hilltop on the British side that served as command post, Lord Wellington watched the fatal cavalry charge through his telescope. "Good God, they've gone too far," he muttered. "They're dying."

He shifted the scope. "Is that Temberlay?" he asked in surprise.

His aide looked. "Yes sir, I believe it is."

The duke squinted across the field again. "So it is. I wonder if he knows his wife is looking for him?"

Chapter 72

⤜∽◦◦∾⤛

"**Y**ou should rest, Meg," the surgeon said. "You've been here all day, and this is only going to get worse. Eat something, come back once you've slept."

Meg ran her hand across her forehead. "I'm fine."

There was a shout as a soldier threw open the door, letting in long fingers of late afternoon sun. She squinted as he leaped onto an empty table just as a wounded man was lifted off of it. His grin was white, his eyes wild in his battle-blackened face.

"We've won!" he yelled. "The Prussians arrived in the nick of time, and by God and Wellington, we've won!"

Joy supplanted agony. Anyone with a voice cheered. Meg sagged in relief. She pushed her way through to the soldier.

"The Royal Dragoons? Temberlay?" she asked.

His face fell, and he shook his head. "They charged at midday. I saw them. They were all cut down."

Meg felt her ears buzz. She stared at the soldier, saw his lips moving, but couldn't hear. There was no hope in his eyes as he described the desperate charge. Her chest drew tight, squeezing her heart. She couldn't breathe. His face receded down a long dark tunnel, and then he was gone, and there was only darkness.

Chapter 73

"**A**h, good. She's awake at last. Fetch someone to see to her, please, Captain." Meg forced her eyes open. A man lay on a cot across the room from her.

"Where am I?"

"I believe it's a storeroom of some kind," he said cheerfully. "Shocking, but it was the only quiet place left to put you—and me. We've been properly chaperoned, I assure you. A young lady was sitting with you most of the night. Lady Delphine St. James. Forgive me for not getting up. I lost my leg yesterday, you see."

Meg tried to sit up. The room spun. "Slowly, if you please, Your Grace. I'm in no condition to catch you if you faint. I'm Colonel Melton, by the way."

A woman bustled in with a soldier. "Ah, madame, here you are at last," Melton said. "This is the Duchess of Temberlay. I'm sure she could use your assistance. Your Grace, this is our hostess. She owns this tavern we're resting in."

The woman appeared to be immune to Colonel Melton's charms. She poured a cup of water and held it to Meg's lips without a word or a smile.

"How long have I been here?" Meg asked, but the woman didn't reply.

"She speaks only French, Your Grace. You've been here since last night. I understand you fainted from your rather heroic exertions on behalf of our wounded. The surgeon says you deserve a medal."

"They don't give medals to women," said another soldier, coming into the room. Melton frowned at him.

"This is my aide, the unchivalrous Captain Allen."

Allen gave her a flaccid smile that didn't reach his eyes. His uniform was spotless, his boots polished. He looked freshly barbered.

"My husband—" Meg said, and swallowed. "Temberlay—Nicholas Hartley. Did you see him?"

She had asked the same question so many times, it felt like the only thing she knew how to say, the only words she could speak.

Melton frowned slightly. "I'm afraid it was all confusion on a battlefield, Your Grace—nearly impossible to see anyone unless he was standing next to you."

"Please," she begged, wanting the truth, bracing for it.

"We lost thousands of men yesterday, my dear duchess. I simply don't know. There are still wounded awaiting aid on the battlefield."

Meg forced herself to stand. "Then I must go to the battlefield." She fought down nausea and dizziness.

"Your Grace—Meg, if I might—the battlefield is no place for a lady. The wounded are being brought to town as quickly as possible. I will have Captain Allen make inquiries."

"Only the dead are left on the field now," Allen said. "You should go home to England, wait there for news."

"I cannot go home, Captain. One way or the other, I must find my husband." She turned to the landlady. "Is there a cloak I might borrow?"

"Dear lady, is there nothing I can say to dissuade you?"

Colonel Melton asked. "A battlefield is a horrific sight."

"No, Colonel, nothing at all," Meg said.

"Then I will send Allen with you. I absolutely refuse to allow you to go alone. If I may be quite frank, there are looters after a battle. You will need protection, and I am ordering Captain Allen to return you to Brussels at once if it becomes too dangerous or upsetting."

Meg straightened her shoulders as she drew the cloak on. "I can bear it."

Allen's eyes flicked over her in disdain. She realized that she still wore the ball gown, now stained and dirty. She smoothed a hand over her hair.

Colonel Melton smiled. "You look lovely, Your Grace. I saw you at the Duchess of Richmond's ball the other night, and considered asking you to waltz. Now my dancing days are over, I wish I had. I sincerely hope you find Temberlay."

The road between Waterloo and Brussels was clogged with a procession of carts, discarded armaments, wounded soldiers, and civilians. There were dead bodies as well, naked white shapes among the trees. Captain Allen pursed his lips. He was missing luncheon for this fool's errand. He waited for the duchess to faint, or cry, or give the order to turn back, but she sat on the cart beside him, white-lipped, pale, with purple shadows under her eyes, searching every face, every scene of horror.

In his opinion, women belonged at home in England, waiting patiently and decently for news. What kind of Amazon had the gall to take herself out to a field of battle? He supposed if she had not been sullying her hands tending the common wounded yesterday, she would have been loading cannons on the field, bare-breasted and fierce.

He wondered if he'd be expected to offer some kind of comfort if—when—they found Temberlay's corpse, if they found it all among the thousands of corpses bloating in the June heat. If the man had not returned to Brussels by now, he was most certainly dead. He only hoped that if they found him, that he hadn't died of horrific wounds as some of these poor bastards had. He was not sure he could bear that himself. His stomach was already roiling at the sights and smells around him, even if hers was not. He fought the urge to turn the cart around, whether the duchess was willing or not.

She called out her husband's name over and over as blank-eyed men staggered past her, but they were too stunned, too exhausted, to care about the fate of anyone else.

As they drew nearer the battlefield, the smell got worse. Allen mopped his face with a monogrammed handkerchief. "It's been several hours, Your Grace. I think it would be best if we return to Brussels. I shall have inquiries made for you."

He shuddered as a wagon moved toward them filled with groaning wretches. He shut his eyes, unable to bear any more broken bodies. He leaned over the edge of the cart and emptied his stomach.

Meg handed the captain her canteen, and her own handkerchief.

"May we put this man on your cart, miss?" a voice asked. Three ragged soldiers blocked their way.

"Of all the insolence! What the devil d'you think—" Allen began, but she laid a hand on his arm, silenced him.

"He's our sergeant, you see, and he fought bravely yesterday," the soldier went on, having her attention now. "Have you at least a sip of water to spare?"

"Get out of the way at once!" he roared at them, and the ragged creature turned malevolent eyes on him.

"We asked politely, sir," the soldier said. "We've been walking since morning. We've had no food and no water. If you and your ladybird wish to go sightseeing, then perhaps you should be the ones on foot, not us as did the fighting and dying."

Allen fumbled for his pistol, fear rising in his empty belly, but the duchess was already climbing off the cart.

"You can't—" he began, but she was reaching for the basket under the seat.

"I have bread and water, a little wine, and bandages." They fell on the bread and water like starving dogs. "I am looking for Nicholas Hartley, Temberlay. Have you seen him?"

"He's a Royal Dragoon," Allen added shortly. "I must insist you get back in the cart, Your Grace."

Meg ignored the prissy captain, and kept her eyes on the soldier. The anger in his eyes faded to wary curiosity. "I didn't see any Dragoons where we were fighting," he said, his voice gruff, but polite.

"Put your sergeant on the cart—" she said, and waited for his name.

He looked suspiciously at the captain for a moment before replying. "Private Alfred Collins. Fifty-second Foot."

"You can't start issuing orders, Your Grace!" Allen said as they hoisted the moaning sergeant onto the cart. Meg shot him a sharp look of disdain as she helped them lift him.

Allen lifted his feet out of the way. "These boots are handmade, and these men are little better than beggars. They were probably thieves before a gentleman put a musket into their filthy hands and gave them some measure of dignity! What if your husband has need of that food, or those bandages?"

"If he were here, I know he'd insist on giving them to these men," she said. "And as for issuing orders, I outrank you, Captain. Not only socially, but also by the fact that I am here with Colonel Melton's blessing. You will take these men back to Brussels and straight to the care of Major Ramsey, the surgeon, is that clear? I shall continue my search on foot."

She watched him pale under her authority, felt her heart sing a little. Private Collins grinned.

"Your Grace, you can't go alone!" Allen argued, looking less arrogant now.

"I'll go with her," Private Collins said.

"You are hardly a proper escort for a duchess," Allen sniffed.

Meg clenched her fist, ready to plant it in his smug face. "There has been enough blood, and enough fighting. I am tired of people telling me what I can and cannot do! I am going to find my husband, do you hear me, Captain Allen? And when I do, there will be no more deceit, no more revenge or mistrust!" He looked baffled. She didn't wait for an answer. She turned and began walking toward the battlefield.

Private Collins bawled out Nicholas's name and regiment to each cart they passed, but no one answered.

In the shadows under the trees, shapes darted in and out of the bullet-riddled foliage.

"Peasant women, stripping the bodies," Collins murmured, stepping closer to her, holding his musket at the ready. He glowered at the scarecrows when they looked up, but did nothing to stop them. They rummaged through packs and pockets boldly, took boots and clothing and weapons, and ignored the curses and threats from the living. They looked suspiciously at Meg as she drew nearer, sat on their haunches to stare, their hands on the body that lay between them like grim undertakers.

As they parted to whisper to each other, Meg saw dark hair spread out across the ground. He lay facedown, his long limbs splayed. His tunic was dark with blood, and the earth under him was soaked with it. Three women were trying to turn him over, strip off his tunic. She saw the blue facings, the gold lace of the Royal Dragoons.

She felt the breath leave her body. "No," she whispered. Fear gathered into a scream, and tore out of her throat. The women crossed themselves as she rushed toward them, and they tumbled backward over one another like carrion birds to escape. They huddled against a tree and screeched as she fell to her knees beside him.

"Nicholas!" she screamed his name, shook him, but he was cold, all life gone. She felt his limbs, trying to find the wounds, hoping somehow she could stop death, make him whole again. She had bandaged so many others, saw them live, walk away. Surely there was time for one more miracle.

"You cannot die! I love you!" she cried over and over again, her tears spilling onto his hair, sparkling.

But she was too late. He couldn't hear her. She would never see him smile again, or feel her heart skip a beat because he'd walked into the room. He'd never stroke her hair, love her—

"My lady, he's gone," Private Collins said gently, gripping her shoulder, trying to pull her away. The scavengers huddled, waiting to return to their prize. One leaped forward and snatched a gold epaulette away. Meg shook off Collins's hand and stayed where she was. "No," she sobbed.

"Why do I find you with another man yet again, Maggie?" asked a tired voice behind her.

Meg spun. Nicholas stood a dozen feet away, mounted on Hannibal. He was filthy, and there was a tattered and grimy bandage wrapped around his head. He was hollow-eyed and exhausted.

She had never seen him look more handsome.

Collins stepped between them, his musket ready. "Are you Temberlay?" he demanded, but Meg hurtled past him to climb the stirrup and throw herself into Nicholas's arms. He held her close. His body was warm, alive, and she could feel his heart beating against hers. She ran her hands over his back, his shoulders, looking for wounds.

"Meg, what are you doing here?" he asked, pulling her into his lap looking into her eyes. Eyes filled with the kind of love she had always wanted. "Are you real?" He wiped the pads of his thumbs over her cheeks, trying to brush away her tears, but they were falling too fast.

"I love you, Nicholas. I had to tell you that."

He smiled slowly, an exhausted parody of his devil's grin. "You walked onto a battlefield to tell me you loved me? Why do you never do things the simple way?" he said, brushing a lock of her hair out of her eyes. "I love you too."

She felt her heart soar. He kissed her gently.

"Your hair is a mess, Duchess, your face is dirty, and I have no idea what you've been doing, but your dress is filthy, and you are still the most beautiful, desirable woman I've ever seen."

"I was afraid you'd be killed." She looked at the body on the ground. "Had been killed," she said sadly.

He held her closer, kissed her. "I'm alive, Maggie, and I love you," he said as if he didn't quite believe it himself.

"When we get home, I will send my grandmother away. I will pay Angelique Encore to leave London and never come back if that's what you want. I want to take you to Temberlay Castle, fill it with our children and grow old with you. Damn London and damn the gossip."

"Is this your husband then, my lady?" Collins asked.

Nicholas extended his hand. "Nicholas Hartley," he said. "Thank you for taking care of my wife."

"Private Alfred Collins, sir," the soldier said, taking Nicholas's hand. "I never shook the hand of an officer before. Or a duke."

One of the scavengers gave a loud sniff, and snatched the dead man's handkerchief out of his pocket to mop away her tears. "Such love," she said in French.

Meg slid out of Nicholas's arms and stood by the body of the fallen Dragoon. "He's someone's husband as well," she said. "Or son, or brother. Someone loved him, is waiting for him. Did he have a ring? I will return it to his family, so they know what happened to him."

The woman clutched her bundle close to her chest. "*Non*. My farm is in ruins, and I have little ones to feed!"

Nicholas dismounted and took a few coins out of his pocket. The woman's eyes lit, and her fingers closed on them. She handed the bundle to Meg and scurried into the trees with her companions.

"Now are you ready to go home?" he asked. He lifted her onto Hannibal's back.

She patted the horse. "Hannibal, how would you like to meet Arabella? Every lady needs a hero."

Nicholas looked up at his wife, and the love in her eyes took his breath away. "Including me," she said. "Forgive me for being too stubborn to see."

"I can't wait to get you alone," he said, then paused. "We need to talk."

"I think we've done enough talking. I know, Nicholas, I've seen with my own eyes what kind of man you are." Her face flushed. "And besides, we won't be entirely alone."

He rolled his eyes. "Don't tell me your mother came with you."

"She's in London." She tilted her head and laid a hand on her belly.

He stared at her. "A child? You came here knowing you were going to have a child?" he demanded as his stomach turned to water. "Our child?" He stared at her flat belly, felt love well up, and swallowed hard. "God, Maggie!"

She smiled down at him. "Can we argue about it later?"

"Don't think we won't, Duchess."

"From now on, I will do exactly as you wish, my love," she said.

"I don't believe that for a minute, Maggie."

She gave him a devil's grin of her own, and he laughed out loud.

He mounted the horse behind her, cradled her in his lap, felt her cheek against his chest, and took the first step on the long road back to the city.

Private Collins marched beside them, and others, the lucky ones, straggled off the battlefield and joined their slow march.

The devil had been paid in full, and it was time to go home.